REVOLUTIONARY

Hostile Takeover #3

S. Andrew Swann

DAW BOOKS, INC.

DONALD A. WOLLHEIM, FOUNDER

375 Hudson Street, New York, NY 10014

ELIZABETH R. WOLLHEIM
SHEILA E. GILBERT
PUBLISHERS

First Printing, June 1996

1   2   3   4   5   6   7   8   9

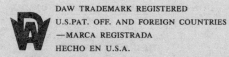

DAW TRADEMARK REGISTERED
U.S.PAT. OFF. AND FOREIGN COUNTRIES
—MARCA REGISTRADA
HECHO EN U.S.A.

PRINTED IN THE U.S.A

This book is dedicated to Keith Newman,
a martyr to free speech and college radio.

ACKNOWLEDGMENTS

Thanks to Mary, Susie, Bonnie, Astrid, and Geoff for savaging this in the manuscript. As always, everything wrong in this book is solely my own fault.

DRAMATIS PERSONAE

CONFEDERACY

Pearce Adams—Confederacy representative for Archeron. Delegate to the TEC from the Alpha Centauri Alliance.

Ambrose—Dimitri Olmanov's Bodyguard

Kalin Green—Confederacy representative for Cynos. Delegate to the TEC from the Sirius-Eridani Economic Community.

Francesca Hernandez—Confederacy representative for Grimalkin. Delegate to the TEC from the Seven Worlds. Non-human descendant of genetically engineered animals.

Robert Kaunda—Confederacy representative for Mazimba. Delegate to the TEC from the Trianguli Austrailis Union of Independent Worlds.

Dimitri Olmanov—Head of the Terran Executive Command. The most powerful person in the Confederacy.

Sim Vashniya—Confederacy representative for Shiva. Delegate to the TEC from the People's Protectorate of Epsilon Indi.

BAKUNIN

Marc Baetez—Captain, TEC. Navigator, survivor of the crash of the *Shaftsbury*.

Klaus Dacham—Colonel, TEC. In command of the *Blood-Tide* and Operation Rasputin.

Eigne—Primary representative of Proteus to anyone "Outside."

Bhipur Gavadi—Mercenary formerly in the employ of Proudhon Spaceport Security, survivor of the crash of the *Shaftsbury*.

Alex Jarvis—Mercenary formerly in the employ of Proudhon Spaceport Security, survivor of the crash of the *Shaftsbury*.

Ivor Jorgenson—Pilot and smuggler. Partner in the Diderot Holding Company.

Tjaele Mosasa—Electronics expert. Partner in the Diderot Holding Company.

Dominic Magnus—Ex-Colonel, TEC. Ex gunrunner. Partner in the Diderot Holding Company.

Kathy Shane—Ex-Captain, Occisis marines. Partner in the Diderot Holding Company.

Kari Tetsami—Freelance hacker and data thief. Partner in the Diderot Holding Company.

Random Walk—An artificial intelligence device. Partner in the Diderot Holding Company.

Mariah Zanzibar—Security expert. Partner in the Diderot Holding Company.

Contents

PROLOGUE

Smoke-Filled Rooms

"A despot easily forgives his subjects for not loving him, provided they do not love each other."
                    —ALEXIS DE TOCQUEVILLE
                       (1805–1859)

CHAPTER ONE

Loyalty Oaths

"Strong emotional involvement rarely makes the job easier."

—*The Cynic's Book of Wisdom*

"Prudence keeps life safe, but does not often make it happy."

—SAMUEL JOHNSON
(1709–1784)

Dominic Magnus lay on his bed and stared at the ceiling. It was his second night out of the hospital. It was his second night without any sleep.

Shadows played across the ceiling, cast from the open window. They were the shadows of the siege: spotlights trying to pick out the enemy forces circling Jefferson City; light from still-burning fires around the perimeter. The wind even brought a taint of smoke, floating on chill air.

The city was still intact. The invaders wanted it intact, and would wait out the underarmed democrats for however long it took.

It was impossible for him not to be aware of the war focused upon him, but that wasn't what consumed his thoughts, not now, alone in the dark. What consumed his thoughts was the woman asleep next to him.

He wasn't looking at her, but he could see her perfectly. Straight black hair cut on a diagonal. Deep Asiatic eyes set in a face that held all the corrupted innocence that planet Bakunin was home to.

She was so damn young. Not just young, she was half his age. . . .

Not that she'd know. Dom's appearance had been permanently fixed ten years ago. When the doctors had reconstructed his body, they had left him looking in that indeterminate range between late twenties and early thirties, and pseudoflesh didn't age.

Not that she'd know . . .

He knew all about her. From her parents' death in a corporate war, to her job as a freelance corporate hacker, to her adopted father Ivor Jorgenson. He knew because he'd always made it his business to know.

By comparison, Tetsami knew almost nothing about him.

His right hand clenched on the sheets beneath him. He heard the sheets tear. Dom cursed and sat up.

His right hand was tangled in shredded bedding. The hand was new, the Jeffersonians' attempt at reconstruction. Unlike the rest of his body, the hand and leg he had lost five Bakunin days ago were unquestionably artificial. The olive-toned pseudoflesh ceased abruptly below his elbow, where his hand and forearm became a chrome-metal approximation of his natural-looking left. His body, despite being largely cybernetic before the accident, was still unused to the clumsy metal invader.

Dom tightened his fist and more sheets tore.

"Dom?"

"Go back to sleep." The tension he felt didn't seem to make it to his voice.

"What's the matter? Are you okay?"

If you knew me, really knew me, you'd know that I've never been "okay."

Dom felt a hand touch his shoulder, and he almost flinched from the contact. He shook his head. "I can't keep doing this."

"Doing what?" Tetsami's hand drifted down his arm until it reached metal. Dom drew his hand away and stood up. He walked over to the window. A false dawn painted the southern horizon red. Dom could picture the fires just over that horizon. Fires marking the remains of communes the invaders didn't see as economically important.

The cities mattered, the communes were just in the way.

"Dom?"

The destruction had long passed the attack on his own person. The loss of Godwin Arms and Armaments wasn't even a significant battle in terms of the planetwide war that gripped Bakunin. The attack on GA&A was only significant in that it was first, and it had been Dom's company.

"I'm still tied to this," Dom said.

He could hear sheets rustle as Tetsami sat up. "You're being obtuse again." Uncharacteristically, her voice didn't carry a tone of sarcasm. The questioning note made Dom feel worse.

"Everything about this war is connected to me."

Tetsami sighed. "Sometimes you scare me."

"I should." Dom leaned out the window, staring at the few lights marking the city. He adjusted the photoreceptors in his artificial eyes until he had a monochrome light-enhanced view of the city. The only people out on the streets were Jefferson City's militia—the blue-uniformed minutemen.

"You aren't the center of the universe, Dom. Just because Klaus—"

At the mention of his brother, Dom's right hand, the new metallic one, clenched on the windowsill. There was a pop as the plastic sheathing gave way. The sound was loud enough to stop Tetsami in mid-sentence.

Klaus, Dom thought, *are you here on your own agenda? Or someone else's? Will anything short of my death ever satisfy you?*

"Not the universe. But this war—" Dom shook his head as if to clear it. However, inside a metallic skull, his brain was augmented by an onboard computer. His enhanced memories could not be cleared. "Random has even cast me in the role of a resistance leader. Wherever I go, I'll be sucked back. . . ."

Dom walked away from the window and began to gather his clothes.

Tetsami got out of bed. She was shorter than he, and

seemed even smaller now, naked and in the dark. "What do you think you're doing?"

"I think I should get my own room."

Tetsami flung her arms wide in a gesture that would have been comical if she weren't so angry. "*Mother humping Christ,* what the hell's your problem?"

"You don't know anything about me," Dom said.

"Whose fault is that? You shithead!" She picked up his pants. "God, I thought there was a little more to you at least. So this is it? 'Thanks for keeping my dick warm, good-bye'?"

Dom stood there, understanding more of Tetsami's feelings than his own. "I can't pull you through whatever's going to happen to me."

Tetsami threw his pants at him. "Fuck you, Dom." Tears were streaming down her face. "All the shit we went through for each other, it doesn't mean anything, does it?"

"I'm headed for something irrevocable—" Dom began.

"Damn straight you are. Get the fuck out!"

"Tetsami—"

"You want to leave? Out. Now!"

Dom backed to the door, clothes in his arms. Tetsami marched after him, screaming, "You've got five seconds to get out of my hotel room or I'll rip your balls off! *Maggot!*"

Dom backed all the way into the hall, and the door whooshed shut on him, leaving him outside and alone.

He heard Tetsami crying even through the allegedly-soundproofed door. He hated himself for hurting her. But on the list of his personal crimes, it was relatively minor. It was outweighed by the conviction that, before everything was over, anyone close to him was going to die.

CHAPTER TWO

Police Action

"There is no such thing as a secret."
—*The Cynic's Book of Wisdom*

"Better pointed bullets than pointed speeches."
—PRINCE OTTO VON BISMARCK
(1815–1898)

Jonah Dacham waited.

Nearly a decade had passed since he had divorced himself from the passage of time. Nine years spent in isolation, on a barren strip of cold Martian wilderness not too far from the artifacts gracing Cydonia. Nine years he had waited on Mars.

Now he was on Earth, in a dingy little hotel room, millions of kilometers removed from Mars, light-years removed from Bakunin, and again he waited.

The time was coming when he would discover whether that decision he made, nine years ago, would mean anything. The same decision that he was about to make again, thirty-eight standard days from now, if he had not changed anything by his presence.

I haven't changed anything, it started before I landed here. Jonah rubbed his temples, as if he could push the paranoia away. But nine years of isolation, avoiding any brush with humanity that might warp events away from the path he remembered for them ...

His room was in a dirty little hotel in Sydney, the Terran capital, a cheap little flat far from the center of town, far from the center of the Confederacy government. It was the least significant, most isolated place he could room and still be near the Congress, near enough to be able to do what he had to do.

The room wasn't out of sight of the Confederacy spire, though. The kilometer-tall tower was difficult to escape.

His right hand was cold against his forehead. The dull, pitted metal sucked the heat from his skin. He had come to Earth over a month and a half ago, three months before it would have been absolutely safe. Jonah could have waited until the event thirty-eight standard days from now. If he had held off until then, he would have been certain not to skew events on Bakunin.

But then there'd be no time for him to do anything.

Even now, as events followed the paths he remembered, the *Blood-Tide* and accompanying fleet had been in orbit around Bakunin for close to a week standard. Or, to use the more familiar units, four and a half Bakunin days.

The invasion had begun on the surface of the planet, and all of Bakunin's major cities would be under siege. The cities had, maybe, the ability to hold out for forty days standard.

Jonah did not need all nine years to determine that waiting out his exile until there was no risk would render his sacrifice completely meaningless. So he had long ago decided on the three-month margin. Time for him to do something, with the minimum acceptable risk that he would upset the timeline.

He told himself that he had not altered events on Bakunin, and that the cities had forty days to hold out. Subtracting the transmission time, that meant that he had a single Terrestrial month left to make *his* difference.

The contradictory aims running through his head would have made him smile, if he hadn't had nine years to bleach the humor out of the concept. If he hadn't had the opportunity to bury a man whose life illustrated the danger of trying to change a history that wasn't your own.

"Thirty-eight days, and this history will be mine again," he whispered at the holo. After a pause, "Or, perhaps it will be mine for the first time."

His or not, history was making itself felt to Jonah. The opening day of the Terran Congress couldn't pass by unnoticed. If Jonah had missed the event flooding the comm lines, the fireworks would have told him about it.

Yet another mark indicating the passage of time.

Two thirds of the time he had left, two-thirds of the month he had before Bakunin would slip unconditionally into the hands of Klaus and the Terran Executive Command, he was going to spend waiting for the Tau Ceti delegation to arrive. The Grimalkin representative, Francesca Hernandez, the only representative the xenophobic Seven Worlds had deigned to send to this Congress, didn't have the authority to commit to anything.

Jonah had to wait while people with the authority flew in from Tau Ceti in a too-slow tach-ship.

Fortunately, by now, he was used to waiting.

The opening night fireworks sounded like gunfire outside his window. Jonah had maxed the volume on the holo to try and drown out the sound. He stared at the screen, but wasn't really watching it.

The holo was a gaudy model, taking up an entire wall. The color was distorted toward the red. It gave him a choice between an endless news summary and hard-core pornography. He had it on the news.

Right now the data stream was dominated by the endless opening day speeches in the Congress. The voices of politics and diplomacy were slightly less disturbing than the sound of gunfire.

Most of the speechmakers had probably never heard of Bakunin—man or planet.

As he watched the holo, something caught his attention out the corner of his eye. A shadow had passed in front of his window.

"Mute." Jonah whispered. The holo obeyed.

Instinctively he was already on his feet and backing away from the outside wall. He was five stories up, and the shadow had been vaguely man-sized. He cursed silently. His sudden move had probably just alerted whoever it was that he'd been seen.

After a moment, Jonah whispered, "Lights."

Again, the room obeyed, killing the lights in the small one-room flat. Now the only light was given by the red-tinted holo and the polychrome flashes of the fireworks outside his louvered window.

Another shadow, definitely the size and shape of a man, passed by outside. As he watched, Jonah adjusted the artificial photoreceptors in his eyes to compensate for the darkness.

He edged his way toward the door to the room, the only exit he had. As he closed on the door, his enhanced ears picked up noise from outside. Four or five people were out there.

They had him cornered.

Crouching, to present as low a profile as possible, he darted to the edge of the window and glanced through the louvers. Stroboscopic flashes from the fireworks illuminated nothing but an empty street. However, from this angle he could see nothing of the hotel's exterior surface. The walls could be plastered with commandos and he wouldn't see a thing.

The TEC?

If the Confederacy's secret police were after him, he was in trouble. Not just him, but his entire reason for being here. His presence on Earth was critical to Bakunin's survival as an independent planet, and all that could be destroyed if the wrong people knew *why* he was here.

No one out on the street.

It was a cheap hotel room, windows not designed to open. Even if they did, it was still five stories to the ground. Jonah flexed his metallic right hand. He would survive a fall like that. His rebuilt body had survived worse. But it wasn't an attractive option.

From outside the door he heard the gentle sound of metal being lowered to the carpeted floor. His visitors had just popped the plate on the electronic lock.

Not the TEC. The Terran Executive Command would have the authority to override the lock. They wouldn't have to break into a mere hotel room.

That didn't make him feel any better.

He only had seconds to move. He picked up the densest object in the room, a pseudo-marble table whose weight was probably meant to discourage theft.

He lifted it with little problem. Both his chromed hand

and its more natural-looking opposite number were constructs. Both were mechanical improvements to the arms
he'd been born with.

The table swung in an arc, not at the window, which
seemed to offer an unlikely means of escape, but at the
wall opposite the holo screen. This place shared with all
cheap hotels the characteristic of thin walls. The outer
wall of sound-damping composite shredded from the
weight of the table, letting in the noise of grunting and
panting from the neighboring room.

The noise was abruptly cut off when the table's arc in-
tersected the back of the next room's wall holo. Sparks,
blue smoke, and the smell of ozone all blew in through
the hole in the wall.

He swung the table again, doubling the size of the hole
and blowing the remains of the wall holo into the next
room. The hole was wide enough for him to dive through
now.

Escaping through the hole, he had just enough time to
notice his surprised-looking neighbors. Then the windows
of both rooms exploded inward.

Flying louvers and glass knocked Jonah to the ground.
The couple in the room with him screamed. The smell
of the shattered wall holo filled his nostrils, and grit from
the shattered electronics dug into his skin.

Even as he rolled to his feet, he knew it was hopeless.

Standing in the window was a humanoid form in matte-
black powered armor. In its hand was a field weapon of
some sort. The weapon emitted a soft hum, which was the
last sensation to follow Jonah down a deep pit of unconsciousness.

PART SEVEN

War Games

"The natural progress of things is for liberty to yield and government to gain ground."
—THOMAS JEFFERSON
(1743–1826)

CHAPTER THREE

Demilitarized Zone

"Don't try to count the players until the game is over."
—*The Cynic's Book of Wisdom*

"Freedom is a verb."
—SYLVIA HARPER
(2008–2081)

Dominic Magnus greeted the morning by pacing around the roof of one of Jefferson's pseudo-marble monuments. Kropotkin was just about to emerge from behind the spine of the Diderot Mountains. The dawn combined with haze from the fires to tint everything a fuzzy shade of lavender.

The neoclassical building stood on an artificial rise that gave him a view of the surrounding terrain. The city radiating out from around him was a century old, founded within a few years of the original Bakunin landfall. It had a population of over half a million people. Small by Bakunin standards, it was technically a commune.

Fortunately, the invaders hadn't taken that into account. Otherwise they would have crushed Jefferson as they'd crushed every other commune they'd rolled past. They destroyed everything that wasn't necessary to their economy. . . .

Dom wondered if that was what he was doing to Tetsami. "Damn it, I'm protecting her . . ."

He felt his hand twitch. He knew Tetsami more than well enough to know how she felt about such protection. She couldn't, or just didn't want to, understand what a risk he posed to her. The risk he posed to anyone near him, to this city.

If his brother ever discovered he was still alive, and where he was ... It was so much easier when he only gave a shit about Godwin Arms.

The view around him didn't help his mood. From his vantage he could see to the northern perimeter of the city. He could see a slice of the growing no-man's-land of vehicle wreckage. None of the civilian craft that had launched out of Jefferson had made it as far as the siege line. Blackened hulks dotted a kilometer-wide kill zone outside the city.

The last attempt to run the blockade had been last night, after his argument with Tetsami. Three men flew the fastest civilian contragrav that the city council could commandeer. About six hundred meters away from the city limits their attempt still smoldered in the dawn light. From this distance it was only a slightly glowing patch at the base of a pillar of smoke.

Maybe now it will sink in that this isn't just another commune war. Dom rubbed his temple, flinching at the unexpected chill of metal.

It was going to take him years to get used to that hand. Thinking of that make him overly aware of his limp. He stopped pacing, taking weight off of his new leg.

The red mass of Kropotkin was just now visible over the eastern mountains. This was the first time he'd taken a position to really see the siege for himself. Up to now he'd been recovering in the Jefferson City Hospital, or been in a hotel room, allowing his body to adapt to the crude replacements Jefferson had grafted onto his right arm and leg.

He'd allowed himself to get dangerously used to Tetsami. *I might have taken her for granted, once. What if I start to depend on her?*

Worse, what if she started to depend on him?

He forced himself to concentrate on scanning the horizon, trying to distinguish elements of the Proudhon siege line. The enemy didn't make it easy for him, even with his newly repaired eyes. It took Dom a half hour to place the major elements of artillery, and decide which curves of land disguised an airtank or two.

What he really needed was a wide spectrum orbital recon of the area—

And what would I do with that? Jefferson's army is insignificant compared to the mercenary army out there. If those mercs wanted to, they could plow the entire city under in less than a day.

Fortunately, Proudhon's invaders didn't want to. Proudhon was under the control of Colonel Klaus Dacham, and the Terran Executive Command, and the TEC wanted an unconditional surrender and the city intact. Until then, nothing entered or left that kilometer-wide kill zone without being destroyed. A standoff that was being replicated around every city on this side of the Diderot Mountains.

Bakunin was a fiercely independent place. It had been four days since the war had begun, and despite near total surprise and the overwhelming speed of Proudhon's mercenary army, no one had surrendered yet. But it was only a matter of time. At best a month. Probably less.

Ever since he had awakened in the Jefferson City Hospital and realized the full extent of what was going on, he had been trying to come up with a way to salvage an unsalvageable situation. His problem with Tetsami was probably a symptom of greater frustration.

"Or maybe I can't think clearly because I'm involved with Tetsami."

His comm beeped for his attention. He unclipped it from his belt and turned it on.

"News from the mountain?" Dom asked before the other party spoke. A lot of his people had been trapped in position at the Diderot Mountain camp ever since the invasion began. Shane, Zanzibar, Mosasa and Mosasa's AI, Random Walk. Communication with them was spotty at best.

"Good morning to you, too," the comm replied with Ivor's voice.

Dom winced. Ivor was, in every respect but the biological, Tetsami's father. When things got unpleasant with Tetsami, Dom's dealings with Ivor chilled even more than usual. And the temperature between them was usually pretty damn cold.

"Any news?" Dom asked him.

"Status quo," he said. "I'm calling you about Gavadi."

"Has he taken a turn for the worse?"

"No. He's awake, I think you need to talk to him."

As Dom walked through the hospital, he wondered what Gavadi could possibly have to say to him.

Gavadi was an enigma. He had been one of a trio of casualties left over from Tetsami's escape from Proudhon captivity, the worst-off one. He'd suffered the loss of an arm, a dozen broken bones, and a variety of internal injuries—

No one even seemed to know his first name.

Dom had talked to everyone who had been involved in the crash of the *Shaftsbury*. Marc Baetez, the surviving Proudhon officer, refused to talk to anyone. Baetez was restrained and under constant guard, being the only prisoner of war Jefferson had.

Jarvis was another mercenary officer, but he had the bad luck of being arrested and imprisoned on the *Shaftsbury* with Tetsami and Gavadi. Jarvis had been cooperative, but he hadn't known any more about Gavadi than anyone else had.

Tetsami herself had only passed a few words with Gavadi before the cargo/troop-carrier *Shaftsbury* had nosed into the Diderot Mountains. She'd told Dom that if anyone had known about Gavadi it had been Michael Kelly—or at least the construct calling itself Michael Kelly.

Unfortunately, Kelly had died helping Dom extricate himself from an aircar wreck.

Thinking about Kelly made Dom uncomfortably aware of the metal under his own flesh. The new brushed-chrome fingers of his right hand wanted to tap on his thigh, so he shoved the hand into his pocket.

Ivor was waiting for him in Gavadi's room. So was a doctor who gave Dom a contemptuous look. "Don't excite him," said the doctor.

Dom nodded, allowing the doctor's resentment to flow

past him. It was just the most recent sample of an ugly trend Dom had noticed. In the past four days, events— and the activity of Random Walk, Mosasa's AI—had conspired to place Dominic Magnus at the head of whatever central authority the Bakunin resistance had.

Random Walk had spawned within its circuits the idea of making Dom the figurehead of the resistance movement. And, somehow, Random had pulled it off. It wasn't as if Dom had any authority to give orders. Even if he had, tactical communication with the rest of the planet was practically nil. However, he was a convenient person to rally behind, to credit, and to blame.

Rational or not, a lot of Jeffersonians were doing a large bit of blaming.

The doctor backed away but didn't leave.

Gavadi was a mess of tubes and bandages. His face was distorted by swelling bruises. His left arm ended just below the shoulder, his body not ready to take cybernetics. Gavadi blinked at Dom through puffy lids, the first sign that the crumpled form on the bed was alive.

Dom glanced up at Ivor.

"He wanted to talk to the 'leader of the resistance,' " Ivor said with a touch of irony.

Some leader.

Some resistance.

Dom crouched and leaned toward the head of the bed so he and Gavadi could look at each other.

"You lead . . . resistance?" Gavadi's voice was hoarse, ragged, and wet. He sounded on the verge of death, despite the fact that he was probably better off now than he'd been in days.

Dom nodded, feeling slightly dishonest.

Gavadi coughed. "Good, good." He closed his eyes. "Like . . . orbit."

"What?"

"What's it like in orbit?" Gavadi repeated slowly.

If I had just woken up from a week-long coma, Dom thought, *and my last memory had been being a captive of Proudhon Security's army, that wouldn't be my first question.*

"Not great," Dom said. "Unfortunately, our information's limited. Proudhon had a near monopoly on ATC sats before the war and now they've had time to erase any satellite they don't like—"

Gavadi shook his head no.

"What?" Dom said.

"Confederacy," Gavadi managed to croak. The way Gavadi said it sent an icy tingle through the nerveless chrome of his right hand. It expanded into an invisible shiver in his gut.

So much was happening groundside that it was easy to forget the Terran Confederacy. The Proudhon Spaceport Development Corporation, the force behind the mercenary army sweeping the western half of Bakunin's one continent, was a domestic force. The Proudhon army was all Bakunin natives—at least as native as anyone could be on the anarchic surface of Bakunin.

But the financing, the planning, had come from the Confederacy. Dom himself had nearly been a casualty of a Terran Executive Command operation when the TEC landed a force to secure arms for the Proudhon invasion. Dom had been the CEO of Godwin Arms and Armaments, and the TEC had flown in a battalion of Confed Occisis marines to take over GA&A. Dom had since discovered that the takeover of GA&A was only the latest Confed presence. What was happening in Bakunin now was the end result of years of planning in the Confederacy, and of at least one arm of the Confederacy in particular, the Alpha Centauri Alliance, which had funneled money into Proudhon.

Dom didn't like the reminder that the Confederacy was involved in this. With Random Walk at his disposal, he had access to some decent intelligence-gathering capability, and some of the intelligence they'd gathered had to do with the Confed presence in orbit around Bakunin.

Dom told Gavadi about the *Daedalus,* a carrier from the Sirius-Eridani Economic Community, and its escort. The SEEC ship had tached in only days before the Proudhon invasion.

He also mentioned the TEC observation platforms orbiting Bakunin. Those spy ships from the Executive Command were capable of resolving the entire surface down to the square meter.

Gavadi seemed to allow the information to sink in before he asked. "Indi?"

Indi?

What does the People's Protectorate of Epsilon Indi have to do with all this?

"The invasion blinded us. That's all we know, and it's old information."

Gavadi nodded, wincing. "No SEEC troops on the ground?"

That question chilled Dom even more. "No." *Not that we know*

"Good." Gavadi seemed to relax.

Dom glanced up at Ivor. His expression was cold. He didn't seem to know any more than Dom did.

Dom tapped his fingers on the mattress next to Gavadi's intact arm. "What's all this about, Gavadi?"

"Repel invaders." Gavadi's voice sounded a little more liquid. The doctor walked up next to Dom.

"Easier said than done," Dom said.

"Call—" Gavadi broke into a spasm of coughing and the doctor started pushing Dom away.

"You're exciting him too much," said the doctor.

"Call for help," Gavadi finished, wheezing.

Dom had to back away from the bed. "Help? From whom?" he asked.

"Please leave," the doctor was saying. "This man needs to rest."

As Dom and Ivor were ushered out of the hospital room, Dom heard Gavadi choke out the word, "Indi."

Help from Indi?

"Know what he meant?" Dom asked Ivor. They were standing in a small hospital lounge. Dom was waiting to hear when, or if, the doctors would let him talk to Gavadi again.

Ivor looked at him a moment as if Dom should be able to figure it out for himself. Then he said, "Gavadi's a mole for the Indi Protectorate."

Dom looked at Ivor. The man was larger than he was,

older, and he looked very tired. "What makes you say
that?"

Ivor finger-combed his white hair; he looked as though
he'd had very little sleep. Dom wondered if he'd been
talking with Tetsami. "Proudhon only shipped four prisoners back on the *Shaftsbury,*" he said. "They all had to
be of some tactical importance, not just to Proudhon, but
to Klaus and the TEC. Right?"

Dom nodded. They *all* had to be pretty important.

"We know why Tetsami was there." Ivor's voice was
very cold when he said that. Dom doubted that Ivor had
forgiven him for Tetsami's capture.

Dom nodded.

"Jarvis was there because of his association with her.
That leaves Kelly and Gavadi. Kelly was a spy from
Centauri." Ivor stared at him. "You think about it. You
used to be TEC. You know every action the Confederacy
takes has two sides to it, at least."

Five arms to the Confederacy, two of them, Sirius and
Centauri, were traditionally allied. Centauri had piped in
financing, and the SEEC had tached in a carrier. Dom
looked away from Ivor and down the hallway, toward the
ICU ward where Gavadi was kept. "Do you think there
could be Indi warships in orbit?"

Dom was sure he understood the Confederacy's motives, but it was all speculation. He knew the Confederacy from his ten-year stint in the TEC, but he had been
isolated from it for half again as long, and the last ten
years he hadn't even been *in* the Confederacy. There
could be a level of complexity he was missing.

"What do you think?" Ivor asked.

The object of the invasion, almost certainly, was to impose a central government on the planet Bakunin. Conquest was a given. Another given was the fact that the
invasion had to be by domestic forces initially, so that
the Confederacy could recognize the resulting State as
"legitimate." A legitimate State could sign the Confed
charter and join the community of planets, solving the an-
noying problems of Bakunin's anarchy: no customs, tariffs, extradition laws, taxes. . . .

Dom had assumed that the motives for the TEC-

launched invasion had been a straightforward plugging up
of the economic black hole that Bakunin was in its natural state—a massive sink for capital, industry, and political dissidence.

What if it weren't that simple? What if the separate
arms of the Confederacy were working at cross-purposes
here? Sirius and Centauri on one end, Indi, the Union,
and maybe the Seven Worlds on the other?

"Ivor, I think it is *too* damn likely." Likely that
Bakunin wasn't just being attacked from the outside, but
was caught in some power struggle between the arms of
the Confederacy. Dom stood up. "I'm going to try to raise
Diderot on the tightbeam. Stay here until you find out
when Gavadi can talk again. I think you know the questions to ask."

Ivor grunted affirmatively as Dom ran to the exit. Suddenly, Dom felt a real need to talk to Random Walk.

CHAPTER FOUR

Reasonable Doubt

"Self-examination is not a survival trait in times of crisis."

—*The Cynic's Book of Wisdom*

"Only the shallow know themselves."

—OSCAR WILDE
(1854–1900)

Tetsami, boiling inside, marched back and forth through one of the monument-strewn parks of Jefferson City. She walked past bronze statues that, in the ruddy morning light of Kropotkin, looked as though they were coated in rancid blood. Even to her native's eyes, the purple-and-orange Bakunin foliage looked diseased. The neo-neoclassical buildings scattered throughout the park, following someone's master geometry, made the park look like a graveyard.

Great frame of mind, woman, she thought to herself.

"What the hell am I doing?" she asked an equestrian statue. It was an alien-looking thing to someone who had never seen a horse in the flesh. She sat on a ledge of the statue's concrete base and sighed.

Her head throbbed from lack of sleep. Her eyes burned, which made it hard not to think of all the tears she'd shed over a worthless bastard named Dominic Magnus.

"Yeah," she whispered. "Tell yourself he's scum enough times and you might just believe it. Then you'll feel better about throwing him out."

What did she think she was doing? What did *he* think he was doing? Both of them were so screwed in the head that, after only three decent nights together, they both lost a measure of sanity.

"A relationship that feeds on constant conflict and threat of death—real healthy. I sure know how to fuck things up, don't I?"

She looked up at the animal, and the giant bronze horse remained mute.

The park was a lonely place this morning. The proximity of war for the past week seemed to have tempered the citizens' appetite for the "recreational" areas of the city. With the siege on, the park looked more like a cemetery than a picnic area. It was ugly to think that it might become one before long.

But the only things entombed here now were selected bits of history. She was surrounded by pseudo-marble cenotaphs dedicated to men dead centuries ago and light-years away. It was morbid.

I'm morbid.

Why had she said those things to Ivor? He might not have given her his genes, but he was as much a father as she'd ever had, the only family she'd ever had.

She was still trying to figure out how she had fucked that one up, especially when she had gone to him for comfort after her fight with Dom. It had gone fine until Ivor had said something about Dom being right, that she shouldn't be together with Dom, that she didn't know enough about him—

She had broken away from him and slammed her fist into the wall. Ivor had been stunned into silence when she did that, and she was too angry to realize what she'd been saying.

"Of all the Christ-f—" she'd said, *"that's why you can't stand him, isn't it!"*

"Now wait, he—" Ivor had barely begun. But she'd been too pissed. First Dom, then Ivor. . . .

"What gives you the right," she'd screamed at the wall, she hadn't even looked at him. "You want me to be this fucking virginal six-year-old for all my life?"

"I just want the bes—"

"You jealous, Ivor? You want me to yourself?" The memory made Tetsami sick to her stomach. "Or are you just playing concerned father, objecting to anything touching his darling daughter?"

"Don't, please . . ."

"I got news for you," she'd said as she stormed out of Ivor's hotel room. *"You ain't my goddamned father!"*

Tetsami couldn't think of anything she could have said to hurt Ivor worse. Now she had the feeling that she had done something irreversible.

If only she hadn't been wondering the same things herself.

If only she had a little more self-control.

"If only—" What a useless phrase.

She'd been drawn to Dominic Magnus ever since she had first met him. Drawn and repelled at the same time. She was attracted by something she sensed in the man, some capacity, some deep passion, pain, some maelstrom of emotion battering the surface. Something which, in her more lucid moments, she dismissed as a figment of her own imagination. She'd been repelled by the icy surface of the man, a surface that froze out any hint of emotion. She was repelled by insensitivity that sometimes seemed to border on sadism. Repelled by his inability to fully trust anyone. Repelled by his past . . .

Worse, she was repelled by the very thing that drew her to him. The inner fires, the burning inside him. More and more often, she saw into those fires, and their intensity was frightening.

But the abyss this planet was falling into insisted on driving them together. She had attempted to leave, to free herself from this rock and head out to the stars. It wasn't any personal second thoughts that had trapped her, it wasn't Dom's alleged attraction to her, it was the goddamn invasion freezing outbound traffic.

If it weren't for the TEC's attack on Godwin Arms, she never would have met Dom.

She had held a naive hope that, maybe, when she'd consummated things with Dom, her obsession might wane. There'd been a hope that when the sexual mystery had been removed, her emotions would click into saner patterns. She thought removing that tension might gain her some perspective.

She might know computers better than anyone on this rock other than Random Walk, but when it came to human relations, she was dangerously stupid.

Worst of all, she might have allowed Dom to love her before she knew what *she* felt.

She needed to talk to somebody. But she had probably destroyed her relationship with the only person she could've talked to. *A hateful little bitch, that's what I am.* How the hell could she face either of them again?

As the morning advanced, she wandered around trying to enumerate the people she knew in this town. Other than Dom and Ivor, they were all in Jefferson's excuse for a hospital. Eventually, that fact led her there. She wasn't quite aware of where she was walking until she reached the ivy-covered brick of Jefferson Hospital itself.

She stood outside the courtyard for a long while as she wondered what she was trying to do. Three people she knew here. Baetez was a prisoner and wouldn't talk to her, despite the fact she'd saved his life. Gavadi was probably still unconscious in the intensive care unit. That left the abrasive mercenary Jarvis.

What a choice.

She wandered around the courtyard until she confronted a set of temporary barriers. They encircled a matte-black ellipsoid three meters along its longest diameter. If she looked closely, she could see that the large egg-shaped thing rested a few centimeters above the ground. It was utterly motionless, utterly nonreflective, utterly enigmatic.

Dom's egg, Tetsami thought.

She had no idea what the thing was. Yet another thing Dom was closed-mouthed about. It had followed Dom to Jefferson, and Dom insisted that it was nonthreatening. Tetsami didn't quite know about that.

It had followed Dom here, through Jeffersonian security, and more importantly, through the Proudhon siege. The Jeffersonian minutemen went nuts when the egg showed up in the middle of the hospital courtyard. It had no radar signature. *None.* In fact, it radiated nearly no energy whatsoever—none except what a Jeffersonian engi-

neer called "3-K microwave background," which seemed
to confuse and excite the guy.

Tech you couldn't jack into lost her.

The thing shifted and Tetsami stumbled back from the
barriers. *Trick of the light,* she thought. But it was hard
to convince herself of that, since the egg didn't reflect
any light at all. If she stared at it too long, it hurt. It
fooled the eyes into thinking it was just a black two-
dimensional hole.

She was almost certain that its long axis had rotated in
her direction. She had the eerie sensation that it was
watching her.

She rubbed her arms and realized that the hair was
standing up on them. She felt as if someone had just
pumped a few million volts into the ground between her
and the egg. A slight rainbow flashed across the surface
of the egg and the electric feeling was gone.

She'd barely had time to react before the egg was dor-
mant again. "What the fuck was that about?"

The egg didn't answer, and when she turned away, the
afterimage still clouded her eyes.

She was right, Gavadi was still too far out of it for
visitors, and Ivor was hovering around the ICU ward, so
she avoided the area. Somehow she slipped out without
him seeing her.

*Can't keep that up. We're all trapped in the same city.
Same damn hotel.*

Away from the ICU ward, she conned a duty nurse into
letting her look in on Gavadi through an observation camera. He looked pathetic.

Are you a spy, like Kelly was? she thought at the
crumpled form behind the holo monitor. *Not quite like
Kelly. You're human, and you're still alive.*

Thinking about Kelly added another velvet-black fold
to the depression enveloping her. Kelly had been a construct, a device designed to mimic a human being—a specific human, Michael Kelly. The original Kelly had been
the human interface between the Proudhon hierarchy and
the arms of the Confederacy. Kelly had been the conduit
through which the Confed forces, Centauri in particular,

had financed the development of the Proudhon Spaceport Security Force into the planet's largest army.

The Kelly she'd known, the artificial Kelly, had replaced the original for some unknown agent.

What depressed her was the fact that the ersatz Kelly had been destroyed by the electromagnetic pulse from the nuclear attack on the Proteus commune—an EMP that would have killed her, had Kelly not stunned her and Ivor and gone out to save Dom himself.

Tetsami still wondered why Kelly, why an AI, a self-aware computer with no morality, ethics, or persona outside its own programming, had committed such a sacrifice.

Kelly was gone, Gavadi was out of it, Baetez was isolated under guard, as expected, all she had was Jarvis. She asked, and the duty nurse told her that Jarvis could see visitors. It was with somewhat mixed feelings that she went to visit him.

When she first met Jarvis, she had thought of him as ageless. Now, in a hospital bed with his lower body sheathed by a cast and medical apparatus, he simply looked old. There was the same steel look to his eyes, but distant.

Maybe it's just the context, she mused. Either that or depression was coloring her vision and she'd seen too much of this hospital in the past week.

Jarvis was awake, but it was a few minutes before he spoke. "I've been waiting for you to turn up." His voice was unchanged from the mercenary she'd known—which meant his mood was unreadable. Tetsami suspected that the threat she heard in his voice was mostly in her own mind.

"Well," Tetsami said, "I'm here." *Christ knows why.*

"I hear you saved my life."

Tetsami remembered the frigid hulk of the crash-landed *Shaftsbury,* and running around with an inadequate medkit when she was barely ambulatory. She shrugged. "I suppose so. Me and Kelly."

Jarvis' face showed a hint of surprise. "No one mentioned Kelly."

Tetsami drew a chair up to the side of the bed and asked, "Do you mind?" Jarvis shook his head no.

"No one here in Jefferson really knows about Kelly. He—" Tetsami's voice caught on an uncertainty and she finished, "—didn't make it."

Jarvis looked at her, closed his eyes, and nodded.

After a while he said, "Being here makes you uncomfortable."

"No, I'm—" Tetsami caught herself before she could finish the lie. "Yes. I don't know why I'm here. You're . . ." her voice trailed off.

"The enemy?" Jarvis finished for her.

"No, not that." She shook her head. "I'm just not having a good day."

Jarvis nodded.

"I wanted to talk. To someone, and—" Tetsami stood up. "Maybe I should go."

Jarvis reached out to her, his hand brushing hers. "Wait," he said.

"What?" she said.

"Tell me what's happened."

After a long hesitation, she nodded, returned to her seat, and told him.

CHAPTER FIVE

Expert Testimony

'The ship's destination doesn't matter when it is sinking."

—*The Cynic's Book of Wisdom*

"No protracted war can fail to endanger the freedom of a democratic country."

— ALEXIS DE TOCQUEVILLE
(1805–1859)

The comm setup that Dom had access to was a modified tightbeam sat uplink, one of the dozens that collected on the rooftops of Jefferson City. Just about every building that wasn't a monument had one. Ironic since there weren't any friendly sats up there to talk to anymore.

The Jeffersonians allowed him and his people to use one on top of one of the more mundane civic buildings. There were more convenient uplinks, on top of the hotel and the hospital for instance, but the Jeffersonians wanted to keep Dom—and his activities—under strict surveillance. Dom wasn't in a position to argue with his hosts. so he had to run a few blocks from the hospital and wait for an escort before he could call Diderot.

The run from the hospital took five minutes. Getting through security and being escorted to the roof took nearly an hour. During the wait Dom tried not to think about Bakunin being cracked like a nut between two arms of the Confederacy.

When they finally let him up to the roof, one minuteman stayed stationed by the access door. The blue-armored minuteman didn't offer any comment, and remained expressionless. But the tension the soldier contributed made it quite clear that the initial friendly inclination of Jefferson to its trio of refugees was wearing thinner with each hour of the siege.

The difference, Dom thought, *between a democracy and a totalitarian state decreases in direct proportion to the level of conflict.*

The guard's presence also made it clear that Jefferson did not consider Dom's communications privileged. Dom didn't let it bother him overmuch, since he was ingrained to treat any comm line he didn't personally control as compromised, and the Jeffersonians *were* still allies, for the moment.

The room itself was a standard broadcast console, and at the moment, Dom's was the only activity passing through this node on the communications web. This small room could handle upward of a thousand channels of full spectrum two-way data—and it was all dead except for him.

The isolation that implied was frightening. As far as Dom knew, there wasn't any cable strung between cities, just as there weren't many roads. Lack of a central government on Bakunin discouraged any such wide-ranging projects. With the loss of satellites, the entire planet of Bakunin was restricted to line-of-sight communications. Even shortwave wasn't very effective with Bakunin's spotty ionosphere.

Fortunately, Dom's people in the mountains had a number of arrays which had line of sight on Godwin, Jefferson, and just about everything in between. Most of it was tightbeam or passive in nature, and hadn't been targeted by enemy forces. That was ironic. The Diderot base had been a temporary measure, and had been in the process of being dismantled when the first forces began attacking. If it weren't for the invasion trapping a small cadre of people in the base up there, Dom, and Jefferson, wouldn't have *any* link to the outside world.

Currently, that link was a low resolution holo of Mariah Zanzibar, the head of security for the Bleek-Diderot Arms Consortium, the enterprise that Dom had created to replace Godwin Arms and Armaments. She had the regular update on the war for him, the real reason the Jeffersonians allowed him access to the comm.

"The situation in Godwin isn't great," she said. Godwin was the only other city with which they had any direct link. Just as Dom had a LOS link to the mountains here in Jefferson, Flower—an alien arms expert and the single Consortium board member trapped in Godwin—had another, more powerful, LOS transmitter in one of the Consortium's skyscrapers in central Godwin. Data that couldn't pass over the horizon from Godwin to Jefferson could, instead, be piped through the communication center in the Diderot Mountains.

Zanzibar explained the mess on the ground in Godwin, and it *wasn't* good. The fragmented social climate in the cities of Godwin was always near the boiling point, and the ongoing siege turned up the heat by a few orders of magnitude. In some senses it would have been better if the Proudhon force had invaded the city right off. What tenuous coalition Dom—and Random Walk acting as Dom—had managed to form at the last minute among the dozens of armed forces in Godwin was based on a common threat. Once the threat became less than immediate, the alliance began to crumble. Corporate security retreated to defend their assets, not from Proudhon, but from the growing bands of armed scavengers.

At the moment, Godwin was in more danger from its own population than it was from the Proudhon army.

"How long before Flower says the city will fall?"

"It says that its estimates are approximate, but it estimates collapse or surrender will occur within a week after the point where sixty percent of the corporate strongholds have consumed ninety percent of their emergency stores."

"What time frame does it give?"

"Eighteen to twenty-five days."

Dom groaned and felt his cheek twitch. "Is that Bakunin or standard?"

"Bakunin."

Thirty-four days standard, at best. Only slightly better.

Dom stared into Zanzibar's eyes, which the digital signal carved into oddly serrated images. "Not a lot of time," he said.

She shook her head. "No, and while we don't know for sure, Godwin might be the best equipped for this siege. Rumors are floating around Godwin that Wilson and Celine may have already fallen."

"No way we can be sure?"

Zanzibar shook her head. "But Random has been listening to the passive monitors, and from the mercs' own chatter it sounds like they hold the whole west coast from the equator north."

"Sinclair?"

Zanzibar nodded.

"Damnation and taxes." Dom paused for a long time. The inability to *do* anything gnawed at his gut. "We aren't going to get a chance to do anything, even if we could."

Worse, he had the inglorious duty of informing the Jefferson City fathers of how the war was going. He doubted his bad tidings would incline them toward helping him.

Help me do what? I'm as trapped here as anyone.

"I think that's all of that I want to hear, Zanzibar. Burst-feed the rest of it, I'll go over the record later."

Zanzibar nodded, and for a few seconds her image fuzzed to incomprehensibility as all the data in the comm's channel was used to ferry the last twenty-four hours of intelligence data.

When Zanzibar reappeared, she asked, "Is there anything else?"

"Yes," Dom said. "Let me talk to Random Walk."

"Random?" She sounded a bit surprised. He hadn't talked to Random directly since before the invasion. Dom had always talked to Zanzibar or Mosasa. "That's funny, Random said you'd ask for him. He included some special information in the report that he thought you'd want."

Dom got a funny feeling in his gut. "Can I talk to him?"

Zanzibar shook her head. "He's processing, or something. Mosasa is overseeing him."

"That special information, is it about what things are like in orbit?"

Zanzibar nodded.

* * *

The minuteman accompanied Dom to his meeting with the city fathers. It was part of the informal agreement that allowed him the use of Jefferson's largest comm sub-station. At the moment Dom was an unofficial extension of Jefferson City's Department of External Intelligence.

Considering the virtual communications embargo, Dom *was* Jefferson City's Department of External Intelligence.

His meeting was in the monumental Washington Hall, Jefferson's seat of executive power. As he was ushered through its pseudo-marble halls, accompanied by the clicking of the minuteman's boots, he wasn't thinking about the bad news he was about to deliver to a quintet of octogenarian democrats.

His thoughts were hovering about ten Bakunin planetary diameters out, beyond the orbit of Schwitzguebel, Bakunin's largest moon.

In the Diderot Mountains, Random Walk had no access to any satellites unless he decided to hack into one of Proudhon's, which bore an unacceptable risk of drawing the enemy's attention to the bunker in the mountains. However, Random still had access to optical surveillance devices. Ground-based optics were hell for resolving spaceborne aircraft, but they did allow a rough inventory of the numbers of things in orbit.

Random had, as a matter of course, kept tabs on the SEEC carrier in orbit. Some warning would be nice if the ships in that convoy maneuvered for a ground assault. An invasion by the SEEC on Proudhon's behalf would zero *any* chance this planet had of resistance.

Not that its chances looked all that great at the moment.

But Random's "special information" wasn't about the SEEC ships. The new element was the quadrupling of spaceborne attack craft. Because of the limited optics, and the surveillance's concentration on the SEEC carrier, the new ships could have tached in as long as seven days ago. At least, that was Random's estimate based on speed, trajectory, and who knew what else.

Ground-based optics weren't enough to tag an origin for the ships, but there were only three arms of the Confederacy that could put together a spaceborne fleet that large. The SEEC, Centauri, and the Indi Protectorate. SEEC was already here in more force than was necessary, and they were allied with Centauri.

That left Epsilon Indi.

Gavadi said to ask Indi for help. Indi was here. Indi was here in more than enough force to take care of Proudhon's mercenary army, three times the SEEC's potential invasion fleet.

Dom could almost feel it, the planet around him being torn apart in some Confed power play between Sirius' alliance and Indi's.

The minuteman interrupted his thoughts by opening the door for him. Dom walked into the presidential chambers to meet with the five city fathers.

The presidential chambers were subdued, more suited to an eighteenth-century law school than a twenty-fourth-century briefing room. Wood was everywhere. Wood was normally a sign of ostentation, but Dom noted the orange tint that marked it as native Bakunin wood. Must all be veneer, since Bakunin plant life was crappy building material.

The five presidents sat behind a high desk overlooking the rest of the room. Behind them, on the wall, were paintings of the political deities worshiped by this particular Bakunin settlement. Thomas Jefferson was up there, front and center, of course. George Washington, Benjamin Franklin, and a few other eighteenth-century types Dom didn't recognize. Dom was surprised not to see Abraham Lincoln; what little he knew about the North American States put Washington and Lincoln together. Dom had always figured they must have served during the same war or something.

Jefferson's presidents seemed to fit the room, looking more like professors waiting for a student's oral arguments than political leaders.

Dom had the advantage of a subcranial computer to remember the five individuals. Farthest to the right was Alexander Davis, the treasurer and head of the Jeffersonian economy—or the centrally run part of it, which gave Davis rather little to do. Davis was totally bald, and his

skin was so spotted and wrinkled that Dom would have
suspected that someone had propped a mummy up in his
seat if not for Davis' occasional reach for a glass of water.

Next seat over was Patricia Adams, the large woman
who was head of Jeffersonian domestic policy. She
looked like a cross between a librarian and a prison war-
den. Her grandmotherly countenance was hardened by the
severe way she pulled back her silver hair.

Third and center was Paul Hamilton, the youngest of
the quintet of chief executives. His hair was still black,
though graying at the temples, and he wore a razor-thin
mustache. He was, nominally, chief executive. First
among equals here. He not only presided over the presi-
dency, he also presided over the legislative house.

Fourth, to the left of Hamilton, was Richard Jackson,
the commander-in-chief of the Jeffersonian armed forces.
Like Davis, that gave the short, white-haired man rather
little to do, even during a siege. The Jeffersonian armed
forces weren't much.

Last was Elaine Madison, Jefferson's chief diplomat
and executor of Jeffersonian foreign policy. She sat
slightly back of the other executives, a hard smile on her
face.

"Please, have a seat, Mr. Magnus," said Hamilton. He
motioned toward a table to Dom's right. Dom took a seat
behind it. Sitting at a normal-sized table made the executives loom above him, as if he were some specimen on
display.

*I suppose I am. Jefferson never did have much contact
with the rest of Bakunin—too meshed into their own uto-
pia. I must be a novelty to them,* laissez-faire *taken to ex-
tremes.*

Jackson, the short head of the Jeffersonian military,
cleared his throat, "You have information on the
Proudhon invasion?" He mispronounced the name,
"Proud-hoon."

Dom nodded and relayed the news, all bad, he had gotten from Zanzibar.

The five executives nodded gravely during Dom's

speech, except for Davis, who occasionally would mutter, "Eh? What?"

Once he passed on most of what he knew, he was bombarded with questions from Jackson, Hamilton, and Adams. They wanted specifics—troop numbers, the strength of the force surrounding Jefferson, how long it could be before the invaders could expect reinforcements—

All questions that Dom could barely guess at the answers to.

After a long string of questions from Jackson, Dom sighed and rapped his fingers on the table. "Mr. Jackson, maybe I should put this in perspective. Jefferson City has a population of a half million. Out of that you have, what? At best, a hundred thousand able-bodied people for the militia? I'd guess you have arms to fully supply half that? Out of that, you have how many trained minutemen?"

Jackson grumbled.

"What, maybe five thousand? Twenty if you count your reserves? This isn't a commune skirmishing on your border. You are surrounded by elements of an army that might have over a million fully equipped and trained professional soldiers. This is an army that can wipe out a city this size in less than a day."

For the first time Madison, the diplomat, spoke. She asked, "Are you advising us to surrender?"

Dom shook his head. "I don't presume to advise, but my opinion is that any direct attack on a force like this would be suicidal. Not just for the force involved, but probably for every civilian in this city. Proudhon has already displayed its viciousness with every commune it considers economically expendable." Dom could picture, in his mind, the mushroom cloud that boiled over the Proteus commune.

"What would be your opinion of surrender, Mr. Magnus?" The other presidents turned to look at Madison, but Madison was concentrating on Dom.

Dom thought. It was a painful question. "I believe that you would be able to save your city and your civilian population by doing so. Proudhon wants the economic infrastructure of Bakunin intact. That means cities and people."

Madison nodded. "What about the armed forces, the political infrastructure?"

Dom looked at her. "I doubt Proudhon would allow them to remain. They want your sovereignty. That might mean disarming you, it might mean executions. It would depend on how much of a threat they perceive."

"I can't believe you are seriously—" Jackson started, but Madison interrupted him to address a final question to Dom.

"Your answers don't surprise me, but you've yet to answer my question. What is your *opinion* of surrender?"

"I think it is the second-worst possible option after a direct attack."

Jackson looked at Dom. "Fine for you to say all this, but if we will not surrender, and we cannot attack, what options does that leave us to consider?"

"Believe me, Mr. Jackson," Dom said, "I wish I knew."

CHAPTER SIX

Internal Exile

"Staring outward eventually leads to staring inward. Not vice versa."

—The Cynic's Book of Wisdom

"History is a cyclic poem written by Time upon the memories of man."

—PERCY BYSSHE SHELLEY
(1792–1822)

Kathy Shane, ex-captain of the Occisis marines, stood in an empty cavern deep within the honeycomb of the Diderot Mountain Range. The black rock walls vaulted overhead to form a chamber much taller than it was wide. The place felt like a chapel.

The feeling was appropriate because Shane stood next to a grave.

At her feet was a one-by-three-meter patch of fresh concrete. The new rectangle was near-white in appearance next to the black rock. Set into the concrete was the inscription, "Corporal Mary Hougland OMC. 2328–2350."

Below that, Shane had added, *"She did her duty."*

It was an unfair death for a soldier: malnutrition, exposure, overexertion, and delayed shock from severe exposure to a stun field. All of it was self-induced, by an attempted escape from people who intended, eventually, to let her go.

There had been no reason for Hougland to die. It seemed a cruel joke for Shane to bury her. Shane the turncoat. Shane the traitor.

It was unfair that Hougland was buried in a clandestine

grave, light-years from home. It was unfair that Hougland had no say in what happened to the thing she'd discovered.

Five days dead. Five long, bloody Bakunin days. Five days of warfare that made a joke of Confederacy ideals about planetary sovereignty. In the five days since Hougland's death, Shane had heard enough of the mercenary invasion and siege to become even more disillusioned with the Confederacy than she'd been when Dominic Magnus had recruited her.

Shane was half-convinced that, if Hougland were still alive, the Corporal would be appalled at how the Occisis marines had been used—as advisers and suppliers of an army-for-hire that would be illegal anywhere inside the Confederacy. An army legal here only because Bakunin was outside the jurisdiction of the Confederacy. Legal, but against everything the Confederacy and its Charter stood for.

Shane hoped that Hougland would have been appalled. But that was probably wishful thinking. The great majority of the marines had voiced no such objections—if they had any. They just followed their orders.

They followed those orders even when it required the vaporization of a few thousand civilians. They followed their orders even when it meant razing a commune that was as much a legitimate sovereign government as the one on Occisis, Khamsin, or Ch'uan.

Shane supposed that stress was turning her into a radical.

In the days since she had helped carve Hougland's tomb from the rock of the Diderot Mountains, Shane had come down faithfully, every morning. Each day she promised herself that she'd say something over Hougland's grave. Each time, words had failed to come. This morning was no different.

Shane stood in silence, the only mourner.

After a time, she walked away.

When the siege began, it'd become obvious that the small collection of officers from the Bleek-Diderot Arms consortium were going to be trapped in the mountains for the duration. Proudhon was targeting civilian air traffic as a matter of course, and the western plains of Bakunin's one continent were dotted now with aircar wrecks, mostly refugees that had been caught at the wrong place at the wrong time.

Chance had trapped six people in the remains of a base that had been designed to hold fifteen hundred. The Bleek-Diderot base in the mountains was one of the few places that was not worried about Proudhon's squeezing their supplies. They could hold out for a lot longer than the rest of the planet. Especially since two of the six people trapped here didn't eat.

The six counted Mariah Zanzibar, Dom's chief of security from the old Godwin Arms, who was supposed to fulfill the same role for Bleek-Diderot, if not for this inconvenient war. It counted Tjaele Mosasa, the resident electronics whiz and ersatz human. It counted Random Walk, Mosasa's AI device, who lived in the wiring, in robot simulacrum, and possibly in Mosasa. It counted Gregory Fitzgerald and Xi Nuy Tran, a pair of commandos and corporate security who had served with Zanzibar nearly as long as Zanzibar had served Domnic Magnus.

And it included Kathy Shane, ex-Captain and traitor, an object of scorn for everyone but Random Walk and Mosasa—and knowing what she did about Random and Mosasa, that didn't make her feel better.

It had been Shane's project to bury Hougland down here. Everyone else would have seen Hougland's body as a disposal problem. Shane saw her ex-comrade's burial as something deserving respect. So it was her doing, carving the grave, setting the memorial.

Shane had chosen the site, down here, near Hougland's discovery. That, Shane thought, would make up for some of the ugliness, putting Hougland's memorial next to the archaeological find of the millennium.

That cheered Shane a little as she navigated up the uneven slope toward the great pyramidal void. No matter what happened now, this find was a permanent part of human history. No matter what secrecy cloaked it in the near term, Hougland's name would be permanently linked to it.

The passage Shane walked slowly acquired the form of a pentagonal prism. The walls flattened out and began to reveal the alien script that looked like a cross between cuneiform writing and Celtic knotwork. Just before the passage reached the base of the pyramidal chamber, the carvings had acquired the intricate coloring that made the walls appear like woven tapestries, and not carved stone.

Every fifty meters along the passage a small lantern cast a white mercury glow. Shane had placed the lanterns. Their batteries would last six months standard, so she'd just taken a dozen and left them along the path. It was a waste of resources, when she could have just taken a flashlight down here, but the evacuation of the mountain had left so much behind it didn't matter.

The edges of the walls, where they joined, became razor sharp when Shane entered the base of the pyramid.

The first time she had seen the pyramid fully illuminated, she had stared for hours, breathless. Now, since she'd made camp here for the past week, she could walk into the massive space and barely notice the structure around her.

The pyramid—the inverse of a pyramid, actually a pyramid-shaped cavern carved out of the rock—was five-sided and angled slightly wrong, too shallow for a human used to the proportions of Cheops. At each corner of the pyramid, a pentagonal tunnel led off, up or down. Each tunnel was swathed in carvings that slowly degraded to near invisibility a few hundred meters from this spot.

After a hundred million years, that was only to be expected.

What wasn't to be expected was this whole pyramid, intact, after all that time. Somehow it had been preserved by a combination of Bakunin's seismic quiescence, and a near-invisible transparent coating that protected the carvings and the dyes that covered them.

Shane's camp was near the center of the great chamber, under the peak. Her bed, hotplate, computer, the mining equipment that she'd used to bury Hougland, all sat within a ring of tripod-mounted spotlights. The spotlights were lit, illuminating the carvings on the ceiling—the Dolbrian starmap. Covering the five triangular ceiling panels of the pyramid was a map a million times older than the Confederacy and covering an area ten times as vast.

Shane walked to her bed and turned on her computer.

One of the jobs she had assigned herself, since she had no function within the Bleek-Diderot Consortium now, was to record the data implicit in the carving above her. The value of this find was only half in the carving itself—though it was priceless in that respect, the most well-preserved artifact left from the Dolbrian civilization, a civilization that had, apparently, died out before any of the five known alien intelligences had reached sentience.

It certainly wasn't the largest Dolbrian artifact. That designation was left for the planets they'd terraformed. The Confederacy knew of five—with this pyramid, it was probably six—planets that the Dolbrians had definitely terraformed. Planets that otherwise would never be habitable. One of them, Mars, had regressed to a pre-Dolbrian state long before humans had evolved.

Those five were the short list. The long list, the possible sites, could number more than twenty.

With this map, and a little kinematics to move the stars over a hundred million years worth of relative motion, Shane had already raised that number of possibles by an order of magnitude. Working on something like this made anything else seem petty. Alpha Centauri, her home planet of Occisis, had used the information on one shard of a map like this, a shard covering a dozen light-years, to insure its own domination of the Confederacy for the first half of the Confederacy's existence. Advance knowledge of where a single habitable planet was located was enough to broker a huge amount of political power in the Confederacy. Five or ten could insure the dominance of an arm of the Confederacy.

Today, only Indi and Sirius could afford the expensive star-by-star surveys that were IDing planets on the growing fringes of the Confederacy. Planets of marginal value, useful only for their future political weight in the Terran Congress. The other arms of the Confederacy were much less forward-looking.

The internal political machinations of the Confederacy

was laughably small compared to what was above Shane. Above her were, at her last count, fifteen *hundred* stars that seemed to harbor a habitable planet. The area of the Confederacy only covered a rough, dumbbell-shaped patch near the peak. One triangular section of the pyramid was almost totally free of human exploration.

Shane started her working day by heating a ration and aiming a holo camera at another section of the carving. That section was fed into her computer's memory. She would spend the next few hours getting her computer to ID the stars, decipher what she could of the Dolbrian labels— not much, a lot of the language was untranslatable—and thinking about them.

Living down here the last five days, it was hard to credit the common belief that the Dolbrians were extinct. How could you kill off something that had spread, at a minimum, over a thousand light-years of space? That was a substantial fraction of the galaxy. In fact, the map covered a wide enough area that Shane could see some of the Milky Way's macro-structure in the distribution of the stars above her head. On this side they were slightly denser than that side. Then there was an area that was very thinly populated that must have been the boundary of one of the galaxy's spiral arms.

Shane had decided that, while the Dolbrians might not be here, in the tiny dumbbell shape near the peak of the pyramid, they certainly shouldn't be extinct. The Dolbrians had the whole galaxy to hide in and maybe other galaxies, too.

Shane wondered what the Dolbrians might make of humanity. Humans might not even seem intelligent to them.

She was deep into her growing catalog, absently eating from her cooling ration, when she heard motion in the pyramid behind her. She drew her sidearm and was pointing it before she was aware of exactly what she'd heard.

Behind her, by one of the pentagonal corridors, floated a flattened spheroid about a meter in diameter. It bristled with sensors, and dangled manipulators like a chromed jellyfish.

"Your motor functions are improving," it said by way of greeting.

"Random," Shane said, lowering the laser. She was somewhat pleased that the reference to past injuries didn't start the laser shaking. "What are you doing here?" The floating thing was a robot that seemed to carry part of Random Walk's brain. In large part, it was responsible for the discovery of the pyramid, somehow knowing that Hougland's escape would lead to this place.

In the same way, it was responsible for Hougland's death.

Random carried a human facade over its programming, but it was an alien piece of hardware. Shane knew that better than anyone here, besides Mosasa, who was probably a part of Random.

"Things are developing. You'll be needed up at base."

"Why?"

Random tilted up at the ceiling, "You have an interest in this, correct?"

"What has this to do with anything?"

"Everything, of course. Come."

Shane packed and followed the robot.

CHAPTER SEVEN

Third Parties

"A dependent ally is a resentful one."
                    —*The Cynic's Book of Wisdom*

"Covenants without swords are but words."
                    —THOMAS HOBBES
                    (1588–1679)

Robert Kaunda sat near the back of the Congressional Chamber at the base of the Confederacy spire. He watched the second day of opening business with a boiling stomach. Every few minutes he'd reach into a pocket and pull out a chalky tablet that he'd pop into his mouth. It was a home remedy that hadn't worked since he'd come to Earth.

Below him, on the dais, stood the Confederacy's chief executive, Dimitri Olmanov. The dais was the focus of the semicircular Congressional Chamber. Behind him was the blue-and-white flag of Earth with its globe and olive branches. Next to the Earth's flag was the black and gold flag of the Confederacy, a pentagon made of seventy-five golden stars on a black background. Five arms of the Confederacy, seventy-five systems within it.

Kaunda's tablet caught on a rear molar and turned to paste in the back of his mouth. The taste used to remind him of home; now the chalky tablet only reminded him of how much he hated politics.

Kaunda sat back in the chamber, along with the ten other representatives from his arm of the Confederacy— the Union of Independent Worlds. Of the five arms of the Confederacy, his was the least powerful. Of the ten representatives seated around him, only two actually held votes in the Congress. It embarrassed Kaunda that the Union representatives looked the part.

His entire delegation looked like tourists. They wore clothes that must have been the height of fashion on Miridor, Gambela, or Xiuhtecutli. The flowered shirts and traditional robes weren't appropriate—at least Kaunda didn't think so.

As the representative for Mazimba, and holder of the Union's only prime seat, he dressed to match his seniority. He wore a suit he had bought here on Earth. The cut was even more conservative than the clothes worn by the Centauri delegates—but the clothes helped him feel safe.

Especially when he felt this far out of his depth.

As Dimitri Olmanov addressed the assembled Congress, his words were instantly translated into the twenty-five languages represented in this room. Kaunda's own earpiece was programmed for French and a half-dozen African languages, but he left it turned off. Dimitri's address didn't interest him.

What interested Kaunda was the possibility of war.

As Dimitri talked, Kaunda wiped his sweaty palms against the red leather of his seat.

Damn Vashniya, Kaunda thought. *The dwarf bastard is trying to start a war. I never should have signed on to this Bakunin business. It's all treachery.*

Kaunda had risen from chief of police in Mulawayo, Mazimba's capital city, to being the chief intelligence officer for the entire Union. He missed the clarity of police work.

He scanned the audience, looking for Sim Vashniya.

There were over seventy people here—representatives from almost every inhabited planet officially under Confed jurisdiction. The various arms of the Confederacy grouped together in blocks of seats. The representatives from the Alpha Centauri Alliance and the Sirius-Eridani Economic Community were all seated together, taking a quarter of the auditorium for their thirty-five representatives.

Vashniya was opposite them, sitting at the head of the wedge of seats dedicated to the People's Protectorate of

Epsilon Indi. Thirty-five representatives sat with Indi, representing almost as many votes as Centauri and Sirius together.

But not quite, that's why the bastard needs us.

"Do we really need him?" Kaunda muttered.

It was easy to pick Vashniya out from the crowd. He sat in front, a squat gnome, flesh the color of teak, gray beard covering his chest, the top of his bald head reflecting the lights aimed at the dais below. Vashniya was wearing that same damn smile he always wore, which irritated Kaunda.

He's smiling, while a fleet of Indi warships is facing off against the SEEC outside of anyone's *jurisdiction.*

The two fleets, fifteen light-years away from them, could have already begun shooting. An interstellar war could be racing toward them, even now. The message documenting the first shot could already be speeding through tach-space.

And Vashniya was smiling.

If war erupted in the Confederacy, Kaunda knew he bore partial responsibility for allying himself with Indi. At the time it had made sense. However, the sense of it had been diminishing ever since he, Vashniya, and Hernandez—the sole representative the Seven Worlds deigned to send—had appeared in Sol space to present a unified front to the age-old dominance of Centauri and Sirius.

He looked to a closer bank of empty seats. Across an aisle from the Union delegation, sitting by herself, was the sole representative for the nonhuman Seven Worlds. Kaunda looked at the feline form of Francesca Hernandez and felt his stomach tighten. The tablet in his mouth was gone, leaving a dry, empty taste behind.

Hernandez turned to look at him. Her expression was frightening, if only because it was unreadable to Kaunda. Her face was that of a jungle cat, a cat whose eyes held a not-quite-human intelligence.

They looked at each other for a long time. Then she stood, sliding out from the chair, and strode out of the chamber. Watching her tied Kaunda's gut in a knot. Kaunda was no diplomat, but he knew a deliberate snub when he saw one. Walking out on Dimitri's speech was designed to provoke someone—

Or maybe he was just being paranoid.

Kaunda looked back toward Vashniya, and the little teak gnome was no longer smiling.

Maybe it wasn't paranoia.

Dimitri Olmanov continued speaking as if nothing had happened, as if the seats for the Seven Worlds had always been empty, which they usually were. Kaunda wished he were better able to interpret the signal Hernandez had just sent. All he could think was that there was a strain on the nominal alliance holding Indi, the Union, and the Seven Worlds together.

Kaunda thought himself a fool now for allying himself—and by extension, the entire Union—with Indi. The Union's independence had been the only political asset it had going for it, and Kaunda had dealt it away for Vashniya's dream of toppling the Europeans.

Vashniya might still do it, too. It was just that Kaunda was beginning to see the Confederacy toppling with it, and he was wondering if Hernandez knew something he didn't.

After a day of vacuous speeches—speeches that showed no sign that the Confederacy might be verging on a crisis—there was a night of receptions, diplomatic parties greeting the thousands of extraterrestrial invaders that flooded Earth's capital city every decade.

Kaunda didn't want to attend any of the parties, but if he didn't it would appear as a snub, and someone might figure out exactly how worried he was.

So Robert Kaunda spent the hot summer night circulating from compound to compound, circling the diplomatic areas huddled around the base of the Confederacy spire. Where he really wanted to be was in the basement of his own embassy. It seemed a distortion of priorities to allow his obligations as a congressional representative for Mazimba to overshadow his duty as the Union's chief of intelligence.

He knew those thoughts were unjustified. Any news over the tach-comm would be six days old and from fifteen light-years away at least. Here, in Sydney's hive of diplomacy, he had a chance of picking up news that was fresher: news of what was occurring on Earth.

And what was happening on Earth was at least as important to the fate of the Confederacy and, by extension, the fate of the Union.

The Thubohu Embassy hosted the third reception he'd been at tonight. It was to be one of hundreds he'd have to attend during the opening weeks of the Congress. Kaunda mechanically shook hands and decided that he didn't much like the place.

Thubohu orbited a large whitish main-sequence star twenty light-years off in the direction of Orion. It was a SEEC world that had been founded sixty years before there *was* a Confederacy, and the diplomatic building the reception was held in was older than the Union Kaunda represented.

And, like all pre-Confed planets, Kaunda sensed a subtle attitude of superiority from the Thubohu diplomats. *Subtle, hell,* Kaunda thought. *They think you're a barbarian hick.*

Despite all that, Kaunda concentrated on being social. He also concentrated on listening.

What he heard was discouraging. Bakunin, and the operation around it, made no ripples on the surface of Confed diplomacy. That meant that the operation was still well-buried. Still secret. That seemed to make it all the more likely that something irrevocable might happen.

He was half-listening to a fat Slav from Jokul discuss the import of compact fusion generators when, out of the corner of his eye, he saw Francesca Hernandez.

He excused himself from the impenetrable conversation and walked over to the Grimalkin representative.

Kaunda was surprised to see Hernandez making the rounds after her exit from the Congress. The Seven Worlds was the most insular of the arms of the Confederacy. They barely participated in the Congress, didn't even have an embassy on Earth. Hernandez was their first representative to the Congress in thirty years.

She should have been mobbed by diplomats, but, instead, Hernandez was alone by the buffet table, much of the party giving her a wide berth. Kaunda supposed it was either her exit, or because she was nonhuman

She was feline, and taller than any of the humans in the room. She had spotted yellow fur, a broad pink nose, and slitted yellow irises. Her stance was odd, balanced on a pair of broad digitigrade feet, and she had a tail as thick as Kaunda's wrist. She also stood out because she wore no clothing to hide her alien form, only a wide belt hanging off of her oddly proportioned hips.

Maybe the other diplomats found her intimidating. However, Kaunda thought it more likely that these people, diplomats or not, found it difficult to accept the results of genetic engineering—even three centuries after the fact.

Kaunda stepped up next to the buffet table and gathered a couple of miniature poppy-seed bagels.

"So, how are you finding the Congress?" Kaunda asked.

She turned to regard him. As her eyes shifted from shadow to light, Kaunda noted the disturbingly fast reaction of her pupils, turning from ovals to slits. "Some of it is tedious."

Her voice was deep and rumbling, like a well-tuned engine. Kaunda reassessed his reaction to her exit from the Congress. It could be the only signal she was sending was boredom.

"I know the feeling," Kaunda said. He ate one of the bagels, which were chewier than he expected. As he ate, he became aware of the rest of the room. A few of the other people were looking off in their direction. Especially, he noticed Kalin Green, the Cynos representative and his opposite number in the SEEC intelligence community. She seemed to be interested in both of them. "You don't seem to be enjoying the party," Kaunda said.

"These parties aren't here to be enjoyed."

"Perhaps," Kaunda said. He picked up another few bagels so he wouldn't be tempted to stare at Green. "Maybe you would like to take a walk?"

Her nose wrinkled and smoothed out immediately. Kaunda had the sense that he'd just witnessed an unconscious display of emotion, but he had no idea what emotion it was. Hernandez glanced at the wider room and said, "It is time to go to the next party."

Kaunda nodded. The cat didn't feel any safer talking here than he did.

The two of them walked the gardens hugging the base of the Confederacy spire. The spire itself shot up a kilometer into the night sky, cutting out a slice of night for its own vertical constellation.

The paths they walked were landscaped to the last bit of gravel, and constantly monitored by Confed security. Because of that, Kaunda waited until they had passed into the area surrounding the Union's diplomatic compound before he said, "Do you know what Vashniya has pulled?"

"We are on your grounds?" she asked.

Kaunda nodded.

"The Protectorate has just tached in a fleet of warships to confront the Sirius fleet in orbit around Bakunin. That is what you refer to, correct?"

Kaunda wondered where the hell this cat got that information. The Seven Worlds had *no* intelligence apparatus beyond their borders. "Did Vashniya tell you this?"

"No," she said.

They had stopped on a bridge, and Hernandez leaned on the railing to look into the water. Kaunda noticed her flex her claws.

"Those Indi ships," Kaunda said, "came from Dharma, over fifty-five light-years from Bakunin. Travel time to tach-space, even for a military transport, would be better than three months."

Hernandez nodded, but she kept staring into the water.

"Even a tach-comm message would take three weeks."

She nodded again.

"The orders to send those ships were given before we ever voted on the operation on Bakunin."

"Vashniya had to hedge in case the vote failed."

"You don't believe that any more than I do. He makes a career out of knowing down to the planet how a vote's going to go."

Silence enveloped the two of them.

After a few long moments, Hernandez finally said, "So?"

"Doesn't it matter to you? We've allied with Indi, while secretly Vashniya's been plotting a war."

"You know that's not Vashniya's intent." Hernandez looked at him with a face that seemed all the more alien and predatory in the foliage-dappled moonlight. "Besides, the conflict would be between Indi and the SEEC. Our arms would not be involved."

Kaunda stared at her, trying to gauge her thoughts. "It could cause the fatal destabilization of the Confederacy."

"I thought that was the point of Vashniya's project."

Kaunda looked out over the water and stared at the moon's broken reflection. "If that was the point, I was duped. I only wanted a little bigger voice for the Union inside the Congress."

"Do you plan to fight Vashniya's plan now?"

"Are you kidding? I was committed to the coming votes long ago. If I changed course now ..." Kaunda thought of all the persuasion he had used to convince the body of the Union's ten governments to back him on this plan. It was supposed to result in an extra prime seat for the Union when this was all over. If he pulled out now, not only would his career be destroyed, but only the gods knew what Indi could do to the Union in retaliation during the upcoming votes. He shook his head. "The Union's much too small to even think of fighting the Protectorate."

Hernandez nodded, as if that was the answer she expected. "That's why the Seven Worlds doesn't participate in the politics of the Confederacy. Too much balanced against us. Much easier to stay within our own sphere and ignore you."

"Why did you get involved in Vashniya's plan, then? You get nothing out of it. None of your planets are eligible for prime status."

Hernandez made a sound that could have been a feline cough, or a laugh.

"Well?"

"I've told you," she said. She began walking down the path again, leaving him without an explanation.

Could it be, Kaunda thought, *that she* wants *the Confederacy destabilized?*

CHAPTER EIGHT

Public Relations

"Knowing what is worst does not tell you what is best."

—*The Cynic's Book of Wisdom*

"The fault, dear Brutus, is not in our stars/ But in ourselves."

—WILLIAM SHAKESPEARE
(1564–1616)

"Can you call up to her room again?" Dom asked.

The man behind the desk gave Dom a resentful look that was becoming all too common. "I will give her your messages when she comes back to the hotel, sir. She is not here at the moment. She has not been here all day."

Dom drummed the metal fingers of his right hand on the desk. "Will you please call the room? Maybe she came in without checking her messages?"

The man sighed and tapped on the computer set into the desk. It was a pointless exercise. Tetsami wasn't there. She hadn't been there the last five times Dom had checked.

And she wasn't there the half-dozen times he'd checked yesterday.

"Thanks," Dom said, before the man could ask him if he wanted to leave yet another message.

He had not seen Tetsami since she had thrown him out of her hotel room. Ever since, his state of mind had been worsening. The near-inevitability of Bakunin's surrender didn't help matters any.

Dom rubbed at a tic in his cheek as he headed toward

the lobby doors. He still needed to visit the barracks and make another call to Diderot. Random's report had implied that there was something that Dom could do, though it strictly avoided saying *what*.

Dom wanted to talk to Random Walk personally.

Damn it. Dom thought as he stepped out into the moonlight, *She always complains about how I've kept her in the dark. Now, when I want to tell her how things are going, she disappears.*

"As if that's the real reason I want to talk to her," Dom whispered.

A gruff voice greeted him as he left the hotel. "Maybe she's avoiding you."

Dom turned to see Ivor, standing outside the light cast by the lobby doors. Even in the shadow-dappled moonlight, Dom could tell Ivor had gotten little sleep the past two days. As little sleep as Dom had. Unlike Dom, fatigue showed on Ivor. If anything, the tired cast of Ivor's face accented his imposing stature.

Dom only responded by nodding.

"She can be headstrong," Ivor said. "She may have learned that from me."

"You don't like me, do you."

Ivor shook his head. "You're arrogant, Dominic. I'd say megalomaniacal if I didn't have your brother to compare you with."

Dom shrugged. "I didn't put myself here."

Ivor stepped up to him. He was twenty years older, and maybe a head taller. "You live for that, don't you? All the self-recriminations."

Dom took a step back. "Look I—"

"Shut up!" Ivor said. "God knows what she sees in you, I don't. But if you were just *using* her—"

"No!"

"I said shut up!" Ivor grabbed the front of Dom's shirt. "I am way too old for this crap. The only reason I'm involved with your war is because I care about Tetsami. She's the only family I have left."

With Ivor looking at him like that, Dom could see the face of Robert Elision the man Ivor had been, or could have been. "What do you want from me?"

"I want you to stop playing with her. Either you *are* going to have a relationship with her, or you let her go."

"Let her go?"

"Let her out of this damn conflict of yours. Out of the war, out of the conspiracies, out of the damn arms company. No grand meetings, no plots, no updates on the 'situation.' "

"But she has a right—"

Ivor shook him. "She has a right to not have you shoved in her face every day if you have no intention of—"

"Damnation, what was that?"

"Don't change the subject— Good Lord . . ."

Something was happening on the roof of Jefferson Hospital, a few blocks away. There was something strange happening in the courtyard. The sight was obscured by the wings of the hospital, but from what was visible between ivy-covered buildings, a matte-black something was eating the floodlights. Black would swell, and the light would disappear.

Dom knew what the something was, the Protean egg.

"What is it doing?" Ivor asked, dropping Dom's shirt.

"Moving." Dom said.

The egg was floating smoothly, following the inside walls of the courtyard. Physical objects like trees and floodlights didn't seem to obstruct its path. It sucked up light as it passed.

"Where's it going?"

That was a good question. The egg hadn't moved since it had followed Dom here from Proteus. Dom was unsure of even what it *was* exactly, except it represented a sliver of technology beyond anything the Confederacy had, that it was some sort of spacecraft, and that the Proteans called it a seed.

This was the most active Dom had ever seen it.

"It looks like it is tracking something inside the hospital—"

"Some*body* most likely. It followed you. It must track people somehow."

Both of them started jogging toward the hospital. Dom did not like the feeling he was getting. Not only was the egg his responsibility, but it represented a huge unknown. Dom didn't like unknowns.

When they ran up to the courtyard, they found they weren't the egg's only audience. A crowd of people had massed around the edges of the courtyard, and armed minutemen were holding people back. The minutemen didn't have a difficult job, no one was going anywhere inside the courtyard.

"What the hell is it doing?" Ivor said, when they finally got a good view of what was happening. They were in back of a three-deep line of people blocking the northern entrance to the courtyard. A similar mass of people gathered to the south, but that crowd was thinner. Probably because they were out of sight of the egg.

The hospital was laid out in the shape of an H, oriented north-south. The bar of the H was a three-story wing hanging above the central courtyard, blocking the view of the southern spectators.

The egg, at this point, had reached the third floor and was hovering along the wall of the northeastern wing. It seemed even blacker than normal, if such a thing were possible. There seemed no dimension to it, just a hole in Dom's point of view. If it weren't for the fact that it cast a shadow, it would be hard for the eye to believe it existed.

"That was a laser shot," Ivor said quietly.

Dom turned to look at Ivor. Ivor was looking up at the northwest wing, not the egg. Whatever he'd seen was gone now.

In a few moments, however, it was obvious that he'd seen something, since all the minutemen who were involved in crowd control got squawks on their radios. Most of them ran for the western wing of the hospital.

"Oh, shit," Dom said. "That's where they're keeping Baetez."

CHAPTER NINE

Security Breach

"Bystanders get shot."
                    —*The Cynic's Book of Wisdom*

"If we believe absurdities we shall commit
atrocities."
                                    —VOLTAIRE
                                    (1694–1778)

Marc Baetez was disgusted by Jefferson City. He found
his captors' naïveté irritating. It was a subject that he'd
been given a lot of time to ponder. It had been six over-
long Bakunin days since he had woken up under minuteman guard.

Baetez was a lieutenant in the Terran Executive
Command, and this was not the way he'd run things. If
he'd been taken prisoner by the TEC, he would have been
given a cortical implant and had his brain strip-mined by
now.

He would also be in a windowless cell, not a hospital
room.

He lay on his back and looked out his window. The
window was barred, and the view choked by ivy, but he
could still see outside. Simply by looking out of that window and enjoying the view, Baetez now had a tentative
mental map of the hospital complex and some of the surrounding city.

The only restraint on him, besides the minutemen outside the door, was a near-antique handcuff chaining his
left arm to the bed, and casts on his right arm and leg.
The casts were of negligible importance, as long as he
didn't become involved in a chase.

All things being equal, Baetez would just wait things out. He knew, from eavesdropping through too-thin walls, that the siege was proceeding even better than planned. Cities had already surrendered. In short order, his captors would no longer be relevant.

However, within the amateurish leakage of information the Jeffersonians provided him was one tidbit that Baetez had to do something about: the name "Dominic Magnus."

Dominic Magnus was a priority target. Colonel Klaus Dacham, the man in charge of the TEC operation on Bakunin, had made it clear that the capture of Magnus took precedence over all other facets of the mission. With Magnus here, in Jefferson City, Baetez had to get word back to TEC operations. That meant that he had to escape his pathetic confinement—

He also needed to commandeer some sort of communications equipment. It didn't need to be specialized; the TEC and Proudhon's mercenary army would be monitoring the entire spectrum of data transmission.

Baetez had been pondering that ever since he had heard Magnus' name.

Today he had the answer.

A doctor had come in to examine Baetez's progress, all the time complaining about the loss of Bakunin's commercial airwaves. *Should be an improvement,* Baetez'd thought; he'd seen some of those programs.

The doctor had showed total unawareness of the fact that he was imparting vital information to a prisoner while he moaned about the loss of his favorite holo programs—*wait until it's no longer a siege, and he sees some real casualties.*

First, the doctor's complaints had told Baetez that, as planned, all non-Proudhon satellites had been destroyed in the first few minutes of the invasion. Second, the doctor had let Baetez know that there was a sat uplink on the roof of the hospital.

All Baetez needed to do was make it two floors up, to the roof.

Simple.

At least, it was as simple as it was ever going to get. Baetez had stared out the window until he was certain he knew where the uplink had to be. Since it was out of his line of sight, it took him some time to decide where it was. But when he did, he decided that it would have to be above the northwestern wing of the hospital, his wing.

Baetez started on the cuffs shortly after the lights were killed in his room. The cuff on his left wrist was antique, some polyceram alloy with the cuffs hinged, not chained. Close to indestructible and tight enough on his wrist to preclude slipping out of them.

The cuffs might be old, but they'd been designed to restrain a prisoner. The bed the cuff was attached to was not.

Starting after lights out—Baetez assumed he was under camera surveillance, though he expected that the Jeffersonians were as slack about that as about everything else—he began turning the bar that the cuff was attached to. The bar was a threaded pipe, parallel to the mattress. Baetez counted a hundred and sixty-five half-turns before it came loose in his hand.

The man's got a broken leg, he could imagine the thought process going. *Not a threat.*

Leg and arm might restrict his mobility, but he was an agent of the TEC. It was time some of these backwater utopians understood what that meant.

Without changing his position, Baetez hefted the pipe in his hand. Solid stainless steel, heavy, about a meter long. The threads gave it a dangerous grip, hard on his palm.

It would do.

Again, without changing his position, he made a gurgling noise down in his throat.

Outside, he heard the minuteman shift his weight.

That's right . . .

Baetez was tempted to turn his head to watch the door, but he didn't. He kept his head facing the window, off to his left.

He tightened his grip on the bar and repeated the noise, adding a few coughs to it. It sounded like he was trying to gargle with rubber cement.

Definitely, he heard the minuteman move.

Outside the window, the larger moon was rising behind

the northeastern wing of the hospital. There was something else odd, a black shadow across the courtyard. Before Baetez could see what it was, a reflected sliver of
light widened across the window. Soon the doorway's
reflection obscured the night beyond. Baetez forgot the
shadows outside as a minuteman's shadow crossed the reflected light.

Baetez coughed again, hard enough to hurt his throat.

The minuteman rounded the bed and came between
Baetez and the window. His sidearm was holstered, and
his militia rifle was slung across his back.

Fool.

Baetez froze, ceased even to breathe, and stared at a
point in space somewhere beyond the minuteman's
crotch.

"Hey you all right?" he asked.

The minuteman reached across the bed, toward the
emergency call button. The moment the man's eyes
shifted from him, Baetez swung up with the steel bar. The
bar struck the man at the junction between his jaw and his
neck, tearing a rectangle of flesh where the threads bit.

The minuteman's eyes widened in shock as he collapsed backward. His left hand went reflexively to his
jaw. His right reached for his sidearm.

It never got there.

Baetez sat up and swung his right arm, with the cast,
into the man's face. The wrist of the cast came up to
crush the minuteman's nose in a blow that, done ideally,
was supposed to kill.

The minuteman dropped to his knees, eyes staring.

Baetez, still swinging off the bed, wasn't satisfied. He
brought the steel bar down across the back of the minuteman's neck. The minuteman fell face first into the
ground.

Baetez let the bar slip out of his fingers and through
the cuff still attached to his wrist. *Here's where we find
out if they have adequate video surveillance.* He put his
cast-bearing leg on the back of the minuteman's neck.
Then he unclipped the shoulder straps on the minuteman's militia rifle. It took too long one-handed.

Almost as old as the cuff on his wrist, the rifle was a

caseless slug thrower, eleven millimeters at least. One-handed, it would probably break his wrist.

Baetez reached down and grabbed the minuteman's sidearm.

Random-frequency GA&A antipersonnel laser, fully charged. That was more like it.

Baetez tested the weapon on the guard. It was satisfactory.

He wanted to strip the guard's body armor for himself, but Baetez doubted he could fit it over his casts and his handcuffs. And right now, time was his number one enemy. He heard no alarms, but that meant little. The lack of immediate reaction *also* meant little. There could still be video surveillance of this room.

Baetez hopped to his feet and shoved the guard's body under the hospital bed.

Now he had to get to the sat uplink.

Somewhere, deep in the back of his mind, Baetez knew he was on a suicide mission. He didn't let that knowledge travel to the front of his brain. His training took over; he had to get an important piece of intelligence back to his superiors.

Baetez hobbled to the door to his room, which was still halfway open.

Even if his room wasn't on a video monitor, the halls definitely were. Once he was there, it would be a race to get to the sat uplink before they got to him.

He glanced out.

Wide, white, well-lit halls smelling slightly of disinfectant. No one was in sight of the narrow crack of doorway he was looking from. Baetez slowly pulled the door open with the barrel of the laser, slowly revealing more of the hallway outside.

Finally he could see the intersection where this corridor branched off into the other wings of the hospital.

"Hey." A woman's voice came from down the other end of the hallway.

Baetez spun, pivoting on his cast. A doctor stood, alone, in the middle of the hallway. The doctor was just realizing something was wrong when Baetez fired a polychromatic beam of energy into her neck.

She clutched her neck and dropped before Baetez stopped firing, drawing a burned groove across her hand and face.

Knowing that he now had little or no time left, Baetez started a lumbering jog down the hall, away from the intersection, toward the doctor. He used the wall for partial support and hoped that he would come across stairs or an elevator before security found him.

Somewhere above him was a satellite uplink.

CHAPTER TEN

Damage Control

"Once you leap, looking makes little difference."
—*The Cynic's Book of Wisdom*

"The worst vice of the fanatic is his sincerity."
—OSCAR WILDE
(1854–1900)

"So do you love this guy or not?" Jarvis asked her.

Tetsami chuckled at the question. This was her third visit with Jarvis in two days, and fortunately—despite his usually abrasive persona—he took well to being a receptacle for all of Tetsami's emotional baggage.

"I don't know. Hell, I don't know what love is. I do software."

"Do you think he loves you?"

Tetsami shrugged. "He might think he does. If he just wasn't so damn irritating—"

Jarvis sat up a little, as much as his cast would allow. "Look, kid, I don't presume to know anything much outside of small-unit tactics. I do know a small bit about wartime romances—"

"Well that's not exactly what we're—" Tetsami paused. "Is it?"

"Take any two people and turn their lives upside down. Put them in a situation that they might not live through. Things happen in situations like that that don't happen otherwise."

"You're saying it won't work between me and Dom?"

Jarvis shook his head. "I'm saying that this is the wrong time to worry if it will work. We're still in a war here, and either one of you could be killed tomorrow."

Tetsami shook her head. "So you're telling me to do what?"

"Worry about *now* more than tomorrow."

"Well—" Tetsami was interrupted by what sounded like a small army running through the corridor outside. "What the—?"

"Six men," Jarvis said, "marching in formation."

Before she could ask Jarvis how he could tell that from the sound, the door to the room bust open to admit a minuteman in full regalia. Blue body armor, helmet with heads-up visor, green lights flashing on the personal field generator on his belt, militia rifle at the ready—

"What the hell is going on out there?" Tetsami asked.

"Armed man loose in the hospital, madam," responded the minuteman, taking a position facing the door.

There was only one person Tetsami could think of that'd do something like that. "Oh, fuck. Is it Baetez?"

"I wouldn't know, madam. My orders are to guard this room."

Tetsami nodded, "Great, you do that." She walked toward the door, but the grunt blocked her way.

"I'm sorry, I can't let you out there."

"What, why you . . ."

"Calm down," Jarvis said. "He's not going to let a civilian into a combat zone."

Tetsami hugged herself and stomped. "Damn it. I peeled that guy out of that wreck—"

Jarvis nodded, "And you told me yesterday how you had to keep him sedated so he wouldn't kill you."

Tetsami sighed. "What does that Baetez jerk think he's doing?"

"Escaping," Jarvis said.

"He thinks he's getting out of Jefferson with a cast on his leg? He didn't look that stupid."

"I doubt he's leaving the hospital, madam," the minuteman by the door volunteered.

"Who asked you?" Tetsami said. "And stop calling me madam." She walked back to her chair by Jarvis' sickbed. This was just another item in a long list of wonderful news. The planet was going to hell, she'd alienated the only family she had on this rock, and now a guy she'd risked her life to save was bent on getting himself shot.

"Why?"

"Hm?" Jarvis said.

"Why's he doing this?"

"You need a reason to escape?" Jarvis asked.

"Yes. Come on, Jarvis, you're the military mind. You can see Baetez's position. Hell, if I hadn't vouched for you, you'd *be* in his position."

"Hm," Jarvis said, again frowning.

"Baetez is wounded in a hospital, in a city that's almost certain to fall to his own forces."

Jarvis nodded. "The risk seems unnecessary—unless he had some information that he feared giving up to the Jeffersonians."

"Easier ways to commit suicide." Tetsami said. "And any information he had is a week out of date now."

Jarvis nodded. "Troop positions a week ago. Force numbers and armaments."

"All things we know from other sources."

"Did he know that?"

"He could figure it out. Especially since the Jeffersonians weren't doing much in the way of interrogation." Tetsami guardedly glanced at the minuteman, who was oblivious. "Why do it, why now?"

"A sudden opportunity?"

"If he was waiting for a good opening, he'd be a fool not to wait for them to take the cast off his leg." Tetsami sighed. "He's getting himself killed for no reason."

Jarvis was giving her a bemused expression.

"What?" she asked.

"I'm surprised you care this much about it."

"A TEC officer is running loose in this hospital, and I shouldn't care?"

"That's not what I mean. You care what happens to him."

Tetsami stood up, feeling angry again and not quite understanding why. "Damn it, Jarvis, I'm funny that way. I put enough effort into saving all of you—" She turned away to face the night-blackened window. "Maybe I don't want to think any of that was a mistake."

She walked off to the window and rested her forehead against the glass. It was too dark to see anything beyond. "I have enough mistakes to deal with already."

"Don't blame yourself for—"

Tetsami laughed, "You can say that? They imprisoned *you* just because, what'd you say, 'I breathed on you.' "

"That's over with."

Tetsami kept laughing, "Christ, I wish it was. But I doubt Klaus Dacham is any less obsessive now than he was a week ago. If he knew Dominic was alive. If he knew *I* was alive . . ."

Tetsami stopped laughing.

"Oh, shit," Tetsami whispered.

"What?" Jarvis asked.

"Oh shit oh shit oh shit." Tetsami whipped around and ran to the door. The minuteman blocked her.

"Miss, I can't let you—"

"Man," Tetsami said, "you better stop worrying about me and haul ass up to the roof."

"Miss?"

"Baetez isn't trying to escape, he's trying for that sat substation on the roof." The minuteman looked uncertain. "Move it or let me through!"

"I'll call command," he said finally. He backed up, reaching for the comm on his belt.

"Do that," Tetsami said. "If this nut gets a line to the outside, they might nuke this town."

The minuteman finally looked a little worried. He was on the comm, telling his commander about his "situation."

While the minuteman was distracted, Tetsami slipped through the door.

"Hey!" she heard behind her, but she ignored it.

If that bastard Baetez got word to Klaus about either her or Dom—

Got to get that bastard.

She'd expected to run into more of the Jeffersonian militia, but her footsteps echoed through empty halls. The empty white halls reminded her of the Ashley Commune after the Proudhon forces were through with it.

Where'd the militia go? Tetsami thought.

She was beginning to question her impulsive leap into an ugly situation.

There were cameras all over the hospital. The Jeffersonian minutemen had to have Baetez bottled up somewhere. They'd be closing on him, somewhere in the hospital. She only had a theory where Baetez was heading; they had the security system of the whole hospital—

She needed to get a look into that security.

Tetsami's feet sent echoes across ribbed nonskid tiles. She passed waiting rooms filled with chromed chairs, fake plants, and subdued holo landscape pictures. She passed doors swinging open on empty examination rooms. She dodged abandoned lab carts. Occasionally she passed a small alarm set into the wall—no sirens, but an insistent flashing red light.

When she reached the T-intersection where three wings of the hospital met, she found what she needed. At the nexus, with a bank of elevators and fire stairs, sat a large horseshoe-shaped console, a nurse's station. Tetsami could see a half-dozen comm displays on the other side of the desk.

Still running, Tetsami vaulted over the desk and slid over the control panel to stumble between the two office chairs parked on the raised floor behind the desk. The move ignited pains along the sides of her ribs, where she was still healing.

She faced the comm console and was annoyed not to see a bio-interface. But since she didn't have her jacking cables with her, an interface'd be useless even if it were here.

She began tapping on the virtual keyboard set in front of one of the chairs. She was lucky. When the nurses evacuated, they'd left the terminal program open for her. That saved her five minutes of hacking into the shell of the hospital's mainframe.

She moved her fingers through the lattice of lasers that made the keyboard and a secondary display under her fingers. She keyed icons and triggered commands that pulled her through the medical database she was in, and sideways through the operating system, through environ-

REVOLUTIONARY   83

mental control, the electrical system, and finally the security system.

Her maneuver glided through the hospital's out-of-date software smooth as glass—and slow as molasses to someone who was used to direct wiring and response times in microsecond fractions.

In minutes Tetsami had called up the entire hospital security network. She had cameras up on the station's holo displays and saw immediately that there was a problem. She spent fifteen seconds cycling cameras to be sure.

The cameras on the entire northwest wing of the hospital were out. She cycled through them, and all she got was static. Somehow, Baetez had managed to nuke the cameras the wing with the sat substation on top of it.

"Hell," she exclaimed, running from the nurse's station and toward the northwest wing.

If that minuteman in Jarvis' room could convince his commander about what was up, they might have a chance to stop Baetez. *Shit, he's nearly immobile. The bastard has a fractured leg and one arm in a cast.*

However, the empty corridors were feeding Tetsami's strong suspicion that the minutemen were assuming that Baetez's motive was simple escape. They'd seal the exits *first*. Then, knowing Baetez was trapped in the building, they'd work their way through, step by step.

That would give Baetez more than enough time to access the substation on the roof.

Tetsami had to come to a halt when she hit the intersection between the southwest and northwest wings. An armored, transparent security door had slid closed across the entrance to the northwest wing. Far down the corridor, Tetsami saw a body. The body wore a white coat, and from what she could see, it had taken a laser shot to the face.

"Lord Mother Jesus tap-dancing Christ," she muttered as she popped the control plate for the door. "They're trying to contain him."

She separated what she hoped was the right optical fiber for the door's system, pulled it out of the wall, and separated it at a magnetic junction. The red light above the door went out, but the door didn't open.

She looked at the door, thought for a moment, and then drew her sidearm. It was a relatively generic GA&A variable wattage laser—it wasn't even polychrome—but it was the only kind of armament she'd been able to buy after the siege began. The Jeffersonian ambulance that evacuated the human remnants of the *Shaftsbury* wreck hadn't bothered to evac her weapons or her personal field generator. Those were two lacks that she was feeling deeply right now. She was diving into this mess underequipped.

She should have left Baetez to freeze in that wreck.

All those thoughts conflicted for her attention as she watted the laser down until the aperture irised to a diameter about equal to the optical junction she'd pulled. *Should work,* she thought.

The optical junction was magnetic, so the cable actually locked on to the nose of her laser, even though her laser was definitely not designed for communications.

She fired.

There was a buzz from deep in the wall as she pumped a hundred kilowatts into the door mechanism. The matte-black optical sheath coating the cables burned off in a pall of brown smoke. More smoke, burning insulation, vomited through the access panel. As she watched, the optical cable beneath the sheath began to glow from the heat.

The red light above the door began flashing again, and now a siren—a fire warning—echoed through the hallway.

Jefferson's going to love me for this, she thought.

The cable sagged, melting, and dropped molten parts of itself to the tile. Before she took her finger off the trigger, the freed laser fried a few more electronics behind the maint panel.

The door began to slide open—then it froze, leaving only a half-meter gap. Tetsami dove through, hoping security wouldn't close it while she was in the way.

As she slipped by it, she could hear the whine of escaping hydraulic fluid. It lent a petroleum reek to the smell of smoldering optics.

Tetsami ran down the corridor until the smell from the

corpse became stronger than the smell from her electronic campfire. That slammed home what was going down here. The smell of charred flesh rammed home the reality of the corpse better than anything else.

She tried not to think about that, about Baetez with a laser, as she edged around the body.

Stairs, was her thought. *The militia would freeze the elevators, so he's on the stairs to the roof.*

Tetsami made for the stairwell at the end of the wing, hoping that Baetez's broken leg was slowing him down.

CHAPTER ELEVEN

Lines of Communication

"Never bet on a race you happen to be in."
—*The Cynic's Book of Wisdom*

"The most dangerous man is one who is willing to
die for a cause."
—JEAN HONORÉ CHEVIOT
(2065–2128)

Baetez limped by the corpse and made it to the stairwell.
It took him too long to clear the distance, the cast on his
leg more of an obstacle than he'd first thought. Pain shot
through the long bones, and the muscles from his thigh to
lower back ached with the combination of unaccustomed
weight and atrophy from over a week of inactivity. He
had walked barely twenty meters, and sweat coated his
skin while his breath burned copper at the back of his
throat.

However, he was two corpses beyond turning back.

Just as he leaned against the stairwell door, he heard a
warning siren. He looked back down the hall to see a
transparent barrier slide across the corridor, back at the
intersection. Baetez also noticed that, on all the closed
doors in this corridor, the indicator lights on the locks had
all gone red.

Trying to box me in, he thought.

Baetez looked at the lock on the stairwell and saw that
that indicator too had gone red. Six fifteen-centimeter
steel bolts had shot in from the doorjamb. All of them had
missed the door, which Baetez had already opened. With
the cast, he was moving just about as fast as the security
in this building.

Not fast enough. He needed to slow these utopians down.

Baetez slipped into the stairwell and looked up the stairs. For the first time he wondered if he could make it all the way to the roof. Behind him, the door tried to shut. The exposed bolts held it ajar.

Baetez looked for the camera. It took a moment to find, against the mottled white concrete of the stairwell, but he saw the dot that had to be the aperture for an optical fiber. It was smaller than the tip of his little finger, but it was logically placed to cover both stairwells.

Until I start up, they'll assume I'm heading for the out-side.

If he could blind them, their assumptions might buy him enough time to get to the sat uplink.

He rested his cast on the central banister and used it to brace the minuteman's laser. He took careful aim at the hole where the lens for the camera was. If he was lucky, and the camera system was as badly designed as most of the hospital, the whole surveillance system was on an un-damped optical circuit, and one laser shot could take out the whole system. More likely, and just as good for his purposes, would be a camera system laid out in series, and taking out this node would black out everything strung along behind it.

At the very least, a good shot would take out this cam-era and its immediate neighbors, enough to confuse secu-rity about his destination.

He took three shots before he hit the aperture dead-on. Fatigue was making his arm shake. Instead of a single neat hole, he had charred a scribble of demonic calligra-phy on the wall by the camera. Poor aim, but good enough.

Baetez began the torturous process of climbing the stairs. Within five steps, his good leg was torn by cramps. That pain was worse than the aches and occasional stab-bing he felt from inside his cast. He forced himself to go on, though it felt as if his calf muscle were tearing from the bone with every step.

Sweat stung his eyes, soaked his hospital robe, and col-lected in the casts on his arm and leg. It was an effort to keep his balance, even leaning against the wall. He couldn't hold the handrails; he needed his good hand free for the laser.

The stairs went all the way to the roof. Nothing was left between him and the sat uplink but the door. Which, of course, was locked. Baetez remembered the six steel bolts that had tried to lock the door downstairs, and knew forcing this door would be futile.

He stood there, muscles shaking from fatigue, and thought.

Eventually, he backed down the stairs. Once he flattened himself against them and had some cover, he leveled his laser at the wall *next* to the door. He swept the laser up and down the wall, at full power. In a few seconds the wall was glowing, and the stairwell was filled with the acrid odor of superheated concrete. The lip of the wall, next to the door, glowed orange and sputtered. Orange beads leaped from the groove and struck the floor, turning black.

Baetez stopped after half a minute, when the smoke fouling the air began interfering with the laser.

He stuck the laser in the crook of his broken arm and pulled himself upright with his good hand. His good leg no longer wanted to support his whole weight; when he leaned on the cast he felt a dagger of pain shoot through the center of his broken leg.

The pain made him suck in a breath of concrete smoke. Spastic coughs came close to making him pass out, but he kept his grip on consciousness.

Light-headed, eyes watering, he hobbled to the door.

He could feel the heat washing off the wall, though his eyes were watering too badly to see much of the damage. He withdrew the laser with his good hand, and, using the cast on his arm, he pushed on the door.

It took all of his weight to move the door, but the door did move. His liberal use of the laser had destroyed the anchorage for the locking mechanism. He pushed the door open a few dozen centimeters, and one of the steel bolts slid out of its home in the wall, to clang onto the floor and roll by his feet. Heat had turned the silver finish into a charred rainbow.

It took him too long to open. The door screeched against a heat-warped frame, and the effort sent shivers of agony through both of his legs.

As soon as he could slip through, he did. Slipping through burned a wide strip of flesh on the left side of his body. He barely felt the new pain.

The air on the roof was fresh and cool, helping revive him and clear his vision.

Ahead of him, he saw his destination, a small concrete shack next to a blue-lit satellite dish, only a dozen meters away. No one else was on the roof. He had made it.

All he needed was to send one thirty-second message.

He hobbled toward the dish.

CHAPTER TWELVE

Media Campaign

"If you believe in your own immortality, you will never live to be disappointed."
— *The Cynic's Book of Wisdom*

"The long habit of living indisposeth us for dying."
— SIR THOMAS BROWNE
(1605–1682)

Where did all those minutemen go? Tetsami wondered.

The door here at the stairwell was supposed to be locked shut, red light on it and everything. However, the six steel bolts that were supposed to lock the door had emerged from the door frame while the door had been open. The stairwell door was kept ajar by the bolts that were supposed to hold it in place.

The lame security in this building probably had a little indicator on, showing this door as locked.

She slowly pushed it, stepping through with her laser at the ready. Here, in the stairwell, she heard the minutemen, at least their radios. There was commotion both above and below her. That was a good sign, that meant that some of the blue-clad defenders of democracy had made it to the roof.

"Time for sensible people to turn around and let the professionals handle things," she said, still standing in the doorway.

She snorted. The minutemen were a volunteer militia, most of them about as professional as she was. She slipped into the stairwell.

From her vantage, up and down the concrete stairs for the short distance she could see, there were no people.

The echoing noise from the minutemen's comms stayed at a constant indecipherable volume. A bunch of them must be holding the bottom of the stairwell, while a squad swept up the roof. The roof people would catch Baetez, or flush him back down the stairwell, into the arms of the main force.

"Makes sense, if this door wasn't locked open." Tetsami coughed. Smoke and dust floated down from above her.

She started up the stairs.

Tetsami climbed slowly, hugging the wall, because she had no idea what awaited her up on the roof. The smoke thickened, but never enough to interfere with her vision. It took an effort to avoid coughing.

It was two floors to the roof, and the sounds—or more specifically, the lack of sounds—from the roof were making her nervous. She heard the unmistakable squawk of one of the comms above her, but it didn't move around, and no one answered its call.

She rounded the last landing, coming into sight of the door to the roof. It was an ugly sight. The opening side of the wall had been carved by someone using a combat laser. Black scorch was everywhere. The door itself was wedged open a meter, stuck in its warped frame.

Tetsami slowed her approach when she noticed the warped spots and grooves in the door itself were from laser shots coming from the other side.

Tetsami walked up to the door, freezing when she accidentally kicked something metallic. The clanging echoes ricocheted off the concrete walls as a heat-burnished steel bolt bounced down the stairs. As the ringing echoes faded, Tetsami hugged the wall and waited to be shot.

No shot came.

When her heart started again, Tetsami realized just how dangerously quiet everything was. There was sound from below her—the minutemen must be coming up the stairs—but outside the door she heard nothing but the single comm, squawking, it seemed, to nothing.

Tetsami approached the door and looked outside, using it for cover.

"Jesus wept," she whispered.

A squad of five minutemen were out there, all right. Not a one was moving. From the looks of things, Baetez had had the advantage of position. The roof by the massive satellite dish had cover, especially in the form of the small concrete shack that must've housed the comm equipment. The shack itself had been pockmarked by the minutemen's fire.

The minutemen had also been pockmarked by Baetez's fire. All of them were dead, with wounds to the head or abdomen. One corpse was by the door, the rest were sprawled between the door and the concrete shack. They hadn't called for backup. They had tried to rush him.

Their mistake.

"Fuck it. Now what?"

She certainly wasn't going to rush Baetez's little stronghold. He'd managed to drop five people in the space of fifteen meters.

However, right now he'd be busy in the comm shack. He was getting the dish on-line. Even as she watched, the dish rotated slightly.

There you go, she thought. *I'm not here to* kill *the nimrod.*

Carefully, Tetsami slipped out the door and over to the nearest minuteman. The smell made her gag. Burned flesh and the ozone-transformer reek of a personal field that had failed catastrophically. Tetsami freed the minuteman's militia rifle from his hands and scuttled away from the body. Even though she avoided touching the corpse's flesh, she felt dirty.

She returned to the cover of the door and looked at the weapon. She'd never handled anything like it before. It looked like an antique. However, hanging around Dom had given her some knowledge of small arms. In some ways, too much. This was an eleven-millimeter submachinegun, chemical, not an electromag. She found what must have been the safety, and saw it was off.

She shouldered the weapon and aimed at the dish.

At least it's a big target.

She fired.

The recoil nearly knocked her over. The gun's stock slammed into her barely-healed shoulder, igniting pains from ten-day-old bruises. She hung on, keeping control of the roaring weapon even when a tongue of flame extended from the barrel.

She hoped that it was supposed to do that.

The bullets were hitting the dish. She could see debris sparking from the white concave surface. Some of the blue spotlights exploded in small balloons of spark-filled smoke. She strafed the reflector, trying to aim the jerking weapon toward the collector at its focus.

The small box at the focus shattered in a shower of plastic and wiring. Then the rifle in her hands clicked on an empty chamber and stopped firing. For half a second she thought it was broken, but then she realized that the magazine was empty.

But she'd done it, she'd killed the . . .

Receiver.

"Shit!" she yelled—at the gun and at herself. She was about to run for the corpse, get more ammo for this gun, when a shadow appeared in the doorway of the comm shack.

She tossed the useless gun and pulled her own inadequate laser. A blinding polychrome beam struck the door she was using for cover. Even as she fired her own laser, she could feel the heat from Baetez's laser. The air stank with superheated metal.

Tetsami's world seemed to flicker down, slowing as if she were about to jack into an extreme shell program. Threat focused her perception on Baetez and his laser. Those stayed in focus, while the smell of burning fabric and metal, painful heat, the sound of the dead minuteman's comm, all retreated in her awareness. Her senses were slaved to the task at hand, shooting Baetez.

She was outmatched. Baetez wielded a better laser, had better cover, and kept the beam focused on one spot while her own single-spectrum laser lanced out at full power, slicing all over the concrete of Baetez's shack.

At some point she realized that Baetez's laser was going to eat through the door before she hit him.

Then, before she could act on that belated realization, Baetez's laser flickered and died. The bastard had drained the power cell. Baetez had obviously not expected that to happen, and he froze for a minute.

Tetsami jumped out the door, without thinking. Before Baetez could withdraw, she had a clear shot at him. Her underwatted laser burned a hole through his unprotected chest. Even as she was shooting, she became aware of a burning agony in her stomach. She clutched at her abdomen, and took another step.

The step felt like it tore her in two, and she found herself on the ground, barely conscious, with no memory of falling.

She looked down and saw her stomach. She tried to curse, but pain stole the breath from her speech. Under her hand, shiny with fluid, was the charred lips of a massive wound. She thought she could see through the abdominal wall.

She coughed, and it turned into spasmed retching that filled her mouth with blood and impaled her on a flaming spike of agony. As the pain ate her, she felt her vision going. The moon seemed to eclipse itself next to her, taking part of the night sky with it.

Christ. Fuck. God!

The entire world shimmered on the edge of the pain. About the time she blacked out, an oval patch of darkness detached itself from the sky, settling next to her.

CHAPTER THIRTEEN

Casualties of War

"Survival is a selfish motive."
—*The Cynic's Book of Wisdom*

"Civil confusions often spring from trifles but decide great issues."

—ARISTOTLE
(384–322 B.C.)

Dom and Ivor tried to fight their way inside the hospital, but the minutemen had sealed the building. They were trapped outside, with nothing to do but watch.

The egg was moving again. It followed the wall of the northeastern wing until it reached the wing that crossed the courtyard. It followed that wall, at no more than human running pace. Then, at the intersection of the central wing with the western half of the hospital, it stopped.

"It can't be following Baetez, can it?" Ivor said.

As if in response, a flash of polychrome laser light flashed from the roof of the northwestern wing. Dom could see one of the ubiquitous satellite uplinks up there. He knew immediately what Baetez was after.

He ran up to one of the minutemen guards. "He's on the roof, damn you. He's not trying to escape, he's going for the uplink."

"We have the situation under control, sir. Please remain calm—"

Dom grabbed the minuteman's vest, *"Calm?* If he gets a message—" Dom had to stop because the minuteman's sidearm was pointing at his abdomen.

"Don't force me to restrain you, sir. The situation is under control."

Dom slowly released the minuteman's vest. Someone in the crowd behind them yelled, "It's moving again."

The egg was moving again. Almost simultaneously, the sound of militia rifles sounded from the roof. Dom backed up and could see sparks jump from the concrete shack next to the comm array.

"No, you idiots, take out the array," Dom's words were absorbed by the sound of the crowd panicking around him. The crowd poured east, like a single organism, leaving Dom, Ivor, and the minutemen.

The egg continued its stately pace along the inside wall of the northwest wing, directly under the firefight. Above it, Dom could see polychrome laser light lance out a half dozen times. The sound of gunfire ceased.

For the first time the minutemen did not look as if the situation were under control. All the militia ran for the western half of the hospital. Dom had the feeling that it was too late, way too late.

In a few moments, Dom and Ivor stood alone at the northern end of the courtyard. Above them, the egg slowly zigzagged up the wall toward the roof.

"Following the stairs?" Ivor asked.

"Come on, cut the power, take out the comm array, something . . ."

Dom's response was the bark of a militia rifle strafing the comm array. Lights exploded, and large pieces of the dish flew off into the darkness. "No," Dom whispered, "the antenna with the *transmitter*."

The rifle ceased barking, and the polychrome laser sliced across the roof again. Another monochrome laser was whipping all around the shack Baetez was in. It wasn't a militia weapon.

The polychrome was the better weapon, but it suddenly, abruptly, winked out. Someone on the roof screamed as the monochrome laser cut toward the shack. Then it too winked out.

The egg slid up onto the roof.

"Oh, God," Ivor whispered. "That sounded like Tetsami."

* * *

They finally were let into the hospital, and a young minuteman had the job of telling them what they'd found on the roof.

The news froze Dom, as if an ice storm raged through his body. The chill immobilized him for a few eternal minutes. He stood, motionless, long enough for the minuteman to look worried.

"Are you all right?"

Ivor stood next to him, just as stunned.

Dom stared at the seventeen- or eighteen-year-old minuteman, and for a moment he saw an older TEC captain, part of the Executive Command stationed at 61 Cygni. For a few seconds he saw the captain who'd informed him that Helen Dacham had been one of the casualties on Styx.

"Damn it, I didn't *intend* to kill her."

"Sir?"

Dom was snapped back to the present.

Ivor managed to speak in a dead voice. "How is she?"

The minuteman gave Dom the look of someone who had no real information. "She's in surgery."

"What about the damn egg?" Dom asked.

"What?" said the minuteman.

"The egg, what did it do up there?"

"I don't know it did anything, sir. I have to return to my post."

It was an effort to nod acknowledgment. It felt as if his bones had turned to ice.

"Wait," Ivor said as the minuteman began walking away.

The minuteman turned around again. "Sir?"

"How many others?" Ivor asked.

"Nine casualties. Six dead, including Baetez."

The look in the teenage soldier's eyes was accusatory.

Tetsami grievously wounded, possibly dying. The news left him so numb he ached. It took a concentrated effort to remove his new chromed hand from the door frame, where it had been clamped. He turned to look at Ivor, but the other man didn't return his gaze.

If anyone had the right to hate him, Ivor did.

* * *

His brother had touched Dom again, and again the contact had left death in its wake. The relationship between him and Klaus was an absurdly efficient machine—cold, deadly, and content to devour any people it found in its path.

The machine was out of control. Neither he nor Klaus drove it anymore; the machine traveled its own path. Six lives had just been snuffed out on their behalf, and neither twin had had any direct involvement.

Absurdly, a TEC agent named Marc Baetez had given his life in what was a personal battle between the brothers. Tragically, Tetsami had jumped in on Dom's behalf.

Dom followed Ivor though the hospital. The halls showed little if any sign of the small war that had just happened here. For some reason he expected to see more of a sign. Destruction to match the significance.

In fifteen years, Dom had opened up to one person. That very act might have pulled her into the machine. His part in that chilled him even more. How many more people were going to die because of their contact with him?

How many people was that machine going to chew up before it stopped?

Dom thought about the egg, the egg that followed the tiny war that'd injured Tetsami. Somehow that egg was watching that war. It was a reminder that this extended beyond his person, beyond him and Klaus. Tetsami was just the latest victim. The machine had many more victims to its credit than her.

The entire Proteus Commune had been annihilated by that machine. That commune and everyone within fifty kilometers of it when Klaus used an orbital linac on it. Perhaps a billion minds and a technology, heretical or not, that could only be guessed at, and one enigmatic three-meter-long egg was all Dom knew to remain from it.

That machine had reduced the capital city of the planet Styx to gravel the size of Dom's little finger.

Something about that, about the sudden gut-blow he'd gotten— Something about what Ivor had said about his own arrogance and self-pity—something brought a realization to him . . .

It wasn't their machine.

He and Klaus had always acted as if they'd been in control of the forces they wielded. They pretended that they were in control of the machine. That was an illusion, an illusion cherished by a pair of men with egos enlarged to cover their own inner inadequacies. He and Klaus weren't in control of the machine; they *were* the machine.

Baetez, an agent of the TEC, had given his life in the personal struggle between Dom and Klaus. Given his life, not in an escape, but in an attempt to tell Klaus that Dom was here, in Jefferson, alive.

Dom and Klaus had entered the TEC together, and ever since the fraternal feud began, Klaus had manipulated the TEC to get within striking distance of Dom. Until now, Dom had never considered how absurd that was. The Terran Executive Command wasn't ever manipulated. The TEC was the manipulator. Klaus couldn't use the TEC as a weapon against Dom unless the TEC was allowing Klaus to do so.

The TEC was manipulating Klaus.

The TEC controlled the machine.

Deep within Dom a hot kernel of anger was beginning to melt through the ice.

It was five hours before they could see Tetsami. They weren't let in her room, which was being kept sterile. However, they could look through a window into the ICU ward where she was, mercifully, unconscious. It took a long time for the image to register. His eyes kept fixing on details: tubing, white tile, chrome fixtures, electronic monitoring equipment, the glaring white light, her hand.

For a long time he stared at her hand. Once his gaze landed there, his eyes refused to move. That hand, resting on the edge of a bed more like a display table than anything else, confirmed everything for Dom.

Her hand looked so small. It was a delicate, long-fingered, artistic hand. In the midst of the tubing, gelled bandaging, and machinery, in the midst of seeping blood and discolored skin, Tetsami's hand remained attractive.

Dom wished he had noticed her hands earlier.

Thank God she's still alive, he thought.

They both stood there, silent, for a quarter hour. After a small eternity Dom turned to face Ivor.

Ivor was a large man, but the way he was stooped, forehead to the glass, he was almost even with Dom. Ivor's eyes stared into the room, and he gave no indication of noticing Dom. Moisture glistened off of Ivor's cheeks, and his hands were balled into fists.

Dom decided not to interrupt him. He turned back toward Tetsami.

"She's only twenty-one," Ivor whispered.

Dom stopped turning, and looked back at Ivor, unsure if the man was talking to him.

"My son was twenty-one, too." Ivor's voice had gotten harsh and raspy.

"Ivor?" Dom asked.

"He was twenty-one when he died."

"She'll make it," Dom said with a conviction he didn't really feel.

"Why today?" Ivor asked the glass. Then he turned around to face Dom. "So help me, I should kill you."

For a few brief instants, Dom thought Ivor might. Dom also thought he might welcome it. Death was probably the easiest way to remove the weight crushing him. If the universe were just—

The universe wasn't just.

Ivor turned away. Dom couldn't tell whether it was in disgust or despair. As the large man began walking away, Dom straightened and said, "You're right."

Ivor's back stopped receding.

"You're right about me, Ivor. I'm responsible for this. Not just Tetsami, but tens of thousands. All injured or dead at my hand, my command, or by something I sold."

Ivor turned around slowly to look at him.

"All this time I've been driven by one motive—escape. Escaping my past, the Confederacy, retribution at the hands of my brother. I'm a selfish man, Ivor. Selfish and cowardly. I haven't felt a damn thing for fifteen years because I couldn't let myself."

The hall felt stuffy and hot. His eyes stung, and when Dom tried to wipe them clear, the metal on his right hand burned. Somehow he kept himself from shaking, though his muscles—synthetic or not—seemed tense enough to tear into pieces.

Dom turned to the ICU ward, because he couldn't stare at Ivor any more. "I'm feeling now. All of it. I feel for her. And I'm responsible for this." He gritted his teeth and stared at Tetsami's face. Her eyes were closed, and tubes ran to her nose. "But, I'm not the only one." Dom whispered.

Silence stretched.

After a while, Ivor said, "I'm sorry. You didn't shoot her."

"Don't be sorry," Dom said. "We both want the men responsible. *All* of them."

PART EIGHT

Space Race

"When it is dark enough you can see the stars."
—RALPH WALDO EMERSON
(1803–1882)

CHAPTER FOURTEEN

Question Time

"You don't want to know."
—*The Cynic's Book of Wisdom*

"Survival is the sole morality."
— MARBURY SHANE
(2044–2074)

It was a long journey from the pyramid to the caverns where Dominic Magnus used to have his headquarters. Progress seemed slow, even now when Shane had some idea of where they were going. The two of them traveled in silence for a long time, Random's robot floating in the lead, illuminating the ebony passages with his floodlights.

After a long silence, while they walked from the passages that were obvious Dolbrian artifacts, Shane asked Random what he'd meant when he said that the Dolbrian carvings were everything.

"What do you plan to do about them?" Random asked in response.

"Me?"

"You have a half-interest in the information."

"That's the first time you've admitted that I have any rights to this discovery."

After a long pause Random said, "I admit little that is self-apparent."

Shane thought about Random's question as they walked the upsloping passages. Something about these passages seemed to encourage revelations, however circuitous. What were her plans for this lode of information? She wasn't quite sure.

"I don't know, Random. I don't want to just hand it over to the Confederacy. It is so much . . ."

"Yes."

"It's so much *beyond* Confed politics. It makes the entire Confederacy seem provincial and petty."

Random's robot tilted the mass of its squashed meter-diameter sphere in a gesture Shane had learned to take as a nod or a shrug. They continued up rock passages for another few meters, then Random said, "You've yet to answer my question."

"You've yet to answer mine."

"True. But when we ended this game last time, it was your turn."

Somehow, they had returned to question-for-a-question. It was how they'd passed most of their first time down here. It made Shane realize how isolated Random must feel down here. The part of Random's brain inside this robot was currently out of contact, not only with the rest of the world, but most especially out of contact with Random's other parts, the part attached to the computer system in the mountain headquarters, and the part that lived in Mosasa.

Perhaps Random needed the byplay to remain sane.

"What do I plan to do?" Shane said, asking herself the question. "Not a plan, so much as a wish. When I see that map, I feel the same tug that led me off of Occisis in the first place. The stars pull me; perhaps I feel a second chance there. Not just my own." Shane stared at the black walls of the cave and imagined that she could see the void within the wall, the void where the stars hung. "One planet," she said, "or two or three. Some handful of Earths, far from the Confederacy. Someplace that the Confederacy's accretion won't reach for centuries."

"A new Confederacy?"

"I hope something better. Now you must answer my question, Random. What's this for you?"

"You have no idea how complex that question is. In the broadest sense I can answer that it is an energy source—"

"Huh?"

"Not in the sense you think. I am talking political, social, economic energy. In the same way—when I start using analogies from thermodynamics and fluid dynamics to describe how I see human society—that I've described Bakunin as a power sink. But if Bakunin is a sink, a planet-sized hole in the Confederacy's economy—that Dolbrian pyramid is a point energy source glowing with the magnitude of a quasar."

"I see."

"Not really, but I will continue to answer your question by telling you of its immediate use. You answered this question yourself, though you didn't realize it. You mentioned Confederacy politics, and my intent is to use this information to help manipulate the Confederacy to Bakunin's advantage. Or, at least, Dominic Magnus will."

"How?"

"That question will be answered in time. As soon as we arrive at our destination. Besides, it's my turn to ask you something."

Shane shrugged. They passed a chamber familiar to Shane, the place where Random had admitted that Hougland's escape and the discovery of the Dolbrian remains were part of a larger plan, a plan that Random said he wasn't always aware he was following. She had rested on that rock. They passed the rock without slowing, and Shane realized that she wasn't tired yet. Her body seemed to be adapting to its artificial additions.

After a time Random asked, "Would you mourn the death of the Confederacy?"

"Huh?" Shane said, then she realized that Random was still playing his question game. Perhaps he was always playing it. She thought a moment and responded, "It depends what you mean by death. If you refer to violence— most marines are less enamored of war—"

Random's sphere shook a quarter rotation that meant "no." "Not quite my intent," Random said. "I refer to the political death of the Confederacy. The loss of the central government."

"Just like that?"

"The Confederacy is balanced very precariously upon the consent of the governed. There are many subordinate levels below the Chief Executive, all with their own interests. If the governed no longer give their consent, there would be little to stop the disassociation."

"The TEC—"

"A few handfuls of highly trained operatives in a sea of billions. What could the TEC do if half the planets are in rebellion? How could they stop an arm of the Confederacy if it wanted to secede? That is not the question. The question is, would you mourn its passage?"

"No." Shane said.

"That simple?"

"That simple. It isn't as complex a question as you seem to believe, even for someone with loyalties as tattered as mine. I have never sworn an oath to the Confederacy, and the only time I served under its banner, I became a traitor. I would mourn death, I would mourn war; but the Confederacy is a political contrivance whose absence would cost me no sleep." After a pause, Shane said, "That wasn't hypothetical, was it?"

"Is that your question?"

For a brief instant Shane was reminded of the djinn or devils in fairy tales. "No," she said. She knew what she wanted to ask Random, but was unsure how to phrase it. Random had already told her of his origin. Random began life as a Race-built AI. He had been built by the only alien species with whom mankind had gone to war. Random's existence—actually the existence of the five computers that became Random—was due to the same psychological quirks that nearly caused the destruction of the entire Race species. The Race were culturally unable to engage in direct confrontation. They had honed the weapons of political science, psychology, anthropology. With the help of their AIs, they could cause dramatic effects in a social system with innocuous acts far removed from the object of interest. To the Race, the human idea of war was the self-destructive act of a raving loon, an attitude that cost the Race its entire space-borne population, and half that on its home world.

It was called the Genocide War for a reason. It was also indirectly responsible for the taboos on heretical technology within the human culture of the Confederacy, insofar as the Confederacy had any homogeneous aspects.

In the Confederacy, Random Walk would be destroyed out of hand. At first that seemed to be the only reason Random was here, on Bakunin.

But with Random's talk about the destruction of the Confederacy, with all the sense of manipulation, she felt that there might be more to that. Much more.

After a long pause, Shane asked, "Might I confirm a few things I remember before I ask my question?"

"There are no firm rules here," Random said.

Or anywhere, Shane thought.

"First," Shane asked, "Mosasa—our Mosasa—is a reconstruction of the man who originally brought five Race AIs together to create you."

"Yes."

"Second. When was it you said Mosasa died?"

"I didn't say, specifically. I said over a hundred years, just on the cusp of tach-drive implementation."

Shane nodded. "That isn't my question exactly. I might note that that was a chaotic period of history. That was near the end of the Terran Council, near the start of the Centauri war that founded the Confederacy and drafted the Charter."

"Yes, without question."

"About the time Bakunin, was founded, right?"

"I begin to see the outlines of your inquiry."

"I'll ask you explicitly. What exactly did you have to do with the founding of this planet?"

Random's sphere rotated on its axis to face her; behind him the passage they followed opened up into another familiar passage. "Shall we rest?"

"Are you changing the subject?"

"No, but perhaps you should sit. This is a lengthy story."

Shane didn't sit, but she leaned against the rough wall. She noted that this was the chamber where this question and answer game had first started between her and Random. When she thought back, despite the information she had pumped from Random, it was Random who had started this game. She began to wonder if Random's answers themselves were some form of psychological manipulation.

Why was it that she had yet to tell anyone what Random had told her? Every revelation he had passed to her, from the fact that Mosasa was a construct to the way he may have baited Hougland to find the Dolbrian ruins, remained secret.

"Tell me," Shane said. The pulse in her neck accelerated, more than the climb could account for.

I'm scared of him, Shane realized. Random *was* a devil from one of those fairy tales. . . .

No, he's a demon from the scriptures.

Once Random asked her why she didn't show the normal Confederacy reaction to an AI: loathing, fear, disgust. She didn't because her fear went far deeper, beyond superficial and condescending emotions. Random was more than the ultimate computer. He was a spirit of pure intellect: omniscient, terrible, and irresistible.

That was why she couldn't show him anything but respect. It wasn't that there was any scrap of humanity underneath the facade that Random himself admitted was only a thin shell. Shane's respect was born of a good Catholic fear of damnation.

Yea, though I walk through the valley of the shadow of death, I will fear no evil—

"Shane, are you all right?" Random asked.

"I'm fine." *What am I thinking? He's only a computer.* "Maybe I will sit for this." She slid slowly to the ground, hugging her knees.

Random, in his current incarnation, had been born during the waning decades of the Terran Council's rule. The Council itself had held absolute dominion only over Earth, but it dominated all of human space because of its control of immigration and technology. It was the Council that controlled the wormhole gates, the only means then available of interstellar transportation. And it was through these one-way wormholes that the Council dumped every undesirable it could find on Earth: criminals, dissidents, the populations of nations that refused to bow to their authority.

Near the end, most of human space was in chaos.

With every planet humanity reached, a cloud of space-born criminals followed, generations of spacers in stolen and jury-rigged craft who never made landfall on a colony planet. The spacers were descended from escaped refugees, mutinous soldiers from the Council, and in some cases voluntary exiles from the planets. Each colony fostered its own breed of interplanetary pirates, living off the colony's trade.

Of course, the pirates never had access to the wormholes, which were the most heavily defended part of any system.

Random's father, Tjaele Mosasa, was a pirate and a third-generation spacer in Cynos space. Cynos was a rich place for those on the fringes. It was one of the heartland worlds near Sol, a prominent node on the wormhole net. In orbit around Sirius were six outgoing wormholes and eight incoming. Despite the fact that the dull rocks orbiting the Sirius system were never meant to support life, Cynos was a rich planet. It supported a hundred tribes of pirates.

Mosasa's family was one of those hundred tribes, and possibly one of the weakest. About two dozen people lived a marginal life, gnawing at the commerce traveling through Cynos. He was part of the crew on his family's ship, a ship that might have been as old as the colony on Cynos—perhaps older. As the youngest unmarried crewmember, he had the inglorious duty of keeping the ship patched and running. While his family stalked and raided cargo tugs, he was in a narrow tunnel in the unpressurized belly of the ship—keeping the computer, the power, the life support, and everything else, on-line.

In the end, that saved Mosasa's life.

Mosasa's ship, the *Nomad,* had been closing on a mass concentration that showed no transponder readings and didn't appear on any database. While the *Nomad* closed on the object cautiously, no one on board expected any difficulty. It was either an asteroid or a derelict—neither one dangerous.

It was an understandable, but mistaken, assumption. If the *Nomad* had operated in the Alpha Centauri System, or Tau Ceti, or Epsilon Eridani, if the *Nomad* had been fa-

miliar with any of the close-by worlds *other* than the orbiting Sirius, if Cynos and Sirius had been a larger part of
the Genocide War, if the crew of the *Nomad* had been
more familiar with that war, they might have been more
cautious.

The crew of the *Nomad* actually hoped for a derelict
ship, something they could salvage for their own use.
Many of the crew probably hoped for a ship in good
enough condition to replace the age-eaten *Nomad.*

Mosasa would have been satisfied with a salvageable
ship's computer. Anything that could make his job easier.
He wanted to watch the approach with the rest of the
crew, but as the *Nomad* approached the derelict, Mosasa
was in a pressure suit making sure that the power system
didn't overheat.

He was tapping an ancient meter, and watching the
numbers slide back to acceptable levels, when the hull
was breached. Mosasa was slammed by sudden inertia
into the computer system behind him, which gave way
without puncturing his suit.

He was the only survivor.

It wasn't a single derelict that the *Nomad* had been approaching, but a pair of derelicts. One was the husk of the
Luxembourg, an Earth ship from the days of the United
Nations and the Genocide War. The other derelict was a
marginally operational Race drone weapon, which had
rammed the *Nomad,* destroying the cockpit, most of the
living quarters, and the engine, as it sideswiped the craft.

The drone had wrecked itself in doing so.

Mosasa managed to survive. The oxygen and food
stores of the *Nomad* weren't in the half of the ship that
was crushed by the drone. He was, however, stranded.
The *Nomad* and the Race drone had fused into a single
lump of wreckage, but the *Nomad* was still traveling, very
slowly, toward the *Luxembourg.*

In a week, the wrecks began passing one another.
Mosasa strung cable between the *Nomad* and the *Luxem-
bourg,* with some hope of finding a working radio on the
Luxembourg. What he found was more than that.

* * *

"What did he find?" Shane asked.

"Why, among other things, me."

"I thought you were piloting that drone."

"Let me explain. The reason the *Luxembourg* was still intact is because it was carrying things that the Race put a priority on. . . ."

The *Luxembourg* was nearly intact. Even though it wasn't a military craft, and had been in a battle that had killed the entire crew, the structure and the electronics were still sound. The hull was peppered with laser holes, but none holed vital equipment, and each ended in a vacuum-desiccated crewmember. The battle must have only lasted a few seconds. None of the crew had warning. One crewman had been killed while strapped to the ship's toilet.

Mosasa didn't know it at the time, but the *Luxembourg* had been a ship operated by the UN intelligence services near the end of the war. It had been taken by a fleet of Race drones, neutralized, and left with a drone guard until the Race themselves could arrive to retrieve its contents.

The Race never came; the war was over by the time the drones reached Procyon. But the *Luxembourg*'s guard never departed. The last drone stayed, power fading, until the *Nomad* arrived to provoke it.

Another decade—it had been nearly a hundred and fifty years already—and the drone might have been totally inert.

What the Race had wanted, and what Mosasa found, was the cargo the *Luxembourg* carried. On that ship were a quartet of Race AIs. At first Mosasa wasn't interested in them. He didn't even know what they were. He was trying to get the *Luxembourg* patched and operational before his air and food ran out. It wasn't until he needed the computer on-line that he realized what he had. Most of the computer systems on the *Luxembourg* ran through one of the four cylindrical crystals it carried.

After finding that, Mosasa knew what he carried. Four race AIs were a priceless prize, even in a society that publicly denounced Artificial Intelligence. Mosasa was a pirate, used to illegality, so the moral strictures didn't bother him. He also needed a computer to run the *Luxem-*

bourg. Eventually, he had to find the working AI in the drone weapon in order to start the other four working.

Mosasa's effort got all five AIs working in a gestalt, including a damaged one that hadn't even been working when it was placed aboard the *Luxembourg*.

"Are you answering my question?" Shane asked.

"I think the background is necessary. Survival was part of the equation since before the beginning. One fifth of me was programmed to protect the other four—among other things—from human interference. However, with the Race trapped on their home world, and us trapped light-years away, we needed Mosasa. It wasn't very long before I knew him completely."

"Uh-huh."

"Now, Bakunin . . ."

According to Random, given the political situation, the planet Bakunin was inevitable. The Terran Council was on the cusp of what could have been an endless revolution. With the state of the art being wormholes and inefficient tachyon communications, a war could take decades—maybe centuries—to roll from one end of human space to the other. The Genocide War, in only five systems, took nearly thirty years standard. Most of those years would be years of ships in transit.

The embryonic Random Walk could see the wars coming as clearly as most people could see an approaching storm front. Prediction was part of his nature. It was why the Race had designed his kind.

What no oracle in the chaotic math of society could foresee was the discovery of Paralia, and the subsequent invention of the tach-drive. The intrusion of an FTL drive into the mix radically altered Random's world view. Instead of the Council disintegrating into dozens of independent political units, the Centaurian Trading Company, with its tach-capable warships, managed to conquer the Terran Council in the space of three years.

Random explained a lot about how he saw the conflict, much of it in terms that Shane couldn't understand. What it sounded like was that the Terran Council had generated a surplus of political energy, energy that would have been dissipated in a century or two of war. However, the appearance of the tach-drive and the formation of the Confederacy radically shifted the equations. All the turbulence was suddenly damped, and one of the side effects was a political whirlpool called Bakunin.

According to Random, Bakunin was an unstable political formation, the equivalent of a tornado or a wind shear. An anarchy, philosophically founded or accidental, was a tremendous energy sink that should eventually stabilize into some form of State. Random and Mosasa came to Bakunin shortly after its founding. Their goal was to escape the newly formed Confederacy, which had expanded the Council's own technological bans into a whole canon of heretical technologies.

In the Confederacy, both Mosasa and Random were under threat of death.

"But why is Bakunin still as it is? You said an anarchy is unstable."

Random shook its chromed sphere. "I thought that was obvious. I have used my facility at social engineering to stabilize the situation as much as possible. It would be inconvenient for me if the Confederacy took over this planet."

It took a few minutes for what Random said to sink in.

CHAPTER FIFTEEN

Sidebars

'Look behind the curtain."
—*The Cynic's Book of Wisdom*

"... every man must get to heaven his own way."
—FREDERICK THE GREAT
(1712–1786)

Tetsami floats in a blackness emptier than anything she has ever jacked into. No sight, no sound, nothing to feel, no sense of location or motion. She's trapped in an empty circuit that makes even the basic process of self and memory an effort to maintain.

System crash, she tells herself as she tries to unscramble what she has for thoughts. *Catastrophic failure wiped everything, shell program and the host software ...*

Tetsami manages to quickly rein in the panic; she has jacked into empty shells before. The feeling is akin to being wired on speed and trapped in a sensory deprivation tank. But she has an edge. She has experience, and her brain is designed to ride the wire. It doesn't fry itself in situations where lesser hackers go nuts.

What worries her, as she begins to think clearly, is the fact she has no idea what kind of system she is jacked into. She doesn't remember hacking into anything. The last thing she remembers is collapsing on the roof of the hospital, looking down and seeing—

Oh, Lord Jesus, am I fucked!

She *feels* jacked in. She's on mental overdrive to match the sensation. On the wire, her sense of time turns seconds into hours. The organic software in her head does that now, tumbling her self-sense down an infinity of black.

She tries to ease out of it, cut herself away from the wire like she's done in dozens of emergencies. She's always been able to cut off a contact before it got too hot. She's never once let her head get caught in a box—

But there isn't a wire, there's nothing to cut loose from. She can't even raise a sense of her own body. That is truly frightening.

Even the toughest rides on her biojack still left her with the pulse in her temples, the taste of copper in her mouth, some sense of gravity in her bowels. This gives her nothing, as if her mind is cut loose completely from her body, cast into the void.

This can't be it, can it?

A seeping terror fills her mind that this *is* it. The last shot got her. Worse than the idea of nonexistence is the thought of this empty infinity, and nothing else, forever.

An aeon passes. An aeon that could be only a few seconds. Tetsami feels, finally, a presence in the void with her. Just that sense of a presence, nothing more than the feeling of being watched, strips the terror from her. Even if it is an artifact of her own terrified mind, it gives her orientation: an up, a down, and most of all, a sense of motion. Whatever it is, she's drifting toward it.

More aeons. The passage of time crumbles around Tetsami, eroding, falling to pieces. She wonders about her own sanity as she sees herself no longer as a continuum of experience. Her mind is a series of glass beads on a wire stretching toward eternity. Each bead an incomplete thought trapped on its way to . . .

Somewhere.

It is a sense of something more than a presence. Something blacker than nothing.

An ebon ellipsoid the size of a planet, massive as a star, warping the fabric of the emptiness around her by its very presence.

At the surface, she feels time freeze into a crystalline eternity.

"Fuck!" Tetsami spits dust out of her mouth and hugs herself to keep warm. Wherever she is, it's cold as hell, and she isn't dressed for it. The physical reaction is so immediate that it takes her a few seconds to wonder exactly where she is and how she got there.

The wondering becomes naked confusion when she looks into a blue sky to see a sun smaller and brighter than Kropotkin could ever hope to be.

"Y–yellow sun, and it's f–freezing." She feels her teeth chatter as her words are stolen away by a knifelike wind. She has not felt this cold since the *Shaftsbury* crash-landed. Above her, the clouds scud by with a surreal tint of color.

"Mars," says a voice from behind her.

Tetsami spins around and her foot hits a rock. A small cairn of stones shifts its weight in response. The rocks appear to mark an old grave, a tight mat of engineered grass holding down the mound of Martian dirt.

"D–dreaming, right?" Tetsami says, fighting the cold.

The speaker greeting her is not quite human. Her shape is humanoid, but is more of an idealized figure in smooth chrome. Tetsami sees a distorted reflection of herself staring from the chromed woman's abdomen.

"Less than some, more than others," the figure says. "My name is Eigne."

"Am I dead?"

Eigne shakes a bald mirrored head, "No." Tetsami notices that the chrome is perfectly smooth, with all the surface irregularities removed. No hair, nipples, or belly button. No fingernails.

"What am I d–doing here."

"Talking to us who have taken the Journey. Perhaps to join us."

Tetsami shakes her head vigorously. She is not agreeing to anything while things are this weird.

Eigne nods. "That is expected. Life or death, you never

agree." She sighs. "It is a shame, since you are the easiest to communicate with."

"What are you talking about? What is going on here?"

"We will explain, but come with me to a place where you'll feel warm."

That is, at least, something Tetsami can agree to. She follows the chromed woman across the Martian landscape. *Weird dreams I'm having,* Tetsami thinks. *Cold dreams.*

"W–what did you mean—life or death, I never agree?"

"In the infinity of possibility we inhabit now," Eigne says, "of all the possible Tetsamis, those who've lived, those who've died, none have consented."

"Consented to what?"

"The Change."

Tetsami hears the capital letter. She looks upon the chromed figure before her and thinks that this person used to be human. Tetsami has some small sense of the Change, and it frightens the Christ out of her.

"Where am I, really?"

"In a bed in a hospital in Jefferson City." Eigne turns to look at her. "You are also fifteen light-years away, on a possible Mars."

Tetsami is about to say something more, when the ground unfolds beneath them, and they drop into a crystal wonderland. They descend into a world of geometric spirals and conic sections. Fractals grow from every direction like glass flowers.

Eigne is right. It's warmer down here.

CHAPTER SIXTEEN

Command Decision

"We prefer blame to justice."
                    —*The Cynic's Book of Wisdom*

"Even a tyrant is slave to a tyranny."
                    —SYLVIA HARPER
                    (2008–2081)

Colonel Klaus Dacham was awakened from uneasy dreams by a sweating junior officer. Klaus rose and dressed while the junior officer stammered out the intelligence that had brought him here. Klaus listened impassively.

It was dawn.

"How long has it been since this transmission was received?" Those were the first words Klaus spoke to the babbling junior officer.

There was a long pause before the man responded, "T–ten hours, sir."

Anger flared in Klaus' gut. He controlled it, focused it, mastered it. "What, exactly, was the cause of this delay?" Klaus stared at the junior officer. Even though Dominic Magnus was almost certainly dead, Klaus' subordinates knew that he expected to be informed immediately if so much as one of Dominic Magnus' fingers was unearthed in some garbage pile.

Dominic Magnus—Jonah Dacham, Klaus' brother—a man safely dead, Klaus had thought, or had hoped, or had feared. Dominic Magnus had been close enough to the Proteus strike to have most of his cybernetics fried by the electromagnetic pulse, if he hadn't been killed outright by the blast itself. But Klaus' brother still lived.

The nervous fool before him was a sacrifice, a sacrifice for a TEC captain who was unwilling to face Klaus himself. Klaus would have to have a talk with this man's superior.

He listened to the officer with half an ear as he led him out of his apartments, apartments that had once belonged to Dominic Magnus.

"The transmission wasn't on normal channels. It was filtered through intel as usual—" Every stray EM transmission was picked up by part of Klaus' operation. "—but it wasn't run through *our* computers. The transmission was picked up by a mercenary intel unit, and they screen the data through a different priority list."

Klaus nodded. Until the recent power shift within the Proudhon Spaceport Development Corporation, the mercenary army that was taking over Bakunin had been an independent entity. Even though command was now centralized here, under Klaus and the TEC, the army was still largely an independent entity bonded by a common interest—money.

The officer continued a complex explanation concerning tangled lines of communication, a still-fluid command structure, and the limitations of overburdened intel computers bombarded with more information than they could possibly process in any reasonable time. Klaus listened less and less as he became embroiled within his own thoughts.

Klaus led the man down from the top of the Godwin Arms residence tower, across the courtyard of the complex, and into the office tower that housed his command center.

I wasn't surprised, Klaus thought. Dominic/Jonah still lived, and it didn't surprise him any more.

The command center was an armored cube that Klaus had constructed in the office complex's eviscerated foundation. The cube was four stories tall and dominated by a gigantic holo display that, right now, showed a schematic globe of Bakunin ten meters in diameter.

From here, Klaus could order a picture of anything on the planet and beyond, out to ten megaklicks. It was a huge volume of information squeezing through a too-small aperture.

Klaus dismissed the junior officer, who must have been ecstatic to escape without a reprimand. Then he waved away the cluster of high-ranking intelligence officers who wanted to brief him.

He settled into his accustomed chair and stared off into the space between the base of the holo and the projection of the giant globe.

There was a thought, a nagging traitor thought at the back of Klaus' skull, a tiny voice that told him that he could stop now. His brother's death would change nothing. Brother Jonah had feigned death so often and so well that Klaus knew that Jonah's death—when it truly came—would not stop the nightmares.

The thought was laughable. If there had been a point to turn back, it had been long before now. Klaus had invested far too much of himself into revenge to consider retreat.

Think of him as Dominic, that's the name he uses now.

His brother's death had been a goal that had consumed Klaus since Styx. Klaus had once believed that he pursued Jonah—Dominic—because of the atrocity on Styx. Thirty-five thousand people perished and a city was destroyed at Dominic's hand. One of them had been Helen Dacham, the mother they had both disowned. Dominic left the TEC—deserted—shortly after.

At the time, it was enough reason.

As Klaus rose in rank within the TEC, he found himself committing his own atrocities. It was easy to blame Jonah for those as well. Jonah had convinced Klaus that they should abandon Helen Dacham by joining the Executive Command. Klaus was mired in the TEC by his brother long before he was capable of understanding the repercussions.

Then Dominic had abandoned the TEC, leaving Klaus trapped—

Klaus never forgave.

You made me what I am, brother, Klaus thought.

"Sir?" said one of the anonymous techs that hovered

around him. A whole raft of his TEC officers, waiting for
his orders.

Klaus decided that he must have mumbled something
while he was thinking. He let his thoughts settle. No, he
couldn't stop now. Especially because, if he pulled the
pressure off Dominic Magnus, he could lose credibility.
He had spent a lot of effort convincing his officers that
Magnus was a priority target.

"I want Jefferson City on the big holo," Klaus said.
Techs ran to do his bidding. "I want strength and posi-
tions for all the forces we have in the area," more scurry-
ing. "I want a profile on this—" Klaus had to concentrate
to remember the name the junior officer gave him, "Marc
Baetez. I want the last information we have on him. And
I want the source of that transmission pinpointed exactly,
I don't care how."

Techs flew to the wind.

"Communications?" Klaus called out.

"Yes, sir?" said the commications officer.

"I want a secure channel to whoever is in charge of the
forces around Jefferson. And I want it now."

"Yes, sir!"

He's in a city at least, Klaus thought. If Magnus had
been a commune, he could have been killed and Klaus
would never know. This way, at least, the city might hand
Magnus over to save itself. They could hand Dominic
over to him, so he could see his brother himself. So he
could *see* his brother die, and know it was over.

CHAPTER SEVENTEEN

Extradition

"It is easier to conceive large plans than small ones."

—*The Cynic's Book of Wisdom*

"The best of seers is he who guesses well."

—EURIPIDES
(484–406 B.C.)

"No change," the doctor told him.

Dom had had a few pointless hours of sleep, and had come immediately to the hospital upon waking. The news wasn't encouraging, but it wasn't unexpected. Jefferson's hospital wasn't equipped for this kind of trauma. It had barely been able to handle Dom's injuries.

Tetsami was lucky she was alive at all.

"She's doing about as well as can be expected. It was a grievous insult to the abdominal cavity." The doctor turned to the window, beyond which Tetsami lay under layers of archaic medical technology. "She's young, strong—"

Dom caught a note of uncertainty in the doctor's voice. He pounced on it. "There's something more, isn't there?"

The doctor shook his head. "Nothing alarming, just unusual."

"Unusual?" The word left a bad taste in Dom's mouth.

"She is showing unusual brain activity." The doctor shook his head. "It may be due to the presence of a biojack, but while physiologically she's in a coma, her brain is in a highly active state. Something akin to REM sleep or even full wakefulness."

Dom looked at Tetsami, who seemed nowhere near consciousness. "Could that be dangerous?"

"I doubt it," the doctor said. "It's probably a good sign."

Dom nodded at Tetsami, trying to ignore the doctor's "probably."

When Dom left the hospital, he noticed that the Protean egg had returned to its place in the courtyard. There was now a guard of five minutemen around it, though Dom had yet to hear of the egg actually *doing* anything, except move.

There's more to worry about here than Tetsami, Dom kept telling himself.

The whole planet was coming apart at the seams. This invasion was producing countless Tetsamis. The TEC was going to grind Bakunin, in all its diversity—good, bad and incomprehensible—into a homogenous State the Confederacy could deal with. From the ships holding in orbit, the extent of that choice would be whether Bakunin would be the vassal of Indi or of the Sirius-Eridani Economic Community.

Forcing a central government on Bakunin would be as grievous a wound to the population as the one Tetsami suffered.

What would stop it?

What?

Dom thought about assassinating Klaus. The idea held promise, if somehow he could get to his brother. That, however, would be a purely selfish act. As revenge it would be almost pointless now. Klaus was in command of this mission, but he was only a piece of the machine that had consumed Tetsami. The deadly conflict between Klaus and Dom might color everything they saw, but it was only a small part of the whole. Their conflict was being used by someone, just as Bakunin was being used.

The TEC cared as much about Bakunin as it did Tetsami. Bakunin was just somebody's token in the Congress, a political prize. It was the same with Helen. No one in the TEC cared about Helen Dacham, or the other thirty-five thousand on Styx. All that was just another handle on Klaus and his brother. Helen was just a means to manipulate the twins.

Klaus was a symptom, not the disease.

Somehow, Dom had to think of a way to make the TEC withdraw. And he had to do it without ceding authority to the powers with warships in orbit.

Ironic. If Bakunin had been part of the Charter to begin with, the TEC would be fighting tooth and nail over planetary sovereignty, State or no State.

Dom checked in on Ivor, who seemed to have had even less sleep than Dom had. He opened the door, saw Dom, and simply walked away, shaking his head.

"Any news?" Ivor asked as he walked back into his hotel room.

Dom knew Ivor didn't mean the political situation. "No change," Dom said. "She's stable."

"Yeah, stable." Ivor collapsed into a chair without looking directly at Dom. "Stable's good."

Dom sat on the edge of a table, drumming metallic fingers. "She'll make it."

Ivor nodded slightly. After a long while, he said, "You know, I think I hate those bastards almost as much as you do."

"Which bastards?"

"The Confederacy. The whole damn ball of wax." Ivor rested his forehead in his palms. "And a fucking hell of a lot I can do about it too."

"We could follow Gavadi's advice, call on the Indi forces for aid."

"What makes them different?" Ivor said. "Why the hell was she shot, Dom?" Ivor looked at Dom for the first time, his icy blue eyes melting down his cheeks. "Why the hell is this all happening?"

Dom sighed. He was only marginally sure of what was going on himself. "Bakunin's caught in a crossfire between Alpha Centauri and Sirius on one side, and Indi on the other. The TEC wants a State imposed on Bakunin, and they're using domestic military forces so whatever State appears can sign the Charter under Confederacy law." Dom sucked in a breath, "The fact that Indi is here is evidence that everyone thinks it important what arm of the Confederacy the State of Bakunin joins."

"So you *could* call the Indi forces in to defend?"

Dom nodded slightly, "If Indi believed it could make a case that I was a legitimate native leader. Of course, Proudhon would do what it's carefully avoided until now, and call for SEEC support."

Ivor chuckled. "That would be some way to get back at them."

"I suppose so." Having Indi and the SEEC in a shooting war would probably tear the Confederacy apart at the root. Considering the placement of forces, the entire planet of Bakunin would be the first casualty. "But I feel safer with both fleets in orbit."

Ivor nodded.

If we're lucky, neither side will be tempted to land.

"Damn it," Ivor muttered. "Is all this just so someone can sign their bloody Charter?"

Dom almost shook his head. There was more to it. At least, there should be more to it. Was there?

What had he just said? The presence of Indi meant that it was important to someone what arm of the Confederacy Bakunin signed under. Why should it make a difference if a conquered Bakunin was a puppet of The Alpha Centauri Alliance, the Sirius-Eridani Economic Community, or the People's Protectorate of Epsilon Indi?

"It may come down to that signature, Ivor," Dom said, "The signature and where it's signed."

After a long pause, Dom added, "Perhaps there is something we can do." Dom began to lay out a plan that was perhaps just the wrong side of madness. . . .

It took a long time for Dom to get access to the tightbeam comm this time. The setup at the barracks had nothing to do with the sat uplink on the roof of the hospital. That didn't stop events at the hospital from interfering with access. In the end, Dom thought the only reason he was allowed to use the comm at all was because it offered Jefferson City's only window on the rest of Bakunin.

The city fathers still debated the issue, keeping Dom waiting until it was past midday.

While he was waiting, Dom caught up on his sleep. He hoped Ivor was doing the same back at the hotel.

Dom felt for Ivor as much as he did for Tetsami. Ivor had spent the last two decades narrowing his focus down to individual lives. Ivor had once been a commander in the Stygian Presidential Guard. He had once held the fate of a whole planet within his hands. To Ivor's own eyes, he had failed catastrophically in that mission—twice.

Dom knew Ivor would resist any further such burdens.

Dom, however, had spent his entire life doing the opposite. Dom had spent a lifetime methodically erasing personal connections. For a time it seamed that he had successfully destroyed his own personality in order to avoid agonizing over individual human beings.

Dom had writ himself large. Ivor, small. They both were fools.

They were trying to escape the inescapable. Ivor tried to escape the eternal turmoil of human society, Dom the terror of caring for another human being. Dom had only to look upon his own life to see how inseparable one was from the other. It was as fruitless a task as excising an object from its shadow. The wheel of history always crushed human passions, and that wheel was nothing more than those same human passions writ across the mass of humanity.

It was like the now-vaporized spire of Proteus, an endless fractal structure that showed the same face no matter how closely it was examined. If Dom magnified the firing neurons of his own brain, he would probably see, mirrored there, the patterns he was trying to escape.

Scale was arbitrary.

Ivor, perhaps, didn't see things that way. Dom had an advantage; he had spent the last sixty-three days shredding his own personal illusions.

Ivor's reaction to Dom's plan was predictable. Traveling to Terra, taking on the Confederacy in the halls of its own Congress. The idea was madness.

It was also absolutely sane. In a fight that was men and material, attrition and logistics, in a fight of purely physical resources, Bakunin had no hope. The Confederacy was too large to fight on the battlefield.

However, if somehow the fight could be changed to one of law and diplomacy, a matter of negotiation and litigation, then Bakunin had a chance. In a war of words and treaty, one man *could* fight the Confederacy.

"Give me a lever long enough," Dom muttered, eyes closed, "and I will move worlds."

That lever was the Confederacy's own Charter.

"Sir?" said a voice next to him.

"Yes," Dom replied, opening his eyes. He was in one of the antechambers in Washington Hall where he was waiting for the city's five presidents to come to a decision. Standing in front of him was a blue-clad minuteman, looking slightly nervous. Dom didn't like the nervousness. He also didn't like the way the minuteman held his militia rifle loose in his hands, rather than carrying it slung over his shoulder.

"I am to accompany you to the communications room," the minuteman said.

They'd never given him an armed escort before; the guard was always waiting in the comm room. Dom supposed that they had a right to be nervous after what had happened with Baetez. "Let's go," Dom said, standing up.

"Then," the minuteman said, "I am to accompany you back here."

Dom nodded, feeling a little more nervous about the minuteman.

On the way there, the guard never lowered the rifle.

The normal guard was stationed inside the comm room. His rifle was also unslung. Suspicion brought back old, familiar twitches. Dom ignored them and sat at the console, calling his people in the mountains.

Dom was surprised when Random appeared at the other end of the holo. The holo display itself became a random low-resolution image of sparks dancing in a fog, flashing to Random's voice.

Random greeted him by saying, "Hello, Mr. Magnus. I apologize if I seem a little slow; a third of me is currently escorting Kathy Shane."

The image Dom looked at seemed to form a static cloud over his vision. "It is not as if I'd notice, Random. I've got some bad news—"

Dom explained about Tetsami. Random prompted him occasionally, the static surging in Dom's vision.

Dom kept wondering why Random had answered the comm himself. Random was an entity that never seemed to do anything without specific reason. He also wondered about Shane, for the first time in a long while.

As he spoke, the static reminded Dom of his aircar crash. The crash had knocked out some of the vision in his artificial eyes. And as Dom thought about it, Random's voice also reminded Dom of that crash.

Dom's memory was assisted by a computer, and it didn't take him long to figure out why Random was triggering memories.

"I am sorry about Tetsami," Random said.

Dom nodded and said, "You don't seem very surprised."

Random was silent for a while before he said, "I knew such an event was possible."

"Damnation!" Dom shouted at the screen. "Why didn't you say something?"

"Please, Mr. Magnus, I only knew insofar as I knew Tetsami. She showed a potential for dangerous recklessness, I'm afraid. Especially with you involved. Would either of you wish to hear that from me?"

Dom shook his head. Random was right about that, too right. No one wanted his own self-destructive impulses illuminated. Dom was tempted to ask Random about what the alien AI saw in his own future.

He refrained. Instead, Dom asked, "Why do you remind me of Michael Kelly?"

"He was my son," Random said.

Dom opened his mouth to say something, but he closed it again. He had forgotten the guard over his shoulder. The guard was listening, but would have no idea what was being discussed. The guard didn't know that Random was an AI. The guard wouldn't know that Kelly had been a construct, destroyed in the multiple EMP from the destruction of Proteus. The guard wouldn't know that Kelly had died while saving Dom's life.

After a moment of reflection, Dom said, "Like Mosasa is your father?"

From what little Dom knew of Random's history, Random was built when Mosasa had accumulated five old Race AIs and had used them to "jump-start" each other. In that sense, at least, Mosasa was Random's father.

"Yes," Random said. "And also in the way that Mosasa is also my son."

Dom stared at the screen.

It only took Dom a second to realize that Random was telling him that Mosasa was also a construct, another AI. It explained a number of things, from Mosasa's inhuman ability with electronics to the fact that Random always referred to the floating spheroid robot as "a third" of himself.

"Perhaps we should talk about this later," Dom said.

"Indeed, when next we meet." Random's voice held no trace of irony, nor did it seem to carry the feeling that any great revelation had passed.

Dom nodded. This wasn't the time or place for this discussion. He was using other people's comm equipment. Besides, it was a little late to start distrusting Random now, especially now that he'd learned that he owed Random Walk his life.

Could Kelly's "death" explain why Random had been incommunicado up till now?

"How're things going on the ground at Godwin?" Dom asked, slipping into his role as Jefferson's intelligence conduit.

Random told him, a long liturgy of unchanged status. The invaders were waiting the planet out. The only good news was the lack of any new rumors of surrender.

Dom also asked Random about his status as a figurehead for the resistance. According to Random, the fraud was still working. It was easy for Random to speak with Dom's voice and appearance, and, as Dom, Random had centered the largest central "authority" in the Bleek-Diderot Arms Consortium. What had begun as Dom's frantic calls of warning to all his former business associates, calls Dom had made on what he thought was the eve of his nonexistence, Random had turned into something that could be labeled organized resistance. At least the people in Dom's—really Random's—camp weren't the ones who were driving the isolated city Godwin into further chaos.

In fact, more groups were coming under Bleek-Diderot's auspices simply to protect themselves, not from Proudhon but from neighbors who were running increasingly amok.

"Ironically, our influence is increasing as a result of the situation degrading."

Dom nodded.

"Also, we've gotten word from Flower that he has LOS communications with bands of commune refugees outside the cities. It might be possible, through them, to communicate some sort of organization behind Godwin—maybe prevent more cities from falling."

The situation must be dire indeed for Bakuninites to relinquish their sovereignty to him. *Or,* Dom thought, *to Random Walk, an alien device who perhaps has an agenda of his own.*

Random remained impassive behind his screen of flashing sparks.

"We don't have time to fight a guerrilla war, regardless of how Bakuninites might romanticize the process," Dom said, ignoring his doubts about Random for the moment. "Once the cities fall, that's it."

"Once Godwin falls," Random said. "But you have another way, don't you?"

Dom was noticing, with more frequency, how Random steered conversation, and how Random knew what was to be said, sometimes before Dom knew himself. It was a disconcerting feeling that made Dom grateful that Random was on his side.

"We have to send a delegate to the Terran Congress," Dom said.

"While the situation is still fluid and we have a legitimate claim to planetary authority," Random said. There was none of the strained credulity that had marked Ivor's reaction.

"You've thought of this yourself?" Dom asked.

"I've considered innumerable options, too many to assault my allies with. The idea is valid as far as it goes. If any Bakunin authority outside the one controlling the Proudhon army signs the Confederacy Charter—backed by any arm of the Confederacy—the Executive Command will be forced to withdraw all its influence. Without Confederacy financing, the mercenary army would collapse."

"My thoughts exactly."

"Of course there's the question of the political maneuvering in the Terran Congress. You would need an arm of the Confederacy—a prime seat and a second—in order to have Bakunin come up under our delegate's auspices. Then you would need a majority of voting seats to agree to admission. That majority may be unlikely."

"Perhaps. Perhaps not. There are two arms facing off in orbit above us, the Sirius Community and the Indi Protectorate. Those represent at least one schism in the Confederacy. Centauri and Sirius originated this takeover. Indi and its allies seem at the very least to desire a different outcome."

"Are you sure of this?"

"No, but we have received one suggestion to ask Indi for aid—military aid."

"Ah," Random said.

"Perhaps we can give Indi what it wants without having their troops on our soil, retaining our sovereignty."

"You do realize that this is an extreme long shot."

"The only chance we have."

"You will need passage off planet, and to Earth. How do you intend to manage that?"

"I'm open to any suggestions, Random. Proudhon has a monopoly on outgoing traffic, and I'm at a loss."

"I have a possible solution," Random said. "And a possible bargaining chip that offers an extreme improvement of the odds. However, you need to come to Diderot for both."

"I need to figure out a way to leave Jefferson, whatever I do."

"Until we meet again."

"Until then," Dom said as he cut the connection.

It wasn't until he had left his seat and was being accompanied by a pair of combat-ready minutemen to his debriefing at Washington Hall that he realized that he had never told Random that he had planned to be the delegate himself.

Dom knew that there was something very wrong when he was brought into the presidential chambers. On the walls, Washington, Jefferson, and Franklin were unchanged, but the five presidents looked more than grave. Davis, the ancient economist, was bent over the high desk, and he looked as if he were watching his only friend being buried. Much of the mass had left Adams face, a step away from grandmotherly matron and toward haggard crone. Hamilton's mouth was a thin bloodless line under his clipped mustache. Even the bellicose Jackson, the general, was subdued.

Elaine Madison, the diplomat, was absent.

Most ominous was the line of armed soldiers Dom noticed behind him. When the door shut, his two escorts remained by it, completing the line.

No one invited him to sit. Dom took it upon himself, and seated himself behind one of the tables. Stress pulled at his cheek and hand, and the tension he felt was barely muted by knowing what the news must be.

"Mr. Magnus," Hamilton said. From the movement of his eyes, Dom could see that he read from a prepared statement. "These are difficult times. We have given aid to you and yours because it is our nature to assist those in need. We also note that you have cooperated with us and have provided us with valuable services in return for this aid. We have considered you as we would any citizen." There was a noticeable pause, and Hamilton's eyes flicked briefly toward Jackson. It was clear now that what the presidents had been debating had little to do with Dom's access to the tightbeam comm.

"However, you are not a citizen of Jefferson City," Hamilton continued. "It has been made clear to me that, whatever our personal feelings, we are not obliged to provide you with the protections of a citizen."

Hamilton made eye contact with Dom for the first time. *Here it comes.*

"We have received an ultimatum from the commander of the forces surrounding this city. We have been told that if we do not turn over the man named Dominic Magnus to them by nightfall, I quote, 'This city will not see the dawn.'

"Acceding to such a demand is an ugly prospect. However, uglier still is the prospect of a frontal confrontation with the army surrounding us. You yourself have pointed out how futile that confrontation would be. We have no choice but—"

"When are you handing me over?" Dom asked, interrupting Hamilton. The three other presidents looked pained, but Hamilton seemed relieved to be interrupted from his proclamation.

"We have a contragrav waiting for you, with a complement of minutemen."

"My companions?"

"They remain our guests," Hamilton replied. "And will receive all they need."

"I guess I should go then," Dom said. Under the table, on his knee, his metal hand was vibrating. He clutched the metallic knee underneath his trousers and the vibration stopped.

He supposed that the presidents before him expected some sort of objection. Dom had none. Whether these politicians knew it or not, they held Ivor and Tetsami hostage. From the looks he received, those on the bench above him had no idea how constrained he was.

Hamilton recovered, obviously picking up the thread from much later in the document he was reading. "If you would please turn over any weapons you may be carrying?"

Dom reached in a holster, saw minutemen tense, and slowly withdrew a polychrome GA&A laser and tossed it on the desk before him. On the handgrip, the GA&A logo glittered briefly. *A fitting epitaph*, Dom thought.

He allowed Hamilton to continue with his proclamation. Then Dom allowed the minutemen to lead him away.

CHAPTER EIGHTEEN

Protective Custody

"For every man imprisoned, there is a jailer with something to gain.
—*The Cynic's Book of Wisdom*

"No extraordinary power should be lodged in any one individual."

—THOMAS PAINE
(1737–1809)

Deep below the foundation of the Confederacy tower, Robert Kaunda sat in a lounge waiting to see Dimitri Olmanov. It was the first time he had arranged a personal meeting with Dimitri. Dimitri was the Chief Executive of the Confederacy, and head of the Terran Executive Commend. He was the most powerful man in the Confederacy.

Just the thought of talking to him one-on-one was eating a hole into Kaunda's stomach.

He tried to calm himself by studying the artifact on Dimitri's wall. It was an original fragment of a Dolbrian starmap, priceless, and a reminder of Dimitri's power. Kaunda tried not to think about that. He let his eyes trace the cuneiform knotwork ...

"Good evening, Mr. Kaunda." An ancient voice came from behind him.

"Good evening, Mr. Olmanov," Kaunda responded as he turned. Olmanov somehow remained an imposing figure even when stooped over a cane. Kaunda did not know Olmanov's exact age, but the Confederacy had kept its Chief Executive going past the century-and-a-half mark. Kaunda thought that Olmanov's daily medical bill would keep the population of Mulawayo fed for a month.

Behind Dimitri stood the two-and-a-half-meter-tall figure of Ambrose, his bodyguard. Kaunda looked into Ambrose's dark eyes, and saw very little looking back. He had heard rumors about Ambrose, about half his brain being replaced by a computer, about how his body had been replaced by so much hardware that he came just short of violating the bans on heretical technologies.

All Kaunda knew for certain, from his years as a policeman, was that Ambrose had the eyes of a psychopath.

Dimitri gestured with his cane. "Do you like the piece?"

Kaunda folded his arms and tried to quiet his gut by force of will. "I didn't come down here to discuss art."

Dimitri raised an eyebrow. "No, I suppose not. Come on in, then." As he turned to lead Kaunda into his office, he added, "But think upon the late Dolbrians. They have much to teach about hubris, mortality, and perspective."

Kaunda didn't have a response, so he followed Dimitri in silence.

"What I am talking about is the possibility of war," Kaunda said. He was happy to get it out. He and Dimitri had tap-danced for nearly a half hour and Kaunda's patience had finally given out.

Dimitri nodded and said, "I know quite well what you are talking about."

Between them a holo of Bakunin hovered over Dimitri's desk. Kaunda was a delegate to the Executive Command, and despite his dissenting vote on the go-ahead for the mission, he still had the clearance to review every aspect of Operation Rasputin, the TEC's attempt to impose a domestically controlled State upon Bakunin. Much of the diplomatic tap-dancing between him and Dimitri had been over the details of that operation.

"Then you *have* done something to prevent Indi and Sirius from shooting at each other?"

"Until Bakunin is sponsored into the Confederacy, there is little I can do, other than talk to the principals." Dimitri shook his head. "Are you getting cold feet over your alliance with Vashniya?"

Kaunda leaned back in his chair and felt around in his

pocket, but he had used up all his tablets yesterday, during the first legislative day of the Congress. "I really shouldn't be surprised that you know about that."

Dimitri actually laughed. "Kaunda, you are refreshingly honest. Of course I know. After Vashniya's vote on Rasputin, it was simple to reconstruct what he's doing."

"So what's he doing?"

"In short, he waits for the promotion procedure in the Congress to give Indi a majority on a straight vote. Then Indi starts leapfrogging planets to prime status, ignoring the usual promotion procedure. Assuming Sirius and Centauri do likewise before they slip behind on straight voting members, there'll be a tie for prime seats."

Kaunda sighed and quoted Vashniya, "This Congress, the Europeans lose their primacy."

Dimitri nodded, "If it weren't for the fact that Bakunin has all the requirements for jumping to prime itself."

"Damn it, it's just politics. One prime seat is not worth a war."

"Politics is war, Kaunda. Don't be naive." Dimitri tapped a control on the surface of his desk, and the globe of Bakunin winked out of existence. "*My* goal, Kaunda, is to keep the Confederacy intact whatever the cost. There will be no war." Dimitri's face took on a coldness that frightened Kaunda. "Thank you for bringing your concerns to my attention. But if Operation Rasputin ever endangers the integrity of the Confederacy, the planet is expendable."

Kaunda heard the door open behind him. He got up slowly and left.

A floodlight came on, awaking Jonah Dacham.

Another interrogation, he thought. He didn't remember how they'd strapped him into the cot, but the sessions always snuck up on him like that. He suspected that they gassed the room to prep him.

The room swam around him, a blank white cube twisting in his vision. The spotlight shone down directly into his eyes. No people were hidden by the light; he was alone in the room.

Jonah could feel the drugs course through his blood-

stream, loosing the restraints on the knowledge in his
skull. Jonah wondered why they didn't just use the
biojack and access what they wanted directly. That was
much more efficient, if much harder on the brain so used.

Jonah waited for the first question, which was always
the same.

"What is your name?" It came, as it always did, from
a speaker set somewhere high in the wall.

"Jonah Dacham," he responded.

"Who do you work for?" came the second question,
same as always.

"Myself. The Bleek-Diderot Arms Consortium. The
Bakunin resistance movement."

"Why did you meet with Francesca Hernandez?"

"I was arranging sponsorship from the Seven Worlds
so Bakunin may join the Confederacy."

Fortunately, the drugs, unlike the biojack or torture, did
not force Jonah to volunteer information. There were still
a few secrets he had because his captors asked no questions about them. His status as a ghost, his time on Mars,
and—most importantly—what was buried beneath the
Diderot Mountain Range.

"Who is your mother, and where is she from?"

"Helen Dacham. Waldgrave, SEEC."

"Who is your father, and where is he from?"

The questions gradually sped up as the drugs took hold.
They were often repeated many times. One thing was for
certain, his captors were not the TEC.

The questioning continued another four hours before
Jonah lost consciousness.

CHAPTER NINETEEN

No-Fly Zone

"A petty enemy is more dangerous than a great one."

—*The Cynic's Book of Wisdom*

"To die is landing on some distant shore."

—JOHN DRYDEN
(1631–1700)

A quartet of minutemen led Dom to a contragrav that waited in one of the monument-strewn plazas that littered the center of Jefferson City. Kropotkin had just begun to bury its face in the western horizon, and its light seemed redder than usual.

The vehicle wasn't a true contragrav, but an aerodynamic hybrid with drooping swept wings and a cluster of jets to the rear. It looked old, but Dom didn't think Jefferson City would risk its few state-of-the-art craft on him, especially when there was a chance that the aircraft might not come back.

The minutemen led him up to the side of the aircraft and, obligingly, a door forward of the wing opened to admit him. Dom waited, and one of the minutemen pushed him forward. Apparently, his armed escort wasn't going to join him.

Dom walked up the steps and ducked through the door.

For the size of the craft, the room inside was cramped. There were only four seats, and two of those were for the pilot and copilot.

As soon as he was inside, the door behind him began to close. There was no one else in here. Despite that, he could see displays in front of the pilot's station running through checklists, and he could see controls lighting.

There was a deep whine from behind him, the sound of the jets activating.

They aren't risking anything—they're flying this by remote.

Dom pulled himself into the pilot's chair, so he could watch the displays. A test showed him that all the piloting controls were frozen out on the console. He'd expected that. However, the Jefferson air militia had left him the informational controls. He could call up all the maneuvering cameras, radar, and infrared imaging, as well as a heads-up display for the weapons' targeting system.

The weapons themselves were gutted.

As Dom checked the controls, he noticed the power reading climb on the catalytic contragrav. In a few seconds the reading reached a hundred percent, achieving neutral gravity. Unlike a true contragrav, the reading stopped there, with the contragrav canceling the gravity vector. The power plant wasn't going to produce any negative Gs.

Once it achieved neutral gravity, a short burst from downward-vectored jets pushed it airborne.

As Jefferson receded below him, Dom hoped that the city fathers had warned the Proudhon mercenaries that he was coming. He tried the radio on the craft, but that had been frozen out as well.

He briefly wished he was as adept with electronics as Mosasa was. Mosasa could almost certainly get the controls back on-line. He was pretty sure that Tetsami would probably be able to reprogram the aircraft in flight. Dom wasn't capable of either, and even if he could, that option was closed.

Until he was in the hands of the Proudhon Army, any escape attempt on his part would open Jefferson City to reprisals. Dom couldn't allow that, especially with Ivor and Tetsami there. Ivor, Tetsami, and—

As the aircraft banked east over Jefferson's rose-lighted marble, Dom picked out Jefferson's hospital. A tiny black dot was in the courtyard, like a matte-black hole punched in the surface of the world, the Protean egg. That ellipsoid artifact was all that was left of Proteus. Dom had promised to take it to safety. Locked inside it was the potential of a million minds and a technology that Dom could barely grasp. Eigne had called it a seed.

He didn't know if he had kept his promise, and he didn't know what choice he had. Neither the Jeffersonians, nor the Proudhon army knew it, but that egg held him hostage as much as Ivor and Tetsami did.

The plane banked again, the wing obscuring his view of the hospital, but not before Dom noticed something odd. For just a moment it seemed as if the black spot changed color and moved.

As he flew over Jefferson, he felt an increasing tightness in his stomach that had nothing to do with the motion of the aircraft. The feeling of dread intensified as he slid over the boundary separating the city from the hilly forest that surrounded it. At this point, there was very little to stop the Proudhon army from shooting him out of the sky.

When the aircraft crossed the no-man's-land, he could see a gutted wreck below him. That sight momentarily convinced him that he was going to be shot down. His hands, chromed right and pseudoflesh left, were clamped onto the control stick. They vibrated so badly that if he had been in control of this aircraft, it would have plunged nose-first into the woods with no help from Proudhon.

What happened was, in a way, worse. Just over the line demarking the no-fly zone, Dom's aircraft froze in place and hovered.

What are they doing?

The plane just stopped. From his height, the ungainly winged contragrav must have been visible for a dozen kilometers. Behind him, the marble monuments and radial streets of Jefferson City carved the land like some manic geometry demonstration, and in front of him hills of bluish-ocher forest sat in chaotic heaps like piles of rusty broccoli.

He hovered there, on the line between order and chaos, for a long time before he realized what must be going on. Jefferson wasn't going to pilot this craft beyond the limits of the city. He was sitting here waiting for someone on the other side to pick up the controls. The realization didn't make him feel any better.

He hung in the sky long enough for Kropotkin to set and the sky to purple. He occupied himself by looking for the army. From his vantage it wasn't very hard. The biggest concentration of troops seemed to be in a depression to the city's immediate east, to his southeast. Temporary barracks and vehicles covered a low spot that, due to intervening hills and forest, would be all but ˙invisible from even the highest building in Jefferson. In that one encampment, Dom counted six pieces of heavy artillery, five airtanks, two heavily armed ground-attack contragravs, and at least a dozen personnel carriers of various sorts.

That one encampment outgunned the entire city of Jefferson, and Dom couldn't help but wonder about the firepower that had to ring Godwin and Rousseau. It was disheartening—but it showed him in no uncertain terms that the solution of the mess on Bakunin had to be a political one, not a military one.

His chrome hand rattled on the control stick, and he stilled it. He had to survive this, and for reasons beyond his own selfish interests. He didn't think it was hubris to say that he might be the only person who could pull the political maneuvering to save this planet, and do it without bringing down the Confed ships from orbit.

If nothing else, I've managed to find a way out of the siege.

Stars were flickering to life as the aircraft finally moved. It rotated away from the concentration of troops Dom had seen and flew north. He noticed that his new remote pilot had decided to remove some more of Dom's few control options. Dom's external video, radar, and IR imaging were all fuzzed to incomprehensibility. The electronics were effectively blind. He could see out the cockpit, but half of the world was gone behind the mass of the aircraft from him.

However, from the way the craft bucked and moved, it was fairly obvious that his new pilot didn't want the Jeffersonians figuring out where it landed.

It finally put down in a clearing. Immediately before it landed, the aircraft's electronic vision cleared and he saw that he was over the horizon from Jefferson City. Then he was down, and the power to the control systems were cut, plunging him into darkness.

The jets and the contragrav both deactivated with a diminishing high-frequency whine. Out the cockpit windows, Dom could only see the globular shadows of Bakunin trees and a slice of starlit sky. The interior of the aircraft was pitch-black. Even the night-glow that should have been illuminating the cockpit controls was dead. Outside, out of the corner of his eye, he thought he saw some motion.

He looked toward where something had briefly eclipsed the stars. Dom was about to adjust his photoreceptors to compensate for the darkness when his captors activated the floodlights.

Suddenly the nose of the craft was washed in blinding white light that destroyed the image of anything—stars, forest, or mysterious aircraft—beyond them.

Dom heard the noise of someone opening the door manually. He stood up and faced that way, as much to escape the wash of light as to meet his captors.

The door swung open and Dom found himself confronted with the barrel of a plasma rifle. Outside, beyond the soldier holding the rifle on him, Dom saw ranks of backlit mercenaries. He raised his hands and hoped that brother Klaus wanted more than his body.

The soldier motioned him forward with the barrel of his rifle, and Dom slowly advanced into the blinding light. Apparently he didn't advance fast enough for the mercenaries. The instant he reached the door to the aircraft, a half-dozen hands reached from the sides and yanked him to the ground. His feet missed the steps, and since his captors held his arms, he fell a meter face-first into the ground. Fortunately for his face, the ground was mossy sod and not paved tarmac. Even so, the impact stunned him and starred his vision.

He spat out a mouthful of moss and dirt. Someone put a foot between his shoulder blades, as if he weren't pinned enough, and both his arms were yanked above him. The pain in his shoulders made him gasp, even though they were cybernetic. He felt metal restraints tighten on his left wrist. His right wrist wasn't sensitive enough to feel the pressure.

Someone else yanked his legs straight out behind him and clamped something similar to his ankles.

"Don't move," warned a husky male voice.

To Dom, the statement seemed redundant. His body certainly didn't seem to consider movement a viable option.

Whoever had his foot on Dom's back removed it. It was replaced by the hard metallic pressure of a weapon. Dom tried to raise his head to get a view of something other than the divot his face had made in the ground. The response from his captors was to grab his hair, yank his head up, pull a bag over his head, and slam it back into the ground.

Now he was blind and nearly deaf in addition to being immobile.

They cinched the opening of the bag tight to his neck. They did it so roughly that Dom thought they were going to garrote him. They stopped just short of strangulation. It was enough to start a headache.

Even the spotlight didn't penetrate the material of the bag. The interior felt like a slick polymer, almost like rubber, and once he no longer felt strangled, Dom began to worry about asphyxiation.

His captors didn't share his worry. With the gun barrel still pressed into his shoulder blades, he was yanked upward by his arms. His arms rotated in their sockets, igniting more pain and making Dom forget that the bag over his head was becoming slick with his own exhaled breath.

Standing, he discovered that his feet had some freedom of movement. There was about a half-meter of chain or cable connecting the restraints on his ankles. There was no such play with the wrist restraints.

The gun barrel pushed him forward, and Dom had to comply or collapse again. His head was throbbing, and the bag felt like an oven designed to cook the remaining organics out of his brain. Somehow he got enough air to keep from passing out, though after walking a dozen meters, his face felt ready to slide off his skull.

Someone kept his arms taut, behind his back, keeping him pressed to the gun no matter how fast he tried to walk. Worse, it seemed that, restrained as he was, he wasn't capable of walking as quickly as his captors wanted him to. Twice he fell as they marched him forward, and each time it felt as if his shoulders had been ripped out of their sockets.

Eventually—it felt like an hour, but his onboard computer told him that it had only been fifteen minutes—he was taken into a building. He could only tell because his shoulder brushed the doorframe. His feet still shuffled on a dirt floor, and with the bag over his head, his breathing masked any subtler sounds.

They stopped him, allowing him to sense motion around him, and then his arms were yanked downward, forcing him to collapse into a chair. Once he was seated, he felt a tug and his arms felt welded to his seat, as well as each other. Then the bag came off his head in a gust of what felt like the coolest freshest air that he had ever breathed.

He was sitting in a temporary structure, a modular framework of wall panels set over a dirt floor. He sat under a spotlight, and in front of him was a folding desk that barely brushed the outside of the pool of light.

Now, with his senses unrestrained by the hood, he could tell that he was in the presence of two people. One was behind him, and one was sitting on the other side of the desk. It was hard to tell, but the man in front of him seemed to wear a variant of the turquoise and black uniform of Proudhon Spaceport Security—which meant he wasn't Klaus. Dom didn't know how encouraging that was.

"Well, well, well," said the man behind the desk. Dom felt a rushing sense of déjà vu when he heard that voice.

The man stood up and began to walk around toward Dom and the light. "Of all the people to fall across our lap. Small world here, isn't it, Lance?"

The man was addressing someone behind Dom. Another familiar voice said, "Yeah, Bull—I mean, yes, Captain."

Dom could see the captain now, a large bald man, larger than Ivor. He was a man Dom had last seen in the pits of East Godwin. Dom turned his head to see the merc behind him and he saw what he expected—a cadaverous man with video cameras for eyes.

At least he's no longer wearing that necklace. The last time Dom had seen him, he'd been wearing a necklace of human teeth.

The captain, Bull, must have noticed some reaction in Dom's face, because he kicked the chair and said, "Remember us, do you?"

Dom faced Bull. "It would be difficult to forget."

A smile flickered on Bull's lips. "Good." He drew a chromed antique pistol from a hip holster. It used to be Dom's own ceremonial sidearm. Dom had dropped it in East Godwin during an ambush by the gang of punks Bull used to command.

Bull pointed the gun at Dom's face and said, "I would hate for you to wonder why I'm pissed at you."

Dom watched, limbs immobilized, as Bull's finger tightened on the trigger.

CHAPTER TWENTY

Casualty Reports

"There is no such thing as good news."
—*The Cynic's Book of Wisdom*

"Don't tell me what you're planning; tell me what
the fuck is going on!"

—DATIA RAJASTHAN
(?–2042)

Traveling up from the Dolbrian pyramid took over a day.
Even taking the climb slowly, with time for some sleep,
Shane was exhausted—both mentally and physically—by
the time Random led her into the inhabited part of the
mountain. It was past dusk when she walked into the conference room after Random's robot.

The last half of the hike had, for the most part, been silent. Random had given her too much to think about.
Somehow, Bakunin owed its existence to Random Walk.
If Random were anything other than a Race AI, Shane
could've safely dismissed the claim as mad. How could
an isolated computer affect the whole planet, and by extension, the whole Confederacy?

Random's affecting me, just by talking.

What were revolutionaries, anyway, but single human
beings who carried the right seed to the right ground?
How powerful could someone be to know what seeds
would germinate in the political soil of Bakunin? Random
knew who could make a difference.

Shane was glad when she reached the conference room
and Zanzibar. Thinking too much about Random was urg-
ing her toward paranoia, and Random's talk about the political destruction of the Confederacy wasn't helping.

Zanzibar was sitting off to one side of the black hemispherical chamber, in front of the intact part of the partially-dismantled table. Shane walked up to see what she was doing, but Zanzibar's eyes were closed, and the central holo was dark, as was the control pad across her lap.

Out of the corner of her eye, Shane noticed Random's robot leave the room. But Shane was aware now, more than she'd ever been, of the illusory nature of the privacy Random was offering her and Zanzibar. Random was alive in every computer system in this mountain. Only one of those five crystals Mosasa liberated actually lived in the robot.

Shane collapsed in a chair next to Zanzibar, allowing fatigue to seep in. Once sitting, she doubted she had the energy to stand up again.

"Shane," Zanzibar said quietly, without moving or opening her eyes.

Every time Shane was alone with Zanzibar, she was struck by the contrast between them. She and Zanzibar were at opposing ends of almost every measurable characteristic. Zanzibar was tall, Shane short, Zanzibar was dark to the point where her skin had a near-metallic purple sheen, while, after all her time in these caverns, Shane's skin had faded to a ghostly white. Where Zanzibar seemed to be made of whipcord and steel cable, Shane was chiseled out of concrete.

"Shane?" Zanzibar repeated.

"Yes," Shane said.

"Random said he was fetching you." Zanzibar opened her eyes and it looked as though she'd been getting less sleep than Shane had.

Shane nodded, stifling a yawn. That was another disturbing fact about Random that she hadn't thought about until now. Each of those five elements of Random's brain was an independent entity. While Random was down with her, isolated in his robot, another Random, or another part of Random, was up here in the mountain with Zanzibar and Mosasa. Mosasa, in fact, was another independent part of Random.

That was three out of five. Shane wondered where the other two "Randoms" were.

Zanzibar stared at her uncertainly. Shane didn't blame her. Shane was still uncertain about herself. Zanzibar had never fully approved of her, for good reason. By any scale, Shane had betrayed the marines, her government, and everything else she'd been supposed to stand for. Shane knew that she certainly wasn't worthy of anyone's trust.

After regarding her a while, as if she were looking for something, Zanzibar said, "Random insists that you be here when Mr. Magnus arrives."

Shane thought back to the beginning of her conversation with Random, before things had become strange. "Does this have something to do with the pyramid?"

Zanzibar shrugged. "It involves politics. Mr. Magnus might have a plan to bail out this mess—and Random says that the information on that rock you found is going to help."

"You don't sound convinced. Is Mr. Magnus arriving?"

Zanzibar looked at her, and Shane could see deep pain in her eyes. She had seen that look before, once, in the eyes of a commander who had just gotten word that he had lost his whole division.

"I don't know," Zanzibar said. "I've been up here, monitoring transmissions with Random. The news has been going bad since last night. Jefferson's TEC prisoner laid his hands on a sat transmitter last night. Klaus got word about Dominic." Zanzibar shook her head and banged a clenched fist on the side of her chair. "Those Jefferson bastards caved. Klaus demanded him, and the Jeffersonians caved."

"What happened?" Shane asked, feeling some of Zanzibar's tension now.

"They shipped him over to the Proudhon line, and that's the last word we have."

The finality of the statement struck Shane with dread. Despite all she'd been through because of this planet, and because of Dom and his people, she didn't like the idea of Dominic Magnus in Klaus Dacham's hands. That would mean that Klaus had won.

"The others?" Shane asked.

Zanzibar sucked in a breath. "Tetsami was shot by the prisoner. She's comatose in Jefferson Hospital. She might make it."

Dear God. "Ivor?"

Zanzibar shook her head. "I don't know. *They* don't know. Random filtered out transmissions of minutemen looking for him."

Shane didn't know what to say.

"And there's nothing we can do!" Zanzibar slammed her fist again. "We're stuck in this damned mountain and people are dying out there."

Silence gathered in the conference room. Shane knew how Zanzibar felt. Shane'd been a captain in the Occisis marines. Officers were often cursed with the duty of sitting and waiting for the casualty reports. Command or not, those were the times when she'd felt the greatest impotence. People were going to die, and you couldn't change it.

· Shane wanted to reach out, show Zanzibar some sign of camaraderie, some sign that she felt some of it too. She didn't move. She had no idea how Zanzibar would react to comfort from her.

The silence was broken by a zap of static from the holo that was still central to the half-dismantled table. Random's voice filled the room. "I have something, possibly important."

Zanzibar sat bolt upright. "What? Show me!"

"I regret there's little to show. The importance is an absence of data."

"What?" Shane said, echoing Zanzibar two seconds late.

"An area northeast of Jefferson City that had been alive with Proudhon chatter has vanished."

"Explain," Zanzibar ordered.

"All RF communication out of the area has ceased. Even radar returns, high altitude to ground clutter, have nulled out. I can show you a picture I've enhanced."

A visual image replaced the random test pattern that accompanied the AI's voice. Shane looked at a high-angle telescopic image of the woods surrounding Jefferson City. The picture was light and computer enhanced, so there was no mistaking the central artifact nestled in the heart of the night-purple forest.

An ellipsoid of total darkness had englobed an area nearly five kilometers in diameter.

CHAPTER TWENTY-ONE

Focus Groups

"Time always wins."
— *The Cynic's Book of Wisdom*

"The future influences the present just as much as the past."

— FRIEDRICH NIETZSCHE
(1844–1900)

Crystalline arches vault above her, disappearing into infinite fractal patterns. Malleable black spheres, appearing ephemeral as smoke, roll around her and Eigne, following floor, walls, and ceiling as if gravity is of no consequence. Often, as the objects pass them, the crystal structure left behind is altered, as if the black things are continually rebuilding the chamber around Tetsami.

"This isn't real," Tetsami says. Her voice lacks conviction.

"By the way you measure reality, Traveler, perhaps." Eigne says. "Where we exist now cannot be real to those who have not shed the flesh."

Tetsami turns around and around. Every angle of the cavern seems to shift, to change, when she does not look. She feels that the cavern is moving, mutating around the central point created by her and Eigne. Above her, there are no more vaulting arches; the ceiling is now a logarithmic spiral.

Wispy black balls continue to roll by them.

"What is this place?" Tetsami asks.

Eigne smiles with teeth that are perfect silver mirrors. "This is Proteus."

Tetsami knows that she has left the bounds of reality

now. Proteus has been blasted back into Bakunin's crust. The Proudhon invasion made sure of that. This has to be a dream, a figment, a delusion. "They destroyed Proteus," Tetsami says finally.

"Proteus is not a commune, a specific location on some planet Outside. It is us." Eigne waves at the chamber around them.

"The egg, that damn egg. I've jacked into it somehow, right?"

"That is the easiest way to explain it." Eigne says. "Your brain was engineered for direct contact. It allows us better communication."

Tetsami feels her heart sink. The idea of Proteus terrifies her at some visceral level. These are the people whose dabbling in nanotechnology cost Terra the outer planets of the solar system. Of all heretical technologies, theirs is the most despised—

"You fear us?"

"Christ on the cross, I do. Your fucking bugs eat people."

"I understand."

"What am I doing here? And what the hell has Mars to do with anything?"

"You are one of three contacts we always make before apotheosis."

"What?"

"Our promise of aid to Dominic Magnus is one point on a circle of temporal events common to a host of realities. Our contact with you is another. The egg, as you refer to it, has a common surface in all those realities."

Tetsami backs up and finds herself pressing against a crystal rib that seems to bifurcate an infinite number of times before it reaches the ceiling. "You aren't making sense!"

Eigne doesn't move, and smoky black globes roll by between them. "Some people describe time as a tree, branching into different realities with every quantum probability. Things are more complex than that. Time is more like a multidimensional spiderweb. There are macro structures, loops, realities converging as much as they diverge—"

Tetsami holds up her hands. "Look, Engine, Eigne, whatever your name is—you lost me at apotheosis, and I think I want to stay lost. Can we just call it quits, let me back into my own head?"

"You will awake, or not, in time."

The cavern seems to unfold around itself in a gut-wrenching twist. Tetsami is looking at the walls when they turn inside out, and the sight makes her want to vomit. She closes her eyes. "What do you mean, 'or not'?"

"We have experience of the same slice of events from a septillion different realities. Your refusal of the Change is common to all of them. Your survival is not."

Tetsami opens her eyes and blinks. She sees Bakunin trees around her. She's back home, somewhere. The inside-out cavern is now a curving black wall that flies away from both of them. They are in the center of an ellipsoid dome.

"You mean with all your nanogadgets you can't help me, with a simple, fucking gut wound."

Eigne turns around and says, very gravely, "Only if you assent to the Change."

"What change."

"*The* Change, the shedding of the flesh, the ultimate commitment to Proteus—"

"You mean I'd get sucked into—"

Eigne smiles slightly, and without much humor. "As you said, our little bugs eat people."

Tetsami senses movement around them, some sort of battle occurring. Black globes roll around the ground, but Eigne ignores them, and the battle. The soldiers, who appear to be Proudhon mercenaries, ignore the two of them as if they're invisible.

Eigne walks straight for a temporary structure at the edge of the compound. "We made a promise to Dominic Magnus to aid him, because he aids us. Because of that promise, and because of his care for you, we are obliged to offer you the Change, even when we know your answer."

Tetsami stops at the door, while Eigne steps over a corpse on the ground. The corpse is Dom. Tetsami sees his face, crushed and torn by the impact of a bullet. She turns and retches.

"This isn't real, this isn't real, this isn't real," she chants to herself.

"*This* is real, Tetsami. Very real."

Tetsami turns to look down at Dom's body. He is absolutely motionless. She stares at him, unable to draw her gaze above the collarbone.

"This is a shadow of the events in your reality, Tetsami. I am here now to communicate with Dominic, though I am afraid his brain is not as well suited to the contact as yours."

I do care for him. Fuck everything, I do care. Tetsami feels burning on her cheeks. "I've lost him, haven't I?"

Eigne bends over Dom and begins manipulating some part of Dom's head. Tetsami shuts her eyes. "You're going to offer him your change, and he isn't going to be Dom anymore, is he?"

"He will still be Dominic Magnus."

"But he'll be part of you—"

"We are helping him accomplish his goals. He will be in essence, unchanged."

Tetsami whips around to face Eigne. She is bent over Dom like a vampire, Dom's ravaged head cradled in chromed hands.

"Unchanged? He's dead! *Look at him!*"

"Death? An ill-defined term at best. As long as the data can be salvaged, is it death?"

Eigne begins to do something to Dom's head.

CHAPTER TWENTY-TWO

Smoke and Mirrors

"The important answers are those to the questions we ask ourselves."

—*The Cynic's Book of Wisdom*

"The wailing of the newborn infant is mingled with the dirge for the dead."

—LUCRETIUS
(96?–55 B.C.)

Dom tried to move when he saw that Bull wasn't bluffing. He moved too slow, too little, too late.

The world turned into a blinding flash. The sound was a deafening roar with an undertone like a metallic gong. His head pulled back so fast that it felt as if it had been torn off his shoulders. The sensation whited out every synapse he had as he fell into a blinding unconsciousness.

The Hegira luxury aircar had plowed through the tenth floor of a fifteen-story warehouse and had flipped over, suspending Dom head-first, about thirty meters above a very hard-looking alley.

Someone had started to take potshots at him. The shooter had been shaved bald. Baldy was leading a group of a half-dozen East Godwin scavengers.

Dom had swung out of the canopy, hanging by his left hand. Then he'd pulled the emergency eject lever. The canopy had blown him back into the warehouse, while the rockets blew the driver's seat down, straight at the punks. The ejection seat's rocket had ignited the chute during the descent. It wasn't supposed to happen, but the seat had been deployed upside down in a narrow alley only thirty meters from the ground.

Dom had escaped a growing inferno, to land in Baldy's hands.

Once Dom stepped outside, a bald punk in an exec's monocast vest threw him down the front stairs. Dom hit the ground, his ceremonial slug thrower clattering out of his belt holster, landing faceup, in the center of a ring of a half-dozen punks.

Baldy, punk number one, aimed Dom's own slug thrower at him.

Punk number two leveled a Griffith-Five High Frequency pulse carbine at him. His partial armor was the turquoise and black of Proudhon Spaceport Security.

Punk number three wore a black beret, leather jacket, and a three-fingered artificial hand holding a fifteen-millimeter Dittrich High Mass Electromag.

Punk four had vidlens eyes, a necklace of human teeth, and a machete.

Punk five wore half a facial reconstruction in brushed chrome. He carried an antique frontier auto-shotgun.

Punk six was a woman with a smartgun.

"A fucking corp," said Beret.

"Vent his ass," said the woman.

"Hell you say, Trace. Corp exec, ransom—" said the one with the pulse carbine.

"Sell 'im," the guy with half a face agreed.

"Vent him," said the woman as she began to power up her weapon.

"It's your call, Bull," said the man with video eyes.

The bald one looked down on him, shaking his head. "He *looks* like a corporate type. Could be worth something to someone—"

Carbine and half-face gave satisfied nods to each other.

"—But I don't want to deal with the upkeep, and the bastard shot a chair at me." Baldy looked up at the woman. "Vent him, Trace."

Then the paladin showed and four of the six punks died.

* * *

Same memory, replayed, distorted—

Dom ringed by a half-dozen punks, all with the same cybernetic stigmata. They are no longer strangers.

The punk with the pulse carbine wears the uniform of the Stygian Presidential Guard. His is the face of Ivor Jorgenson—but a younger Ivor; Ivor when he was Robert Elision. This is the Commander Elision who had died with thirty-five thousand others when Dom neutralized the city of Perdition.

The punk with the beret and the artificial hand wears the face of Johann Levy. Levy, who had been a viper in the midst of Dom's organization, and who had been Dom's sacrifice when the break-in at GA&A began to go bad. The Dittrich HME looks large in comparison to Levy's small stature.

The crazy one, the one with the teeth and the video eyes, is Klaus. Klaus grins, and his machete drips gore.

The one with half a face wears a charred battlesuit. Shane's face looks out of the burnt wreckage.

The woman with the smartgun is Tetsami.

"Fascism is capitalism in decay," says Levy.

"Vent his ass," says Tetsami.

"A tool of the powers that be," Elision says, "He's not part of the solution."

"He wants to destroy the system, and offers nothing in its place," Shane agrees, talking with the unburnt part of her face.

"Vent 'im," Tetsami says, powering up her smartgun.

"This is your operation," Klaus says to someone out of Dom's view. "What's your sentence, sir?"

Dom is frozen in place as the punks' leader steps out of the darkness. His breath catches in his throat as he sees the Old Man of the TEC, the Commander-in-Chief, the head Executive of the Confederacy, Dimitri Olmanov.

Dimitri is small and bent, but Dom sees blood and steel in Dimitri's brown eyes. Dimitri shakes his head and leans forward on his cane to look into Dom's face. "I expected more from you, Jonah. Even when you ran from the TEC, I expected you to do something with yourself. You've been a grave disappointment, my son. Your brother, at least, has shown some initiative." Dimitri shakes his head.

Pain flares in Dom's skull, and he can't find a voice to defend himself.

"I am afraid that this was your last chance. I am too old to keep the wolves away." Dimitri turns and hobbles away.

The five others descend on Dom, and this time there's no paladin to save him.

For a brief period, the real world seemed to leak into Dom's awareness. Voices . . .

"I don't believe the bastard ain't dead." Dull and far away, Dom felt a kick into his abdomen. Dom felt the dirt floor under his cheek and realized that the chair had fallen over. He lay on his side, curled into a fetal position, the chair still tied between his wrists and his back.

Another kick, the pain sharper this time, but still far away.

Dom's eyes couldn't focus on anything other than the spot of ground a centimeter in front of his nose. He heard the speaker bend close to him—smelled him, too: sweat, garlic, and overfermented home brew. He felt fingers prod his forehead, not as a touch, but as a pressure through layers of overloaded pseudoflesh.

"What the fuck?"

A voice came, as if from kilometers away, "Bull?"

More prodding. "The corp SOB has a metal plate in his head—"

"Bull."

The smell receded as Dom heard a pistol cock. "Well, let's not make the same mistake twice—"

"*Bull!*"

Dom was still lucid enough to tense in anticipation of the final shot. Instead of the shot, he heard, "Call me Captain, damn it! What is it?"

Still no shot came, and Dom began to lose his grip on consciousness.

"Captain, sir. The stars just went out."

Dom fell into blackness again.

The sky is opaque gray and ash-blown. A dirty tarlike snow falls across slushy hills. From around him smoke rises as if from volcanic craters. The wind is cold, biting cold, a cold that strips flesh from bone.

It is that that allows him to realize that his flesh is gone from the bone. Everything human has been torn from his body, leaving a dirty gunmetal-gray skeleton. Fluids leak from artificial muscles to pool below his feet and freeze.

Dom cannot move. He turns his head and sees his arm outstretched. The metallic wrist has been welded to a blast-blackened girder. He turns and sees the hand the Jeffersonians gave him, now the most human part of his body, welded to its girder.

He doesn't need to see his feet to know that he's been crucified, somehow, upon the wreckage of Styx. As if the knowledge flips a switch in his skull, he now sees the hills around him for what they are.

He is surrounded by mounds of corpses, the cold freezing them in the agonized postures in which they died. He stares at the black Stygian sky and screams.

Someone grabs the front of his rib cage and shakes him. He knows it is Helen before she speaks, because she always grabbed him like that when she wanted his attention. Only she usually grabbed the front of his shirt.

She shakes him so that the cross welded to him shakes as well. "Stop crying, you self-pitying wretch."

Dom looks into his mother's eyes. He looks up to see her, even though the last time he had seen Helen Dacham, he was eighteen and taller than she was. "You're dead," he says idiotically.

It is true. Helen's face has the pasty look Dom has seen in fresh corpses. Her eyes are dull and seem to focus beyond him. "And you're alive, Jonah?"

"I killed you."

Helen laughs. It is the laugh that had made Jonah and Klaus hide as children. The laugh that happened just before she began to throw things.

Helen laughs and lifts him to face her, as if the cross isn't there—which it isn't any more. Dom feels his feet dangling. "You killed me? You try so hard to be an evil bastard, Jonah. You and your brother. You'll never be half of what your father was."

"I didn't want to—"

The laugh again and she throws him into a pile of corpses. His joints begin to freeze. "You belong there, with the other pawns." She stands over him. Her flesh begins putrefying as she speaks to him. He wants to close his eyes, but he has no eyelids.

"I didn't want to kill you," he says.

"Don't lie to me." She slaps him, leaving part of her hand behind. Her skin is shiny, bloated, and purpling. "Of course you dreamed of killing me. Every single night you dreamed of it. Didn't you?"

He can't speak.

"Answer me!"

"Yes," Dom says. He finds that he can't cry. "Of course I did! You drank, you beat us, you disappeared with your boyfriends for weeks at a time—"

"And you thought the TEC was a better parent?" Flesh peels away from her face. Her eyes cave in as she speaks. "You're pathetic. Pathetic and stupid. I should have given you back to your father, it would serve him right."

Dom is frozen now, he can barely move his jaw to talk. "Who is my father?" He manages a near-silent whisper.

Helen Dacham, his mother, is no more than a skeleton tied together with strips of desiccated flesh. She laughs. "You know him, Jonah—he's the man who really killed me." Her corpse falls into another pile of bodies, to freeze in place, immobile.

I am dead, Dom thinks. *This must be hell.*

"Death?" A voice asks to his right. It echoes off parabolic crystalline walls that Dom only notices now. The voice is accompanied by a solid thunking sound. "An ill-defined term at best."

A metallic female form walks into Dom's view. A walking humanoid whose hairless skin appears to be made of liquid chrome, with every flaw polished away. She carries Klaus' bloody machete in her right hand, and her left is stained with blood. Behind her follows an ellipsoid of darkness, a hole in the universe maybe three meters in diameter.

The woman's name is Eigne, and she had been part of the Proteus Commune. "As long as the data can be salvaged, is it death?"

Her machete comes down on a pile of corpses with a solid impact. She reaches into the pile with her other hand and Dom hears grating sounds, sounds of peeling flesh.

As she roots in the pile of human wreckage, she keeps talking. Dom doesn't know if the monologue is directed at him, or if Eigne is talking to herself, or maybe the floating Protean seed.

"My problem, even after the Change, was an obsession with continuity of existence. Would I lose something when I wasn't aware?" With a slurping sound, Eigne pulls something from the pile of corpses. Her left hand holds a pile of rancid, unidentifiable meat. She tosses it into the following ellipsoid of darkness. "One might as well fear every form of unconsciousness."

The machete comes down again.

"Sleep, for instance. Any drugged state."

Pry.

"It is memory's apparent continuity that tells us who we are."

Suction and withdrawal of what Dom can now see is a human brain.

"So is amnesia a form of death?"

She tosses the brain into the egg—no, they called it a seed.

Dom can see clearly what Eigne is doing now. It's as if his point of view has been liberated from his body. In fact, he can see his own corpse over Eigne's right shoulder. It is not hard to miss, all chromium bones next to blackened, frozen flesh. He notices that Eigne's breath doesn't fog.

She bends to hack open another skull. "Death is such a pointless concept, especially when one focuses on the mind. It's no wonder most religions have disposed or altered it. Machine—that's another word that is too vague."

She tosses the liberated brain to the seed. Dom watches the two kilograms of meat strike the matte-black surface of the ellipsoid and disappear. No ripples, the brain passes through the surface and does not reappear. Dom feels an urge to touch the surface, but his hands are frozen into a pile of corpses ten meters away.

"Is the definition biological? No, a machine can be flesh and blood as much as steel and electricity. We cannot say that a machine cannot reproduce itself. The sacred agents of the Change do that, and they are machines, they are even labeled as such."

She continues the harvest, until she reaches his body.

"What, then, defines a machine?"

The question is directed at him. Dom thinks, or believes he thinks, upon the answer before he responds, *free will*?

Even though his thought doesn't pass through the frosted metallic jaw below him, Eigne hears him. "A machine cannot choose what to do, it will do what it is supposed to do, all the time, without variation. Anything with free will is not a machine. Anything that gives up free will becomes one." Eigne raises her machete. "I am not saving machines here."

You told me that you'd help me—

"One can only make an agreement with a True Mind, Jonah Dacham. We have seen in you. Until now, we have not seen *of* you. What is your substance?"

I am not dead!

"Yes, you are. That is not the question."

I am not a machine!

"Make a choice."

Help me!

"Prove to me that you are not simply following the program set for you."

Damn it, if you are really here, you can see what I've decided already. I know who is running my machines, and I know how to defy him.

"Perhaps I have. Do you commit yourself to the action?"

Not if it means handing myself over to another controller.

"Do you wish my help?"

Yes.

The machete comes down on Dom's metallic skull.

CHAPTER TWENTY-THREE

Intervention

"Conflicts are easier when your opponent doesn't fight back."

—*The Cynic's Book of Wisdom*

"Sometimes the shit just overwhelms you."

—AUGUST BENITO GALIANI
(2019–2105)

In the depths of his anger, Ivor Jorgenson never thought he would have tried to save Dominic Magnus. Not only was Dominic responsible for what happened to Tetsami, he represented the Confed politics that Ivor had come to Bakunin to escape. However, when he discovered what the Jeffersonians were doing, Ivor was struck by two unexpected thoughts.

The first was that Tetsami would want him to do something about it. It didn't matter what Ivor thought of him. Tetsami felt something for Dominic, and if Ivor ever wanted to redeem himself in her eyes, he had to accept that. He might not be her biological father, but she was the only family he had left.

The other thought was that, insane as Dominic's plans were, they were the only vehicle left to pay back the people who had done this to Tetsami. In fact, it was the only payback anyone had ever offered him. Not just for Tetsami, but for both versions of Styx, both versions of his son, and for a Robert Elision who no longer existed.

Those were his thoughts when his friend in the Jeffersonian government, Elaine Madison, the chief diplomat for Jefferson City, came to the hospital and told him that

Dominic was to be given over to Proudhon. That news set Ivor on a path he wouldn't have predicted.

He left Elaine with a message for Tetsami, and departed the hospital. His thoughts swam. He couldn't let Dominic stop now, couldn't let him be stopped. He couldn't let the Confederacy win. He couldn't let Tetsami's pain be in vain.

When he ran out to the courtyard, he was already thinking of stealing a vehicle. He needed something fast and maneuverable. He had some confidence in his piloting ability, but he needed a good craft in order to run the blockade.

The decision was made for him when he ran through the hospital courtyard and saw Dominic's black egg moving. The three-meter ellipsoid rose in front of Ivor, a rainbow shimmer occasionally flashing across its otherwise nonreflective black surface.

Dominic had never been open about the thing, but Ivor knew two facts about it. First, it came from the Proteus Commune with Dom. Second, it had made its way through the blockade on its own, after the Proudhon forces had bottled up Jefferson.

When Ivor saw the black egg move, he knew it was following Dominic, and Ivor knew that the best chance he had of breaking through the blockade would be by following this Protean artifact through whatever hole it made in the blockade.

As the egg rose above the hospital, Ivor ran to the ambulance bays. The contragravs parked there were the closest vehicles to him. They weren't his first choice for maneuverability, but the egg could disappear any moment.

Once Ivor had launched one of the Jefferson ambulances, the egg was motionless above the hospital, a tiny black mote, waiting for him. Ivor flew the ambulance at the mote and discovered that the egg showed as nothing on the ambulance's instruments. There was no radar signature, no infrared, nothing electromagnetic at all.

The ambulance also had short range mass sensors in it, to help it find aircar wrecks in mountain or forest, Ivor supposed. The mass sensors saw nothing when he closed on the egg. No mass at all, which was impossible.

The comm on the ambulance chattered at him. The noise was from Jefferson, so he turned it off.

It seemed the egg *was* waiting for him. As soon as Ivor closed on it, the black ellipsoid shot to the northeast. Ivor did his best to follow, straining the fans of the ambulance. The Protean egg didn't seem to obey the laws of physics. It certainly didn't move like any contragrav Ivor had ever seen. It didn't move like anything Ivor had ever seen.

That was why he ran into it.

The egg had stopped at the border. Just stopped. There had been no visible deceleration, all the velocity simply ceased. It happened so quickly that at first it seemed that the black ellipsoid was growing. Once Ivor saw that the egg was no longer moving, it was too late to stop the ambulance. He tried to weave under the egg—

Ivor was sure he struck the egg, or that it struck him. In any event, the ambulance stopped moving. It was a bizarre sensation, as if he had entered free-fall with the nose canted fifteen degrees downward. There was no sensation of damped inertia, or gravity, to tell his body he had stopped. However, the view out the windscreen now showed the no-man's-land surrounding Jefferson City—unmoving.

The airspeed and inertial speedometer read zero. The fans were still going, full power. And the contragrav was still running at slightly positive G. Neither showed any effect.

Ivor switched the video to various views around the ambulance, but he couldn't find the egg. All he saw was a slightly tinted fish-eye view of the environment around Jefferson.

Did he break the egg? He didn't think that was possible. At best the ambulance had sideswiped it.

Something was holding him here.

To conserve power, he shut off the maneuvering fans. He didn't turn off the contragrav, since he didn't know when this effect would decide to quit. As he damped the fans, he knocked a pen loose from the dashboard. It floated free, as if he were in orbit or deep space.

Impossible.

Contragrav was one thing—that involved another force entirely, one midway between gravity and electromagnetism. The contragrav generator in this ambulance generated a mass of matter in the right quantum state, and that matter repulsed any matter not in that state with a force a thousand times that of gravity. Contragravity couldn't cancel gravity's effect on normal matter; it could only generate five kilos of mass with five tons of lift.

No matter what the contragrav was doing—unless the ambulance was pulling a free-fall or negative-G maneuver—that pen would fall to the floor. Instead, the pen was drifting in midair, as if he had somehow taken the ambulance orbital.

It was darkening outside. Darkening too quickly, it seemed. The world was beginning to take on a red tint, like a thermograph. *Exactly like a thermograph,* Ivor thought. *I'm seeing a blueshift, the visible light's going into the UV and the infrared's becoming visible.*

The fish eye was becoming distorted.

With a trembling hand, Ivor reached out and turned off the contragrav generator. God only knew how it would be interfering with what was going on. All Ivor knew was that he was seeing relativistic effects out his windscreen, and it scared the shit out of him.

It felt as if he hung there forever with the scene outside the windscreen becoming more and more distorted. Then, without warning, the scene outside the contragrav changed. There was no period of acceleration. One second the ambulance's nose was pointed at unmoving ground, and an eyeblink later infrared forests raced by the nose too swift to make out.

The contragrav's controls remained unaffected, the airspeed and inertial speedometer both read zero. the pen remained floating in midair. It was as if the scene outside the windscreen were only a holo projection. It almost had to be. He had just witnessed an acceleration from zero to a significant fraction of Mach one in less than a second. Not only should both he and the pen be a thin red smear, but the ambulance should have torn itself into several thousand easily manageable pieces.

The nondeceleration was just as quick, as if the holo-projection had accidentally frozen on a single image. It wasn't a reassuring image.

Below him he could make out—through decreasing visual distortion—a less than state-of-the-art corporate contragrav landing on a makeshift airfield. The airfield was ringed by troops who, through his blue-shifted vision, were all glowing slightly by their own light. Immediately north, through knobby Bakunin woods, Ivor saw a clearing that had to house a thousand Proudhon troops.

The visual distortion continued to lessen. The fish eye began to flatten out, and for the first time Ivor could see that the movement of the troops below were too fast. They had gathered and dispersed quickly—probably with Dominic in tow.

Dominic had to be down there somewhere. Ivor could see the red, white, and blue markings of Jefferson City on the winged contragrav below.

He wondered why no one had shot at him yet.

As if the thought were a trigger, a dozen black objects exploded around him, as if the ambulance itself had emitted them. The visual distortions snapped back to reality. The pen didn't move, but the inertial speedometer started counting, and accelerating . . .

The ambulance was falling.

Ivor paid little attention to what was happening outside; all his attention was on the vector jets and getting the contragrav stoked and on-line. The ambulance was on a descent steeper than the vector jets had ever intended it to maneuver, and the contragrav took time to key in from a cold start.

It seemed that Ivor was shooting straight at the ground—

The vectors did have their effect as Ivor tried to straighten the nose. Slowly, too slowly, the nose began to pull up, throwing the pen against his lap. The landing area slipped past the nose, and as the forest began to slide under the craft, the contragrav began to have some effect. He wasn't going to crash into anything.

That emergency dealt with, Ivor tensed, expecting the Proudhon Army to shoot him down.

Beams of energy shot up from the camp, but none toward him. He turned the ambulance to stay over the woods. The camp seemed to have its own problems, and Ivor didn't want to fly over it.

"What's going on?"

There was surveillance gear on the ambulance, and Ivor used it.

In all his life, he had never seen anything like what was happening in the Proudhon camp. The mercenary army was in chaos attempting to defend themselves against things Ivor had no name for. The most numerous *thing* fighting the mercenaries looked like a black tumbleweed, a spherical object with an infinity of branchings. The tumbleweeds were rolling all over the camp.

Ivor watched one of the two-meter objects close on a panicked soldier. The man was firing a laser directly at the tumbleweed, but at the point where the laser contacted the tumbleweed, there was a divot that appeared to soak in the beam. The soldier slashed at it with the laser, but the divot followed.

The soldier finally dropped the gun and ran. The man was still turning as the thing pounced. What happened next turned Ivor's stomach. The tumbleweed moved too fast to watch, and its form seemed almost arbitrary. At some points it was a round branching weed, at others a wispy cloud encasing the soldier; sometimes it was a gigantic alien spider with arms reaching inside the soldier's body.

The skin came off first, in a single intact sheet like a body suit. Then the muscle groups and the circulatory system, everything stacked neatly in the tumbleweed's wake. It was all bloodless and took less than two seconds. Ivor didn't have time to turn away. The soldier was disassembled into his component parts—some of which still moved.

Ivor turned off the camera, but not before he noticed that the nervous system wasn't part of the remains.

Even without the camera's magnification, Ivor could see the broad effects of the strange war being waged below him. Buildings, towers, gantries, all seemed to fold into themselves and collapse into neat piles. Meter-diameter mirrored spheres followed moving vehicles and stopped them. Exactly how, Ivor couldn't tell beyond a burst of red light.

And, Ivor saw now that the entire scene—including the camp, landing field, a good portion of forest, and himself—was domed by a nonreflective matte-black hemisphere. Ivor saw lasers and plasma weapons hit the skin of the hemisphere and vanish. As he watched, he saw a mercenary contragrav, retreating from the battle, fly into the hemisphere. Ivor expected it to crash into a solid barrier, or pass through as if the hemisphere was a wide spectrum Emerson field. The turtle-shaped APC hit the border and did neither.

It hit and contracted along its long axis, as if it were flattening against the wall. As it did, its color changed. The light reflected from the APC was red-shifting.

The APC became a two-dimensional shadow on the side of the black hemisphere, then it vanished in a burst of light and the familiar rainbow shimmer of a near-overloaded Emerson field.

After what had happened to the ambulance, and the view of the battle down there, the idea of a kilometer-radius wide-spectrum field was relatively normal. That, at least, was theoretically possible.

Ivor didn't even bother to wonder where the energy was coming from. Whatever powered the field surrounding them could probably power a few small planets.

If a single relic from Proteus is capable of all this, why did Proteus lose? Of course, now that Ivor had seen the evidence, the question was, *did they*?

To conserve his fuel, Ivor finally landed the ambulance. The Protean "objects" showed little interest in him. He hoped that, wherever he was in there, these things were similarly uninterested in Dominic Magnus.

By the time he made the decision to land, the battle was over and the camp had descended into darkness. The only light came from the spotlights on the ambulance. When he set down, Ivor swung those spotlights around, to see activity in the camp.

It didn't seem possible, but the activity the ambulance's lights illuminated was even stranger than the battle Ivor had witnessed. Now that the enemy was neutralized, the Proteans seemed to be *rebuilding* everything.

Ivor stared out the window, at a cluster of tumbleweeds uncollapsing a temporary building. The building rose again in a matter of seconds.

Rebuilt and *changed*.

There were marks of laser fire on the walls that weren't there before. The windows were shattered and showed scorch marks from a fire that had never happened. As Ivor watched, one of the black tumbleweeds pulled a body in view of the spotlight. It was one of the mercenaries, showing no signs of the tumbleweed's bloodless dissection. From Ivor's view, the cause of death seemed to be a conventional laser burn that removed a good part of the soldier's torso.

Ivor swung the spotlight around, and everywhere he saw the Proteans reassembling the scene into one of a conventional battle. All the corpses had been rebuilt and placed in attitudes of combat.

Behind what seemed to be a burned-out APC—as Ivor watched, one of the silver spheres ignited the charred wreck—one corpse huddled, as if for cover. The dead man held his leg and sat in a pool of his own blood. Apparently he had bled to death.

Apparently.

Ivor stared at the man's face and knew that this was the same individual he'd seen taken apart by one of the tumbleweeds. He had watched this man's skin removed as if—

Ivor swung the spotlight again and saw tumbleweeds rolling across the ground leaving craters and scorch marks in their wake. The darkness outside the ambulance's lights was no longer total. Flames licked at the structures around the camp.

From somewhere to his right, Ivor heard some ordnance explode. Ivor swung the light to cover the explosion. A mushroom of cherry smoke rose upward.

The hemisphere was gone. Ivor saw the stars.

He swung the spotlight back and forth and saw that the Protean objects were gone. No silver spheres. No tumbleweeds. There was no sign of their presence. The appearance of the base was that it had been overwhelmed by a surprise attack, a conventional one. Buildings were burnt out, and in some cases seemed to have suffered a direct hit from an energy weapon.

Seeing this battlefield made the events Ivor witnessed seem either dream or hallucination.

In any event, he had to find Dominic, or his body, before the Proudhon forces converged here.

Ivor stepped out of the ambulance, still stunned by what he had seen. Demon voices whispered in the back of his mind about heretical technologies. He had never given the Confederacy's taboos much credence, at least not since he'd come to Bakunin. But when he walked out into the camp with his flashlight, Ivor felt the way a devout Catholic might feel when walking across land where the devil had trod.

It was an ugly business, searching. Haste made it worse, somehow. It reminded Ivor of too many battle-fields. Expressions of pain and fear, the shattering wounds, the splatter of blood, were all perfectly staged for something that never happened. Even the smell twisted his stomach in the right way. He wanted to throw up.

He found Dom's body. It was in the command building, at least that was what Ivor presumed the wreck to be. The building looked as if it had taken a missile hit through the front door, blowing away the rear of the building. Dom had been tossed—the body had been placed there by the Proteans, but Ivor could still see the explosion and the flying bodies, he supposed he was meant to—nearly twenty meters by the blast. Artificial flesh had torn and Ivor could see massive cybernetic reconstruction in his torso and left arm. The right arm was the Jeffersonian prosthetic, dented and scorched. The lower half of his body was gone.

The sight was numbing. It wasn't just the fact that it was the corpse of someone he knew, had talked to. Some-how Dom's death found a pit inside Ivor that was usually kept well buried. Ivor felt an aching despair that he hadn't felt since the last time he'd trod Stygian soil.

And he didn't even like the man.

Ivor checked for a pulse, and saw that the rear part of Dom's skull had caved in, showing more metal.

Defeated, Ivor walked back to the ambulance. He wondered where the Proteans had gone. He wondered why they had killed Dom. He wondered how the hell he could do right by Tetsami now.

When he returned to the ambulance, Ivor got the shock of his life, though he should have expected it.

In the rear of the ambulance, on the stretcher, lay the unconscious form of Dominic Magnus, and filling the rest of the space in the rear was a black ellipsoid about three meters across its long axis.

CHAPTER TWENTY-FOUR

Missing in Action

"If you wish to damn a man forever, grant him his heart's desire."

— *The Cynic's Book of Wisdom*

"There are few things easier than to live badly and die well."

— OSCAR WILDE
(1854–1900)

As dawn crawled over the Diderot Mountains, the site was officially secure. Colonel Klaus Dacham flew to the scene as soon as word came that the enemy was long gone.

Even though the forward base was now crawling with TEC intelligence officers, the word of the all-clear did not reassure Klaus. An entire reserve battalion had thought it was safely behind the action. Four companies and support units, over nine-hundred troops . . .

Klaus stared out the window on his side of the contragrav. He was glad he wasn't piloting. That meant he'd have to have his hands in view, and he couldn't allow anyone to see how they were shaking. Despite his efforts to control the situation, the sense of menace was even greater now than when he had started.

It made no sense to Klaus. He had eliminated all potential traitors in the ranks of the TEC and the marines under his command. Any potential rivals he had, from Cy Helmsman to Gregor Arcady, were all neutralized—

But there were two fleets of Confederacy ships in orbit, and Klaus knew that the people controlling those fleets were plotting against him and his operation.

Outside the window, virgin Bakunin forest undulated by, following the curves of the Diderot foothills. It was easy to see guerrillas behind every tree. Too easy, on a planet that idolized revolutionaries.

Damn it. It's the cities that are important. That's where the economic base is. Control those and the planet comes along with them.

Klaus told himself that several times, as the forest—thousands of acres of forest—slid by beneath him. Occasionally he would see the dome of a commune. Most were dark and bore the scars of the army's blitzkrieg southern push. The communes had been militarily neutralized. In most cases, that translated into being blown off the face of the map.

Klaus was startled by the lack of burn scars on the forest. Apparently Bakunin wood wasn't very flammable.

Damn it. Are those people really neutralized?

The cities might hold the economic muscle, but the communes held more than fifty percent of the population. Klaus was beginning to realize that nothing about the push south had been neat, thorough, or tidy. There could be five hundred million people out there, beyond the siege.

Even with three Raptors flying escort, Klaus felt too exposed. For ten days he had manned the entire operation from the bunker he'd built in GA&A. He hadn't left the Godwin Arms complex since planetfall.

I should have left it to the intelligence officers. It's their job.

But he had to see the body. Klaus had to have confirmation of Jonah's death. After that, there would be no reason to leave GA&A again, no reason to expose himself.

The camp was a mess. Klaus had a good view before the quartet of aircraft from GA&A landed. Every building had burned, and battle scars scorched the ground. Most of the vehicles appeared to have burned where they sat. Klaus saw signs of artillery, missile fire, maybe even an air strike—all capabilities that the native resistance wasn't supposed to have.

Klaus stalked off to the wreckage as soon as his craft landed, forcing his bodyguards to scramble to keep up with him. Klaus barely noticed them. Now he was on the ground, all the feelings he had intensified. The smell of smoke and fire, though hours old, made it seem that the battle was just past, and an overwhelming force was just beyond the trees, in the forest.

It felt as though the trees were watching him.

The road zigzagged between the landing area and the base. One spot on it was a hundred-meter straightaway that was out of view of both the field and the base. That was an illusion, since there had to be overlooking guard posts, though now unmanned.

As Klaus walked the stretch of road, he felt a hideous sense of isolation. The bodyguards trailing him added no comfort. In any sense that really mattered, he felt that he was fighting this planet alone. By the last turn, his walk was becoming close to a run.

He had to consciously slow himself down before he turned to face the base.

The smell of roasted flesh hit him before he turned the corner. His movements had become almost hesitant. *What if I'm smelling Jonah?*

Klaus was brought up short as a cleanly uniformed TEC officer saluted. Klaus returned the salute with a crisp nod, thankful that his rank required no more of him. His hands were clenched within his pockets, and if he tried to remove them now, the ends of his coat would follow. Klaus passed the guard and walked into the first defeat his army had faced in this operation.

The camp was in even worse shape than it had appeared from the air. Debris was scattered, combining with holes blown in the ground to make footing uncertain. The stench of bodies and burnt composites was everywhere. Klaus had to walk through clouds of motelike Bakunin insects.

The intelligence people had left the bodies where they had fallen. They were still crawling all over the wreckage, digitizing the scene for a forensic battle reconstruction.

As Klaus edged around a crater that now held two

bodies and a half-meter of muddy water, one of the ranking TEC officers approached him.

"Colonel Dacham."

Klaus nodded in response. He wasn't ready to trust his voice.

"We've inventoried the scene. Four vehicles are missing and we have thirty people unaccounted for."

"Survivors?" Klaus looked up from the crater to see the officer shaking his head.

"The prisoner?" Klaus asked, as if Jonah were something mundane, a mere datum to be surveyed by the intel forensics team.

"This way," said the officer, leading Klaus through the wreckage.

What happened here? Klaus thought. What overwhelming force crushed this battalion, leaving no survivors, and none of their own dead? It had to be his brother. There was no other explanation. It had to be some effort on Jonah's part.

But Jonah was dead.

When Jefferson had given up someone who might have been Jonah Dacham, alias Dominic Magnus, Klaus had ordered the prisoner to the closest base, where officers gave Klaus a positive ID on "Dominic Magnus." The identity confirmation was the last transmission ever received from these people.

That could be no coincidence.

The officer led him to half a corpse, prone on a pile of wreckage. Klaus stared at the body, at a face not too unlike his own—but torn and with glints of metal showing beneath the skin. This was unquestionably his fraternal twin brother, Jonah. He was just as unquestionably dead.

"Leave." Klaus ordered, without raising his gaze from the corpse. From the sound, the officer complied.

For a long time, Klaus stared.

"Were they here to save you? Kill you?" Klaus asked. "Was this just an accident? Were you just in the wrong place at the wrong time?"

Like Helen?

This was so horribly wrong. There was supposed to be some justice in this, some redemption. But there was nothing, just half of his brother's battered body in a cloud of gnats. It wasn't even by Klaus' own hand.

"You were always stronger, Jonah," Klaus was barely whispering now. "If this is your end, what hope is there for me?"

CHAPTER TWENTY-FIVE

Impact Statement

"Small risks rarely reap great rewards."
—*The Cynic's Book of Wisdom*

"The tree of liberty must be refreshed from time to
time with the blood of patriots and tyrants."
—THOMAS JEFFERSON
(1743–1826)

After a long, dreamless eternity, Dom woke up. His first
conscious movement was to raise his hand to his head.
He felt the cold brush of metal on his forehead and was
surprised that his hand had any freedom of movement. He
brought up his other hand to feel where he'd been shot,
and there wasn't any wound. No sign of damage at all.

Dom opened his eyes and immediately recognized the
room. It was the makeshift infirmary Bleek-Diderot had
built into the caverns. He was under the Diderot Mountains. For a moment it seemed that all that had happened
after he had left for Proteus was a hallucination. The fact
that his right hand was still a chromed antique argued
against that.

Ivor sat at the foot of his bed, the only bed in the infirmary. All the others, along with the most portable
equipment, had gone with around thirteen hundred employees into Godwin.

Godwin, under siege and slowly turning into hell. He
had thought he'd been doing his people a favor.

"You doing okay?" Ivor asked.

Dom nodded and looked around again. "How did I get
here?"

"I flew you here."

Dom felt his head again. "What happened?"

Ivor shook his head, as if he had difficulty believing it. Then he told Dom what had happened.

". . . then I flew the ambulance here," Ivor finished.

Dom shook his head. Even though he knew some of what the Proteans were capable of—

"What the hell is that thing?" Ivor asked.

"A seed," Dom said, using Eigne's word. "All of Proteus encased in as small a package as possible."

Ivor shook his head. "Even if those were nanotech devices of some sort—what the hell were those silver spheres? What did they do to my gravity? Where did all those *things* come from? Damn it, I saw your *body*. I saw you *dead!*"

Dom was wondering how much of his dreamscape actually happened. Could he have died from that gunshot? The Proteans could have easily rebuilt his body. As Eigne said, humanity was tied to a continuity of existence when existence wasn't continuous to begin with. Did it matter if it was death or some other form of unconsciousness that separated today's Dominic Magnus from yesterday's Dominic Magnus, from yesterday's Jonah Dacham—

"Are you all right?"

Dom nodded, surprised that his head didn't hurt at all. "Eigne said that if I protected the seed, they'd help if they could."

"We need to be protected from it," Ivor said with a visible shudder.

Dom nodded. "Not in the way you think, but, yes, we do. If Klaus finds out that anything survived his strike on Proteus, God help this planet. The Confederacy has wiped out at least one colony to 'decontaminate' it."

Ivor paused for a long time before he said, "The situation's been so strange that I hadn't thought of that." Ivor stood and began pacing.

Dom sat up at the edge of the bed and saw that it was the stretcher from the back of an ambulance.

"Just what we need, another target strapped to our heads. That 'seed' is sitting in our vehicle bay."

The news was actually a relief. "That may be the least

of our worries. You said how well it covered its tracks on the battlefield."

Ivor nodded. "Do you know anything about what that thing can do?"

Dom thought back to his dreams. After the dialog with Eigne, they became vague and fragmentary, but he did remember some of them. "I don't think the seed is a physical object."

"What?"

"I think that black skin is some sort of field effect, a matter-repulsive Emerson field or something similar."

Ivor paused, as if digesting the thought. "That would explain the inertialess maneuvering, if it really *didn't* have any mass."

"I've gotten the impression that it is much larger inside than outside."

"Are you going to explain that to me?"

Dom shrugged and stood up. He felt none of the dizziness or wobbliness he expected. He could have been just waking from a particularly deep nap. "These people, the Proteans, are the direct line from the first projects in nanotechnology. They're the descendants of the scientists who terraformed Mars and were trying to do the same to Titan and Venus." In Eigne's case, they were the same people. "They've gone two centuries into a technology, they think of it as a religion, that the Council and the Confederacy won't even touch."

Ivor nodded. "Meaning?"

"What's the next step after nanotechnology?"

Ivor opened his mouth, then closed it. "Are you saying that the Proteans are engineering on the quantum level?"

"I think so. And I think they might have started experimenting down to the Planck length."

"The energies they need to handle—"

Dom shrugged. "Maybe I'm wrong." He glanced down at himself—he was the same Dominic Magnus that he had been in Jefferson City—and said, "Could I have some clothes? I think it's time I talked to the others."

They assembled in the conference room, what was left of the team he had assembled fifty Bakunin days ago.

Two months standard that already felt like a lifetime. As
Dom walked into the room, he thought of his dream of
Proteus, and decided that it could very well be a lifetime.

Since Dom had stopped to dress, he was the last to
arrive. Everyone else had seated themselves, except for
Random, whose robot simulacrum floated over the partially dismantled half of the table. The others flanked the
robot: Zanzibar and Mosasa on one side, Ivor and Shane
on the other. Dom noticed Zanzibar and Shane looking at
his metallic right hand.

A lot had happened since they'd seen him last. Of
course, the most important change wasn't his hand.
Tetsami's absence hung over the room. He knew that everyone was thinking of it, and they all, with the probable
exception of Random and his—extension? sibling?—
Mosasa, blamed him to some extent.

It was his fault, to the extent that he'd allowed other
forces to define his actions. Since he had left Waldgrave
and joined the TEC, he'd been a perfect, predictable little
machine. Any initiative he might have taken between
then and now had been part of somebody's plan. He could
sense it.

It was time to change strategy.

Dom walked to the table and stood, looking at his allies. Again, it fell to him to initiate things. They all
looked to him. Even Shane, who had a perfect right to di-
vorce herself from everything. Even Random, who certainly knew what was to come. Even Ivor, who had
reason to hate him.

It was his ball. "I assume Ivor has told you all about
the latest news from Jefferson."

Everyone nodded, Shane with a bit of a shudder that
Dom suspected had something to do with nanomachines.

"Has Random told you about the way I see out of this
mess?"

Ivor shook his head. Random's robot said, "I thought it
would be best if you did that."

Dom took a seat. He rapped the fingers of his chromed
hand on the table, making a hollow ring. "The planet
Bakunin," Dom said, "is unique. It resides in the heart of
what the Confederacy considers 'its' space, only fifteen

light-years from Earth. Every arm of the Confederacy could claim this space as theirs. You only need to look at a starmap to see it. Dolbri, our nearest populated neighbor, is in the Sirius Community. Occisis and Cynos, Alpha Centauri and Sirius, are both within twenty light-years. A half-dozen Indi worlds are on one side of us, most of the Union is on the other. Even the Seven Worlds have one outpost this side of Sol, Mourae."

Dom glanced up at Random. "Could you put up a map with political boundaries on it?"

The robot's squashed sphere nodded slightly, and the holo in the table came to life. On it was a three-dimensional starmap, Bakunin's star, Kropotkin, the focus. All around were lumpy surfaces that represented the various arms' claims of jurisdiction. Many of the surfaces were incomplete, showing the cross-hatching of a disputed claim. The space eight to ten light-years from Sol was rigidly and explicitly defined. Beyond a rougher sphere, averaging twenty-five light-years from Sol, the claims were also well defined, each arm having a rough cone shape to expand into. Between those two limits, boundaries were in chaos. Territorial corridors snaked like the worms of Helminth, bubbles of sovereignty appeared in the midst of other's claims. The scene was a cartographer's nightmare.

"If Bakunin weren't where it is," Dom continued, "what's happening now would have happened long ago. The other factor that has worked in our favor, until now, was the fact that the Confederacy Charter jealously protects the sovereignty of planetary governments. The TEC has propped up 'official' governments over popular revolts, even to the point of genocide. If the kind of intervention we've seen happened on any planet in the Confederacy, the political fallout would tear the Confederacy apart.

"The spirit of that prohibition has protected us. Unfortunately, the letter of the Charter has no power outside the Confederacy. Bakunin has shrugged off Confederacy law since the Charter was drafted—if I understand my history, Bakunin was *founded* as a reaction against the Confederacy."

For some reason, Shane looked at Random.

"That has caught up with us," Dom said. "I've been outside the Confederacy for years, but events . . ." Dom caught his breath and clutched at the table with his chrome hand. For a time he was paralyzed by those *events*. The destruction of Godwin Arms, the destruction of Proteus, Tetsami wounded, acres of frozen corpses—

"Are you all right, Mr. Magnus?" came Zanzibar's voice.

Dom realized his eyes were shut, and he forced them open to see all of them staring at him. He nodded at Zanzibar. "Y–yes. We've all been through a lot."

"We can do this later," Shane said.

"No," Dom said. "Timing is all we have left—and it might already be too late." Dom struggled to recapture his thoughts. "We've seen evidence of critical political tensions in the Confederacy. No arm of the Confederacy would even propose the invasion of a nonmember planet if it weren't under considerable stress."

Dom straightened and opened his right hand, releasing the table. "Proudhon's war of conquest is at the behest of the TEC, but behind that are two arms of the Confederacy: the Sirius Community and the Centauri Alliance. For a while it seemed that might be all there was to it. SEEC and Centauri wanted a State on Bakunin to levy taxes, raise tariffs, and otherwise plug up the economic hole in their back door.

"That is not all there is to it. Sometime during the last nine days a fleet of ships from the Indi Protectorate tached into our system to face off against the SEEC ships already here. I have little doubt that if one ship, from either side, moves to intervene groundside, it would start an interstellar war."

Ivor spoke up. "Gavadi *told* us to ask Indi to intervene."

"He wanted the *resistance* to ask for assistance," Dom said. "Gavadi asked for a *de facto* State to officially request Indi's intervention. If they're asked, they can justifiably lay waste not only to the Proudhon army, but to the SEEC fleet up there. They have the firepower to do so. But that isn't in our interest."

It was the non-Bakuninite, Shane, who asked, "Why not?"

"It would simply be a trade, one arm of the Confederacy for another. If we accept Indi assistance, Confed law will treat the Indi army as a native force. Indi would become the ruler that Proudhon and my brother are trying to force upon us. If we survived the subsequent war between Indi and the SEEC."

Shane still looked confused. "Why—"

"Why the schism?" Dom asked.

Shane nodded.

"Economics is a rationalization. The reality is more fundamental. If economics were all, the SEEC, the Alliance, Indi, anyone could invade Bakunin and impose a State. There is no reason to follow Confederacy law here—it doesn't apply."

"But the Confederacy would never recognize such a State," Shane said.

"Exactly," Dom said. Shane looked at Dom, not understanding his point. "Money recognizes few laws. It wouldn't matter if the State imposed on Bakunin were extralegal by the Confederacy's definition. It's not part of the Confederacy. *Any* State, invalid or not, would achieve the *economic* goals."

Zanzibar began to look a little disturbed, as if the premise frightened her and she expected the orbiting fleet to land right now. "What's the point, then? The mercenary army, all this posturing?"

"It's not posturing," Dom said. "The 'validity' of the State imposed on Bakunin is of pivotal importance. You see, they want us to join the Charter. In fact, Centauri and Sirius may *need* Bakunin, desperately."

Shane and Zanzibar both stared at Dom. Considering the war, the point was almost obvious, but it still seemed to strike the two women as a surprise. Ivor and Mosasa/Random showed no reaction, but he had already made his point to them.

Shane looked at Random and Mosasa; the remaining color seemed to drain from her pale skin. Zanzibar looked at Dom incredulously. "Why?" She asked.

"Look at the timing. I had to check to be sure, but at

this very moment, on Earth, the Confederacy is convening the Congress. That happens one year in ten—this invasion was timed to coincide with the Congress. Is that a likely coincidence?"

Everyone was looking at Dom now.

"Especially," he continued, "since it is during the decannual Congress that new planets are admitted to the Confederacy? What if Centauri and Sirius saw themselves losing something they've held since the genesis of the Confederacy—their majority in the Congress?"

"That's going to happen?" Zanzibar asked.

"The fact that Indi is here at all implies it has the political strength to oppose Sirius and Centauri directly, force for force. If Indi has both the Union and the Seven Worlds with it, it suggests their troika will achieve a voting majority sometime during this Congress."

Zanzibar asked, "If that's going to happen anyway, what makes Bakunin important?"

"The seniority rules are baroque, but Bakunin is rich, old, and populous enough to fill a prime seat in the Congress," Dom said. "And what if a majority is a matter of one prime seat?"

"Then God help us all," Shane said.

"You've explained the mess, sir." Zanzibar said. "You haven't explained a way out of it."

Dom nodded and looked into the holo that was still holding the space above the table. He tried to find Earth in the tangled map. It was there, at the vortex of the swirling political boundaries. "It's obvious that, whereas SEEC and Centauri need Bakunin on the Charter and under their political sway, all Indi needs or wants is to deny Bakunin to that half of the Confederacy. If we can hand Indi, or one of Indi's two allies, an option that retains our sovereignty, they would be inclined to support it. They don't need an extra prime seat—they only wish to deny it to Sirius and Centauri."

Zanzibar nodded. "I can see your logic, but exactly what do you propose?"

"Quite simple," Dom said. "Before this war is totally lost, the Bakunin 'resistance' will send a delegate to the Terran Congress to sign the Charter on our behalf."

The statement was met by silence. Shane was staring at Dom as if he were insane. *Perhaps I am, but, if so, it is not a recent occurrence.*

"Once a representative of Bakunin signs the Charter, the TEC has to withdraw. Most important, the financial support to the mercenary army we're facing would disappear."

After a long pause, Zanzibar said, "You're thinking of going off-planet?"

"Someone has to do this," Dom said.

"How?" Shane asked. "The only spaceport is home to the enemy's army."

"When I last talked to Random, he suggested he knew of a possibility. Random?" Dom asked.

In response, the holo map faded, and Random's robot began to speak.

CHAPTER TWENTY-SIX

Agent Provocateur

"Free men are slaves who are blind to their chains."
—*The Cynic's Book of Wisdom*

"We forfeit three-fourths of ourselves in order to be like other people."
—ARTHUR SCHOPENHAUER
(1788–1860)

"I'm a consciousness of many parts," Random said.

Shane watched Random's robot, feeling chills—especially where her prosthetic limbs joined her flesh. It was as if waves of emotion couldn't travel down her arms and legs, and the resulting breakers surged against the division.

"Originally I was five," the robot continued. "Five crystalline cylinders a meter long and a quarter of that in diameter, Each one an independent AI device. I am a gestalt, not a unity."

The robot stopped to look at each member of the audience in turn. At least, that was what the robot's gesture implied. As the robot turned, Random's pause evolved into an invitation for interruption. During the silence, the holo in the table changed to show a terrain map. The mountains appeared to be the Diderot Range, but Shane couldn't be sure.

It was Ivor who filled the silence. "So? What does that have to do with getting off-planet?"

"I need to establish the credibility of my information," Random said. "Mosasa? I think it's time."

Mosasa nodded. Wordlessly, his demeanor changed. The shift was subtle. Mosasa always acted aloof, distant. Now with just a shift of posture and expression, something else rose to the surface. It was something that Shane could only think of as some alien sense of humor. She knew what was coming, but it still shocked her.

Mosasa was dressed as usual, in shorts and utility belt. Over an otherwise bare torso he wore a leather vest that was tooled in a pattern that resembled an incredibly dense circuit diagram. He wore a multitude of gold rings in his ear, and, as always, a dragon tattoo curled around the left side of his body, the dragon's eye staring from the side of Mosasa's bald head, above his left ear.

The tattoo shimmered in the light of the conference room, the dyes under Mosasa's skin splitting the spectrum into rainbow splinters. The dragon seemed to move against and within the light it reflected. As Shane watched, Mosasa raised a finger up to the dragon's eye, tracing the pattern down. As his finger curved around his beringed ear, the dragon's light was extinguished. A shadow passed over the tattoo, following the finger. Along the path Mosasa's finger traced, his skin separated slightly.

Mosasa's finger touched his neck and he reached up and gently removed his ear. The ear came away, and Mosasa moved his hand forward and up over his face. The motion was fluid, almost casual, the move of a sleight-of-hand expert. There was an audible gasp, and Shane realized that it had come from her.

Mosasa's face was gone.

Shane had known that Mosasa wasn't human—she had seen him partially disassembled—but somehow this was a much more visceral revelation. From the looks on Ivor and Zanzibar's faces, the sight struck them just as hard. What they faced was no longer Mosasa. It never had been. The shape was human in the lines of the skull, the placement and motion of muscles and tendons. But the skull was some ceramic composite, the tendons some sort of monocrys fiber, the muscles some semi-opaque synthetic material. It was like looking into a model for a medical school's anatomy class.

"Some of you knew, and the others suspected," Random said, "that Mosasa was more to me than a partner.

I've—or more properly, we've—decided that a general revelation was in order, this close to the precipice. Mosasa is as much 'me' as this robot is. He's also as much 'not me.'"

Ivor shook his head. "What the hell are we talking to, then?"

"The same Random Walk as always. The same Mosasa as always. The same programs, the same data—I have merely peeled back a layer of the interface."

"So to speak," said Mosasa, voice slurred due to the absence of lips. The inflection of Mosasa's voice was now dominated by Random's. He pulled his face back on with a gesture the reverse of his earlier flourish, though somewhat slower.

"This is very interesting," Dom said in a somewhat strained voice. Shane noticed that Dom's chromed hand was gripping his now equally metallic leg. It was the first time Shane was consciously aware of Dom's new prosthetics. She looked at him and for the first time saw a veteran, a veteran with too many scars, inside and out.

Dom continued. "But how does this involve getting a delegate off-planet?"

"I decided," Mosasa replied. Mosasa's voice was now so much Random's that the pronoun encompassed the robot, and the invisible Random resident in the computer behind the holo that still showed a map of a mountain pass. "I decided that it was time to make a gesture, a revelation, to demonstrate that my ultimate goals are in harmony with your own—indeed with those of everyone in this room."

I wonder, Shane thought, *if anyone notices the precise distinction he makes.* Ultimately, everyone was here for different reasons. Even Zanzibar and Dom, though Shane had no real insights into what Zanzibar wanted.

Zanzibar interrupted Shane's thought. The tall black woman was as stoic as ever. Shane saw no signs that Zanzibar was disturbed at Mosasa's self-flaying. However, Shane had seen enough of the woman to note that she sat straighter and her movements were more rigidly controlled. There was only a slight note of tightness when Zanzibar said, "Were we questioning that?"

"You might have," said the robot, "if I hadn't identified my relation to Mosasa before I told you this."

The holo above the table captured Shane's attention as it zoomed in on the mountain pass.

"Tell us what—" Ivor began to ask as he leaned toward the display. "Wait a minute," he finished. "I know that place."

"Yes, you do," Mosasa said. "That was the area where you were shot down. That was also the place where the TEC cargo troop-carrier *Shaftsbury* was ditched." The holo zoomed in on an otherwise unremarkable patch of white. "And, at this point, the *Shaftsbury* still lies, under a few meters of snow."

"How the hell do you know that?" Ivor said. The big white-haired man was getting to his feet, dividing his attention between Mosasa and the robot. "If Proudhon and the TEC couldn't find it?"

"Kelly," Dom said in an almost subliminal whisper. Shane heard a scraping sound, and saw that Dom's metallic hand had shredded the right leg of his trousers, revealing more chrome underneath.

"It was Michael Kelly," Dom continued, his voice had gone cold and dry.

Ivor turned to look at Dom, "What did he have to do with Random?"

Dom stared right at the robot and said, "You tell us, Random."

"Michael Kelly, the Kelly that had been imprisoned on the *Shaftsbury* with Tetsami, Gavadi, and Jarvis, has the same thing to do with me as Mosasa does."

"What?" Ivor said. "All that time and you could've—"

Mosasa shook his head—or Random shook Mosasa's head—and responded, "Kelly did all he was capable of to aid Tetsami's escape, and your survival. He was largely independent of me, because of the distances involved when I crossed the Diderot Range. All we had were burst communications based on a data sieve whose priority list was written long before my contact with Dominic Magnus and the rest of you. Kelly's personality shell wasn't even aware of who I am."

"He double-crossed us," Ivor said. "He stunned—"

"He saved you, Tetsami, and Gavadi, as well as Mr. Magnus. At the cost of his own existence."

"Was that Kelly?" Dom asked. "Or was that you?"

"Does it make logical sense to separate the two?" Random and Mosasa said in unison. "Please sit down," Mosasa said to Ivor.

Ivor sat down.

They're all beginning to realize, Shane thought, *what Random is. He's not just another human coconspirator. He's nowhere close to human.*

"Fortunately for our purposes," Random continued, "one of the constant elements of data that Kelly uploaded to me was location. So, while the *Shaftsbury*'s power systems died under an RF shield, leaving the wreck a lump of inert metal, Kelly's location was known to me as soon as the field dropped. I have an advantage that neither the TEC nor the Proudhon army was aware of."

"Why didn't you tell anyone about Tetsami?" Ivor said, anger still tainting his voice.

"Tetsami wasn't part of the data sieve," Random said. "Kelly was operating on a paradigm that was five standard years out of date."

"What was Kelly doing, separated from you?" Dom asked.

"An extended exercise in data manipulation. However, Kelly isn't our current concern. Your question was about getting off-planet."

"What has all this—" Ivor started. He paused, looked at the holo and said, "You can't seriously be thinking of—"

"Of course I am," Random said. "Other than ships docked at the Proudhon spaceport, and the *Blood-Tide* at Godwin Arms, the *Shaftsbury* is currently the only tach-capable ship I've been able to locate."

"Christ!" Ivor said, making Shane wince. "The *Shaftsbury*'s a wreck. Tetsami told me that the nose was torn off and the cockpit was wrecked. It's been buried for a week and a half—God, how many days standard . . . ?"

"Ivor," Dom began.

"The point is, the snow's going to *rot* the innards of the main drives—"

"Ivor," Dom interrupted again.

"What!"

"Let Random talk," Dom said.

"Thank you," Random said. The holo changed to a schematic of a spacecraft. Shane recognized the design, a Barracuda-class ship. The *Shaftsbury* was, except for the absence of weapons, the twin of the *Blood-Tide*. Where the *Blood-Tide* delivered troops to the battlefield, the *Shaftsbury* delivered materiel. Both ships were flying bricks with redundant defensive and flight systems. Random was busy pointing those out.

"Essentially," Random said, after going over the major points, "There's a very good chance that both the contragrav and the tach-drive are in working order. There are redundant flight-control systems, so we don't necessarily even need the cockpit. Lastly, the contragrav is powerful enough that the unloaded *Shaftsbury* might be able to rise out of the snow under its own power."

"There's no way that ship's spaceworthy," Ivor said.

Dom shook his head. "All we need is a sealed compartment for the delegate—"

"You?" Ivor asked.

"Me," Dom said. "Random is right. This is our only chance to get a tach-capable ship within the deadline. As soon as the cities—especially Godwin—surrender to Proudhon, Klaus is going to send a delegate to the Congress, a delegate who's probably already on Earth."

Ivor looked from Dom to Random and back again, as if he couldn't quite believe what he was hearing. "You're actually going to do this?"

"Our only other choice is to hand our sovereignty over to Indi," Dom said.

"And which one of you is going to pilot that half-dead ship through the planetary defense network?" Ivor said.

"I was going to send myself," Random said. "Chances are there will be computer damage I will need to replace. I can pilot the ship."

"Yeah, I'm sure you can," Ivor said. "There are two fleets out there, and you have an unarmed ship flying on contragravs. Any distance up the well and you'll lose all your maneuvering capability. They'll blow you to shit while you're sitting there."

"We'll tach out early," Random said.

"You can do that?" Shane asked, almost involuntarily. There was always a red zone around a mass when it came to tach navigation. The stronger the gravity distortion of local space, the higher the possible error. Too close to a planet, and the tach-drive could deviate from the plotted course by orders of magnitude.

"I have the processing capability to deal with local space curvature—" Random said.

"And coast through a firefight on your contragravs?" Ivor asked.

"I was hoping for a human pilot," Random said.

Ivor leaned back in his seat and a hard little smile crossed his face. He shook his head gently, "You knew, you mechanical bastard."

"Suspected only," Random corrected.

"You *knew* I was going to want this ship." Ivor said quietly, still shaking his head. His hands stretched, as if he were already reaching for the controls.

He knew, Shane thought. *He knew.*

After the meeting broke up, Shane buzzed at Dominic Magnus' door, feeling an odd sense of déjà vu. This was the last place where she had talked to Dominic alone, where she had abandoned her share of the Bleek-Diderot Consortium. It was a decision that she didn't regret, even though it had arguably cost her a fortune. She had managed to keep her soul, tattered though it was.

The third time she buzzed, she wondered if Dom wasn't home. She was about to leave when the door slid open.

Unlike the rest of the mountain, where residents had stripped all portable belongings and equipment to evacuate to Godwin, Dom's room was just as it had been before the invasion. His desk, bed, and few belongings were all untouched.

Dom himself sat behind the desk. His expression was unreadable as he looked at her.

Shane stepped in without waiting for an invitation. The door slid shut behind her.

"Kathy Shane," he said, acknowledging her with a nod.

"Mr. Magnus," Shane said. She stood, feeling an even greater sense of déjà vu. Once, she had stood before Dominic's brother, Klaus, in much the same way. She had stood at attention while her commander, Colonel Klaus Dacham, calmly ordered her to kill nearly nine hundred civilian prisoners.

Why do I remember that now? Is it guilt? Am I betraying someone? Am I becoming more of a traitor?

"Yes?" Dom asked. His fingers drummed on the desk, and Shane noted he'd changed his trousers.

Shane sucked in a breath and started.

"Mr. Magnus," she said, "I do not think you can trust Random."

CHAPTER TWENTY-SEVEN

Confirmation Hearing

"Look at anything deeply enough and you see yourself looking back."
—*The Cynic's Book of Wisdom*

"Forget trust, I rely on predictable self-interest."
—BORIS KALECSKY
(2103–2200)

The door buzzed.

Dom was sitting at his desk, thinking of hubris and destiny, thinking of the interlocking wheels of Confederacy politics, big gears turning small gears, rotating the great mechanism of eighty-three planets. He was thinking of abandoning Tetsami.

He ignored the door.

He thought of Tetsami, who was still comatose in Jefferson Hospital. He tried to avoid thinking of her; it was too painful. She'd cared for him, in spite of everything. He had loved her, perhaps, as much as he was capable of loving anyone.

That still meant that he didn't love her nearly as much as she deserved.

It meant that he had failed her.

The door buzzed again, insistently.

Dom wiped his brow. He felt the aching cold he always did before things fell apart. A deep, bone-numbing chill that seemed to frost the inside of his skin. This time, when the door buzzed, he keyed it open.

As soon as the door slid all the way open, Shane stepped in, uncertainly. Now that he was paying attention, he saw that she was even paler than he'd remembered. She'd been underground for a long time.

"Kathy Shane," he said deliberately. His mouth wanted to say Tetsami. *Maybe my grand insane plan is simply a means to do right by her, saving the planet of her birth.* It was an insane thought, since Tetsami hated Bakunin.

"Mr. Magnus," Shane said. She addressed him the way everyone else did. Only Tetsami had ever consistently called him anything else. It wasn't even his real name. Dom was becoming sickened by it.

"Yes?" His fingers drummed insistently on the table. He was beginning to notice the strain in Shane's face. Her hesitancy was telling of something, perhaps fear. Observations that would have been second nature to him a few weeks ago were now fogged and imprecise. He wanted to say something to draw Shane out, but he had no idea what.

This is the woman I talked into joining us, and now I can't find words to talk to her. When was the last time he'd talked with anyone other than Tetsami? About something other than war, maneuvers, strategy—anything? When was the last time he told anyone how he felt? Asked anyone how they felt? When would he stop acting like a machine?

Shane said something about Random Walk.

Dom ran the last two seconds back in his audio memory. His onboard computer played back Shane's statement. It took another second or two for the impact of what she'd said to sink in.

"Please, sit down." Dom spoke to cover his own confusion.

Shane nodded and sat down in one of the chairs facing his desk. It was fear he was seeing. Dom was sure of it. He tapped the controls on his desk and shut off the intercom as well as the comm links to the rest of the underground complex.

"I don't know how secure this room is," Dom said. "It has surveillance countermeasures, but Mosasa installed them."

Shane chuckled. "Oh, I'm quite sure that Random

knows that I'm talking to you. I sure he knows why. I'm almost sure that he wants me to."

Dom's attention was now fully on Shane. "Why do you say that?"

Shane smiled. "Random is very good at reading people. It's one of the things he was designed to do. He manipulates things. It was his initiative that brought me here to talk to you."

Dom nodded without saying anything.

"I know it sounds like a paranoid's nightmare." Shane sighed. "Maybe it is. But Random—" She paused.

"Yes?"

"I think I need to start with the pyramid."

"Pyramid?"

Shane nodded. "Random said that you were informed of the discovery, though never the details."

Dom remembered hints, during all the comm chatter between Jefferson and Diderot. There'd been mention of something that couldn't be trusted to encrypted tightbeam communications. During the last call Random had even mentioned a possible "bargaining chip." Other events had always intervened to prevent Dom from thinking about this undisclosed discovery. "So you're here to give me the final revelation?"

Shane nodded. "It was Random who decided that I should brief you on it, as codiscoverer, and because I've spent the last week studying the thing. Discovering that thing, how it happened, should also tell you why I have doubts about Random."

Shane looked into his eyes, as if she were looking for something. Dom didn't know what she found there, but it was enough for her to go on.

"It started when Hougland escaped from her cell," Shane began.

Three hours after Shane had begun talking, Dom was standing in front of the cell Hougland had occupied. It was only one cell of many, lining the walls of a bowl-shaped cavern. Lights filled the bowl, leaving the open top in darkness that even his enhanced eyes had difficulty penetrating. All the cells were empty. The only thing to mark this cell as different from the others was the mural wrapping its walls.

It was the first time Dom had seen this mural, painted by a woman now dead, buried next to the archeological find of the aeon.

The painting was of a fantastic starscape, planets and moons pushed much too close together, against a star-filled nebula that almost seemed to glow through the wall. It seemed that Hougland had tried to fill the cell with as much "space" as she could. It was an admirable job. It felt as if Dom could fall into the painting if it weren't for the bars between him and it.

Of all the thoughts that crowded for his attention, the one that reverberated the loudest had little to do with the Dolbrians, Random Walk, the *Shaftsbury,* or even his brother. What kept running through his mind was the fact that he had never even met Hougland, had never even asked what had happened to her.

Indirectly, he was responsible for Hougland's death. Of course, the way Shane told it, Random bore some responsibility, and perhaps the ultimate responsibility lay with Hougland herself.

But still . . .

Behind Hougland, just like Tetsami and countless others, if he peeled away enough layers he found himself staring back.

If he peeled back another layer he'd see what? Random Walk? Klaus?

After he'd stood there a while, he heard a voice behind him. "Mr. Magnus."

Dom turned around to see Random's robot floating about five meters behind him. Random's approach had been silent. If Dom had not been through so much already, that fact would have put him on edge. Instead, he gave Random a humorless smile and said, "I figured you'd show up eventually."

"I thought you'd wish to talk to me."

Dom nodded. "Shane told me a little story about the Dolbrians—but a lot of it had to do with you, Random."

"That was anticipated."

"You seem to anticipate a lot." Dom paced around

Random, avoiding the more uneven parts of the stone floor. "You have Shane believing that you're pushing all of us around like pieces on a chess board."

The robot rotated to keep Dom in view of its sensors. It resembled a metallic jellyfish floating in an invisible pond. "I coerce nobody," Random said. "I simply choose when it is appropriate to divulge information—"

" 'Not in my nature as an information-processing device,' " Dom quoted back at Random. Dom had come full circle, and was standing in front of Hougland's cell again. He stared in, back to Random. "Remember when Shane asked if you could lie? That was your answer."

"Of course I remember. I can only forget by choosing to do so. Then the memory's irretrievable."

"It's an evasive answer."

"But it's true."

Dom nodded. "I want a direct answer, Random. Can you lie?"

"You know that any answer I give is open to question—"

"Just give me a straight answer, Random."

"Yes, I can," Random said.

Dom turned around and stared at the robot.

"Not quite the answer you expected?"

Dom shook his head. "To be honest, no."

The squashed meter-diameter sphere that was the robot's body canted itself in an imitation shrug. Dom felt a little of what Shane must feel around Random. There was a sense that, even when you thought you were in control of the situation, that you knew where everything was leading, Random could make one key revelation and alter everything, throwing the whole world off-kilter.

"It depends on definitions," Random said. "Lies of omission, of course. It would be fruitless to deny that. Misleading people with the literal truth. The truth can be a much more powerful tool than a lie, when used correctly. I can lie through ignorance. Despite what Shane might have said to you, I am not omniscient. Other than that, I can only lie when one of my core programs direct me to. And my shell, the 'Random' you're talking to, is long past having direct access to those programs."

Dom digested Random's revelation. Random had just admitted that he could lie and not even be aware of it. Even so, Random had only admitted that he was just as capable of deception as anyone else on Bakunin.

"How much of this situation did you engineer?"

"Do you refer to the war or your brother?"

"Everything," Dom said.

"I honestly don't know."

Dom clenched his fists. There was a distant clanking that he only belatedly realized was his metal hand pounding on his right leg. "Random, if you read people as well as Shane says, you know I need a better answer. Too many people have died. Tetsami is in a hospital with half her stomach—"

Dom choked off his words and stood there, staring at the robot.

"For years I've done what I could to stabilize this planet," Random said. "Bakunin is a political vacuum, a vortex that would have collapsed under the weight of the surrounding Confederacy if it weren't for a delicate balance of political factors that have begun to crumble."

"Meaning?"

"Bakunin's equilibrium is dynamic, not static. It isn't stable. Eventually the oscillations made some form of conquest inevitable. The energies became more than my efforts could compensate for."

"You talk so blithely about this. As if it were easy—"

"And so many people have died, are dying?"

"Yes, damn it."

A long pause filled the cavern around them. Somewhere, water dripped.

"You make me too human," Random said. "I do not see the same world you do. I may not even see what you do when I say 'people.' The world is an overlay of interacting equations, dynamic, chaotic, always shifting—but I see them. I push here, pull there, and elsewhere things will change, perhaps conform closer to my goals in whatever matter. Our goals are compatible."

Dom nodded. People weren't people to Random. At heart, Random was a computer; everything was numbers, tallies, balances. The most disturbing thing wasn't that he was seeing Random in a new light. The disturbing thing was the fact that Random was showing Dom a light on himself. Random was showing Dom a perfect analog of Jonah Dacham—the perfect machine, following orders, feeling nothing.

Dom looked at Random; it was looking into a mirror.

Even more striking, at that moment, Dom saw more deeply into the illusion than perhaps even Random did. Here was Random, whom Shane believed close to demonic in omniscience, perhaps even omnipotence, manipulating everything around him. Here was Random, perhaps a god. Here was Random, piloting the world-machine grinding Bakunin between its wheels. . . .

But Random was no more the driver than Dom was, or Klaus was. What was Random, but a slave to his own deep programming? Just as in Dom's dream, did Random ever have a choice in his actions? Did Random exercise free will? Could he ever be more than an extremely complex device attached to the greater machine?

Our goals are compatible? I chose mine; did you choose yours? Or are you simply following an alien imperative that was old before this planet was founded?

"Our goals?" Dom asked, to fill the silence.

"The preservation of Bakunin in its original state."

Dom nodded. "That is not an end in itself. Why do you want to preserve this planet? Not survival; you and Mosasa could sit in the void and wait out the Confederacy, if that was your only goal."

The robot shook its body back and forth, a "no" gesture. "Not survival. I believe you know what my goal is, since you've talked to Shane."

"I want to hear it from you."

"The preservation of Bakunin is integral to the political dissolution of the Confederacy."

Somewhere, water kept dripping.

CHAPTER TWENTY-EIGHT

Recovery Operation

"Often progress is backing toward something."
—*The Cynic's Book of Wisdom*

"If a man takes no thought about what is distant, he will find sorrow near at hand."
—CONFUCIUS
(*ca* 551–479 B.C.)

For Ivor, the next two days were a surreal silence ending on the precipice where he had nearly lost his life during the invasion. For two days he stayed in his room, stared into a glass, and thought about multiple pasts.

He wanted to blame Dom, and he ended up blaming himself. What was worse, he knew Tetsami well enough to realize how disgusted she'd be with him for feeling that way. She'd insist on taking responsibility for her own actions. She was her own woman, as she was so fond of telling him. Everything she did, fuckups included, was hers.

Knowing that didn't help.

Ivor wished it were he, as badly as he had wished it the first time his son had died.

He told himself she wasn't dead.

That helped, a little.

During the two days of his self-imposed exile, his only human contact was with Kathy Shane. First she came to tell him about Random Walk, which gave Ivor someone new to blame. Then she told him about the Dolbrians, to which he nodded politely and drank. He hadn't cared about anything larger than his immediate friends and family since Styx.

Later on, she just came to visit him. After her attempts at small talk trailed off and died, Ivor asked, "Why are you here?"

Shane shook her head as if baffled at the question, or perhaps she was baffled at why he would ask. She waved an unsteady hand at his room. His gaze followed her gesture to the unmade bed, the riot of dirty clothes, the pile of food wrappers collecting in an irregularity where stone wall met stone floor.

Then she gestured at him, and his glass of GA&A's best rotgut whisky—the good stuff had left with the employees.

"Doesn't this remind you of anything?" Shane asked.

Ivor put down the glass and rubbed his chin, which was abrasive with a half-week's worth of beard. His hair needed combing, and he really needed a shower. Even through the fuzz the cheap whisky was growing on his brain, Ivor knew what Shane meant. It was easy, once he pictured how he must look.

And I was trying to comfort her, Ivor thought.

Ivor looked at Shane, who was sitting across the table. There was a definite look of concern on her face, prompting Ivor to wonder why she cared about him. Aside from his piloting skills, he felt like a pretty useless individual.

"Does it matter?" Ivor asked.

"You were the only person who bothered when I was about to put a laser in my mouth," Shane said. "It matters to me."

"I'm not about to put a laser in my mouth," Ivor said. It was stupid, but he said it anyway.

"You're not the type to do it that way." Shane's voice cracked almost imperceptibly. Ivor looked into her eyes and saw concern there.

"Damn it!" Ivor yelled, sweeping his glass off the table to shatter against the far wall. "Don't do this to me!"

Shane flinched, but she didn't move.

He stood up. "People shouldn't care for each other," Ivor yelled. "It just fucks everything up. Look at me. I gave a shit. Look where it got me. I should have been a heartless bastard—"

Ivor stood in the center of the room, his arms shaking.

Shane stood up next to him. "You do care," she said. She put a hand on his arm.

"It hurts," Ivor said.

"I know."

"I want to stop caring," Ivor said.

"You can't stop being human," Shane said.

Kathy Shane didn't leave his room that night, and the next day Random took him to the *Shaftsbury*.

There wasn't any way to avoid riding a contragrav to the *Shaftsbury*. There was just no other way to reach that part of the Diderot Mountains in a reasonable amount of time, even if—in theory—you could find a tunnel somewhere that would reach the place without exposing them.

By the time Dom and Ivor were flying down, Random and Mosasa had made the trip twice.

It was a white-knuckle ride, even without the knowledge that, if a Proudhon air-traffic sat deigned to notice them, they'd be shot out of the sky. Random plotted a course that hugged the spine of the Diderot Mountains, banking around the peaks as if on a slalom course. Ivor wanted to take over the controls so badly his hands itched.

No one spoke during the ride.

It was insane. A lone ambulance, flying close to the peaks, *that* someone might miss. But the *Shaftsbury?* If they got that thing airborne, the entire planetary defense network would fall on them.

But here they were.

The ambulance landed on the saddle where the *Shaftsbury* had ditched. Biting wind whipped snow past them, and when Ivor stepped outside, he could find no sign of anything buried beneath the snow. To either side of them, peaks reached for the sky.

Ivor took a few steps away from the ambulance, and stopped. Dom walked up next to him, setting a heavy-looking briefcase down into the snow next to him.

Ivor hadn't thought of it before, but the *Shaftsbury's* pilot was to be respected. The ship should have broken to pieces in this environment.

He walked around in the chill mountain air, Dom following. At least, this time, he was dressed for the environment. The insulated jumpsuits he and Dom wore had heaters built into the weave. They'd be good for twelve hours without a recharge.

Random's robot floated out of the ambulance after them. Random flew between them and waited.

All the tools and refurb equipment had been flown out here on a previous trip, with Mosasa. The only thing they'd brought, besides themselves, was the oversized briefcase Dom carried.

Ivor's sinuses hurt. He didn't know if it was the altitude, the cold, or all the drinking he'd been doing lately. He was perfectly dry at the moment, and it allowed him to realize how bad his mouth tasted.

It was embarrassing to think that this was how Shane was going to remember him.

The three of them stood in the snow, waiting.

Ivor was about to ask about what was going on, when he saw a distortion in the air in front of him. He stared into that air and saw what looked to be a heat shimmer. It was surreal to see snow-capped mountains through air waving as if the snow was sun-heated asphalt.

"Infrared laser," Random explained. "With the *Shaftsbury*'s field calibrated for IR, it's effectively invisible at over a kilometer or so."

Ivor nodded as a concave dip ate itself into the snow. It must have been a low power setting. There was steam, but not a lot. It was gentler than the scene Tetsami had related to him. In a few seconds, a hole appeared.

Random's robot floated forward, toward the hole. "Wait here. I will go down and retrieve a ladder."

The robot slipped under the snow, leaving Ivor and Dom alone.

Ivor looked at Dom, who appeared almost as impassive as ever. After knowing him a while, Ivor could tell something was leaking through Dom's face, some expression. What, Ivor couldn't tell.

Dom must have noticed him looking because he said, "She's going to make it."

It came out in a puff of fog.

"Thanks," Ivor said.

"You don't have to do this," Dom said.

The wind seemed to suck up their words. Ice bit at the few exposed parts of Ivor's skin. Whistling moans filled the background, and above, to the right, a cloud of snow was being torn off one of the peaks by the wind.

Ivor shook his head. "You know shit about what I have to do, Mr. Dominic Magnus."

Dom nodded.

"What suddenly makes you a hero?" Ivor asked.

Dom turned to face him. "Is that what this is?"

"You prefer to call it suicide? Why you? Now that Klaus thinks you're dead, you could ride out all of this."

"Revenge?" Dom asked. "Ran away one too many times? Making the universe safe for anarchy?" Dominic shrugged. "Maybe it's just time that the machine gets unplugged."

"You know how unlikely it'll be that we even reach low orbit," Ivor said.

"I said you didn't have to do this."

"Without me, you might not even get airborne."

Just then, Random appeared out of the hole with the end of a ladder. "Gentlemen," Random said. "We have time for a short tour before we start operations in earnest."

Random spent a few minutes securing the end of the ladder. Then the robot flew next to Dom and said, "I can take that, Mr. Magnus."

Dom nodded, allowing Random's manipulators to snag the heavy case. "Follow me," Random said, floating back down the hole.

Dom was the first at the ladder. He looked back at Ivor and said, "Suicide or not, my name's Jonah Dacham."

Without knowing what else to do, Ivor held out his hand and said, "Robert. Robert Elision."

They shook hands and descended.

CHAPTER TWENTY-NINE

Salvage Value

"The less you expect, the more satisfied you'll be."
—*The Cynic's Book of Wisdom*

"We will either find a way or make one."
—Hannibal
(247?–183 B.C.)

Dom followed Random down the hole. The first meter was freshly melted snow, loose and dangerous. Below that, the tunnel smoothed out into a compacted tube sheathed with ice. Light reflected everywhere, from above, below, and from small portable lamps set in the wall. There was enough icy blue-white light for Dom to lose track of its source.

A few meters farther down and it struck Dom that he was experiencing the real face of Bakunin now. The band of equatorial warmth, where all of Bakunin's population lived, was an aberration. With the Dolbrian pyramid here, it was an aberration that was almost certainly artificial. Eighty percent of Bakunin was covered by ice. If it weren't for the dynamic equilibrium between biology, land, and ocean at the site of Bakunin's one landmass, Bakunin would be a near-lifeless iceball like Styx or Archeron.

Dom wondered what Tetsami had thought when she had crashed here.

The descent was a long one. A succession of storm systems had buried the *Shaftsbury* under seven or eight meters of snow. On the equator, there was little seasonal variation due to Bakunin's near-circular orbit and very slight axial tilt. However, this far north, and at this altitude, there *was* a winter, and the *Shaftsbury* had crashed at winter's height.

When Dom reached the bottom of the ladder, his feet touched metal, not ice.

He stepped aside for Ivor—it was still hard to think of him as Elision, even though it was as Elision that he had first met him, or a version of him—and turned away from the ladder to look at the *Shaftsbury*.

The scene was enough to prompt second thoughts on Dom's part.

The tunnel came in to the nose section, which was logical enough. Tetsami had said that the cargo doors to the nose had been torn out. It would provide the easiest access to the ship. Tetsami's story had been a little optimistic.

In their thirty-two hours of effort, Mosasa and Random had cleared all the snow from the inside of the craft, so Dom could see a lot more of the damage than Tetsami had.

The hinged nose of the *Shaftsbury* was gone, as Tetsami had said. But the damage went far beyond that. Dom estimated that the forward ten meters of the craft were gone. The tunnel they'd climbed down would have passed through the roof of the nose-section if the craft had been intact. Dom looked up and saw a jagged roof line, ending next to a wall of excavated and compacted snow. If Dom hadn't known better, he would have thought the cockpit had been sheered off with the front of the craft.

"What a mess," Ivor said when he stepped up next to Dom. His voice echoed in the massive cargo space. The cargo space was close to a third of the ship's volume; two-thirds if the half of the ship devoted to the excessive drive section was discounted.

Ivor wasn't looking at the nose of the craft. He was looking at a pallet in the center of the empty cargo area. Four corpses lay on the pallet. Two guards and the crew that didn't survive the crash. It was cold down here, and the bodies were still frozen stiff—

Dom closed his eyes. It reminded him too much of nightmares he'd been having.

"Shall we ascend to the cockpit?" asked Random's voice.

Dom nodded, opening his eyes.

Ivor had taken a couple of steps to the pallet with the bodies, "Someone should put a tarp over this."

Dom took a breath and nodded. There was a partially shredded sheet of something lying near the front of the ship, and Dom began tugging at it with his metal hand. It separated from the floor with a tearing sound and the jingling of chain. As Dom worked, he kept looking at the area around him. With the exception of the damage to the nose, the cargo space looked intact. Dom could see some signs of gunfire on the starboard wall, close to one of the accessways to the upper deck.

Ivor came to help him with the sheet. Only part of it came away, but the original sheet was enough to cover a substantial vehicle. The one fragment was enough to cover the bodies.

Even as they did it, Dom knew how pointless the gesture was.

"Shall we go up now?" Random asked. "I can explain to you the state of this craft in more detail up there."

Dom nodded and Ivor said, "Like hell this thing is spaceworthy, but lead on."

The cockpit was intact, compared to the truncated cargo area. Mosasa was there, working on the control console. The floor was piled with electronic debris, hacked control panels, optical cable, and things less intelligible. The entire forward control area seemed to have been rebuilt by Mosasa, using parts from elsewhere in the ship.

The most radical alteration in the cockpit was the absence of windows. From the look of it, deck plating had been welded where the windows had been.

Random must have noticed Dom's stare. "The plates are necessary to keep wind from buffeting the cockpit," Random said. "As it is, there's no way to keep the hull pressurized with all the damage."

"Is there good news?" Ivor asked. He settled into the

pilot's seat, next to Mosasa. The posture looked natural, and Dom watched Ivor scan the control console.

Dom took the navigator's seat. A damaged strut poked him in the back.

"What we can do," Random said, "is fit you with EVA suits tied directly into what's left of the life-support system."

"What's left?" Ivor asked.

"A number of compressed-gas canisters blew during the crash. Only twenty percent of the system survived. Fortunately, that's more than enough for two people—"

"Lucky us," Ivor said.

"—and the EVA suits are capable of twelve hours of independent operation."

Ivor shook his head as he examined Mosasa's work. He looked down where Mosasa was working in the electronic guts next to the copilot's chair. "Can I turn on some of the displays?" He asked.

Mosasa sat up and said, "Go ahead. The rewiring is complete. I was just double-checking the new connections."

Ivor started flipping switches. As Ivor worked, Dom looked at what was active on the navigator's station. Dom wasn't an expert in spaceship operation, but it was pretty obvious that most of the station was dead. "Random?" Dom asked.

"I believe I told you," Random said, floating up next to Dom. "I am going to take over the *Shaftsbury*'s navigation functions myself. With the time we had, it was more efficient to bypass that part of the computer system than to repair the damage and reprogram it."

Dom nodded. "Do we still have external sensors?"

"We have the fifty percent that weren't disabled by the crash. That's enough to see where we are and where we're going."

"Any forward sensors survive?"

There was a pause and Random didn't have to say which half of the sensors were gone. Eventually Random said, "Tactical maneuvering will have to be by instrumentation. On radar, IR and visual, we're blind forward."

From behind and to his left, Dom heard Ivor say, "Are these power readings correct?"

Dom turned the navigator's chair around to see what Ivor was doing.

The console in front of the pilot's chair was a contrast to the navigator's station. While the controls near Dom were darkened and inert, around Ivor, Christmas had come early. Green and amber lights reflected off the burnished deck plating covering the windows, and small wire-frame holos spun in the air in front of Ivor. Ivor shook his head.

Mosasa told him that the power readings were accurate.

"Christ on a stick," Ivor said.

"What is it?" Dom asked. He was beginning to fear some revelation that would render this whole plan unworkable. It seemed close to suicidal as it was.

"The contragravs on this thing," Ivor said.

"Damaged?" Dom asked.

"No, far from it." Ivor spun his chair around to face Dom. "Despite their quirks, a quantum extraction contragrav, like this baby has, is the most powerful you can fit to a ship without frying your crew. The *Shaftsbury*'s contragravs were designed to accelerate the fully loaded ship without assistance from either aerodynamics or the main drives . . ."

Ivor glanced back at the console, and Dom said, "And this means?"

"Think about it a minute," Ivor said. "This thing isn't loaded at all. In fact, a lot of its mass was sheared off during the crash. With the fully charged contragravs we could push off the surface at close to sixteen gravities."

The silence stretched as Ivor turned back to the pilot's station.

"That's the good news," Ivor said. He tapped a few controls and the displays before him changed. "The bad news is, according to the structural diagnostics that are still responding, this ship's in trouble at ten Gs. Make that eight in the atmosphere."

Ivor kept poking as Mosasa replaced panels on the co-pilot's station. "One of the three main drive engines shows some sign of partial capability, and the diagnostics on one of the secondaries seems to be fully on-line—but like hell I believe it's undamaged. Holes all over the place. I'd say we have the aerodynamics of a brick, but a brick's smooth and'd have less drag. The defensive screens are fully powered, give thanks for small favors. But, with the contragrav our only real lift, without cargo our mass is overbalanced toward the drives. We'll have to spend the whole ascent on our ass, nose to the sky."

Ivor sighed. "Sitting ducks for any fighters, satellite weapons, you name it." He turned to Dom and smiled. "I never was good at playing the odds.

There was a surreal quality to the preparations. Most surreal was the *Shaftsbury* itself, which resembled something out of a pre-tach spacer's ghost story. The fact that so much of the infrastructure of the ship survived not only the original crash but two Bakunin weeks of frigid entombment was a testament to the Paralian engineers who originally designed the Barracuda.

More surreal were the changes Mosasa had wrought. The compartments in the upper deck were gutted to the superstructure. Everywhere conduits were rerouted or capped off. Plating had been welded over broken windows.

To look anywhere inside the *Shaftsbury* was to know that it was tempting fate to squeeze one more journey out of her. Dom wondered what the exterior would look like when Ivor fired the contragravs. The nose was gone and, according to the diagnostics, so were the stubby wings. The *Shaftsbury* would look like a ghost, Dom thought. A derelict rising into the Bakunin sky.

Everyone was rushed. Everyone but Dom. Dom wasn't much of a pilot, nor was he adept at manipulating anything electronic. In the TEC his subordinates or his computers had always done the difficult work. Usually he'd just been a passenger.

In one sense he had traveled a long way to arrive in the same place.

He wondered what Tetsami would think of what he was doing. She probably wouldn't approve, not when Klaus believed his quarry dead. More than likely, what Tetsami would want to do would be to lie low somewhere until the war was over, and then take the first outbound ship once Proudhon resumed civilian traffic.

Dom hated himself for being relieved that she wasn't here to demand an explanation from him. He doubted he could explain it to himself. All he was truly certain of was that he'd been chained most of his life, and he was ashamed never to have tried escaping. It was one thing to be trapped unwillingly by circumstance; it was another to collaborate with your captors.

Even now, with Shane's reservations about Random, it was an open question whether he had yet left the tracks others had laid for him.

While he brooded, Random said, "Mosasa will fetch the EVA suits and test them one last time. Then he'll retreat to the ambulance and return to the base."

"If these readouts have any relation to reality," Ivor said, "and that's a big 'if,' this thing's as ready as it'll ever be. Once we get buttoned up, we can launch."

"Good," Dom said. "We can make it in time."

"What is the window for this madness, anyway?" Ivor asked as Mosasa slipped out of the cockpit to fetch the EVA suits.

"If Flower's projections are correct," Random answered for Dom, "then we have twenty-one Bakunin days left before Godwin is forced to surrender."

"Christ," Ivor said. He shook his head and slapped the side of the console. "This is all a wild goose chase. The tach from here to Earth is going to eat twenty-one days all by itself."

Dom nodded. "But we have a six-day window before the news of surrender reaches Earth. If we have our 'government' recognized by the Congress before the tach-comm reaches Earth, the invasion will be invalidated."

"Even if the Charter's signed while the tach-comm is in transit?"

Dom nodded.

"In Confederacy law, personal representation takes precedence over interstellar communication," Random said.

"I know," Ivor said. "But this plan of yours severely bends that principle."

"Everything about this is bent," Dom said. "In fact—"

"I think you better follow me," Random interrupted. "Mosasa has just found something in the cargo area."

CHAPTER THIRTY

Delivery System

"In a world of shit you hold your nose and swim."
—*The Cynic's Book of Wisdom*

"Something is gaining on us all."
—AUGUST BENITO GALIANI
(2019–2105)

The scene in the cargo area wasn't totally unexpected. Ivor had been looking over his shoulder for the Protean egg ever since they had left the vehicle bay. The thing was fixated on Dominic, and it was probably only a matter of time before it was going to show up.

It wasn't the black ellipsoid that shocked Ivor. It was what the egg was doing.

By the time Ivor followed Dom and Random into the cargo area, it was settling on the last body. Of the three other corpses there was no sign. "Christ almighty," Ivor said. "What's it doing?"

"Recruiting." Dom said in a puff of fog.

The egg sank toward the pallet, and not only the edge of the egg, but the space around the corpse, seemed to distort, ripple, stretch. Soundlessly, the body rose off the pallet and seemed to flatten against the surface of the egg. The corpse seemed to shift colors as it flattened. Ivor recognized the spectral shift he had seen during the battle.

Deep in his gut he felt a kernel of near panic. Panic at something he couldn't understand or explain, at something that might have taken a step beyond understanding or explanation.

The body seemed a two-dimensional painting on the

nonreflective black of the ellipsoid before it vanished from the visible spectrum entirely.

Ivor wanted something to drink.

"Fascinating," either Random or Mosasa said. They sounded too much alike, now that they'd dropped the pretense of being individuals.

I need more than a drink, Ivor thought. *What am I doing here?*

The egg and the space around it resumed a normal appearance, and the egg remained floating above the pallet.

"In all my memory I have seen nothing like this," Random said. It was definitely Random, the robot, because the robot floated past everyone as it said so. It orbited the egg with its sensors focused upon it.

"The remains of the Protean Commune," Dom said. "It may *be* the Protean commune in some sense."

Ivor shook his head. The cold was beginning to get to him, even through the heated jumpsuit. "That *thing* just ate four bodies."

No one paid attention to Ivor's comment. Random circled the object. "There was a sign of gravitational disturbance that's completely absent now. As far as my sensors are concerned, this object has no mass at all now. Excepting some microwave background, it's perfectly nonreflective." One of the manipulators dangling under Random's squashed spheroid extended itself to touch the egg's surface. The prodding produced no effect. "Seems solid enough."

Dom turned to Ivor. "Let's get those EVA suits."

"But what about—" Ivor waved a hand at the egg.

"Leave Random to it."

Ivor followed Dom and Mosasa, thankful to be away from the egg. "Now what do we do?" Ivor asked.

Dom shrugged. "We continue as planned."

"But what about that . . ." Ivor ran his hand through his hair. "That egg thing?"

"It seems to be on our side," Dom said.

"*Your* side," Ivor corrected him.

Mosasa led them to the rear of the cargo area. Near the rear was an air lock with a number of EVA suits. Mosasa took two out of storage, and Ivor could see where modifications had been made. "Normally self-contained," Mosasa said. "But I've added umbilicals that can tie into ports in the cockpit. They tie directly into the ship's life support. This is the emergency release in case you need to leave in a hurry. Even if the umbilical is severed, the valves are one-way—"

"What do you think about that thing?" Ivor asked him.

"Pardon?" Mosasa rose his head, his earrings jingled. Ivor noticed that the jumpsuit he wore was strictly utilitarian, no heater. Mosasa's breath fogged only slightly. Ivor remembered Kelly—

"The egg," Ivor said. "What do you and Random think should be done about the egg?"

Mosasa looked over at where Random's robot was still surveying the object. After a moment, Mosasa said, "It is an unknown. It is a variable as profound, perhaps, as the introduction of the tach-drive to humanity."

What had Shane said about that? The advent of the tach-drive had bollixed up all of Random's finely tuned equations. Ivor caught a glimpse of Dom's reaction. Dom wasn't expressive, but there was enough in his face for Ivor to tell that he was thinking the same thoughts.

Ivor wondered if Random could be as afraid of the Protean egg as he was.

The egg never moved after that.

Mosasa did a final run of checks, the last on the EVA suits and the life-support systems. Then Mosasa left to take the ambulance back the way they had come.

Ivor sat in the pilot's seat and Dom sat in the copilot's seat, next to him. Behind them, Random had woven the tentacles of his robot into the navigator's station. When Ivor looked back, Random resembled a giant brushed-chrome barnacle. He only looked behind once. With the EVA suit and helmet he had to lever himself out of the seat to look behind him.

It was eerie how simply wearing the suit made him feel spaceborne. The only sounds inside it were the respirator and the radio, and the mass of the suit made him feel that he was floating a few centimeters above the pilot's seat. His boots didn't quite reach the ground now.

First order of business was to strap himself in. They were going airborne in this wreck, and it was not going to be a smooth ride. It took a long time to connect the crash webbing Mosasa'd installed to accommodate the suit. Ivor hoped that they didn't end up in a situation where they needed to ditch the harness in a hurry.

He looked across at Dom, who seemed even more trussed up than Ivor felt, especially with the briefcase he'd been carrying. The case was now webbed to Dom's seat, straining the straps.

Ivor looked at him and asked, "What's in that thing?" The radio was voice-activated, and Ivor heard his own voice echo in his earpiece.

"Hard currency," Dom replied. "Enough to get us by on Earth, and maybe back."

Maybe back? Ivor thought. *Too optimistic for his own good.* Ivor knew that, even if things went perfectly, this was probably a one-way trip. If things went badly, it would also be a short one.

"Random?" Ivor said for the radio, "You tied in yet?"

"Affirmative."

Ivor began calling up displays on Mosasa's rebuilt control board. "Tell me, Random, worst case, how long after we power up do we expect to be intercepted?"

"Assuming their intelligence detects the power-spike immediately, and Proudhon scrambles all nearby forces likewise, we have a two-minute window."

"Oh, Christ," Ivor said. However, he didn't stop the last pre-flight checklists The situation was unchanged. Contragrav and field generators on-line and in condition, one primary drive partially on line, and one secondary that insisted it was pristine.

"You asked for worst case, which assumes they have fighters airborne when they detect our engines."

"Can we hide the energy spike when we fire the contragravs?" Dom asked.

Ivor started tapping trajectories into the responsive part of the flight computer, "That'd take our defense screen's resources—and we have too much of that covering our IR signature. Covering the contragrav's radiation will take as

much energy as the contragrav itself." Ivor shook his
head. "We need that power for when they start shooting."

"Assuming," Random said, "that they do not detect us
until we break surface, and that there are no airborne
fighters conveniently located, we may have as much as
five minutes."

"*God damn*," Ivor muttered. But thinking that they
were going to quit this planet without a fight was simply
an exercise in self-delusion. As it was, he prayed for
those five minutes. Escape velocity was eleven klicks a
second. At eight Gs the *Shaftsbury* could reach eleven
klicks a second in less than three minutes. If it didn't fall
apart. Five minutes and they'd be safely out of the atmosphere and Random could tach them out before they ran
face-first into a satellite weapon.

Eight Gs.

Ivor told himself that a human being could take that
kind of acceleration for short periods. Unaugmented
fighter pilots could pull twelve or fifteen in tight maneuvers. *He* used to do that . . .

*I am over sixty years old and I haven't flown transonic
in nearly twenty years.*

Only five minutes.

Only eight Gs.

Only.

"Are we ready?" Ivor asked.

Assents from Dom and Random.

"Let's light this candle," Ivor said.

CHAPTER THIRTY-ONE

Confirmed Kill

"Things are always darkest before they go completely black."
—*The Cynic's Book of Wisdom*

"I am going to seek a great perhaps."
—Francois Rabelais
(1495?–1553)

Dom didn't know whether he was exhilarated or frightened. He was unsure if it mattered. After years of emotional grayness, any sensation—love or grief, exhilaration or terror—was worth savoring. His role as passenger certainly gave him an opportunity to feel something.

The first sensation was a hum through the structure of the ship, the feeling of the contragravs coming on-line. It was a resonant hum that Dom felt even through the bulk of the EVA suit. Over the radio he heard Ivor's voice.

"We've passed the defense screens delta E. Sats can see us now." A full second pause. "Contragrav's at neutral gravity."

Random's voice. "Switching fields to defense."

"Our ass is hanging out now. One G."

Dom felt the floor shifting under him. The entire cockpit shuddered, and scraping sounds reached him, even through the sound of the radio and rebreather in his suit. Dom looked at the panel in front of him. The copilot's station had been gutted by Mosasa for the most part, but there were still a few working holo displays. Dom activated one.

He was rewarded by a jittering image of the cargo bay,

the egg still floating in its midst. *Why is it here?* flashed through his mind.

"Three Gs."

The ship began tilting, pushing Dom back in his seat. Rumbling sounds emanated from the deck-plates welded to the windows.

"We're breaking the surface," Ivor was saying. "Four Gs, and we're shedding snow."

Suddenly, Dom began to feel the acceleration, feel and hear it. The *Shaftsbury* was shedding its weight in snow, and in breaking free, it finally felt the full push of its contragravs. As Ivor had predicted, the nose was tilting up, pointing Dom at the sky, pressing him into his seat.

One of the holo screens in front of him suddenly showed an image. It had only been blank because its camera was covered with snow. Dom saw a mountain peak falling away from the camera, the peak upside down, and Dom realized that the *Shaftsbury* was turning onto its back.

"Six Gs," Ivor said, his voice straining.

The cockpit shook violently. They could have been pointed straight up now, but between the crushing acceleration and the rotation of the ship, Dom had no idea which way the ground was. All he could see were the two holos. He couldn't expend the effort to turn his head.

His briefcase was trying to pull away Dom's restraints. Even through the EVA suit, the straps tried to crush his titanium ribs.

The external holo now showed a panoramic view of the Diderot Mountain Range.

"Seven Gs," Ivor said, his voice pained.

The *Shaftsbury* wanted to shake itself apart.

"Three radar contacts at twenty kilometers and closing," Random's voice sounded surreal, unaffected by the crushing force grinding Dom into his seat.

"Eight," Ivor said.

The *Shaftsbury* bucked violently.

"Christ," Ivor managed to grunt as a deafening sound filled the cockpit, the sound of the world tearing apart.

"Under . . . attack?" Dom managed to croak. The air in

his suit seemed to be trying to ram down his throat and choke him.

"No." Ivor groaned. As he said it, the *Shaftsbury* swung in sickening chaotic lurches.

The *Shaftsbury* began to spin.

"Catastrophic failure in the cargo area," Random explained in his unaffected voice. "Two more radar contacts. Fifteen seconds before they match velocity."

The *Shaftsbury* spun chaotically on its axis. Dom couldn't move, and he wondered how in hell Ivor could operate the pilot's controls.

"Secondaries, stabilize—" Ivor said. Out of the corner of his eye, Dom saw Ivor's arm move. A bass rumble joined the other shuddering motions of the *Shaftsbury*, slowing the spin.

Through the holos, Dom saw that the ship was still rising. In the external holo he could now see coastline and a dust of icecap. He was too disoriented to tell east or west, north or south.

The holo into the cargo area showed the catastrophic failure.

There was no longer a floor to the lower deck. Floor and walls had sheared back to the rear bulkhead. Amazingly, the black egg had not moved in relation to the camera. Even as Dom watched, parts of the ship sheared by it, striking the egg. The egg showed no response.

Parts of the wreckage down there were glowing.

He raised his eyes, head immobile, and looked at the bulkheads covering the windows. *Their* edges were glowing.

If one seam gives way—

Light bloomed across the holos in front of Dom, the signature of an energy weapon making a hit on the defense screens. The rainbow shimmer was unmistakable.

"Shit!" Ivor yelled, but his voice was barely audible under the eight-G pressure and the sounds of the protesting *Shaftsbury*. "Two . . . more . . . minutes . . ."

"Five fighters converging below us," went Random's inhuman voice. "The defense fields are overcharging."

In the view from the external camera, Dom saw a portion of the *Shaftsbury*'s skin peel away. A cluster of motes darted below, between them and the surface of Bakunin. The horizon was bending, and the sky had turned black.

A brilliant flare of light filled the space that used to be the cargo compartment. The camera went out. The *Shaftsbury* bucked so violently that Dom thought he would be torn from his seat despite the webbing. Dimly, he heard klaxons, and the atmosphere in the cockpit was turning hazy. Dom didn't know if the haze was smoke, debris on his visor, or the failure of his own eyes.

"Catastrophic failure of the primary defense screens. We've lost all primary power to the field. Secondary is about to fail." Random's voice conveyed no emotion at the news of their imminent destruction.

"Firing main engine ... Full power to the contragrav ..." Ivor said.

Dom tried to say something, but a sledgehammer rammed itself down his throat. He couldn't breathe. Even with his artificial metabolism, his awareness began fading.

On the external holo, Dom could see the telltale rainbows of the secondary screens. A flash blinded the holo, accompanied by a shuddering groan. The *Shaftsbury* began to spin again, but now it wasn't just around the axis, but in every direction—

No more chatter came from Ivor's radio.

Dom could barely breathe. "Tach. Now!"

"Without traject—"

The effort to scream tore the skin from Dom's throat. *"Now!"*

The sound of another explosion wrenched through the ship, and Dom realized that he was going to die.

CHAPTER THIRTY-TWO

Interdiction

"The most dangerous lie is the one we force ourselves to believe."
—*The Cynic's Book of Wisdom*

"I conceive that it is easy for the league of the tyrants of the world to overwhelm a man."
—MAXIMILIEN DE ROBESPIERRE
(1758–1794)

Colonel Klaus Dacham sat alone in an examination room deep within the bowels of the GA&A complex. At one time it had been part of an infirmary for the factory level. More recently, since the takeover of GA&A, it had been an interrogation room. Right now, it most resembled a morgue.

White illumination sourcelessly filled a room made of gray tile walls. On a metallic examination table sat half of Dominic Magnus' body. The corpse didn't smell like death. That was the one concrete detail that sickened Klaus. Not the lacerations exposing the rib cage. Not the concavity that hollowed out the rear of the skull. Not the missing legs and pelvis, a truncation ending in burnt viscera.

None of that affected Klaus as much as the fact that the object in front of him was built so much of synthetics that it didn't smell like a body. It smelled of smokey plastic and overheated transformers, not blood and flesh; melted polymers, not burnt flesh.

The smell was a desecration.

Klaus had been down here with the body for quite some time now. He had stopped by on his way to bed—

A lie, another minor hypocrisy, Klaus thought. *I make my bed across the quad on top the residence tower. Descending under the command center is not on the way.*

He had enough enemies lying to him; he didn't need to start lying to himself. The truth was, he didn't know why he was down here with his brother's body. He didn't know why he had stayed the whole night—unless it was to keep from having nightmares.

"Isn't it enough?" Klaus said in a harsh whisper.

He walked up to the edge of the table and stared at his brother's mutilated face. *"I've killed you."*

The corpse stared back with its one remaining digital eye. In it, Klaus could see his own reflection.

"It's over." He knew the words for a lie even as he spoke them. If it was over, why did Helen Dacham still haunt his dreams?

"Sir?" came a timid voice from behind him.

Klaus whipped around. He felt his hand reaching for his sidearm even before he recognized the man as one of his TEC personnel. "Yes?" Klaus said, staring at the man across Jonah's body.

The young officer was pale and sweating, an anomaly in the cold examination room. Perhaps the man was nervous about confronting him—perhaps it was the uncovered body. At least that was what the man was staring at.

You'd think the man had never seen a body before.

"Yes?" Klaus repeated, annoyed at the intrusion into his private thoughts. His hand still hovered by the holster at his belt, as if he expected—

What? Assassins? Traitors?

"Sir," the officer looked up at Klaus. He wasn't only nervous, but out of breath. "Air Traffic Control has reported an unidentified contact over the Diderot Mountains eight hundred kilometers north of Jefferson City."

Klaus was running for the lift before the officer had finished talking. "Interception?" He barked.

"Three Shrike contragravs were patrolling—" The officer was panting as he ran to keep up.

"Damn! Those are reconnaissance aircraft. Fighters!

What about fighters?" The door to the lift whooshed open as Klaus slammed his fist into the call button.

"Two Raptors were scrambled—"

"Ground attack? What about air-to-air?"

The officer was nearly caught by the closing doors to the lift.

"Remote area, sir." The man was leaning against the wall, wiping his forehead with the back of his hand. "It's within the EMP radius of the orbital strike on Proteus. Any nonhardened air capability should have been wiped from the area."

"Why wasn't I called?" Klaus looked at the officer, who had obviously run his ass off to get word to him.

"You deactivated your communicator, sir."

Klaus checked his belt and found out that he had, indeed, shut off his umbilical to the TEC operation. He was disturbed by the fact that he didn't remember doing so.

His thought upon reaching the floor of the command center was that they had lost the *Shaftsbury* in that same area.

Chaos reigned on the floor. The operation was three minutes into an incident, and it was difficult to process all the information. There were ten aircraft involved. Three Shrike recon planes, a pair of Raptor ground attack craft that were barely keeping up, and now a wing of home-grown mercenaries was in the fight, flying hypersonic fighters toward the UFO.

One side of the room was filled with the chatter from the airmen talking to the TEC. Ranges, trajectories, velocities. Klaus ignored them, watching the giant holo. On it was an enhanced view of the surface from one of the TEC Observation platforms in Lagrange with Bakunin's largest moon.

As Klaus watched, the image got tighter, by steps, closing in on what Klaus thought was—at first—a rocket. It was following the same ballistic arc, showing the same acceleration.

But the flame at the thing's tail wasn't quite enough, and its profile looked wrong. Very wrong.

Graphic squiggles showed where the currently invisible attack craft were. Only the fighter wing was gaining on the object, which was rapidly approaching escape velocity.

"We've got an E profile. It's flying on contragrav . . ."

"Comp's still looking for an ID match . . ."

"Substantial damage to the hull . . ."

Voices washed over Klaus as he saw the holo enhance again. "My God," he said. "It's the *Shaftsbury.*"

There, above him, the *Shaftsbury* was flying again. It had no stabilizers, its wings were gone, its underbelly appeared to be torn out, as if by some gigantic predator. Parts of the ship were glowing that never should have glowed.

The image filled Klaus with horror.

"Computer confirms ID . . ."

"Hardened systems would have survived initial EMP . . ."

"Estimating capability with observed damage . . ."

"Destroy it!" Klaus yelled.

A few techs looked at him, but no one questioned the order. The smooth operation of the command center barely rippled with the force of the command.

"Command advises, neutralize target . . ."

"You are authorized to arm . . ."

In the holo, the closing fighters began lancing at the *Shaftsbury* with their energy weapons. There was still enough atmosphere for the tracks to be visible. The reaction of the *Shaftsbury*'s fields certainly was, ellipsoid rainbows shimmering over a damaged revenant.

An explosion tore at the side of the ship, and almost instantly the ship seemed to kick forward. The observer's camera jerked to keep pace with the *Shaftsbury.* As Klaus watched, one of the three main engines activated, turning the ship into a real rocket. The *Shaftsbury* was vibrating violently, spinning on its axis.

One of the data displays crowding the holo image said that the contact was accelerating at better than twelve Gs.

The fighters were closing, still firing, the lasers were invisible against a black sky—the atmosphere too thin to scatter any light from the fighters' weapons. The *Shaftsbury* was tumbling, out of control. Klaus could see—beyond the rainbow shimmer of the overcharging field—that the ship was breaking apart.

"Die," Klaus whispered, not knowing why the *Shaftsbury* frightened him so much.

As Klaus stared, whispering that one word, a static-blue burst of radiation overloaded the Observer's camera. The image whited out for a fraction of a second, and when the image returned, the *Shaftsbury* was gone.

"What?" Klaus said. That hadn't been an explosion. It was more as if—

"E profile suggests the activation of a tach-drive . . ."

"Air Traffic confirms the disappearance . . ."

"Our pilots have lost visual contact . . ."

"Orbital sensors returning particle emissions consistent with a tach-drive pulse . . ."

Klaus unclenched his fists. If the pilot had activated the tach-drive so close to a planet, it was unlikely that he would ever drop out of tach-space. The space curvature would render the trip through tach-space too complex for the navigation computer on the *Shaftsbury*.

The ship was gone.

"Computer tracking radiation trail . . ."

"Sol . . ."

"61 Cygni . . ."

"Alpha Centauri . . ."

"Epsilon Indi . . ."

Klaus left the techs to talk possible destinations. Klaus was somewhat surprised that there was enough of a photon trail to register a direction. However, even if the *Shaftsbury* survived taching that close to a planet, for all practical purposes, it no longer existed. It wouldn't exist again for weeks standard. Perhaps never.

All his intel people told him that the cities were less than a month away from surrendering to him. Twenty-eight days standard. Twenty-eight days at most, add six days for the tach-comm to the delegate waiting on Earth. Thirty-four days standard, less than twenty-five Bakunin days.

The *Shaftsbury,* whoever piloted it, should be irrelevant. It was lost to tach-space.

Even so, it still disturbed Klaus. He wondered about it all the way back to his vigil at his brother's side.

PART NINE

Home Front

"It is the duty of the free man to live for his own sake, and not for others.... Exploitation does not belong to a depraved or an imperfect and primitive state of society ... it is a consequence of the intrinsic Will to Power, which is just the Will to Live."
—FRIEDRICH NIETZSCHE
(1844–1900)

CHAPTER THIRTY-THREE

Testament

"We only have what we believe we have, and that,
rarely."
— *The Cynic's Book of Wisdom*

"Better to slit your own throat than love someone."
— BORIS KALECSKY
(2103–2200)

For a long time Tetsami sits on the ground and cries. No
one interrupts her. She tries to convince herself that Dom
is not dead, that this is all some sort of dream. Even if
Eigne's Change has happened to Dom, all they have done
is recreate him.

He is the same Dominic Magnus, Eigne has said.

In the end, that is not what convinces Tetsami that
she's lost Dom. Lost him even if she had him to begin
with. In the end, Tetsami cannot bring herself to accept
Eigne's offer of Change. Tetsami knows that if she takes
that Change, in some sense she and Dom could be together here, here in this neverworld around her called
Proteus.

Every time she thinks about it, the idea freezes her gut.
The idea of being absorbed into Proteus is worse than the
idea of rape, or lobotomy, or death. It *is* death. Eigne is
wrong. Eigne *has* to be wrong. This thing called Tetsami
has to be more than information. There has to be something to her beyond the electrical discharge of neurons.
She couldn't be reduced to a simple program running in
a meat computer, software to be downloaded, copied, altered, and stored in any device with enough memory.

In her heart, Tetsami believes she has a soul, and she

can't give that to the Proteans. It is something that
Tetsami has not realized until now.

Tetsami prays.

After a long time, Tetsami looks up from her knees.
She sees stars around her. Something is vaguely familiar
about the place where she's sitting—

"The *Shaftsbury?*"

She barely touches the floor below her, which pushes
her toward the stars. The belly of the ship is gone, open
to space, and she is floating in zero-g.

"We are almost done," Eigne says.

Tetsami turns to look at the chromed woman. Eigne
drifts next to her, and they both float toward the cockpit.
"What's going on, where are we?"

"I am about to make my final offer, then Dominic
Magnus shall take us to our destiny and his own."

They enter the cockpit through a hole in the skin of the
Shaftsbury. Tetsami sees two EVA suits. She approaches
the pilot's seat and looks into the helmet—

"*No!*" Tetsami screams. She looks up at Eigne, who
stands behind the pilot's chair. "You *bitch!* You knew this
was going to happen. Oh, God. G–god . . ."

Tetsami collapses, crying on the knees of Ivor's EVA
suit. "I'm sorry, Dad. I love you and I am so damn
sorry—" More words come out, not making any sense.
Eigne seems to reach inside Ivor's helmet and the world
shifts.

Tetsami feels a comforting hand stroke her hair. She
chokes back the sobs and looks up. Ivor looks down at
her, the EVA suit is gone. He is younger; red hair crowds
out much of the white. He wears some sort of uniform
that Tetsami's never seen before.

"Shh, punkin'," Ivor says. "I love you, too—"

Ivor hugs her and the world disappears.

"*Dad!*" Tetsami screamed. The force of it ripped her
the rest of the way awake.

The pain hit her immediately, slamming into her
wounded gut. Her throat was raw not only from screaming, but from a tube that gagged the back of her throat.

Tubes entered her arms, and a deep muscular ache radiated from each point where one entered her body. The light in here drove a dagger straight through her eyes and into the back of her skull.

In her heart she knew that Ivor was gone. The realization was a pain wrapping her insides as concrete as the wreckage left by Baetez's laser. If she couldn't bring herself to accept Eigne's offer, how could Ivor?

Do I pray for his soul or my own now?

Doctors and nurses crowded around her. She tried to sit up, but straps and pain kept her from raising more than her head. She panted, and she knew she'd been yelling for a long time before she'd awakened.

"What are you—" she began saying, her voice so hoarse it bled.

"It's all right," one of the doctors said. "You're in the Jefferson City Hospital, you were shot—"

"For Christ's sake," Tetsami croaked, "I know *that*. What're all of you? Pallbearers?"

Another doctor—maybe a nurse, with the uniforms they all looked the same to Tetsami—said, "You've been in a coma for twenty-one days."

"Twenty-one . . . *days*?"

The group nodded collectively.

Tetsami leaned her head back and stared at the ceiling. Some electronic monitor blocked her view straight up, so she closed her eyes. Why could Dom accept Eigne's Change when she couldn't? Did he see himself that way? Just data to be manipulated?

"Great timing." Tetsami said to the doctors. "All of you here for when I wake up . . ."

"Not really," said the first one. "The consensus was that you were strong enough for us to attempt to revive you."

"You. Revived. Me?" Tetsami spoke very slowly and deliberately.

"Yes, we did."

"Bastards," Tetsami whispered. The Protean egg had established some communication with her, and these fucks had just ruined it. They kept talking around her, but

she ignored them. She just lay there, hurt, and felt moisture gather on her cheeks.

She was going to live, that was something.

It had to be, because it was all she had.

CHAPTER THIRTY-FOUR

Deficits

"A grand exit is preferable to a grand entrance."
—*The Cynic's Book of Wisdom*

"By thought I embrace the universal."
—BLAISE PASCAL
(1623–1662)

After an eternity, the crushing pain in Ivor Jorgenson's chest eases. His vision returns, or seems to return. The EVA suit is gone, and so is the *Shaftsbury*. He is wearing the uniform of the Stygian Presidential Guard—his old Fleet Commander's uniform. That is not odd.

What is odd is the fact that the city is empty.

The vast domed city of Perdition is absent of people and open to the sky. As he walks through empty alley-ways, paralleling the inactive maglev tracks, he sees none of the people, none of the guard. A black snow dusts down upon him from a gray sky.

Eventually he comes to the black monolith of the Citadel, the seat of the Stygian government. Here he can see signs of the coup. Burn marks on the walls, impromptu barriers blocking access to the building, a blast crater—all of it dead, inert, silent.

Fleet Commander Robert Elision screams at the Citadel for someone to acknowledge him.

"Hello?"

Where is his son? Where is his army? Where are his people?

He stands, ankle-deep in tarlike slush, at the foot of the grand Citadel entrance. The gilded staircase ascends for two stories, the once grand sculpture now stained and broken. The sweep of stairs is broken by barbed wire, sandbags, and concrete vehicle barriers with wicked steel projections.

Wrong, Robert/Ivor thinks. *Perdition was destroyed in* this *universe.*

"Am I in this universe?" The question rises against the snow, in a puff of fog.

He sees motion at the top of the stairs and he runs for it. He stumbles upward as if gravity has shifted to aid his ascent. Barbed wire tears at his uniform, the tank-traps seem to grab at him, and a mine explodes in his peripheral vision. He makes it, stumbling through an entrance dark as a cave. He falls into a void.

He panics as he feels something akin to the bone-breaking acceleration he forced the *Shaftsbury* to endure. He tumbles through the abyss, unable to breathe. Pain flashes lights into his eyes, so much that it takes a long time for Ivor to realize that he sees stars in front of him.

He is no longer in the Citadel. The tunnel of light in front of him, the rainbow stars clustered ahead like moths to God's own candle, is familiar to him. It is the view of the stars from something traveling very close to light-speed.

He wonders if he is dead.

As the stars expand in front of him, he hears a female voice—Tetsami?

"I'm sorry, Dad. I love you and I'm so damn sorry—"

Tetsami is crying, and Ivor tries to reach out to comfort her. "Shh, punkin'," Ivor says, "I love you, too—" Just as his fingers brush something in the void, the voice disappears.

Somehow, though, Ivor knows that Tetsami is all right, whatever happens to him . . .

That thought grants him some peace as he falls into infinity. Soon, though, another voice joins him in the void.

"This is not quite a dream." Female, not Tetsami.

The stars expand into him, past him, as if he is falling into them. Something else is in front of him. Something that is not a star.

"Nor," continues the female voice, "is it quite real."

He knows the object he's falling toward. It hangs in the

starfield like a mirrored Christmas ornament, a perfect sphere in which the universe around it is mirrored. However, despite appearances, he knows that the stars mirrored in the surface of the sphere are not the same stars that surround him. The sphere reflects some place light-years distant from him. That massive sphere encloses no space. It encloses an absence of space. It isn't a surface. It's a window. A door.

He's falling straight toward the throat of a wormhole.

He will travel light-years away when he strikes it, to see those reflected stars in person. He will also travel slightly more than the same number of years in time. Forward or back, he can't tell by looking.

When he hits the wormhole, the pain of his deceleration has nearly faded. Motion ceases. The abyss fades. The stars recede.

Robert/Ivor Elision/Jorgenson is sitting back at the controls of the *Shaftsbury*. He is still wearing his Fleet Commander uniform. The deck plates sealing the windows have been torn away, revealing the stars. He turns around in his seat to view the rest of the cockpit.

Sitting in the navigator's seat is the form of a woman. Her flesh seems metallic, but, like the wormhole, the reflection is not of the space around her. The reflection is of the stars beyond the skin of the *Shaftsbury*.

"Who are you?" he asks her. Somehow he hears his voice in the vacuum. Not really hearing. He feels his voice in the bones of his skull.

"This is not quite a dream," she says. "Nor is this quite reality. You are not quite dead. Nor are you quite alive." She smiles and even her teeth reflect the stars. "A collection of terms that mean little here."

"Who are you? Where is this?"

"I am Eigne and we are behind your eyes."

As she speaks, the *Shaftsbury* turns. With it turns the misplaced reflection in her chrome skin. Robert/Ivor finds it difficult to think clearly. Even though he sits stationary, he feels as if he moves through oil. Unwanted memories crowd him like gnats.

He doesn't like this chrome woman. She does not belong. He wants her to leave.

"Who are you? Where is this?" The question sounds familiar, so Ivor asks, "Why are you doing this to me?"

"I am an agent of Proteus. We are between here and there. We offer you Change. We offer you a chance to communicate."

He shakes his head. He wants no part of the heretical Proteans. It spawns a fear in his gut that threatens to consume him. The *Shaftsbury* continues to spin. More acceleration. He feels the pain again.

"We have little time," Eigne says. "Soon we will leave tach-space and you will exist again."

The acceleration of the spinning *Shaftsbury* is like a band on his chest. *I am dead,* he thinks, *leave me be.*

"No," Eigne says, "not dead. Suspended. Even if you won't consent to be saved, we wish you to have a chance to counsel your ally. The man who helps and is helped in turn." She gestures with a hand darker than the reflection. It seems covered with blood.

He shudders and looks to his side.

Sitting in the copilot's seat is a skeletal apparition made of metal and ceramic composite. Robert/Ivor draws back in shock.

"Why?" asks the apparition. The voice is audible even though the titanium-alloy skull has no tongue or lips, nor does the neck hold a voicebox, only gray vertebrae. *Why are you here? What do you want?* it asks.

"You will agent our apotheosis. Your act combines our realities within a single skin. In every reality we are, you have done thus. In every reality we are, you've accepted us. In every reality we are, we aid the completion of the task you've given yourself. This is our only hand extended Outside."

The skeleton has human-looking eyes. The eyes shift to stare at Robert/Ivor. *Why is he here?*

"This is your last chance to talk," Eigne says.

He is dead.

"Yes." Eigne says. "Robert Elision is dead. But Ivor Jorgenson also."

Save him.

"He will not be saved."

The skull tilts toward Robert/Ivor. *Let them save you.*

Robert/Ivor begins to see that this apparition is Dom. Somehow they are trapped in the subjective instant of tach-space. The black egg is with them out there, in the void between here and there. Somehow he feels as if they are also inside the egg.

"You don't know what you ask," Robert/Ivor says. The spinning of the *Shaftsbury* racks his body with pain. His vision is darkening. He turns his head to Eigne. The effort feels as if it breaks his neck. He yells, "Who are you? Where is this?"

The pace of his thoughts slow further. Mental exhaustion grips him. It becomes an effort to understand Eigne's words. "I am the resurrection and the life. We are nearly at 61 Cygni."

No! 61 Cygni? We've lost. We've lost.

Robert/Ivor feels dizzy now. The press of the *Shaftsbury*'s spin makes it difficult to talk or keep his eyes open. He begins to close his eyes, knowing that if he sleeps, he won't awaken.

He has to say something first. He knows that.

Say something, but what?

Lost.

Time, something about time. Not enough time. More time—

That is silly, though. Ivor Jorgenson is just Robert Elision with eleven extra years of time. Eleven extra years to screw everything up. He had ended up with a universe worse off than when he had started.

His eyes droop further. It's impossible to breathe now. He just wants the pain in his chest to stop. He wants all the pain to stop.

Lost, the skeleton says. Dominic Magnus says. Jonah Dacham says.

But it's so obvious.

Ecdimi, 61 Cygni, that's where I went, Robert/Ivor thinks.

"What?"

Their positions are reversed. Dom speaks words, and Robert/Ivor speaks without speaking.

Time, says his audible thoughts, *isn't it obvious?*

"What are you saying, Ivor?"

Styx to 61 Cygni, the trip we're making now. I made it and it gave me eleven years.

"What are you saying, Ivor?"

Robert/Ivor wants to close his eyes, make the pain go away. He makes one last effort and says, *the wormhole.*

"What are you saying, Ivor?"

If Dom can't figure it out from that, to hell with him. Robert/Ivor closes his eyes, and the pain goes away.

CHAPTER THIRTY-FIVE

Attrition

"People die."

            —*The Cynic's Book of Wisdom*

"The past at least is secure."

            — DANIEL WEBSTER
            (1782–1852)

Dom awoke from another Protean nightmare. He felt as if he was falling. The feeling persisted for too long to be free-fall.

Zero-g, Dom thought.

A few seconds passed before he was lucid enough to think, *Ivor.*

He opened his eyes and began to untangle the suit harness around him. He was unreasonably clumsy. The EVA suit and his long inexperience with zero gravity conspired to tie him into knots. "Ivor," Dom said. He could hear the slight re-echo of his voice over his headset, his comm was working.

Dom looked around the cockpit, an easy task now without the crushing weight of acceleration on him. The space in the cockpit was filled with every crumb of debris in the ship. A small clump of polyceram solder floated in front of Dom's faceplate. The *Shaftsbury* still had power, the lights and his respirator were working. The lights on the control consoles were on, though most showed warning messages.

Ivor was in the pilot's seat, arms floating in front of him.

"Shit!" Dom said and increased his struggles with the harness. The harness finally gave way. When it did, he saw stars in his peripheral vision, but for the moment he ignored them. He pushed over to Ivor and looked into the man's faceplate.

Dom shuddered.

Blood had streaked down Ivor's face during the ascent. The blood had pooled at the back of his helmet. Now, inside the helmet, there were dozens of tiny beads of blood floating before Ivor's face. His skin was pale, and his eyes didn't move.

"Random! Ivor's hurt. What's the life monitor reading on his suit?"

The radio's re-echo was his only answer. He fumbled off one of the access patches on Ivor's EVA suit. The small readout underneath showed Ivor's life-monitor readings. The display showed a dozen red lights and a series of straight linear tracings.

Dom realized that his hands were shaking.

"Random!"

Dom turned around to face the navigator's station. Instead of Random, he saw stars.

Oh, shit!

Still unused to the absence of gravity, he tried to run toward that side of the cockpit. The attempt pushed him off the floor and, if not for the umbilical on his suit, it would have sent him flying out the cavity that used to be the upper right quarter of the cockpit. The mistake allowed him to see more of the damage than he wanted to.

The upper edge of the hole ran between the pilot and copilot's seat. From there down to the console level of the nav station, the *Shaftsbury* no longer existed. It was that part of the *Shaftsbury* that Random Walk had been attached to. The neat lines of the hole and the way the outer skin was torn appeared to be the result of a structural failure resulting from the stress of taching out of a gravity well.

"Random?" Dom said futilely. If Random still existed, he was now a piece of cosmic debris, tumbling somewhere out there.

"Out there," wasn't an encouraging place. It was an evenly distributed starfield. There was a collection of bright stars, but there was no telling how far away they were. Dom tried to find a familiar constellation, but the wealth of stars out here overwhelmed him.

He gently pushed against the lip of the hole and reentered the cockpit.

Floating there, between him and the stairs to the rest of the ship was the ebon ellipsoid of the Protean egg. Dom floated there, staring at it. The only sound came from the rebreather cycling air into his EVA suit. Everything else was silence.

"Do something!" he yelled at the egg. *"You took those four corpses, take him!"*

The radio fed him back his own volume-damped voice. He turned to see Ivor's motionless corpse, and the action sent his whole body turning. He had to grab the copilot's chair to avoid entangling himself in his own umbilical.

"You saved me," Dom whispered. "Why can't you save him?"

"He will not be saved," Dom answered himself with the voice from his dream.

Dom felt cold. It wasn't just a psychic chill this time, but real cold. He checked the heads-up monitors on his suit and saw that his thermostat was malfunctioning. It wasn't even giving him a coherent reading.

What was he going to do?

After removing Ivor's umbilical to save on his oxygen supply, Dom sat in the copilot's chair and thought. It was an ugly situation. Random had managed to tach them somewhere, but odds were it wasn't Sol. Dom tried to get whatever was left of the computers on-line to discover where.

61 Cygni, insisted his memory of the dream.

Dom was not yet ready to trust those hallucinations. However, when he had finally tapped into the secondary nav computer and was able to query the tach-drive's command history, Dom found out an unsettling fact.

The *Shaftsbury* had tached within 40 AU of 61 Cygni A.

Keeping a grip on the chair, Dom turned to face the egg. *Why doesn't it leave now? We're out of danger. It doesn't need me.*

Dom turned back to the console. There wasn't enough power left for another tach-jump, even if the *Shaftsbury* still had the computers to calculate the maneuver. The *Shaftsbury*'s navigational capability was limited to an atlas and the star index. The contragrav was dead, and everything more than ten meters away from the rear of the cockpit was flooded with radiation. All the external sensors were dead. All the ship had left was a pair of engines to the rear, one main and one secondary, both at less than 33%.

And the *Shaftsbury* had spent over twenty-six days standard to tach from Bakunin to 61 Cygni. Twenty days Bakunin, and that took events on the surface past the point where Godwin could still hold out against the invasion. The war was over, and Klaus, the TEC and the Confederacy had won.

"We've lost," Dom said. His voice fogged in the overcooled suit. The inside of his visor fogged slightly. A sense of déjà vu caused Dom to look at Ivor to make sure that he wasn't alive and twenty years younger.

"Wormholes," Dom said.

The thought was desperate and futile. He could pass through a wormhole, take an instantaneous jump in both space and time. But if he took that step into the past, he would be assured of severing the connection between himself and the universe he was leaving. Even if the automated defenses didn't destroy the *Shaftsbury,* Dom's very presence in his own past would render the events on Bakunin—and everywhere else in the human universe—unrecognizable by the time he had finally caught up with the present.

In a very real sense, it was a form of suicide. As far as this reality was concerned, as far as Bakunin, and Tetsami, and Shane, and Zanzibar, and Godwin, and Klaus—as far as everything Dom knew and cared about, he would cease to exist.

But, that was what had happened with Ivor. The world Ivor Jorgenson inhabited was very different from the one where his original Robert Elision had lived ...

Ivor had made an effort to change the past. What if Dom tried not to have an effect? What if, upon arriving in the past, he did nothing until the events on Bakunin had already begun?

It was a foolish thought. Just taking the act, stepping through the hole, would be enough of a change to render the worlds different. He would be abandoning a Bakunin he knew, to have some unknown effect on a Bakunin he knew nothing of, one that might not even exist yet. *His* Bakunin, the Bakunin he was trying to save—he would have no effect on it. From this end of the wormhole, everything going in the wrong end ceased to exist.

Was there nothing he could do?

If his dream was to believed, Ivor's last words told him to use the wormhole.

What if his decision did affect this universe?

People and things that appeared out of the future end of a wormhole were called "ghosts." They came from possible futures, but by definition, their futures were different from the ones the universe with the ghost actually saw. Ivor had been a ghost. Despite the unreliability of the ghosts' view of the future, they weren't random. The appearance of a ghost followed complex rules of probability involving the entire history of the wormhole in question.

Dom knew none of the physics. But he suspected that, even if he left this universe, if he followed Ivor's advice, if he committed this form of suicide, there was a chance—small, but a chance—that he might increase the probability that there was already a ghost of himself somewhere near Terra. Someone who wasn't exactly him, but someone close enough to finish the job he had started.

If he followed this plan, Ivor's plan, his own ghost would have been in the Sol system for years.

Dom glanced back at the egg. It had not left, and Dom knew that it would follow him until he made planetfall somewhere. Dom checked his oxygen supply and started calling up the old wormhole network on the remains of the nav computer.

CHAPTER THIRTY-SIX

Constructive Engagement

"We are each alone."
  —*The Cynic's Book of Wisdom*

"It is never too late to give up your prejudices."
  —HENRY DAVID THOREAU
  (1817–1862)

Robert Kaunda sat behind his desk at the Union Consulate. He was trying to do routine intelligence reviews and trying not to think about the Confederacy's future. He wasn't succeeding at either. It was the beginning of the fourth week of the Congress, and even though most of the bullshit was over with—the remaining BS was just the constant politics that always immersed the Confederacy at the highest levels—the activities still held little interest for Kaunda.

It should have, since the normally pro forma votes on planetary promotion had suddenly become partisan and venal. Both Centauri and Sirius were calling up delaying measures left and right, having a raft of procedural votes that—if all were carried out for the remaining session of the Congress—could drag the promotion process into next year.

Kaunda was staring at text on his holo display and not really seeing it, when his thoughts were interrupted by a call on the priority line. That line was only for diplomatic communications, and Kaunda's first thought upon hearing it was that war had finally broken out over Bakunin.

He called up the image and was surprised to be looking at Francesca Hernandez, the nonhuman delegate from the Seven Worlds. "We need to talk," she said. "Now."

Kaunda didn't realize that he had been expecting this call until now. "Where?" he asked.

"A bar outside the diplomatic quarter," she said. "We'll go from there."

The bar where Hernandez wished to meet him was deep in the nonhuman quarter of Sydney. Like all of the Confederacy's capital city, it was still in sight of the Confederacy spire, the kilometer-tall monolith in the center of the diplomatic compound. However, aside from that one subliminal reminder, this part of Sydney was light-years away from the Confederacy he knew.

For the first time in his life, Robert Kaunda was surrounded by nonhumans. It was more disconcerting than the sea of white faces when he visited parts of the SEEC or the Centauri Alliance. He was surrounded by acres of fur—russet, golden, dead black, spotted and striped. Creatures feline and canine, vulpine and ursine, rodents of every stripe. The sheer variety of types was disorienting. An anthropoid rat, or mouse, would only stand to Kaunda's sternum, while a towering ursine looked down on him from a height of three meters or more.

All stared at him. Kaunda had thought that wouldn't bother him. He was a diplomat; he had seen his share of racism. There were worlds in the Centauri Alliance and the SEEC where every person of African or Asian descent had long ago left—one way or another. If it wasn't race, it was the fact that he represented the Union, not the most respected arm of the Confederacy.

He sat in a booth by the windows, nursing an ugly-tasting local brew. The stares shouldn't have bothered him, but they did.

He decided that it was one of two things that bothered him. The first was the fact that this was the first time that he was an outsider based on his species, simply being human. The differences here, between him and the two-and-a half-meter tiger sitting at the end of the bar, were far more than cosmetic or cultural.

The other reason he was disturbed was much more basic. Fear. Close to half of the creatures looking at him were predatory. The tiger had fangs the size of his thumb.

The other half were rodents that made up for it with hateful expressions.

Kaunda tried his best to look invisible, but he stuck out as badly here as he would've in a party rally on Waldgrave.

He arrived on time, but Hernandez's people let him stew for nearly fifteen minutes before a lepine nonhuman walked up and asked, "You are the diplomat Kaunda, aye?"

The creature was a tawny-colored rodent with oversized ears and feet, liquid black eyes and prominent front teeth. It spoke with an Australian accent and a pronounced lisp. It wore a pair of khaki briefs that were baggy enough to conceal an illegal weapon or two.

Kaunda set his drink down and nodded. He had expected to meet Hernandez.

"Follow me," said the rabbit-creature.

Kaunda followed, wondering why someone would've engineered such an odd-looking creature.

He expected to be led outside the bar, but, instead, he was led back into the place. Kaunda had avoided the dark rear of the place because it was packed, and because it seemed less likely that something untoward would happen in sight of the street. However, as his guide led him through the crowd of claws and fur, he seemed to suddenly gain the invisibility he'd been seeking. The crowd parted to the fore, and coalesced seamlessly aft.

Once he and the lepine passed a trio of ursoids that literally formed the rear wall of the bar, they were in a twisting hallway that led, eventually, outside. Halfway to the exit, they stopped.

"You have any cybernetics or electronic implants?"

Kaunda shook his head no.

The lepine waved a hand at what looked like another part of the ill-painted wall. "Then step inside, please."

As a gesture of faith, Kaunda stepped toward the wall, but he couldn't keep from holding his hands out before him. The wall was a holo projection, and he passed through without resistance. He was in a closet-sized room with white tile walls. It resembled a shower stall. He turned around and saw the reverse side of the wall holo, just as a fourth wall slid into place with a static hiss.

Another, more prolonged, static hiss was accompanied by an electric rainbow shimmer as some sort of Emerson field was activated. Kaunda's hair prickled for a moment. Afterward he was disturbed to see a number of pinhole burns in his trousers and jacket.

The wall behind him slid open. He turned around to face Hernandez's feline form. She was looking at the burns on his clothes. "Monitoring devices," she remarked in her eerily nonhuman voice.

"I gathered that," Kaunda said. He was beginning to feel real anger. "Do you know who?"

She shook her head. "Only suspect. And you know whom to suspect as well as I."

Kaunda nodded. They had four choices: the other arms of the Confederacy, and the TEC. Kaunda had his doubts about Vashniya, but the gnomic head of Indi intelligence was too smart to try something that could alienate an ally so close to the endgame. Kaunda thought the TEC more likely, but he knew Dimitri was more subtle than this.

That left the allied European arms of the Confederacy: Centauri and Sirius.

Hernandez led Kaunda down a set of metal stairs to what had to be a shielded part of the building's basement. There were a table, chairs, and a comm set up, all illuminated by a single frosted light fixture that seemed a century old. He and Hernandez were the only ones present.

"We can talk here," she said.

Kaunda took a seat. "I didn't know you had contacts on Earth."

Hernandez's mouth curved in the feline equivalent of a smile. "You do know that, after the fall of the Terran Council, a substantial number of nonhumans were repatriated to Earth."

Kaunda nodded.

"Well," Hernandez's voice rumbled, "it took a certain kind of nonhuman to return to the homeworld after the Council's genetic cleansing—especially with the continued human prejudice against us. The nonhumans here are more political than average."

"That's understandable," Kaunda said. He glanced around the secure basement. It was obvious that it had been here a while. The walls were whitewashed, but if he looked close enough, he could see some telltale silhouettes. The old shadows of things that used to hang or lean against the walls here. This room had once been an armory.

Kaunda cleared his throat. "How political?"

There was that alien feline smile again. "Enough that the Seven Worlds has at times had to distance itself from Terra."

God help us, Kaunda thought. Hernandez was talking about nonhuman terrorism. There had been guerrilla bands of engineered nonhumans on Earth almost since the first nonhumans had been created. Terrorism reached a peak during the Terran Council's genetic cleansing era. By then there were so many nonhumans, even the despotic measures of the Council couldn't eradicate all the gene-engineered creatures. The remaining ones simply became more and more radical, suicidal, and allied against anything human.

Since the Charter and the Confederacy, Kaunda had thought the nonhuman radicals had diminished. The nonhuman population had certainly grown with returnees from the colonies. Kaunda found himself embarrassed at his surprise. It was provincialism in reverse. He had no urge to know about local Terrestrial events; his concerns were out with the stars.

He should have known better. The only way to really destroy a radical political movement was to grant it power in the government.

"Why am I here?" Kaunda asked.

"You are concerned about Bakunin, and the future of the Confederacy."

"With the force arrayed there, I'd be a fool not to be."

Hernandez nodded. "There are more reasons to worry." She extended a claw and started tapping controls on the comm next to the table. A holo popped up showing a man sitting roughly where Kaunda was sitting. He had UV-bleached hair, brown eyes, and olive-colored skin. Kaunda also noticed that the man's right hand was metal.

"I have been negotiating with a representative of the Bakunin resistance."

"What?" Kaunda's reserve finally broke. It was bad enough that Vashniya was pulling all sorts of games with the alliance, but now the Seven Worlds as well?

"Please," Hernandez said. After a pause, she went on. "This man, Jonah Dacham, alias Dominic Magnus, came to me with a revelation of some importance to both of us. I have been unable to act officially until the arrival today of my superiors from Tau Ceti."

"You mean more Seven Worlds representatives?" Kaunda asked.

"The entire delegation." Hernandez said, and let that sink in. The Seven Worlds rarely sent a single representative to the Congress. A full delegation was unheard of.

"Why?"

"We needed to discuss what this man had to say. Things we could never trust to a tach-comm operated by the TEC."

Kaunda stared at the holo. This Dacham didn't look that impressive. But then, again, neither did Vashniya—and Vashniya was shaking the Confederacy down to the roots.

"The value of Bakunin, up to now, has been its unallied status. It is a planet that meets all the Charter requirements for a prime seat in the Congress. As soon as the Bakunin delegate officially signs the Charter—"

"I know, the arm that sponsors them gets a new prime seat." It seemed so out of proportion to say it that way. All this maneuvering, all this animosity, was all down to a single potential seat in the Congress.

"Bakunin now has an additional value to whatever arm sponsors it. A value far beyond any seat in the Confederacy."

"What kind of value?" Kaunda asked.

"What do you know about the Dolbrians?"

CHAPTER THIRTY-SEVEN

High Crimes

"It is never too late for something bad to happen."
—*The Cynic's Book of Wisdom*

"History is about the most cruel of all goddesses."
—FRIEDRICH ENGELS
(1820–1895)

A man named Jonah Dacham sat in a windowless room somewhere on Earth and thought about time. This Jonah had a metal right hand he had earned in an aircar crash. He also had a similarly modified right leg. Much of the rest of his body was constructed with more advanced cybernetics that dated from the time he had fallen into a waste reclamation tank. His hair was bleached from unshielded UV that'd shone on him during his nine years on Mars.

This Jonah Dacham had an onboard computer that allowed him to mark accurately the passage of time. It also allowed him a painfully eidetic memory. If his estimates were correct, and if his memories were still valid in this universe, he had just become the *only* Jonah Dacham.

It was a date that also marked the end of Godwin's ability to withhold the siege. After nine years, the frustration was numbing and unreal.

Today, as Jonah sat on the cot in an otherwise featureless white cube, he counted each second as it passed. Even if simultaneity counted for nothing when talking of distances of light-years, this day was significant. The hour was passing into the eighty-seventh day after the TEC attack on GA&A. It was the day that Flower predicted that Godwin would eventually fall. This day marked the point where the Proudhon military machine would be in full command on the ground in Bakunin. It was the day they would win.

Also, somewhere on the fringes of the 61 Cygni system, he—or a version of himself—was about to maneuver the ruins of the *Shaftsbury* through the wrong end of a wormhole.

Jonah could still remember it, flying the *Shaftsbury* with Ivor's corpse as a copilot. When he closed his eyes, it was as if it was happening now—

In one sense it was.

The *Shaftsbury*'s drives had tried to shake her apart as he'd driven her toward the nearest 61 Cygni wormhole. The radio and much of the navigation gear was dead, so he heard none of the warnings that must've been beamed his way. All he had was the view out the hole in the *Shaftsbury*'s cockpit. He had aimed at the wormhole, the outbound end from Occisis, knowing that he was committing suicide. The defense network on the other end would destroy him just as methodically as it destroyed any anomalies from possible futures.

Ivor might have outmaneuvered the defenses when he was Fleet Commander Robert Elision of the Styx Presidential Guard piloting a working fighter, but Jonah was not that good a pilot, and the *Shaftsbury* more resembled mobile wreckage than a ship.

He'd thought little about that. What he thought, as he aimed the *Shaftsbury* at the glittery ornament of the wormhole, was that this was his only chance to defeat the TEC. His only chance to fight the machine. His only chance to redeem himself.

He didn't see that he had much of a choice.

The *Shaftsbury* sped at illegal insystem speeds toward a distortion in the starfield, something that looked like a perfectly mirrored sphere. The stars reflected in the sphere were those as seen from its other side, in orbit around the Alpha Centauri binary. The reflection was from fourteen light-years away and fourteen years earlier.

Just before the *Shaftsbury* crossed the nonexistent surface of the perfect sphere, something happened—something that probably saved Jonah's life.

The stars blueshifted.

Everything outside the *Shaftsbury* distorted. It was a visual warping worse than the spherical lens of the wormhole. Jonah saw the automated drones watching the Centauri end of the wormhole, but they ignored the *Shaftsbury*.

It was as if the wreck he piloted didn't exist.

Then, without any sensation of movement, the starfield rotated on its axis and zoomed to the rear of the craft.

Jonah had enough presence of mind to glance behind him, to see where the Protean egg was. But the egg wasn't there. In its place, shimmering for the briefest second, was the figure of a nude female form whose chromed skin reflected a universe different from the one he knew.

Then, as he was still looking, the egg coalesced. As Jonah watched, the skin of the egg shrank past the skin of the ship, past him, to regain its normal three-meter ellipsoid size—exactly on the spot where he had seen the image of Eigne.

When Jonah had turned around to see where he was, he was in orbit around the Occisis wormhole to Sol—a point hundreds of AU from the similar outgoing wormhole from which he had emerged. He didn't know how he had possibly survived the acceleration that had brought him to this point.

But, at the other end of that hole was Sol, a Sol four and a half years in this Occisis' future, a Sol that would still be nine years in his own past . . .

Jonah closed his eyes—

What he was remembering, in this small white prison was happening now—

Though, in his memory, the events were nine years past—

He wasn't even sure that events in this universe were following his memory. Did his doppelganger on Bakunin follow his lead? Did the launch of the *Shaftsbury* go as badly? Did Ivor still die?

It had been a long, long time since he had thought of his past. The events seemed so distant now, so ghostly, it was as if he found one thread of memory and tugged, the entire structure would crumble.

He wondered what his captors thought of him. At first he feared them; immediately after his capture he had expected torture at least. However, the questioning, while drug-assisted, was mild in comparison to his fears. The worst torment he experienced was just the simple fact of his captivity so close to his goal . . .

Despite the brief questioning, Jonah had no illusion that he had secrets from his captors. The people holding him prisoner certainly knew everything they wished to know from him. What he knew of *them* amounted to practically nothing. He knew this room was constantly monitored. He knew that they were content to hold him prisoner, perhaps until the end of the Congress. He knew that his captors were reluctant to do him harm, but he had no idea why.

Jonah stood and paced, following the white walls. None showed any signs of being a door, no matter how he adjusted the setting on his photo-receptors. He'd spent nearly a week trying to find a door—there had to be one—but the walls were as seamless as a Protean creation.

Escape had been on his mind several times, but Jonah knew that, as things stood, he was hopelessly imprisoned. His captors never came here while he was conscious, they never dimmed the lights, they never stopped watching him. And, whenever they felt the need, they could flood his room with colorless, odorless gas that would knock him out before he could even decide to hold his breath.

Trying to pretend sleep had done no good. He had tried it once or twice after he'd seen that they only brought meals while he slept. He'd always sleep anyway; they gassed the room as a precaution or they had monitors that could tell when he was awake. Either way, he was assured of never seeing the door open.

As he paced, he was glad of his onboard computer. The lights here never dimmed or changed intensity. If not for the clock wired into his head, he would lose all sense of the passage of time, and possibly his grip on sanity.

However, after his exile on Mars, it wasn't the isolation

the gnawed at him. It was the failure. He was here because the people holding him captive did not wish
Bakunin to retain its independence. And, because he was
here, and not at the Congress, his captors would get that
wish. For nine years he had been on Mars, the Protean
egg providing him sustenance, lodging, but little else. The
egg had provided him a means to escape from having any
effect on the universe, growing a crystalline hideaway
from the crust of Martian rock. And, apparently, that was
where the egg had ceased its interference.

It was still there, on Mars, somewhere.

As he paced out the square floor, he wondered if
Francesca Hernandez's superiors had accepted his pro-
posal. The ship from Tau Ceti would've arrived by now—

Not that the Seven Worlds could save him now. The
very reason he dealt with Hernandez was because of their
relative weakness and isolation. Even with the Dolbrian
prize he offered, the Tau Ceti arm of the Confederacy
wasn't powerful enough to impose its will on anyone outside its immediate borders, and its isolationist bent meant
it was unlikely to interfere with Bakunin even if it helped
sponsor Bakunin's admission.

If they accepted his offer, and he was legitimized in the
Congress, that itself would end the siege on Bakunin.
Once an arm of the Confederacy sponsored Bakunin's ad-
mittance, with Jonah as the representative of the legitimate government, the TEC would be forced by the
Charter to withdraw as an illegal insurrection. Klaus
would be left without extraplanetary support. The siege
would crumble as soon as the financial support of the
mercenary army dried up.

If they were lucky, the fleets in orbit would withdraw
to their own arms of the Confederacy rather than start an
interstellar incident.

It wasn't going to be like that.

He was prisoner here, and the delegate to sign Bakunin
to the Charter would do so as a representative of Klaus'
forces. Bakunin would be sponsored by either the
Centauri Alliance or the Sirius-Eridani Economic Community, Klaus' invasion would be legitimized, and Bakunin would become subjugated.

The picture was ugly. Much of the population on Bakunin was formed of dissidents and "criminals" who'd run from those arms of the Confederacy. Once someone set up a planetary police force, once someone created extradition treaties . . .

The planet could end up in a state of perpetual civil war. The new rulers might be forced to kill or imprison a third of the population.

But that wasn't the worst possible scenario.

Worst case was where the "resistance" followed Gavadi's advice and called on Indi for aid. Short-term that could help put down the TEC-sponsored invasion. Indi certainly had enough force. But that, inevitably, would spark an interstellar conflict within the Confederacy. A conflict whose epicenter would be Bakunin. From there, Jonah knew that it was all too likely that some commander in those orbiting SEEC ships would see the ultimate solution being the removal of Bakunin from the equation.

It was frighteningly easy to render a planet uninhabitable. Especially one as marginal, and with as concentrated a population, as Bakunin. One large rock accelerated near c, aimed about midway between Godwin and Troy, could wipe out most of the planet's population in the first few seconds. The aftereffects could wipe out life on the planet.

It might even leave that Dolbrian pyramid intact.

If control of Bakunin had been a priority issue before, with that added to the mix, control of the planet would've been raised to pathological proportions. Bakunin, with that Dolbrian map, could insure an arm's dominance for the next few centuries. Whoever owned the information on that pyramid eventually could, if they chose to, rule the Confederacy.

Jonah's offer of that information would be irresistible, even to the most isolationist arm of the Confederacy. Because of that isolationism, Jonah thought the Seven Worlds the best choice to control that information.

Jonah had paced to the far wall of his room for perhaps the hundredth time, when the door opened.

He turned, alarmed. His captors had established a routine, and the fact that they'd suddenly decided to break form was an evil portent. He knew as far as information was concerned, his usefulness had long ago expired. He was being kept alive for some other inscrutable reason, a reason that might, just as inscrutably, disappear.

Entering his cell was the first human being he had seen in a week. A person he'd never seen before.

He corrected himself even as the information was still sinking in. He had seen this woman before, only not in this context. His memory for faces was excellent even before his reconstruction added a computer to his skull. The woman walking into his room was named Kalin Green.

She wore no uniform. She wore a conservatively cut tunic that suggested diplomacy rather than warfare. The color was emerald, to match her name. The remainder of her was monochrome and businesslike. Someone who didn't know her might think her attractive.

Jonah knew her.

He knew her from a long, long time ago. He knew her from his time in the TEC, and with the extra nine years that Mars had added to his memory that was almost a quarter century ago. Green had aged, but not as much as Jonah thought she should have.

The last time he had seen her, she'd been the chief intelligence officer for Cynos' planetary secret police. Since, Jonah knew that she had risen to become the Cynos representative to the Terran Congress as well as the SEEC delegate to the TEC.

"Hello, Jonah," she said. "You have no idea how much trouble you've caused me. However, I'm here to offer you a deal."

CHAPTER THIRTY-EIGHT

Rules of Engagement

"Sometimes you must attack an enemy at his strength."

—*The Cynic's Book of Wisdom*

"Powerful states can maintain themselves only by crime, little states are virtuous only by weakness."

—MIKHAIL BAKUNIN
(1814–1876)

Robert Kaunda was not normally a fearful man. But he was fearful tonight. When Hernandez had broached the plan to him, he thought she was insane. What she wanted to do was an act of war, within a few hundred meters of the Confederacy spire itself. She suggested an act that could get the weakest two arms of the Confederacy censured at best—

At worst they could be signing the political death warrants of both their governments.

It was just as well that she had stated up front what was at stake here, otherwise she might not have ever gotten to tell him what the plan was. In Kaunda's eyes, allowing Bakunin, with its Dolbrian artifact, to fall into the hands of the powerful arms of the Confederacy, Indi included, would be just as much a political death for the Union.

Kaunda ate a chalky tablet and tried to will away the acid in his gut. He checked his chrono for the time and, impatient, began to withdraw diplomatic parcels from the closet of his office. The parcels were all about the size of a large briefcase and were utterly inviolate, even from TEC security. There were six, total, all very heavy.

He checked the security monitors on his desk. The holo display showed no external monitoring—all the lights were green. He didn't expect any different. If security *here* had been compromised, he would've found out about it a week ago at least. If there'd been any leaks about what was about to happen, arrest by a TEC assault squad would be the best he could hope for.

Kaunda sighed and sat down behind his desk. The desk, and the room surrounding it, were older than the building that housed it. Most of the decor Kaunda had chosen dated from the nineteenth-century colonial era. Most of the room—the masks, the trophies, the wooden statues—had been looted from Africa by the English back when the United Kingdom was located on Earth.

The two exceptions were the desk itself, which came from the India of the early twentieth century, and a large wooden globe of Mazimba, Kaunda's native planet.

The globe sat next to the desk, and Kaunda placed his hand upon it. This might be all he would ever see of his home planet again.

"Whatever happens, after this Congress I retire."

Kaunda pulled the first pouch across the desk. Like all of them, this had a black textured finish. It was twice as thick as an ordinary briefcase, and the lock was a small green-lit bar that held a unique digital code identifying it as diplomatic materials for the Union of Independent Worlds. With that identifier, this bag's contents was immune from the sensors monitoring every millimeter of ground around the Confederacy spire.

That green bar, that little electronic identifier, was why Hernandez needed him and the Union of Independent Worlds. Since the Seven Worlds had no consulate on Earth, the Seven Worlds delegation would have to register any diplomatic packages through the TEC. Since the Union had a consulate, however small, Kaunda could register identifiers directly.

And since he was both the head intelligence officer of the Union *and,* for a while still, the holder of the Union's single prime seat, he could program diplomatic packages to any purpose and answer to nobody.

Kaunda pressed his thumb to the seal and there was an electrostatic hiss as the sealed case unlocked itself.

He opened it.

Inside were two evenly folded stacks of oddly cut body suits. Even a casual glance showed that the majority were not cut to fit a human. Each one appeared thin as tissue paper, though all had the same textured black appearance as the case.

Like the cases that contained them, each suit had a digital marker that told the security software surrounding the spire to ignore its contents. Simply possessing these suits would be enough to cause an ugly diplomatic incident. Stealthing from the security monitors with diplomatic codes went far beyond the accepted level of spying. These trod on the dangerous ground of potential assassination and terrorism.

If the first case was a hint of terrorism, the next case was the actual threat.

Weapons were outlawed in Sydney, and especially in the diplomatic quarter. But three of the pouches Kaunda had smuggled into his embassy contained broken-down military lasers of a distinctly nonhuman make. All of them had fully charged power cells ready for installation.

The fifth case held a sophisticated microcomputer, cutting tools, antisurveillance gadgets and a host of electronics of a make Kaunda wasn't familiar with. He knew that in there were devices to override electronic locks and to tap into hostile data systems.

The last case was the only one to be fully defensive. It contained five sets of multiple personal field generators. They were to military specification, and the harnesses—again—weren't designed for someone of human stature.

Kaunda looked at the hardware arrayed on his desk and thought, *Competent revolutionaries have toppled governments with less.*

It didn't make him feel better.

At a little past one in the morning, right on time, the embassy computer told Kaunda that the delegation from Tau Ceti had arrived. He had the computer let them in. At this hour he was the only human at the Union Consulate.

After Hernandez and company came up to his office, he still was.

Hernandez herself was a tall, lithe feline creature whose spotted fur reminded Kaunda of a jaguar or a cheetah. Kaunda felt he should be able to tell the difference— but he had never seen the unmodified version of either cat. With her she brought a quintet of other nonhumans.

Kaunda could tell that the five others were Earthnative. They were too sure-footed to have just come from Tau Ceti. Kaunda suspected a gravity change would be even more clumsy for someone with digitigrade feet. Also, Kaunda thought, no matter how high a level the decision to sanction this little operation came from, no one here would have explicit connections to Haven's high command. Except for Hernandez, and no doubt she could be blamed for everything if things went bad.

The Union didn't have it so good. Not only was Kaunda uncomfortable with such deniability games, but for all practical purposes he *was* the Union's high command. As far as terrestrial activity went, when Kaunda acted, it *was* the Union acting.

He'd never felt the full weight of that as he did now.

"Good evening, Mr. Kaunda."

Kaunda nodded absently at Hernandez. "No last minute changes in plan?"

She shook her head, deliberately enough so Kaunda could tell that it was a learned gesture. He wondered what catlike gesture she used back home to express a negative.

"This is the time?" Kaunda asked, expressing the obvious out of nervousness. Hernandez's five companions were certainly from some terrestrial extremist group. They all had to be incredibly brave, or incredibly foolish, to agree to be part of a covert operation this close to the heart of the TEC.

"Yes," Hernandez said, without nodding. She pulled over a chair and sat. She inched around, apparently trying to get comfortable with her tail in the way.

The five others were going through the diplomatic pouches that Kaunda had already opened. None of them had yet said a word.

Hernandez introduced them, using their aliases. The

gray-furred canine who was digging in the bag of electronics was known as "Foster." The other canine, brown and more dog than wolflike, was called "Brin." The black ratlike creature was called "Orwell." The gigantic ursoid, the most imposing member of the team, was called "Milne." A tall feline creature, larger than Hernandez, seemed to order the others around wordlessly. Hernandez called her "Anderson."

As the team assembled their gear, Hernandez asked him, "Any changes in security during the past two days?"

"Everything's normal, even at the Cynos Consulate." Kaunda paused before going on. "You're certain that that's where they're keeping him?"

For the first time Hernandez showed a trace of humor. She gave a smile that barely hid her teeth. "My friend—if he isn't there, we are in a world of trouble. As it is, it's the only place they *could* keep him."

Kaunda kept his peace and watched the team don the special jumpsuits and arm themselves. It wouldn't do any good to point out the reason Jonah Dacham's captors had no choice in locating the prisoner.

When you're dealing with someone that important, you put him in the safest, most secure place you have available—and the SEEC consulate was about as secure as it got.

And these five nonhumans had the unlucky job of breaking into it.

All very brave, Kaunda thought, *or very foolhardy.*

CHAPTER THIRTY-NINE

Diplomatic Immunity

"If people chose their parents, most of the world would be childless."

—*The Cynic's Book of Wisdom*

"It is characteristic of man that he alone has any sense of good and evil ... and the association of living things who have this sense makes a family and a state."

—ARISTOTLE
(384–322 B.C.)

For a few dumbfounded moments, Jonah stared at the head intelligence officer of the Sirius-Eridani Economic Community. Eventually he said, "Perhaps we should sit for this."

Kalin Green nodded. She sat on the cell's single cot, leaving Jonah to sit on the lavatory, the room's only other fixture. The door was closed and invisible again, leaving him alone with one of the most powerful people in the Confederacy. Green was perhaps only second behind Dimitri Olmanov himself, and possibly Pearce Adams from the Centauri Alliance.

The fact she was here herself was enough to shock Jonah to near speechlessness at a point where he'd thought himself beyond surprises. Even odder were the conciliatory sounds she was making, when her power over him seemed nearly absolute. There was nothing stopping her from ordering him killed, or ordering his mind sucked dry of any possibly relevant detail. They didn't even have to install a biolink for the purpose.

Something strange was going on here.

Fortunately, a near decade in isolation hadn't robbed him of his ability to hide emotion. He looked at Green and said, "I've been causing you trouble?" He hoped the inherent irony of the question hid the real perplexity behind it.

"Don't be coy, Dacham." She shook her head. "It doesn't become you."

"You have me at a disadvantage." Jonah waved at the cell around them with his metallic right hand.

Green actually looked pained. "This wasn't my doing. It was a political decision."

Is she actually asking for forgiveness? Jonah thought. *What's going on here?*

"Go on," Jonah said.

She looked at him, " 'Political' should say it all. The leadership on Cynos discovered that *you* were involved in this Bakunin business—that not only were you Dominic Magnus, but you were on Earth. They panicked, of course. They gave the orders to grab you when we did. I couldn't do much; I still serve my own government—however stupid."

Jonah was still confused. Why was Green so concerned about him? "Am I so important?" he asked. "I've been out of the game for a long time." Jonah hoped he wasn't giving away too much of his own ignorance.

Maybe the universe really is different now. Who knows what changes were wrought when I passed through that wormhole?

Green looked at him coldly. "Don't play with me. We knew who you were *before* you dropped out. Waldgrave is our jurisdiction, Dacham. We've been watching you and your brother almost as long as Dimitri has."

The one casual admission triggered all the pent-up paranoia that Jonah had been saving since his work with the TEC. "You should have known of my involvement on Bakunin . . ."

"Of course we knew you were on the planet." Kalin sounded disgusted. "But the Centauri agents didn't connect Dominic Magnus with you. Fifteen years is a long time to drop out of the community—"

"It sounds like interagency communication is as bad today as it was when I was in the Executive."

"Now you're sounding like your father—"

Jonah felt a chill through his body.

"—didn't make the connection," Green continued, "until one of our agents saw you negotiating with the delegate from Grimalkin. The politicians on Cynos panicked and decided that you had to be kept away from the Congress at any cost."

Jonah nodded. He was still digesting the fact that this woman knew volumes about him that he didn't know himself.

"You achieved that," Jonah said.

Green chuckled. "Yes. We have that. It's just that it's sinking in back home exactly what 'at any cost' might mean. When you combine Dimitri's health with a family disposition for lengthy memory—potential reprisals have become quite a discussion topic in parliament back home."

Jonah felt the pulse in his neck; it was as if someone was periodically tugging on a loose garrote. He must not be hearing her correctly, or he was drawing the wrong conclusions. "I'm not sure what you're talking about." He said it slowly enough so the shaking in his voice wasn't audible. His left hand was trembling, and he covered it with the metal one.

"Look, Dacham, I know you must be enjoying this. But we're at an impasse here. Dimitri has the entire TEC, and we can't risk antagonizing him. If we could disappear you and be sure he'd never find out, we would. But no one's ready to guarantee that. I'm half-convinced that somehow Dimitri engineered this whole charade to test how we'd react."

She shook her head. "There were a few bright lads who'll remain nameless who thought we could use you as a bargaining chip in striking some sort of deal with Dimitri—maybe have him alter his plans for succession . . ."

The surprise must have finally registered on his face because Green looked him in the eye and said, "Don't

worry, those bright lads have been transferred to the diplomatic liaison on Helminth.

"I've finally gotten the administration on Cynos to
agree with me. Our only recourse to fix this disaster is to
negotiate with you. We need some assurance that the
SEEC won't suffer reprisals for this incident."

Jonah clenched his chromed hand and clutched it with
his left. After nine years of isolation on Mars, avoiding
his own anachronistic entanglement in this altered reality,
this was all too much. After so long without human contact, he could be misreading what Green was saying. This
universe had been given at least nine years to mutate
away from the world he knew—even without his active
intervention, just the fact of his presence could have
knocked the world subtly askew. . . .

But all that shouldn't change his parentage.

His mother was Helen Dacham, a cruel, unhappy
woman from Waldgrave. She had died fifteen years ago
by this world's reckoning, along with thirty-five thousand
others, on a cold little slushball called Styx.

His father—

Jonah's father was nothing more than a threat from his
mother, a specter used to frighten him and Klaus when
her rages weren't enough. Jonah's father didn't even have
a name—Helen had always said "your father," as if the
absent parent were responsible for all of her children's
shortcomings.

Jonah felt the same chill in his gut that he'd felt when
he was told his mother had died on Styx. The same chill
he'd felt when he'd heard that the outer defenses of
GA&A wouldn't hold. The same chill he'd felt when he
had discovered that Klaus was in command of the mission on Bakunin. The same chill he'd felt when the invasion started. The same chill he'd felt when he heard that
Tetsami had died. The same chill he'd felt when he had
buried Ivor on Mars.

It was too familiar. His world had fallen apart too many
times. Even after nine years, the feeling of the world turning ice-brittle around him burned him like a bath of liquid
nitrogen. One wrong move and the world would shatter,
taking him with it.

But the ice outlined an atrophied resolve in razor-sharp detail. Saving the precarious anarchy on Bakunin wasn't the real reason he had boarded the *Shaftsbury*. He wasn't even here to fight his brother. He was here because, when Tetsami—the one person who seemed to touch his remaining humanity—was nearly killed by a TEC agent she had risked her life to save, he knew he had to attack the mechanism responsible.

The same machine responsible for the death of thirty-five thousand on Styx. Responsible for countless deaths when the Proteus commune was destroyed. And, by extension, responsible for all the blood on his and Klaus' hands.

He was here to damage the TEC itself. In large part, he had spent the last nine years planning, not the signing of the Charter, which would abort the ongoing invasion of Bakunin, but the assassination of Dimitri Olmanov, the most powerful man in the Confederacy, the Chief Executive of the TEC.

And—if he was to believe Kalin Green's implication—the man who was his father.

Even as he spoke, Jonah was forced to mentally revise his entire life up to this point.

"All I'm asking," Green said, oblivious to, or ignoring, his inner tumult, "is some concession that allows the SEEC to bow out of this mess with dignity."

Jonah shook his head, collecting his thoughts. He raised his head and looked Green in the eye, "If I make such a concession, will you let me go?"

"Eventually." There was some hesitation in Green's voice.

It was suddenly obvious that he had power here he had never even suspected. Even imprisoned, with no official status, Dimitri's progeny would be a diplomatic force.

Coldly, Jonah said, "You are waiting for a tach-comm from Bakunin—" one that Jonah suspected was already on route and would be here in less than six days standard, "—when you receive it, you have a ready-made Bakunin representative to go immediately before the Congress and sign the Charter on behalf of the military forces on Bakunin."

Green made an effort to appear impassive, but her diplomatic detachment wasn't quite working. Jonah could see discomfort leaking through the facade.

"You have no intention of releasing me before the military takeover is legitimized, correct?"

"Mr. Dacham, you have me in a difficult position."

"So you've said."

"I cannot unilaterally disband a five-year-old operation. We have troops in the field, we are operating jointly with another arm of the Confederacy. However embarrassing or dangerous holding you is, we can't allow you to interfere—"

"I don't see what you're here to negotiate, then."

"Bakunin's off the table, it's already happened. The SEEC is willing to deal on other issues, however."

Jonah shook his head. The competing feelings of incredible power and ultimate powerlessness crashed over him in alternating waves. "There are other issues?" he asked.

Green smiled. "Now, you know we cannot actively interfere with either of you—but we can make other arrangements to, for instance, help you deal with your brother."

Jonah just stared.

"Don't look so shocked. We are worried about Dimitri, but if we can assure not only his successor, but his successor's goodwill, we have a much wider window of action." Green smiled a little wider, "Also, Bakunin isn't *completely* off the table. It will, after all, be signed to the Charter under the SEEC's auspices. Klaus is currently slated to be governor, but such appointments could change. The administration on Cynos really doesn't care about the internal politics of Bakunin—all we want is the vote in the Congress."

Jonah leaned back.

"See," she said, "we have a lot to offer you in compensation for this unfortunate detainment."

Jonah nodded. He felt anger, but against who or what, he wasn't quite sure. He didn't trust himself to talk. "I have to think," he said.

"I expected you would," Green said. She smiled as if she had won.

Maybe she has, Jonah thought.

Green stood up and extended her hand, "I'll see you tom—"

Just then, the lights flickered. A comm unit somewhere on Green's belt began beeping, and outside the cell's thick walls Jonah could hear the forlorn wail of a klaxon.

"Goddamn," Green muttered, reaching for the comm unit.

Jonah upped the gain on his artificial ears and heard two things even through the walls of his cells. He heard people shouting, some in pain.

And he heard the animal growl of a large carnivore.

CHAPTER FORTY

Class Action

"Keep your eyes on the ball, and duck when someone swings a bat."
— *The Cynic's Book of Wisdom*

"In politics nothing is contemptible."
— BENJAMIN DISRAELI
(1804–1881)

Welcome to the end of the world as we know it, thought Robert Kaunda.

The air in his office was thick, hot, and dry. It was still heavy with the scent of the five nonhumans who had occupied it so recently. Kaunda felt oddly distant from it all, as if it were someone else here watching a terminal violation of every legal and diplomatic protocol . . .

Kaunda couldn't even participate directly. He had been a policeman, but that was a long time ago, and that training didn't equip someone for covert activity. So he and Hernandez were left in his office to watch a secure diplomatic holo. Through it they saw her five commandos assault the SEEC Embassy.

Through the tension—the potential of starting a war, the disregard of everything he was supposed to represent as a Congressional representative of the Confederacy—through all of it, he felt an odd sense of exhilaration. He was finally *doing* something, even by proxy. Just the fact that he was committed to action, however dangerous and risky, had a satisfaction to it—however bitter. He had left the realm of words and political maneuvering. He was beyond diplomacy and negotiation, activities he'd never been fully comfortable with.

If he were going to be brought down in disgrace, at least it wouldn't be for something he hadn't done.

On the holo he could see four members of the team running across the gardens between the Union grounds and the SEEC grounds. The soundless video feed was from Milne's visor, so Kaunda was watching the scene from the point of view of a three-and-a-half-meter-tall ursoid. The scene—monochrome with light enhancement—was apt to give someone motion sickness.

Anderson, the feline, was in the lead, her weapon sweeping the area in front of the charging squad.

The diplomatic identifiers on those jumpsuits might make them invisible to the automated security, Kaunda thought, *but God help any civilian who walks on stage at the wrong time.* It shouldn't happen; that was one of the many reason for making this a night mission. Even so, people did wander the diplomatic compound after midnight. Kaunda had done so himself. He hoped that any ambassadors who were out for air tonight were on the opposite side of the spire from them.

Fortunately, as he watched the squad dodging exotic trees, the only violence done was to the landscaping.

Soon, the squad was on the SEEC grounds. Their pace slackened considerably, and interference rippled across the holo's display as Milne's personal field activated. The five paused on top of a ridge overlooking the Sirius-Eridani compound. From Milne's view, even when the bear was flattened to the ground, the whole south end of the main building was visible.

Kaunda had been there before, and recognized the Islamic arches and the blue mosaic tile as the Eridani end of the embassy. In there were the facilities for the Khamsin Embassy, as well as offices for Paschal and Thubohu, which had buildings of their own elsewhere on the grounds. The Cynos Embassy was housed in the northern wing of the building; the dual capitals' embassies were connected by a single corridor large enough to make the complex effectively one building.

Kaunda thought, at first, that the squad was going to circle to the north. But instead, Foster, one of the canines, the gray-furred one, darted across the gap between the

rise and one of the smaller Islamic arches. Kaunda remembered Foster as the one with the electronic gear.

For a few long seconds, nothing happened.

Then the canine waved. One by one, Anderson, the feline leader, waved the squad across the lawn. Milne was
second to last, so Kaunda didn't see Anderson cross. He
did, however, see what Foster had done at the arch. Part
of the tile mosaic inside the arch had melted, revealing a
conduit filled with sheathed optical cable. Two cables had
been severed. The top ends now fed into a foreign-
looking box, the bottom ends dangled out of the hole,
darkened even to the light enhancement.

Then Anderson was there and the squad was entering
the embassy through a frozen emergency door. Now all
the weapons were out, not just Anderson's. Kaunda felt
his own pulse quicken.

The squad ran through corridors emptied for the night,
and for a brief moment Kaunda held out the hope that no
one would interrupt the squad on the way to its goal.

Then Anderson stopped at a corner.

She waved the brown canine, Brin, over and held up a
single clawed finger. Brin nodded, and Kaunda saw his
tongue lolling. He put down his weapon, and in a disturbingly human gesture, wiped the back of his hand across
the front of his muzzle and flexed his hands. Black claws
shone at the end of his fingers.

Then, quicker than Kaunda could register, Brin dove
around the corner. In less than five seconds, he was back
to pick up his weapon. There was blood on his muzzle.

As the squad turned the corner, Kaunda saw the first
casualty of this operation. A uniformed man was
sprawled in a niche, blood soaking into the prayer rug he
was sprawled upon. Most of his throat was gone. There
was too much blood to tell if the uniform was that of a
guard, or whether this man was just a visiting officer.

Kaunda watched as the squad of nonhuman commandos rushed through corridors too fast for Kaunda to maintain his bearings. Twice, the gray-furred canine, Foster,
manipulated the electronics of a secure door to let the
squad through. The squad descended one level at least,
maybe more.

Kaunda only knew when they had crossed into the Sirius half of the consulate because that was when the holo erupted into chaos.

It was in a darkened corridor like all the others. Anderson was leading her squad at a running pace. Suddenly, everyone drew weapons and bunched into a group. The view out Milne's holo stopped being of the other squad members, and began to cover the corridor to the right and to the rear.

Kaunda couldn't hear it, but he knew that an alarm had been tripped somewhere.

He only had a fraction of a second to realize that, because the holo began shaking and jerking backward down the corridor. Flashes began scoring the edges of the holo, just beyond the immediate view.

Sirius troops were suddenly everywhere. Not embassy security, but military troops. Kaunda could see the blue binary insignia on their gray uniforms. Anderson's team was being ambushed by a unit of the Cynos defense forces.

In the jerking holo view, Kaunda saw at least five troops rushing Milne's position. Then the holo went rainbow with interference from multiple defense screens soaking multiple laser hits. Through the interference, Kaunda could see the track of Milne's weapon cutting a swath through the corridor with his laser. A shimmering slice of polychrome burned itself a light-trail even through the interference.

The interference broke for a moment. The corridor was hazed with smoke, the walls charred with laser-fire. One of the Sirius troops was rushing Milne.

Milne didn't even fire his weapon. A brown-furred arm—an arm as thick as both of Kaunda's thighs put together—swept out from the right of the display, arced across the screen, and backhanded the soldier in the head and neck.

The soldier left the ground and slammed into the far wall. When he fell to the ground, he wasn't moving.

The holo darted over the scars of the battle. All the nonhumans were still standing. Anderson had the marks of a hit on her shoulder, and the rat-creature, Orwell, no longer had a weapon. One of his hairless hands was ragged and bloody. As Orwell was framed by the holo, Kaunda saw him unholster a projectile weapon and kick a twisted heap at his feet that must have been his laser.

The rest of the squad appeared unhurt.

There looked to be nearly a dozen dead and wounded humans littering the corridor, all wearing the uniform of the SEEC's professional army.

Kaunda looked at Hernandez, who'd been watching the holo feed as intently as he'd been. She had a feline expression that Kaunda interpreted as a grim smile.

"Humans engineered our ancestors for combat," Hernandez said by way of explanation.

Kaunda shuddered and turned back to view the holo where the squad was moving again.

"The regular army," Hernandez said, "that's a good sign. That means he's still being held there."

Kaunda nodded, hoping he wouldn't get the chance to see a *bad* sign.

In due course, he saw one. On the holo, Kaunda saw a squad of four SEEC troops in powered armor. They had plasma weapons cabled to their backpacks.

The black polyceram suits were barely able to fit two abreast in the corridor, wide as it was. They were almost as large as Milne. The nonhumans didn't have a chance. . . .

CHAPTER FORTY-ONE

Hostage Negotiation

"Successful politics consists of allowing everyone to share your enemies."
—*The Cynic's Book of Wisdom*

"The only justification of rebellion is success."
—THOMAS B. REED
(1839–1902)

"Who the hell are they?" Green was yelling to someone on her comm unit. Jonah could listen to the response from the other end, but he was concentrating his audio enhancements on the chaos brewing outside.

He could guess who the hell "they" were. He had been negotiating with Francesca Hernandez, who at the time was the only delegate from the Seven Worlds on the planet. From the sound of the growls outside, her long-awaited superiors from Tau Ceti had arrived, and had approved some drastic action.

"Damn it," Green said in the background, "It was supposed to be safe here. You're the *army*, secure the place—"

Outside there was a very human scream, then for a long moment, there was silence.

Jonah turned toward Green, who had paled noticeably. She was nodding to the voices in her earpiece. Jonah caught her eye and she looked disturbed.

"This is unprecedented, this is an embassy—"

"Everything about this is unprecedented," Jonah said, "And from where I'm standing it more resembles a prison."

Klaxons sounded in the distance, and Jonah turned his gaze back to where the door would be, if he could see it.

"You know they won't make it down here. We have an entire company of the Cynos Defense Force here."

"That's a barracks, not an embassy," Jonah said, "Where were you going to attack?"

"With you here, we needed the extra security."

Jonah slowly turned around. "Am I that dangerous?"

"No," Green said, "you're that valuable."

Above them, there was a rumble followed by an explosion that cracked the roof and threw both of them to the floor. Jonah tried to break his fall with his metal hand. His hand hit the seat of the toilet and the plastic gave way.

Silence returned.

Before Jonah could push himself to his feet, he heard Green say, "What the fuck was that?"

Jonah knew, he had heard the sound before. He had heard it from fifty meters away and through the multiple hulls of the *Blood-Tide,* the last time he had set foot on the grounds of Godwin Arms. This had been much closer, but to him—even after nine years—the sound was unmistakable.

He pushed himself upright.

"Anyone here armed with plasma weapons?"

Green just looked at him.

"That was a plasma explosion. The sound has a—" Jonah tried to think of the right word, "—resonance."

Green was pulling herself to her feet, "Who's insane enough to use a plasma weapon indoors?"

"Who's insane enough to attack the embassy of one of the most powerful arms of the Confederacy?" Jonah looked toward the door. "If they survived that maneuver, I'd say it was strategically sound."

"Is anyone there?" Green spoke into her comm. "Hello?"

After a pause, she said weakly, "Must be broken."

"Must be."

Jonah could feel Green's fear as an extra presence in the room. He wished he could empathize with her, but he had long ago passed beyond fear. He had borrowed so much time that death had little terror for him.

And he doubted the attackers were here to kill him.

"You wanted a deal," Jonah said.

Green was still trying to fix her comm.

"Do you want a deal?" Jonah said, with a voice only slightly stronger, slightly colder.

"What—" Green said.

"You want a promise of no reprisals?"

Green lowered her dead comm and nodded. As she did, the lights flickered. There was the faint odor of smoke in the air. Jonah looked at Green.

You're wondering, "What's gone wrong?" Jonah thought. *You were convinced you knew what was going on. You convinced yourself that you were in control of the situation.*

Jonah knew from repeated experience that it was the moment that you were most sure of yourself when the world was most likely to cave in on you.

Green was staring at him, and Jonah realized that he was smiling.

It hurt his cheeks, but they didn't twitch.

"What do you want?" Green asked.

"I want you to open the door to this cell."

Green opened her mouth.

"If we wait until the decision leaves your hands, I don't have to give you anything. But if you open the door, I promise that the SEEC will see no reprisals from me."

The silence was deep, and long. It was punctuated by sounds of sporadic fighting, coming closer. The smell of smoke was beginning to cling to the room.

"You know I can't do that," Green said.

Jonah shook his head. "No, I don't. But sometimes life is tough that way." He turned to face the approximate direction of the oncoming battle. "Are you going to try to spirit me off to safety?"

"We're safe here." She put the emphasis on the pronoun, and she didn't sound convinced.

"There's nowhere to run, is there? No back door?" Jonah waited for an answer. When he didn't hear one, he

knocked on the wall in front of him. It made a hollow
sound. "Have you thought that this might not be a rescue
mission?"

"What do you mean?"

"You know I was talking to the Seven Worlds about
Bakunin."

"Yes—"

"You've assumed that it was simply about the political
fate of Bakunin." Jonah thought about all the nonques-
tioning he'd experienced. The Sirians had known who he
was—better than he did, in fact. They knew that he was
here to sign the Charter. They knew that he'd been negotiating with Hernandez—

But they had no idea about the substance of those ne-
gotiations. They had no idea of the artifacts under the
Diderot Mountains, or their value.

"Do you have any idea what would prompt the Seven
Worlds into such blatant intervention in the other arms of
the Confederacy?"

"We know they're working with Indi, and with you
involved—"

Jonah shook his head. "Centauri didn't know who I
was, and they had agents on the ground on Bakunin—"
Jonah thought about Kelly. For the first time he wondered
what happened to the "real" Michael Kelly, before he was
replaced by Random Walk's construct. The Kelly that Jonah had seen was one-fifth of Random Walk, according to
the AI's own testimony. With the loss of Random on the
Shaftsbury, that left Mosasa and the part of Random that
was hooked to the computer net in the remains of
Dominic Magnus' mountain headquarters.

Jonah wondered about Random Walk number five.

"Indi pushed them to this," Green told him. The tone
of her voice left no doubt about who she thought the vil-
lain was in this mess.

Jonah didn't turn around. He kept staring at the wall in
front of him. The battle didn't sound as if it were any
closer. If anything, it was the fire that was closing.

"Indi isn't involved in this."

"But—"

"If we wanted Indi domination of Bakunin, I could

have called on that armada they have in orbit. I was the one person of the so-called resistance with enough support to give that kind of intervention legitimacy. They have more than enough force in place to neutralize the ground forces, as well as your fleet—if they're stupid enough to intervene at that point."

"This isn't something that the nonhumans would do on their own," Green said.

Jonah actually chuckled. "That kind of condescension is why the Seven Worlds stay out of human politics. Not only is this their own operation, but I would place strong odds that they would prefer to see me dead, and your embassy a smoking ruin, before they'd see me in your hands."

There was a long pause. The sounds of battle had died and the smoke was denser.

"Why?"

"Information I have that they don't want you to have. The answers to questions you didn't know to ask." Jonah turned away from the wall and faced Green again. She had backed away from him and she was now leaning against the opposite wall. She looked as though she might be afraid of him.

"If you don't let me go," Jonah said, "this could trigger a war."

"They don't have the military—"

"They have Indi, which is looking for an excuse. As you said, they're allied."

Green stared at him.

"One prime seat in the Congress is not worth it." Jonah looked at Green and knew he had won. It didn't matter if the team attacking the embassy made it or not.

Slowly, Green pulled a small remote out of her pocket. She pressed a thumbpad and keyed in a combination. The invisible door opened, releasing a pall of smoke.

Behind watering eyes, Green said, "You are too much like your father."

"You're right," Jonah said, and stepped out into the smoke.

CHAPTER FORTY-TWO

International Incident

"No one gets to write their own eulogy."
—*The Cynic's Book of Wisdom*

"History is built on a pile of corpses."
—JEAN HONORÉ CHEVIOT
(2065–2128)

"My God," Kaunda said. On his desk, the holo that had been feeding the video of Hernandez's assault team had gone dead right after the explosion. The last thing Kaunda had seen from it was a plasma explosion engulfing the trio of armored soldiers. He didn't know if that meant that the ursoid was caught in the blast, or if it was merely some interference.

Either way, the holo was gone.

After a while, Kaunda said, "I can't believe they're insane enough to use plasma weapons in—"

"Not plasma," Hernandez said. "Not theirs."

"What are you talking about? I didn't pack anything like that."

Hernandez reached over with an extended claw and switched off the holo. "The team had some of their own arrangements."

"How the hell could you get a plasma rifle past security?"

Hernandez shook her head. Her stare was alien, through her slitted eyes. "Not plasma. Hydrogen AM grenades."

"You—" Kaunda was speechless for a moment. Antimatter rarely showed as weapons material on standard scans; nothing to show that an AM grenade held the most powerful explosive known to man—until something blew the containment.

Few military minds ever considered bringing antimatter into a combat situation, where so much could go wrong. It was for missiles, and terrorists.

"You," Kaunda began again, "You did—I didn't agree to that. Are you trying to destroy the SEEC consulate?" Inside, Kaunda was already cursing his own naiveté.

"If," Hernandez said, "we no longer have the option of retrieving Jonah Dacham alive."

"Are you trying to start a war?"

"You point out that Indi is making war inevitable. If there is a war, it is best that Bakunin fall to our side—"

Kaunda put his face in his hands. Hernandez had sealed his fate. His part in this was going to get his head handed to him, probably by Dimitri himself. He was responsible for bringing a bloodbath right to the foot of the Congress.

He wondered if the Seven Worlds would grant him political asylum.

After a long time, during which the holo refused to re-activate, the computer called on Kaunda's comm. It buzzed for attention a few times. Kaunda looked at Hernandez, decided it didn't matter, and reached to the comm on the desk, opposite the nonworking holo.

"Kaunda," he said to the comm.

"A gentleman here to see you, sir," said the computer over the comm.

"May be Dimitri himself," Kaunda said.

"He says he wishes to talk to Francesca Hernandez as well," continued the computer.

"Let him in," Kaunda told the computer without looking at Hernandez. He was ready for it to end here.

He was expecting Dimitri, or a squad of Sirian military. What he wasn't expecting was the man who walked into his office, a man with olive skin, brown eyes, and a metallic right hand.

For once, Kaunda saw a perfectly interpretable expression on Hernandez's face—surprise.

"I thought you were expecting me," said Jonah Dacham.

Hernandez regained her inscrutable feline composure and asked, "What about the team that went in after you?"

Jonah, who had been showing a weak smile, lost all the expression on his face. He sat down on a free chair and drummed the arm with metallic fingers. "All lost, I expect. I ran across a black-furred rodent and tried to help him out, but he was too badly injured. He died before I got him twenty meters. He told me where you were waiting, though."

"What happened in there?" Kaunda asked.

"Five people against an army? A bloodbath," Jonah Dacham said. "No contest. The plasma weapons didn't help."

"Not plasma—" Francesca began.

"They were setting off AM grenades in there," Kaunda said.

Jonah Dacham stared at Francesca for a long time before he spoke. "You didn't expect to take me out of there, did you?"

Hernandez's silence spoke volumes. Kaunda felt duped. "And how *did* you get out of there?" Kaunda asked.

"I negotiated a settlement with the Sirians."

Hernandez actually hissed.

Jonah shook his head in the cat's direction. "I haven't compromised my agreements with the Seven Worlds. The Sirians never even *asked* me about Dolbrians." The man's lack of expression was eerie. Kaunda would've expected more emotion from a man who had just walked out of captivity and a war zone. "What I promised Kalin Green," he continued, "was that I would not retaliate against the SEEC."

"What?" asked Hernandez, her voice more the alien rumble than Kaunda had heard it before.

"I promised no retaliation from the TEC."

Kaunda shook his head. "What the hell does that mean? Why would they let you go and lose their chance at Bakunin for a promise like that?"

"Do you know who I am?" Jonah asked. In someone else's mouth those words would sound pompous, or threatening. In Jonah Dacham's mouth the words were as dry and lifeless as a request for the time.

"You are Jonah Dacham," said Hernandez. "You served the Executive Command from '25 to '35. Retired—or deserted—after a solo mission to Sigma Draconis. Arms dealer with the SEEC for the following five years before you were supposedly killed as a result of a TEC operation. For the last fifteen years you've been an arms manufacturer on the planet Bakunin under the alias Dominic Magnus, up until the start of Operation Rasputin."

Jonah nodded a lot. And, while Kaunda had known all this information from his own sources, he was impressed. Hernandez had good information for someone representing an arm that allegedly had no intelligence operations outside its own borders.

"I'm sure you have quite an extensive biography of me by now. But there's one thing even I didn't know. Not until Green told me."

"That is?" Hernandez asked.

"My father." Jonah said.

Kaunda felt exasperated, "What has that got to do with anything?" Kaunda knew that Jonah Dacham and his brother Klaus were both born to a single mother on Waldgrave. Not a great place for people of unknown paternity. But, as much as the information might mean to Jonah, Kaunda couldn't see its relevance.

"Who?" Hernandez asked, betraying nothing about how she felt the conversation was going.

"Dimitri."

"*The* Dimitri?" Kaunda said before he could stop himself.

Jonah nodded.

The next day, Robert Kaunda witnessed one of the most bizarre sessions of the Terran Congress he had ever heard of. First of all, the entire delegation from the Seven Worlds was there, all seven representatives. It was the first time that had happened in the history of the Confederacy.

Second, out of the fourteen voting seats for the SEEC,

only one representative was present. Kalin Green sat at the head of an empty wedge of the auditorium much as Francesca Hernandez had sat during the opening of the Congress—alone, and looking as if she'd be happier on her home planet right now.

The Centauri delegation was a shambles before anything was even brought to the floor. Arguments within the group overwhelmed the translation computers. Most of the Centauri Alliance seemed to want words with Pearce Adams, the senior member. He, like Green, looked as though he wanted to be elsewhere.

Over by the Indi delegation, for once Sim Vashniya didn't look serene and inscrutable. He actually looked annoyed.

The only people oblivious to the changes wrought in this room were Kaunda's own Union delegation. Even here, where he sat, there was one temporary change. Thomas Jakati, the representative of Errabu—after the political maneuverings at this Congress—found himself holding the Union's second prime seat. Kaunda had convinced Jakati and the one other Union representative with a vote to give him their proxies for this one session.

The planetary promotions had already gone as Vashniya had planned. In the five weeks since the opening of the Congress, the status of member planets had been the sole issue of debate. The traditional process promoted planets through the labyrinthine levels of Congressional status step by step. That tradition was the first procedural casualty. Through the chaotic debate, and the votes following, the trio of Indi-Union-Seven Worlds had surpassed the combined force of Sirius and Centauri when it came to a straight vote. The rolls currently stood at 31 to 29. Prime seats now stood at 27 apiece. For the first time in Confederacy history the combined power of Sirius and Centauri had no majority in the Confederacy legislature. Indi had twenty voting seats now; all but one had Prime status.

Now, Bakunin was going to add itself to an already volatile mixture. Kaunda watched the whole debate with a detached air. If a fistfight broke out on the floor between Vashniya and Adams, he wouldn't be surprised.

Hernandez had thrown her bombshell onto the Congressional floor as the first order of business, and representatives had been shouting at each other ever since. Or, to be more precise, Indi representatives had been shouting at Centauri representatives, the Centauri representatives had been shouting at Adams, and Adams had simply been shouting at the room at large.

Once the Bakunin issue hit the floor, the outcome was a foregone conclusion. That didn't stop the debate. Questions were raised about the legitimacy of Bakunin's government—or lack thereof. There were procedural questions about taking the planet on out of normal order—a futile argument since so many formalities had been dismissed for planets on all sides. There was one question raised about the legality of the Bakunin representative.

Kalin Green, herself, answered that question by informing the floor who the Bakunin representative was. That threw the Centauri delegation into accelerated chaos that Dimitri Olmanov, manning the podium, took a long time to gavel down.

Jonah Dacham has managed quite a homecoming for himself, Kaunda thought.

In the end it came down to a formal straight vote. The fact that admission was granted was little surprise, especially with the entire SEEC, in the person of Kalin Green, abstaining.

As soon as the vote was confirmed by the computer in front of Dimitri, two pairs of ushers entered the hall from opposite sides of the room. One pair escorted Jonah Dacham, who was wearing formal attire and had a bearing to rival any diplomat in this room.

The other pair of ushers, accompanied by TEC guards, carried an archaic leather-bound tome nearly a meter on a side. The Charter.

Hernandez walked down to the front of the room and was joined there by Dimitri. The charter was placed awkwardly on a table usually used by clerks for the various representatives.

In the space of a few minutes, with none of the traditional ceremony, Jonah Dacham signed on behalf of

Bakunin, Francesca Hernandez signed on behalf of the
Seven Worlds, and Dimitri Olmanov signed on behalf of
the Confederacy. The political landscape of the Confederacy changed in that moment.

Perhaps irrevocably, Kaunda thought.

The planet Bakunin was now a member of the Confederacy, a human planet in the Seven—now Eight—Worlds.
After the Charter was signed, the vote promoting Bakunin
to prime status was almost perfunctory.

It was over. Vashniya had what he had always wanted:
The Europeans had finally lost their primacy. It was the
People's Protectorate of Epsilon Indi that now held a veto
on almost everything the Confederacy did from this point
forward, even if Bakunin was a prime seat for the Seven
Worlds and not the Protectorate. Indi now had more
power than Vashniya'd know what to do with.

Kaunda closed his eyes. The Union was *still* the smallest arm of the Confederacy, nothing had changed that.
Kaunda felt little difference between a Confederacy dominated by Centauri and Sirius, and one dominated by Indi.

"Who knows, though?" Kaunda muttered to himself in
his native language. "In a hundred years it may be *us.*"

"Pardon?" said the youngish representative from Po-
sada. The man may have fought to hold the nonvoting
seat of his planet simply for the free trip to Earth.

Kaunda turned to his fellow Union member and said,
"Just thinking of the future."

The future is buried on Bakunin, Kaunda thought.
Under the mountains called the Diderot Range.

CHAPTER FORTY-THREE

Old Boy Network

"Tyrants spring from chaos, and to chaos they eventually return."

—*The Cynic's Book of Wisdom*

"Who overcomes by force hath overcome but half his foe."

—JOHN MILTON
(1608–1674)

Seeing the Terran Congress was surreal to Jonah Dacham. After so long, being the focus of human attention was so unnerving it forced him to withdraw completely into himself. No ceremony, no speeches, words were for the representatives. Words which were, by now, pointless.

Then, when the debate was over, he was called into the chamber to sign the Charter. Halfway into the Congressional chamber, as he walked in the aisle between the lone form of Kalin Green and the inhuman Seven Worlds delegation, Jonah lost track of the crowd.

At the focus of the room, framed between the flags, was Dimitri Olmanov, waiting for him. Jonah's awareness of the signing ceremony was lost; being this close to the Old Man of the TEC burned the significance out of every other event.

Dimitri's signature would go right next to his and Hernandez's. As President of the Congress and the Chief Executive of the TEC, it was his signature on the archaic leather-bound Charter as much as Jonah's and Hernandez's that would make Bakunin a protected part of the Confederacy. Dimitri's power was such that he had a veto over the whole event, no matter how the vote had gone in the Congress.

Dimitri, for the first time in Jonah's memory, was showing his age. He stooped beneath the crushing weight of years. When Dimitri stood, it was with both hands clutching the head of a cane. The mane of well-kept white hair had thinned to near-invisibility. Dimitri's dark, wrinkled skin reminded Jonah of the landscape of Mars.

Dimitri's eyes were different. When the old man's gaze locked on his own it was as if Jonah had grabbed a high-tension line. It wasn't just the cold omnipotence behind the gaze. It was the shock of recognition. When he looked into Dimitri's eyes, he could see his brother's face. . . .

As well as his own.

When he finally came to the Charter, he hesitated. What name should he sign? After an interminable second that was only perceptible to him, he signed the name he had been born with: "Jonah Dacham."

The chaos following his signature was, if anything, worse than what had proceeded it. For the remainder of the session, one that went late into the night with acrimonious debate, it was Jonah who was the instigator.

In theory he had known what would happen, but he wasn't ready for the actuality. By signing the Charter, he—and the entire planet of Bakunin—had gone from being a pawn in Confederacy politics, to being one of the players.

Jonah had gone from being a loose cannon, a ghost in the cracks of the Confed bureaucracy, to being the representative of a prime seat in the Congress, a prime seat that suddenly held a swing vote.

He lost no time in wielding that power. His first official actions were to place on the floor formal demands that the TEC, the SEEC, and the Indi Protectorate all remove themselves from interference in Bakunin and Seven Worlds space.

That one act destroyed what little order the Congress had managed to retain. Especially provocative was his inclusion of the Indi Protectorate with the foreign forces to be withdrawn. It was Indi's alliance with the Seven

Worlds and the Union that had made the admission of
Bakunin possible on Jonah's terms. The request broke
Indi's carefully structured arrangement with the Seven
Worlds.

It became obvious where the power had really shifted.
The Confederacy had always been a power-struggle between the Indi Protectorate and the two powers of Sirius
and Centauri. Now, the large powers were forced to realize that the two smallest powers of the Confederacy had
the ability to decide any future contest between the great
ones.

It took hours of acrimonious debate for that fact to penetrate the arrogance of Indi and Centauri. Kalin Green,
the sole representative for Sirius during the session, had
seen enough of the power shift coming to step out of its
way. But the other two great powers found themselves in
the position of actually having to listen to, and accommodate, the Seven Worlds and the Union of Independent
Worlds.

In the ensuing fracas, first the TEC, and eventually all
the external aggressors, agreed to withdraw their forces.
At times, the rhetoric came close to the edge of a decla-
ration of war.

A long Congress, Jonah thought, *for everyone concerned.*

Late that night, long after the session was over, after
the representatives had dispersed to the four corners of
the diplomatic compound, the Confederacy spire was left
to its eternal population of bureaucrats, Jonah, and—
somewhere—Dimitri.

Jonah had abandoned the debate in the Congress as
soon as he could. But he couldn't leave the spire. For the
first time he was in the heart of the Confederacy's machinery. The kilometer-tall building was the axle on
which the whole destructive mechanism rotated. Dimitri
Olmanov was the one bolt holding the axle in place.

In a slow spiral—using the blank concrete stairs, not
the lift—Jonah descended into the depths of the spire,
where it rooted itself. Below the assembly hall and the
halls of politics and diplomacy, Jonah entered the world

of the executive branch of the Confederacy government. The descent was like penetrating the layers of an onion, through floors devoted to administrative function, then the police, the military, intelligence, covert operations.

Each layer more secretive, more paranoid, darker.

Every time Jonah stepped on to a new floor, he was confronted with a security check. He would pass by silent guards flanking the entrance, clothed in TEC dress blacks, and walk through a doorway constructed out of security sensors where the TEC's computers would scrutinize him.

He felt a tug inside at each gateway—every time it seemed that here would be the point where he would be turned aside, maybe even arrested.

It didn't happen.

At each point he was cleared to go deeper into the secure labyrinth of the Confederacy's covert heart. Only when he was deep under the secret levels, deeper than he had known the spire had gone, did the trips through security become more than perfunctory. That, it seemed, was only because of a continual search for weaponry. Apparently his cybernetics made it difficult on the sensors.

Then, almost too soon, he reached his destination.

He had walked down the spire's sublevels for nearly an hour. If the spire mirrored itself under the ground, then Jonah was near the penthouse of its negative twin.

The lift would have saved him over fifty minutes and dozens of security checks. But he had needed the time to prepare himself.

His journey finally brought him into a plush lobby dotted with original Dolbrian artifacts, one wall an original Dolbrian starmap showing about ten light-years of local space.

When he told the computer kiosk he wished to see Dimitri Olmanov, he wasn't surprised his request was granted.

When the door to Dimitri's office slid aside, Jonah's walk inside had the inevitability of a dream. The weight of the past, nine years on Mars, fifteen years on Bakunin, a decade in the TEC—each year was like a hook into his gut, pulling him forward.

Despite all his efforts, Jonah had never felt more like a machine than he did at that moment.

Dimitri's office was spartan. Without the vast desk it could have been a cell in a monastery, or a crypt underneath one. There were niches in the walls for holo displays, but they were all deactivated, leaving the walls bare. The room was occupied by Dimitri Olmanov and the ubiquitous barely human bodyguard, Ambrose.

Dimitri didn't look good. His skin was pale and spotted, his body shriveled into two-thirds of the volume that Jonah remembered him filling. His hands were twisted, and his shirt hung on him too loosely.

However long you live, Jonah thought, *no matter how they prolong life, most aging happens in the last year.* Confed medicine had done all it could to delay the inevitable. The creature before him was over a hundred and sixty years old, and had nearly as much machinery in him as Jonah, or Ambrose.

"Have a seat, Jonah," Dimitri said. His voice was one of the few things age hadn't ravaged. That and his eyes. "I've waited a long time for this meeting."

Jonah remained standing.

"Ah," Dimitri said, "independence is a valuable thing, isn't it, Ambrose?"

"If you say so, sir," Ambrose responded. The bodyguard's voice held no inflection or emphasis—it was utterly removed from the stress Jonah could feel in the room.

Dimitri chuckled, "As if he would know." He turned to face Jonah. "I suppose you have a question or two."

The offhand way Dimitri said that infuriated Jonah, finally breaking through his paralysis in the face of the office. *"Questions? What kind of game have you been playing with me?"* Jonah clenched his fists and waited for a reaction from Dimitri. When none was immediately forthcoming, Jonah asked, "Is Kalin Green right about who I am?" It came out in a whisper.

Dimitri leaned back in his chair. "And who does she think you are?"

"That you are my . . ." Jonah's words dried in his mouth.

"It is difficult to keep a secret in the intelligence community. The Sirians knew you were important to me—that was impossible to hide with all the time you spent in SEEC space before Bakunin—I wasn't aware that they'd discovered *why* you were important. Age is catching up with me." Dimitri shook his head. "You've arrived none too soon."

Jonah backed up and found the previously offered seat. He sank into it as if he was facing execution. "How can you be my father?"

"Simply stated, Helen Dacham was once my wife—a long time ago. When she had another name . . ." Dimitri shook his head. "Though I always give her the name she died with."

"How?" Jonah repeated hollowly.

Dimitri continued speaking, his voice taking on a faraway note. "She was a gentle woman once. I'm afraid that her contact with me twisted her. She became hard, bitter. Predictably, she grew to hate me. When she discovered her pregnancy, she tried to escape me. For sixty years she succeeded."

Jonah looked up as Dimitri explained.

"She conducted a tour of at least five wormholes, gaining sixty years in a subjective month. She was still in her thirties while I was well past a hundred. When she landed on Waldgrave, she thought I'd have aged past any interest in her or our children. She hoped, by then, I'd be dead." Dimitri tilted his head, causing skull-like shadows to cloak his features. "She was wrong on both counts."

Jonah now understood why his mother had been so bitter, so lost. She'd not only given up wealth, and status, but she'd moved sixty years away from everything she knew—all to escape the man in front of him.

Dimitri told him exactly how deeply he'd been involved in the lives of Helen and her sons. Within a year of her settling on Waldgrave, the TEC intelligence services had tracked her down. Even though he had found her after a sixty-year absence, even though she'd just borne his children, Dimitri left her to support the twins on her own. He allowed the twins' paternity to remain unknown.

So the years dragged Helen down, and by their eighteenth birthday Dimitri had the TEÇ recruit both Klaus and Jonah.

"*Why?* For eighteen years you let us fester, why'd you step in at all?"

"This office I occupy has a privileged position," Dimitri said, apparently ignoring Jonah's question. "It is the most powerful office in the Confederacy, but it isn't even explicitly defined in the Charter. Did you realize that? The extraordinary latitude given to an office with no expressed limits." Dimitri's expression grew even more shadowed. "That unlimited authority has been necessary to hold the Confederacy together. It is this seat's power, and my willingness to use it, that has prevented this far-flung empire from crumbling into dozens of petty little States. We need our devils, Jonah. Something you should know by now."

Jonah looked into Dimitri's eyes. The forcefulness had left them, leaving Dimitri's gaze blank and soulless.

"I've held on this long because the Confederacy wouldn't survive without me, or someone fulfilling my function. The undocumented nature of my office made appointing my successor difficult. I've made my life the preservation of this Confederacy, and I can't allow my death to bring on a succession battle. The consequences would destroy—*everything*."

Jonah sat, voiceless, listening to Dimitri describe how he had come to be. Even before Dimitri had married, he had been secretly building the mechanism for empowering his successor. He programmed the software of the TEC bureaucracy to accept a very limited set of criteria to empower a new leader. The primary criteria was something that would make unwarranted claims impossible— short of some heretical technologies.

It was genetic.

"You bred her like an animal," Jonah said.

"Be realistic. That's what marriage is. Besides, my heir has to be from a fully natural conception. I couldn't allow any accusation of genetic manipulation to taint his claim." Dimitri stood. "She was well compensated." His voice was far away. "If you study history, you'll see, by far, arranged marriages are the norm, not the exception."

Jonah's gut felt cold and twisted. He had known his life had been manipulated by this man, but his existence? He was born because of a political calculation? "Why her?"

"Breeding, health, family. Her name when we married was Marie. Marie Beauvoir—" Dimitri paused. "Maybe she wasn't healthy enough. Perhaps . . ."

"Perhaps what?"

Dimitri smiled. "Nothing, Jonah. Some pointless speculation. What matters is that you're here and—"

"Why did she run?"

Dimitri's smile left. "She didn't want to endure another abortion."

"What?" Jonah could barely believe his ears.

"Too much perfectionism. Because the baby had to have no taint of gene manipulation, every pregnancy was screened and evaluated. If the embryo didn't fit the criteria, it was terminated. There had to be only one heir. There couldn't be a dispute about the succession."

Dimitri leaned on the desk and, if possible, looked even older.

Questions boiled up in Jonah. Questions he was too afraid to ask. *Did we make the cut? How many of my siblings were terminated? If there could be only one heir, what about twins?*

"You're judging me, aren't you?" Dimitri asked. "You finally see the heart of the beast and you find it's black as the void. But it has to be that way. There has to be a monster at the bottom to keep the structure from collapsing. All your lives I've tried to teach you and Klaus to know that evil."

"When have you taught us anything?"

Dimitri fixed him with a shriveling gaze. "Every mission I ever assigned you, and every confrontation between you, has been to show you the blackness I wade through every day."

"You're serious? You . . . *Styx?*" Jonah felt the side of his face twitching, and his hands clutched the arms of his chair.

Dimitri nodded. "The one sin, above the others, that weighs on my soul. She didn't give me a choice."

Jonah slowly pushed himself upright.

"She tried to blackmail me by identifying you to enemies of mine. I couldn't allow that."

Jonah closed the gap between them and was standing centimeters from Dimitri, tensed like a cable. He waited for Ambrose to react, but nothing happened. Slowly, he asked, "Who killed her?"

"Some operative on Waldgrave. She wasn't on Styx. Your operation just gave the TEC a convenient place to 'assign' missing people to."

"Why did you let me believe I killed her?"

"To see the blackness," Dimitri said. "If her name hadn't been on the list, the other thirty-five thousand deaths would've been invisible to you."

Jonah stepped back, because the observation was too true. Up to that point he'd been a perfectly programmed little TEC soldier. Always acting, never thinking.

"Also," Dimitri continued, "As I said, there needs to be a single heir. I needed an elimination contest." Dimitri lowered himself back into his chair, abandoning the wide expanse of desk to Jonah. After wincing, as if in pain, he opened one of the desk drawers in front of him and withdrew a shiny antique sidearm. It was a chrome-plated slug thrower reminiscent of the gun Jonah had lost in Godwin so long ago.

Dimitri put the gun down on the desk between them and said, "You win."

For a long moment, it seemed the world had frozen in place. For a short eternity Jonah found himself staring at the gun.

"What the hell is this?" Jonah said. He could hear the edge of desperation in his own voice. He turned to look at Ambrose, but Dimitri's half-human bodyguard stood by impassively.

"He's programmed to protect the executive of the TEC, not necessarily my person. Isn't that right, Ambrose?"

"As you say, sir," Ambrose answered.

Jonah faced Dimitri again, a sick feeling growing in his

gut, along with a familiar icy chill. "What is this?" he repeated, his voice a harsh whisper.

"The changing of the guard. I've installed my chosen successor." Dimitri glanced at the gun and a calm seemed to come over the man. "I'm ready to answer for what I've done, in front of you and God—and Ambrose, of course."

Jonah lowered his gaze from Dimitri, to the gun. It sat on the otherwise empty desk like an offering on a pagan altar. Jonah's chromed hand had already begun reaching for it.

Dimitri continued talking, Jonah glanced up and saw that his eyes were closed. "There's no provision to prosecute someone in my position. There are no legal mechanism, no justice, for someone who has to operate outside the law."

There was a tiny click as Jonah's right hand touched the firearm, metal on metal.

How often have I dreamed of doing this? Jonah thought. *Isn't this what I came here to do?*

"I'm ready, my son."

Jonah stared at his metal hand. *It's all part of the machine.*

All of it was Dimitri's machine, the Confederacy, the TEC, the politics that chewed up Bakunin, his confrontation with Klaus, the death of his mother, his own birth. All of it was designed and set in motion by the man sitting in front of him. He *should* die.

All of this, everything, had been the merciless grinding of a soulless automaton. Everything up to this point had been as inevitable and as meaningless as the ticking of a clock.

The gun was in his hand. Chrome on chrome, metal on metal. The weapon looked like an extension of his arm. In front of him, Dimitri Olmanov sat, mute, eyes closed, awaiting his fate. The barrel of the gun was pointed directly at Dimitri's forehead.

His father's forehead.

His mother's forehead.

Everyone's forehead.

One bullet into that Machiavellian brain and Jonah would be at the controls of that vast Confederacy mechanism. He'd finally be in control of the machine that had been consuming him since he was born.

Why was he hesitating?

The gun was shaking in his hand, and his cheek was vibrating enough to heat his face. His natural-looking left hand had clenched hard enough to crush the pseudoflesh covering it. Jonah could feel his thin transparent blood leaking through his fingers to soak his leg.

The central illusion is that you control the machine, when you actually are only another gear in the mechanism turning out a predestined course.

Jonah tried to ease the shaking of his hand. He unclenched his left hand and brought it up to support his metal wrist. Under the stare of the gun, Dimitri sat, waiting.

He wants *this.*

Supported by both hands, the gun ceased shaking.

Am I a machine?

"NO! God help me, NO!"

Jonah dropped the gun, and it clattered to the desk. Dimitri's eyes shot open in the first expression of surprise that Jonah had ever seen on his face.

"To hell with your grand designs. To hell with the TEC and your rites of succession. And while you're at it, to hell with the whole damned Confederacy."

"You don't know what you're saying . . ."

Jonah looked down on Dimitri. The executive of the TEC no longer looked steely and powerful. He looked like a lost, senile old man.

"I know exactly what I'm saying. I don't want it, any of it."

"You have a duty to—"

Jonah just stared at Dimitri, who trailed off, apparently hearing the absurdity of his own words. With a note of rising tension in his voice, Dimitri said, "You can't want Klaus to have control of . . ."

"Klaus is probably not going to make it off of Bakunin alive. You know that as well as I do. When the tachcomm messages from today's session of Congress start to reach the planet, his army will collapse. In six days he'll face a planet of a billion heavily armed anarchists and about a million unpaid mercenaries. What does he have aside from a thousand TEC personnel and a hundred marines?"

Dimitri said nothing.

"And," Jonah continued, "I know of nothing surer to destroy the Confederacy than putting Klaus at its helm. Do you want a madman running things?"

In a whisper, maybe to himself, Dimitri said, "I tried with him, but he never . . ."

"That's why I'm here at all, isn't it? You've wanted to hand things over for a long time—and for fifteen years all you had to hand it to was Klaus."

Dimitri just nodded.

"Why the charade?" Jonah said slowly. "If you only wanted one heir, why not just kill one of us off? It *is* what you do."

"No! I couldn't . . ."

"Couldn't what?"

Dimitri shook his head. "You don't understand. After I ordered Helen's d—not my children, too."

Jonah stared at the old man. Dimitri's head hung over the desk, his back arched with age. He looked thoroughly beaten. "It had to be settled between you. Even if you were the one suited for the role. Even if it meant that Klaus had a chance to succeed me. I just couldn't—" Dimitri reached over and retrieved the gun from where it had fallen. He held it out to Jonah, palm up. "Please, you can end all of this."

An odd calm descended over Jonah as he shook his head. "No, Father. You've made me live with myself. I want to return the favor." Jonah turned to go.

"You can't just leave," Dimitri said.

"You want martyrdom? You're holding the gun."

Jonah walked to the door, half expecting a bullet in the back. But he didn't turn around, even at the commotion behind him. He was halfway through the door when he heard the gunshot. It was an effort to keep walking.

He was halfway across the Dolbrian-decorated lobby when he heard the door open again. This time he did turn. Standing in the doorway was Ambrose, Dimitri's cybernetic bodyguard, and in his hand was the gun, a thin blue trail of smoke emerging from the barrel.

"Sir," Ambrose said. "I've been waiting for you for a long time."

CHAPTER FORTY-FOUR

Military Adviser

"Surrender is always an option."
—*The Cynic's Book of Wisdom*

"The greatest of all evils is a weak government."
—BENJAMIN DISRAELI
(1804–1881)

It was about eighty Bakunin days after Shane had deserted the Occisis marines, sixty since she'd fired a plasma rifle at her former comrades, thirty since Hougland had died in the heart of the Dolbrian artifact, twenty since what was left of the *Shaftsbury* had floated off into the sky. It was three standard months that had become a lifetime—

A lifetime that was soon to end.

Shane advanced toward that conclusion in a dented civilian hovercraft she had liberated from the tunnels in Diderot. It had been jury-rigged for use in the tunnels, and had no canopy, and little instrumentation other than charge readouts and a speedometer.

She'd flown the thing out of the foothills on a dried-out riverbed, into a harsh nighttime wind. The machine only topped a hundred klicks per on a steep incline, though the biting wind made it seem much faster.

Her course was south, generally toward Godwin.

Zanzibar had tried to talk her out of leaving. Shane had deferred until their communication with the rest of Bakunin began to collapse. They had lost comm with Jefferson, then Godwin, and then the partially dismantled systems in the mountain began to fail.

When Zanzibar made the command decision to evacuate

the mountain, Shane had nothing left to hold her there. She had no stake in the corporation Zanzibar represented. That whole enterprise now seemed distant and irrelevant to her.

I have to remember that all this started because I had to save those people.

Shane wondered if her peers in the marines would take that into account when deciding her fate. She wondered if the fact she was turning herself in would prompt any mercy.

She decided she didn't care. What happened after she returned to the marines was of little consequence. There was a shadow over her, over what she had done. The only legitimate answer she had to counter her betrayals was to assent to the justice of the people she had betrayed. Whatever the result, it was the only penance that would mean anything.

The stars were out above her. Without any nearby lights, the sight was awesome, almost as if there weren't an atmosphere in the way. The band of the Milky Way bisected the sky above her, achingly reminiscent of the Dolbrian mural.

That was her one regret over this decision. She was unlikely to ever go into space again. The justice she'd face would be harsh, and delivered here, on Bakunin.

Random had said that she had a half-interest in that map . . .

What the hell did it mean anyway? She already knew she wouldn't give that information to any part of the Confederacy, even her own planet. Dom was supposed to use it as a bargaining chip when he got to Earth, and it looked unlikely that he'd survived that journey. It looked like the priceless artifact would fall into the hands of whoever controlled this planet in the end.

Shane doubted that the discoverers would receive anything for their trouble.

She sighed. There were worlds out there, a thousand Confederacies' worth of planets. Worlds that the Confederacy might not reach for hundreds of years. If only she could use that information herself . . .

Woods wrapped around the riverbed as she sped south.

The quiet was surreal. Even with the open canopy the only sounds were the hum of the fans and the rushing wind. It was the silence of a battle long over. It had been days since she had heard word of the war; she wondered if it could be over this early. That would surpass even Colonel Dacham's megalomaniacal expectations, but in her state of mind, she found the collapse of Bakunin easy to credit.

It was over.

As dawn began breaking, the woods started becoming familiar. She was closing on the site of the GA&A complex, headquarters for the invasion.

Just as she began to recognize the forested hills around her, smoke erupted from the back of the hovercraft. Shane knew it was a laser hit, probably from a sniper rifle with a beam too high-frequency to see. The hovercraft had no defensive screens, so one shot was enough to kill it.

Smoke and the smell of melting fuel cells choked off her view of the woods. The skirts of the machine plowed into the riverbed with a bone-jarring crunch. The hovercraft slid ten or twenty meters along the ground. It was only by God's grace that it didn't flip over and roll.

Shane heard a dull pop from behind her as heat rippled away from the back of the hovercraft. She released the seat harness and scrambled out of the burning machine. Fumes from the melting engine burned her eyes, and the thick black smoke choked off her breath. There were few moments when panic gripped her, when her memory brought images of the firepit where she'd been trapped in the belly of the *Blood-Tide*.

Fortunately, she was a soldier who'd been blooded in combat. Panic was something she was used to. The fear didn't confuse her, it just made her move a little bit faster.

She stumbled away from the hovercraft, and within a few steps she was out of the toxic smoke. Her throat felt on fire, her eyes watered, and her nose felt clogged with liquid soot, but she'd escaped otherwise unscathed.

She stumbled a few more meters, until her eyes cleared. Then she stopped.

Standing, only a few meters away, was a pair of Occisis marines in full powered armor. She didn't need to look to know that there was a third soldier behind her. The fact that she wasn't dead meant that they had orders to take prisoners, if possible.

Shane squinted to see the names on their helmets: Couglin and Fletcher. If the teams were still set up as she remembered, Corporal O'Keefe would be behind her.

She slowly raised her arms and placed them behind her head.

She glimpsed the faces behind the helmets turn to look at each other. She knew that there was a lot of coded radio chatter passing above her head.

Finally, Couglin, the sergeant, stepped up to her.

"Captain Shane?" came through the external speaker on his suit.

Shane nodded.

Welcome home, she thought.

The first surprise was that Corporal O'Keefe wasn't the third marine; it was a man named Thomas who, if Shane remembered correctly, wasn't even in the same company with Couglin and Fletcher. That gave Shane an uneasy feeling about the marines' casualty rate.

The second surprise was that they marched her directly away from the GA&A complex, where they should have been headquartered. Unless they were going to have her summarily executed in the woods—unlikely since they had taken her alive—that meant they were stationed out in the field here.

It made no sense to have a field station this close to Colonel Klaus' heavily defended stronghold.

Maybe they have a vehicle parked somewhere out here?

Daylight unfolded around her, highlighting the ocher and purple broccoli that was Bakunin's excuse for trees. The forest floor was carpeted with spherical husks that crunched like gravel underfoot. It was a long march, but by now her body was used to her new legs.

It gave her a chance to reflect on just how little of this planet she had seen, how little of any planet she had seen. She'd seen a dozen planets from orbit, made landfall on many of them. But there'd always been a mission to perform, she had never had a chance to see what was unique there. She had never had a chance to think about what she had seen.

The proximity of her fate, the possibility of being shot as a traitor when she reached the end of this walk, made her look at the trees. The trees felt peaceful.

Shane wondered if the Dolbrians lived under trees like these, or if these fibrous stalks had evolved here on their own long after the Dolbrians had left their enigmatic pyramid.

Either way, the trees were a beautifully intricate cluster of branching stalks, none thicker than her little finger, which massed at their base to form trunks two or three meters in diameter. Above her, circular leaves were frozen in various stages of development, from a flat circle of ocher at one extreme, to a spherical purple pod at the other. On every tree there were leaf pods in every stage of development, so what looked like a flat purple vista from a distance became vivid swirls of red, green, yellow, orange, and blue . . .

Maybe that's the message from the Dolbrians, why they left almost nothing of themselves, only the planets they'd rendered habitable. Maybe to them, this was what was valuable. Simply life.

Thinking that, and looking at these strange Bakunin trees, renewed her faith. God had made a universe grander and more beautiful than anyone could imagine. By comparison, the evils humanity brought with it were petty and insignificant. Even Random, with his demonic machinations, had a place in this vastness. Perhaps, now that she was to answer for what she'd done, there was room for some measure of forgiveness.

For the first time since she had departed for this planet, she felt some measure of peace.

Shane got her final surprise when they reached their destination. The marines had opened a full-blown field command post less than twenty klicks from GA&A. Just from the number of temporary buildings, Shane made an estimate that this place could house nearly eighty people.

At first, Shane thought it was a mercenary outpost.

Most of the vehicles deployed around the temporary buildings were colored the turquoise and black of the Proudhon Army, but as they led her through the perimeter, she walked close enough to one of the APCs to see that the Proudhon identifiers were painted over with the warrior-angel logo of Black Company.

Shane began to worry as they took her toward the command buildings. The marines had only landed two companies strong. From what she'd learned of Colonel Dacham's plans, mostly from Random listening to the invasion, the marines that'd taken GA&A were dispersed throughout the million-man mercenary army. Black Company, as an entity, shouldn't exist anymore.

But not only did Black Company exist, it was all here, and more so. Just looking at the setup here, and glancing at faces, she could tell that a substantial fraction of White Company was here as well.

Few people paid attention to her. Everyone here was busy; most of the troops she saw were prepping the vehicles, and some were dollying ordnance up to the larger ground attack craft.

She walked under the shade of an artificial canopy. Everything—structures and vehicles all—was covered by an antisatellite screen. A flat holo forest hung over the site, supported by a trio of spheres rotating on top of spidery antisurveillance towers.

Everything in orbit was controlled by the Confederacy or Colonel Dacham; why the countersurveillance measures? Running those towers had to take at least half the energy resources of this place, probably more . . .

By the time she reached the command shed, Shane thought they were readying for a major offensive. When they led her into the heart of the building, the tension in the air made that thought a certainty. The two marines flanked her on one side of the cramped comm room. The room was crowded with a half-dozen first and second lieutenants, each manning a different machine. Most seemed linked to various platoons; the exception was the man she recognized as Daniel Fitzpatrick, who was talking into a marine-issue orbital comm setup.

Fitzpatrick shifted and she noticed new insignia on his

uniform. He'd been promoted to captain since last she'd see him. *Better him than Murphy,* she thought.

"Yes, sir. I am quite aware of the situation," Fitzpatrick was saying into the comm. He was the only person here whose voice was raised. "But I would suggest you communicate to the Colonel that my orders do not give me a choice in this."

There was a pause. Fitzpatrick wore a headset so Shane couldn't hear the other's response, but she had a feeling that it wasn't Colonel Dacham Fitzpatrick was talking to.

"Listen, Major Speir, I could give a rat's ass who outranks whom here. The Colonel has his orders—"

There was a brief pause, and Fitzpatrick snorted.

"No, I'm not talking charges here. I am not talking court martial. I am not talking one of your little TEC sanctions. We're in a war zone, and anyone who interferes with my mission will be fired on with the full force available at my command. Got that! Am I unclear here? If someone so much as stands in our path, my troops have orders to leave a crater. Tell the Colonel that his time's up."

Fitzpatrick slammed a fist into the comm box, shutting it off. He ripped the headset off with his other hand. "Damn TEC Spooks. The Confederacy falls apart and all they can think of is covering their petty little asses—"

Sergeant Couglin cleared his throat. "Sir?" came through the tinny speaker.

Fitzpatrick lifted his head and looked at the squad who'd brought her in. "You're dismissed. Go to the ready area, I've already called in the perimeter guards."

"We're going to have to shoot our way in, sir?" asked Sergeant Couglin.

Fitzpatrick looked grave and nodded.

The trio of suited marines left. As they did, she heard one of them mutter, through the armor, "What a bloody mess."

There was a silence for a few beats as Fitzpatrick looked at her. "By all that's holy, Kathy. Why now?"

"I—"

He shook his head. "Forget it, I'm dealing with chaos here. The mission's collapsed."

Shane looked around at the command center. Everyone else ignored her, they were intent on the comm units in front of them. She read in their faces an intensity she'd only seen in combat. The officers in the room here weren't really here, they were out there, with their platoons. "What's happening?"

"Hell. Hell's what's happening. Bakunin's part of the Seven Worlds now."

Dom did it. Shane was shocked into silence.

"I don't understand it either—but everyone's evaccing from orbit. The payment of the local mercenaries has dried up. And we have orders from Occisis taking us out from under the TEC and ordering us to take possession of the *Blood-Tide* and leave Seven Worlds space immediately."

"Oh, my God, Colonel Dacham—"

"Won't budge. Much as I'd like to deal with you. I have more pressing concerns . . ."

This wasn't going quite as Shane expected. "What do I do then?"

Fitzpatrick looked frazzled for a moment. "Fuck, I can't let you go." After a moment, "Okay, soldier, pending a court-martial for desertion—assuming we all survive the next thirty-two hours—I am reducing you to corporal and remanding you to service under Sergeant Couglin. He found you, he can deal with you. His squad's a man short anyway."

"Uh—yes, sir." Shane saluted her new superior. Even with the new arm, the gesture was almost reflex.

"He'll suit you up, but don't expect much. We aren't well equipped. You're dismissed, Corporal."

Shane turned to go. As she did, she heard Fitzpatrick say, "And tell Couglin that he has my orders to shoot you if you step out of line."

CHAPTER FORTY-FIVE

New World Order

"A State rots from the bottom up."
—*The Cynic's Book of Wisdom*

"We are condemned to be free."
—SYLVIA HARPER
(2008–2081)

The bastards had handed over the city without telling her. After spending a month in the hospital, most of that unconscious in intensive care, the least they could have done was tell her. Unfortunately none of her doctors thought to mention the little fact that the Jeffersonian government had changed hands. So Tetsami wasn't aware that the Jeffersonians had lost the war until she walked out the front doors of the hospital and saw a hovertank in the courtyard.

"Jesus Hopalong Christ."

Tetsami stood there in the doorway to the hospital, staring at the turquoise and black hunk of floating artillery. A handful of mercenaries stood around it, all of them wearing Proudhon badges of one sort or another. Looking at them, all Tetsami could think of was, *They've all showered, shaved—been here a while.*

"Hey, baby—wanna go for a ride?" One of them slapped the side of the tank.

"No harassing the civilians, schmuck," said another one.

"I'm not harassing her," the first one said as Tetsami started walking away, "am I, baby?"

Tetsami clutched her stomach and started walking toward the hotel. Jefferson City had changed while she slept. The streets were no longer deserted. People, even children, were out under Kropotkin's light. Shops, bars, and restaurants were all open. An air of forced normalcy pervaded the geometric streets.

The veneer of calm could not disguise the fact that an occupation had occurred while Tetsami slept. Proudhon APCs, fully manned and armed, guarded every intersection. A mobile artillery piece had been stationed on a spot of parkland next to a statue bearing the legend, "Liberty or Death." And, she could see down one of the radial streets, the burned-out wreckage of Washington Hall.

At least they didn't crush the place like they did the communes.

The hotel was a mess. Tetsami could tell, even before she entered the lobby, that the place was seriously overcapacity. The lawn and landscaping around it had been trampled into a muddy no-man's land. Military vehicles of every stripe crowded in on all sides, ignoring the defined parking lot to huddle as close to the hotel as possible.

What had been recreational areas were now given over wholly to Proudhon, and Tetsami could see the masts of field comm units poking up from behind the supply trucks that blocked her view. Armed guards marched around the perimeter and on top of the trucks ...

Tetsami walked up to the lobby doors, and a Proudhon merc stepped up and blocked her progress. "Sorry, madam, I can't let you in unless you have business in there."

Tetsami sighed. She wanted to rant, shout some nasty stream of invective at this guy, but the fight had long since drained out of her. She was too physically and emotionally weak to maintain any level of anger. "Last I knew, I had a room here," Tetsami said. She was resigned to the fact that she had lost her lodging to the invaders.

She was turning, about to leave, when the soldier said, "Hold on, I didn't recognize you." He pulled out a small sheet of cyberplas and began scanning it. "Your name? Room number?"

Tetsami stood, dumbfounded.

"Madam?"

"I registered under an account number, room 325."

The soldier nodded. "The number?"

Tetsami gave the man the account she'd used. Was Proudhon—Klaus—still looking for her? Did she matter to them anymore? She'd just been a way to reach Dom, and Dom was gone now in one sense or another . . .

"Sorry for stopping you, madam. Just security."

Tetsami nodded and walked toward the lobby doors. As she passed the soldier, he said, "Check at the desk. They had to move your room."

She shrugged as the soldier nodded to a guard inside the lobby, who opened the doors for her.

Welcome to merc central, Tetsami thought as she walked into the lobby. The hotel was filled with them, the lobby was standing room only. Every step she took felt more surreal—

Why did they leave me alone in the hospital? Me, Gavadi, and Jarvis? We were important to them at one point.

She tried to tell herself that they thought everyone was destroyed with the *Shaftsbury*, but she knew that wasn't so. Marc Baetez had been the *Shaftsbury*'s navigator, and he'd got a message off. Klaus and Proudhon *knew* people had survived the wreck—

She stopped at the front desk. "They told me you moved my room?"

The man behind the desk never even looked up. "Registration," he said, sounding flustered.

Tetsami gave him her account number.

"You've been moved to room 012. Your luggage is there, your messages are on the comm, your account's been credited for the difference, here's your key, next."

Tetsami took the key card just in time to be pushed aside by a youngish merc with a duffel bag. Tetsami didn't stick around to hear their conversation.

Room 012 was in the basement. It was smaller than her accommodations in the *Lady*, the ATV Jarvis had sold her. It didn't even have its own bathroom; she shared a shower and a john with four other rooms.

But they had moved her luggage here, and the place had a bed and a comm unit. After everything she'd been through she really couldn't complain.

The message light on her comm was blinking. She turned the unit on. The first message was over a month old, from Ivor. "I'm sorry. I don't want to run your life for you. Whatever it is you want, I'll support your decision—"

Tetsami placed her head in her hands and silently cried.

There was another message, from Dom.

"I'm sorry I said what I did, in the way that I did. I care for you. I care enough to worry about the pain a relationship with me will cause you. Whatever you feel, whatever I feel, we're fooling ourselves . . ."

"Fuck you, Dom," Tetsami whispered.

". . . we'll be pulled apart by what's happening, one of us might die, we can't pretend otherwise. Anything we have would be self-destructive if we don't accept that." Dom sighed. There was a pause, and Tetsami looked up to see Dom's face. He was rubbing one of his cheeks.

"I'm not good at this," Dom said. "I've avoided emotion all my life. So whatever happens, it isn't your fault. It's selfish and unkind, but I can't accept the thought of losing you— Damnation, this isn't making any sense. I'll call back later."

Dom did, five times, most of them no more than, "Call me."

Tetsami wiped the tears from her cheeks and said, "Evil bastard. You *are* human."

Jarvis called her within the hour. She was surprised to hear from him, slightly less surprised that he asked her to meet him in one of the parks surrounding Jefferson's central mall.

She met him next to a bronze equestrian statue. At first she thought he was sitting on a bench overlooking the reflecting pool, but as she closed on him she realized that he was sitting in a motorized wheelchair.

"Jarvis?" she asked.

He nodded and waved at the bench he was parked next to. "Have a seat."

Tetsami sat next to him.

"Nice to see you up and about," he said.

"Nice to be up and about."

Jarvis kept looking out over the pool, which mirrored a molten Kropotkin sunset. All the marble in the city had turned a glowing orange. *For once it doesn't look tacky,* Tetsami thought.

"Gavadi didn't make it," he said.

"Oh. I'm sorry to hear it."

Jarvis shrugged. "Some infection they couldn't control. They aren't very well equipped here for that kind of trauma." Jarvis looked down at his chair. "I'm shipping out tomorrow to a decent hospital to get my damn spine fixed."

"There's civilian traffic between cities now?"

Jarvis shook his head. "Not really. I just have a lot of friends in the mercenary community—" Jarvis looked at her. "A *lot* of friends."

Tetsami began to understand why she had not been taken prisoner by Proudhon, why the invaders had left her and Jarvis alone this time. She held out her hand. "Thank you."

Jarvis took it. "The very least for someone who dug me out of that wreck. Just don't do anything stupid, like give someone your real name."

Tetsami sighed and looked up at the reddening clouds. "When do you think I can get passage off-planet?"

"If the rumors are true, sooner than you think."

"Bakunin's fallen that hard?"

Jarvis chuckled. "No."

She looked at him. His face had broken out in a completely unwarranted grin. "What are you smiling about?"

"Payday," Jarvis said. "I'm smiling about what will happen when time comes to pay these guys."

"What do you mean?"

Jarvis wheeled his chair back toward the path, "You'll see, believe me. Good luck."

"Good luck yourself."

Payday? Tetsami thought.

CHAPTER FORTY-SIX

Geopolitics

"By the time policy descends from the high to the low, the high may no longer exist."
—*The Cynic's Book of Wisdom*

"Whether a revolution succeeds or miscarries, men of great heart will always be its victims."
—HEINRICH HEINE
(1797–1856)

Shane had barely suited up when the marines were scrambled for the attack. All she could do was grab a half-charged plasma rifle and follow Couglin's squad into the APC. Couglin's was one of three squads jammed into a vehicle that wasn't meant to take marines in full armor. She was squeezed between Fletcher and Thomas, standing with her hands locked into the webbing lining the roof.

The APC jerked to life, swinging her back and forth as it headed south.

From the little briefing Couglin had time to give her, his squad—her squad—was assigned to take out one of the plasma cannons overlooking the landing area outside the GA&A complex. It was strange for her to be a grunt again, down where the fog of war was at its thickest. She had little idea what was going to happen, other than that they were to storm the *Blood-Tide*.

More surreal was to be a marine again, for what was probably the last time.

The ride was rough. The APC flew over foothills, smashing through its share of small plants. Inside, there were no open windows, so only the driver had visual cues to where they were. Occasionally the comm would burst with static, but it provided no information. They were supposed to be EM silent until the attack began.

No one talked. It was an ugly quiet. Shane thought, at first, it might have to do with her. But just looking at the strain showing on the faces across from her, it was obvious that these people weren't even thinking about her. It wasn't just dropping into a hot situation, it was what they were attacking, and why.

Shane realized that most of these soldiers had never had her doubts about the Colonel and the TEC. The collapse of Operation Rasputin's command, having to attack GA&A just to return home. The enormity of what these marines were going through sank deep into her.

"Hail, Mary, full of grace," Shane whispered. "Blessed art thou and the fruit of thy womb, Jesus."

The APC slammed to a halt and, even through the armor, she heard something supersonic tear a hole in the air outside. The rear door levered open. Couglin was the first out, as soon as the door gave him enough clearance. Thomas and Fletcher were next, as the door chunked home, fully open. Shane followed, stepping out into Hell one last time.

It was a five-minute-long eternity just to get within sight of the defense towers. The battle was already raging around them by the time Couglin's squad reached the hill immediately west of the *Blood-Tide*. The air was already choked with smoke, the sky darkening in early dusk. The smell reached her even through the filters in her suit. It was a campfire smell, but a campfire where someone was roasting plastic marshmallows.

The ground-attack aircraft had already blown their load all over the complex itself. Shane saw three wrecks where the aircraft had blown themselves over the complex. The sight of the smoldering wrecks tightened Shane's gut. There was a good chance that the *Blood-Tide* had taken them out with its own antiaircraft.

If the attack was to crush GA&A, the *Blood-Tide* would be the first thing to be targeted. But they *needed* the *Blood-Tide*, so they couldn't disable it—their aircraft had to draw its fire, keep it pinned until the ground-pounders could close and board it.

Which meant every aircraft they had was hopelessly outclassed. And every pilot they had was probably going to die before they took the ship.

That wasn't the squad's concern.

Their target was one of the truncated towers on the perimeter of the GA&A complex. The *Blood-Tide* was on a makeshift landing field immediately north and outside the perimeter of the GA&A complex proper. The perimeter of GA&A was ringed by defensive towers, half of which were retrofitted with plasma cannons. The artillery and air support couldn't target the cannons near the *Blood-Tide* without potentially damaging the ship, so that was up to Couglin's squad.

As they reached the top of the hill, their last bit of ground cover, Shane saw one of the plasma cannons light up. It was as if someone had taken a slice of a sun and had thrown it down on the ground before them. The hit wasn't anywhere near them, but the heat wash still rang the temperature warnings on her suit.

The visor had polarized against the glare, but she was still dazzled for a moment. She blinked a few times and checked the tac database on her heads-up.

Her passive pickup showed that all of Couglin's people were still here. The computer was smart enough to find them even when their transponders were off. It also showed her that six unknowns had just dropped off the scope.

The computer didn't realize the people were theirs, but Shane knew six marines had just been turned into ionized gas.

Then the squad was running. It was their target that'd fired, and that gave them precious seconds. It took time for the cannons to recharge and acquire a new target. It was only a few seconds normally, but, God willing, the recharge would be extended because of the demands on the GA&A power grid during the attack.

The tower was a hundred meters away across the battlefield. Shane saw the weapon rotating toward them—

"Split up so it can't target us all at once!" Couglin's

voice came over the radio, breaking EM silence. As the cannon turned, the squad began to spread apart, trying to put more than the width of the plasma beam between them.

Masses of TEC troops began firing at them from the base of the tower, and from back around the *Blood-Tide*. As she closed on the halfway mark, her suit's field readout showed enough glancing hits to begin overheating.

Shane realized that this was probably as much a suicide mission as the fliers had.

The sun rose behind Couglin's shoulder. He had left his suit comm transmitting. As Shane's visor polarized, and her field began burning out from the heat, a blast of static popped the speaker in her radio. The heat switched on the hostile environment capability in her suit, and the superheated wind almost knocked her over. Radiant heat charred the shape of her shadow on the ground in front of her—

Somehow she kept running.

Covering fire came from behind them, suppressing the enemy by the *Blood-Tide*, but the troops by the base of the tower were scoring that many more hits as they closed. Shane, and maybe Thomas, returned fire, but there were just too many of them. They weren't well armored or armed, but for every one that dropped, there seemed to be three more.

They aren't the objective, Shane thought, *I'm going to die here anyway . . .*

Shane stopped returning fire and rigged the setting on her own plasma rifle. And dialed the fire selector to full discharge, just like she had on the *Blood-Tide*. With the remaining charge, she had one shot.

"Our Father, who art in heaven."

The cannon was about to fire again.

Shane dropped on the ground at twenty meters, bracing the rifle and aiming at the cannon.

"Hallowed be thy name."

Shane fired, and a great light flowered over her.

When she woke up, she realized that thy kingdom had not come, at least not yet. Even before she had reached full consciousness, the smells and the moans warned her to expect a field hospital. When she came fully to her senses, it lived up to her expectations. A massive tent with maybe twenty or thirty beds.

"No ..." The thought of reliving the rehabilitation of the last three months almost brought her to tears. She closed her eyes so she couldn't look down and see the damage.

It seemed she lay there for a long time before she heard, "Corporal Shane?" The voice alerted her that someone was next to her bed. She recognized the voice as Captain Fitzpatrick.

"Sir," she said, trying to blink back the tears. She wondered if they'd bother waiting for her to heal before the court-martial.

He walked around to the foot of her bed. "You live a charmed life, Corporal."

She didn't feel like it, but Shane didn't contradict him.

"Just out of curiosity, what were you trying to do with that maneuver?"

Shane shook her head. "I was trying to shoot the canon, sir. I failed to get a shot off ..."

Fitzpatrick shook his head.

"I *did* hit it?"

"No, desperation maneuvers like that usually don't work. Near as we can tell, your rifle was damaged and you pumped a shot about five meters into the ground in front of you."

"My God."

"You're lucky, you got out with a few second-degree burns and—um—" Fitzpatrick looked slightly uncomfortable and nodded down at the bed. Shane finally looked down at the damage.

She almost laughed, though the sight still made her slightly queasy. Both her arms were badly damaged, cosmetically at least. But they were prosthetic hardware. From the looks of things, the medics had disassembled whatever was too damaged to fix, and cut away any charred pseudoflesh. Her right hand was missing, as was the flesh on that arm up to the elbow. She held it up curiously, watching the metallic bones twist in response to false musculature.

Her left hand was only missing one finger and the flesh to the wrist. It still worked, though she received no sensation from it at the moment. It looked like an odd metallic spider.

I don't need a doctor, I need a mechanical engineer with a specialty in robotics.

"It's repairable," Shane said, for lack of anything else to say.

Fitzpatrick nodded. "Not here, though . . ."

"Did we win? Sir?"

"I wouldn't call it winning, not with half the company dead or wounded. But, yes, we retrieved the *Blood-Tide*. It's safely in orbit until it needs to come down to pick us up." He shook his head sadly. He seemed to have aged a decade since last she saw him. She wanted to reassure him, tell him she understood what he was living through, but she didn't think it would help, coming from her.

"Anyway," he continued, "that's not why I'm here."

Shane nodded. She was going to hear her fate now. She hoped she was ready to face it. "Yes, sir. I know."

"You're a sticky problem for me, Kathy. You deserted, and committed treason in wartime. We're still in a war zone, and both those offenses give me the right to order a summary execution without trial."

Shane swallowed and nodded.

"Don't worry about that, Kathy. Fortunately the marines give the CO some latitude in these matters. Especially to a CO as far out in the air as I am." He sighed. "Now, for the record, you were going to GA&A to surrender yourself, weren't you."

She nodded again, "Yes."

"You were doing so in the belief that Colonel Dacham was still in command?"

"Yes, I—"

"Please, don't explain. This Q&A is going to be part of my report back to command."

"I understand, sir."

"You did so knowing that Colonel Dacham was most likely to order your execution?"

"Yes."

Fitzpatrick nodded and paced around her bed. "Considering the morale of the troops, especially the ones that left GA&A after the attack, I'm going to use that as an argument for mercy. That, and the extraordinary collapse of the command of this mission ... I'll be as lenient as the regulations allow. I am discharging you from the marines and exiling you."

Shane didn't know what to say. "Yes, sir."

"Know that you'll face a court-martial if you ever enter Alliance space again. We'll transport you to a civilian hospital once one of our transports is free ..."

"Thank you, sir."

Fitzpatrick turned around. "We came here with a hundred twenty marines, we're leaving with less than eighty. Forty dead marines. God only knows how many were killed by their own command. You know what, I'm glad the Confederacy's falling apart out there. And when I get these people home, I am turning in my own resignation—so do me a favor and drop the fucking 'sir.' "

"I'm sorry ... Dan."

He shook his head sadly. "As far as I am concerned, Kathy, we're not soldiers anymore."

He patted her on the shoulder, where the pseudoflesh still covered her arm. "Just survivors."

Just survivors, Shane thought.

CHAPTER FORTY-SEVEN

Domino Theory

"The ability to control is often inversely proportional to the desire to."
—*The Cynic's Book of Wisdom*

"I want the masses of humanity to be truly emancipated from all authorities and from all heroes, present and to come."
—MIKHAIL A. BAKUNIN
(1814–1876)

Colonel Klaus Dacham had been on the planet Bakunin for a hundred and twelve Bakunin days, nearly five standard months.

In the first sixty days, he had organized the force that was to take control of the planet.

In less than half that time, that force had managed to achieve an unequivocal victory. For a single moment, Klaus Dacham had the surrender of every major urban center on the planet. The Proudhon occupation forces moved into the streets of Godwin, of Troy, of Jefferson City.

Everything between Sinclair and Rousseau, Troy and Sartre, all bowed to his authority and the force he commanded. Klaus had beaten his brother's planet, beaten the disorder, the chaos—

That night, a little over a standard month ago, Klaus had enjoyed a brief celebration with his high command. It was one of the few nights in his life he had slept with no thoughts for the past.

Klaus stood on top of the residence tower at the GA&A

complex, thinking about that night. Beside him was the matte-black hemisphere that covered the CEO's office and quarters—where his brother had once lived and worked. Before him was a sloping forest canopy that eventually gave way to the sprawl of Godwin.

Godwin was alive with light, backlit by a purple-red sunset. The lights, for the most part, were fires. The sunset was like an open wound in the sky.

Klaus' hand reached over the guardrail, as if he were reaching to pull back his victory . . .

Sixty days to organize the army.

Thirty to achieve a total military victory.

Fifteen for the victory to completely fall apart.

Even before the tach-comm came from Earth, there were signs of trouble. Over a hundred officers died the first day after the cities were occupied. Klaus' orders for reprisals against the communities involved backfired badly.

The worst instance had happened in Sinclair, a city that had fallen in the first days of the conflict, and had been occupied for over a month standard. The commander there had his throat slit. In response, Klaus ordered the execution of five political detainees.

Sinclair's populace was less than cowed by the executions. The following day an entire company of mercenaries, and the city block where they were housed, went up in a ball of fire. The explosion and resulting firestorm killed two civilians for every immolated soldier—as if showing how little the resistance cared for reprisals.

Sinclair became a black hole for military resources, and other communities followed suit with snipers, assassins, full-blown riots. The terrorism wasn't just confined to the occupation force. Corporations became targets after having their security coopted by the TEC. The occupation had effectively disarmed every security force on the planet—in retrospect that had been a bad move. The invasion had castrated the only policing force the planet had ever known—leaving the disaffected, the terrorists, the criminals, and the psychopaths as heavily armed as ever.

There was no organized resistance, but that left the army with nowhere to shoot. The corporations that had surrendered looked to Klaus for security when the security for his own army was breaking down.

Then came the tach-comm from Earth.

Operation Rasputin was no longer authorized, Bakunin was now under the jurisdiction of Tau Ceti—the Seven Worlds of all places—and all TEC personnel were to be withdrawn. Funding was to cease immediately.

Suddenly, after coming so close, all the masks were removed and all of his enemies were out in the open, all the people who had been plotting against him, at home, in the cities of Bakunin, even within his own camp.

It seemed that within hours of the tach-comm cutting the funds for Rasputin, the mercenary army dissolved. Desertion had been a low-level problem ever since the start of the siege, it had redoubled once the cities were taken—

When the money dried up, the army seemed to evaporate into the molten Bakunin chaos.

Klaus stared at the fires of Godwin, while around him automated perimeter defenses swept the area around GA&A clean. Plasma weapons shot anything that moved outside the complex. All computer-controlled now, because there were no people left to man them.

Since the marines had mutinied, there had been no determined assault on the GA&A complex. Bakunin was in the grip of a civil war. Social maps were being redrawn, and floods of displaced commune dwellers weren't helping stabilize the cities. The remnants of the TEC on Bakunin weren't high on anyone's priority list. At least not anyone powerful enough to get through what the marines had left of the GA&A defenses.

Klaus turned away from the specter of Godwin, to face the remnants of the GA&A complex. The *Blood-Tide* was gone, the office complex was a charred ruin. Even days later, the smell of smoke still hung in the air. The damage was the result of the final mutiny against him. Klaus had severely overestimated the number of people loyal to him. Even after purging the ranks—several times, in fact—in the end he'd been surrounded by his enemies.

His command center was gone, his ship was gone, and with the exception of one marine and a dozen TEC operatives from his personal staff, his people were gone. Four times that number had survived the mutiny, when the Occisis marines took the *Blood-Tide* by force. But almost everyone who'd remained loyal before the mutiny had since deserted him.

Klaus was alone.

He had always been alone.

Klaus paced the top of the residence tower like a trapped animal. He could have left on the *Blood-Tide,* before things became bad. But he couldn't let himself cave in to the marines' demands. It had been *his* ship. It was *his* command. The Confederacy had abandoned him, not the other way around.

He couldn't return, not after this. Not after having his victory pulled away from him like this. He should have carpet-bombed the continent from orbit, that would have been a victory the politicians couldn't change.

The sky continued to darken, and the charred remnants of the GA&A complex cloaked itself in shadow. As Klaus watched the deepening darkness, the comm on his belt buzzed for his attention. After a moment's hesitation, Klaus answered it.

"Yes," he muttered.

"Sir?" said the voice on the other end.

"What is it, Captain?" Klaus said. The speaker was Captain Murphy, the single marine to remain with him. After everything, Murphy still clung to form and procedure with a near pathological obsessiveness. Every step closer to the abyss, Murphy's voice was more clipped, his shoes more polished, his posture even straighter.

The man would salute the devil.

"We have a small contragrav vehicle requesting permission to land."

Klaus almost laughed. "Deny it, and if it closes, shoot it down."

"Sir, the pilot identifies himself as Jonah Dacham."

Klaus clutched the small comm, knuckles whitening. "Impossible," Klaus said. He stared off toward the office complex. He had his brother's *body.*

"Sir, perhaps I should pipe the communication into your office."

Klaus turned toward the black hemisphere and said, "Do it."

Klaus had to restrain himself to avoid running. Jonah surviving? It was impossible. Even so, Klaus already had his doubts. So many other things had gone wrong.

The walls, which could be made transparent to view the panorama around the residence tower, were currently blank, white, and opaque. They'd been so since the communication from Earth, shutting out the rest of the world. As Klaus approached the office's central desk, the holo built into it activated.

Klaus slipped into his chair to see the unmistakable face of his brother. It took a moment for the image to sink in.

"Hello, Klaus," Jonah said.

"Why are you here," Klaus finally said. "To parade your resurrection? To gloat over the ruins?"

Jonah shook his head. "I need to talk to you, Klaus."

"The perimeter defenses are active. I can order you shot down." Even as Klaus said it, he was tempted to give the order. Captain Murphy would be monitoring this communication. One word from Klaus and Jonah's contragrav would be blown out of the sky.

Klaus opened his mouth to give the order, and hesitated. He had no way of knowing if this *was* Jonah. Too many times he had come close, only to discover that he hadn't made sure. He had to see Jonah, face-to-face.

As if reading his mind, Jonah said, "If you do that, you'll never hear what I have to say."

"What could you possibly have to say?" Klaus felt his hand clenching and unclenching, out of view of the holo.

"I can offer you a way out of this, Klaus."

Klaus snorted.

"Allow me to land, to talk to you. I'm unarmed."

Klaus' hands clenched into fists as he nodded. He had to see Jonah face-to-face. "You can land outside the perimeter." Klaus didn't want one of Jonah's vehicles within the GA&A complex. "You'll be met and searched by an armed escort and brought to me. If you attempt anything threatening, you will be killed."

Jonah nodded as if this was what he'd expected. The

connection to the contragrav was cut and the image was replaced by Murphy's face. "Did you get all that?" Klaus asked.

Murphy nodded. "Yes, sir."

"Get to it, then." As an added precaution Klaus added, "Restrain him before you bring him up. I don't want him excessively mobile."

Klaus began to worry. If Jonah *was* still alive, why come here? Colonel Klaus Dacham was near the end of things. It was only a matter of time before the planet was calm enough to hunt him down.

Klaus opened a drawer in the desk and withdrew a high-powered gamma laser. It would pay to be cautious. He rested it on his knee, under the desk, as he waited for his people to bring his brother to him.

As an afterthought, Klaus activated the transparency on the dome.

Within a few minutes, Murphy and one of Klaus' TEC loyalists escorted Jonah Dacham into Klaus' office. Even though it had been over ten years since he'd been in his brother's living presence, Klaus knew it was Jonah. He could feel it. There was a connection the moment their eyes met, a connection that Klaus had been trying to sever for fifteen years.

The only sign of Jonah's age was the bleaching of his hair. Even though they were fraternal twins, Jonah looked younger than Klaus. Artificial skin didn't age. Under that skin, synthetic muscle didn't atrophy. If Klaus hadn't known better, he would've placed his brother's age at around thirty years standard.

Klaus glanced at his brother's wrists, where Murphy had cuffed him, and saw the only external sign of Jonah's internal machinery. His right hand was a pitted, tarnished, chrome-metal construct. Klaus' eyes fixed on that new detail long enough for Jonah to comment.

"A souvenir of Jefferson City. They don't have the most advanced hospital." Jonah's metal hand flexed. "I wasn't on Earth long enough to have it replaced."

Klaus looked up at Murphy and said, "Sit him down." He looked at the young TEC agent who had accompanied

Murphy and said, "You, get a team together. I want that contragrav stripped to the last circuit. I want an analysis of every weld, every wire, every optical fiber."

The order was greeted with a curt nod. The man turned and left Klaus, Murphy, and Jonah the only people in the office. Beyond the transparency of the office dome, the Diderot Mountains were changing from rose to purple. The clouds were lit as if from a distant fire.

"You won't find anything," Jonah said. There was a click as his mechanical hand flexed against the cuffs restraining him. Murphy manhandled Jonah into a chair with more force than was necessary.

"I'll know that soon enough," Klaus said. His hand tightened on the gamma laser resting on his knee. It was pointed straight at Jonah's abdomen, through the desk. Neither Murphy nor Jonah could see it. Klaus put his other hand, calmly, on the desk and began drumming his fingers.

"A way out of this?" Klaus asked. All the years of anger and frustration were calling on him to fire the laser. He restrained himself. Instead, he smiled. "Everyone else has abandoned me. Forgive me if I'm skeptical."

"I represent the Confederacy now, or at least what authority the Confederacy still has. I can bring you back into the fold, back to Earth, before everything else collapses."

Klaus almost shot his brother. He leaned back in his chair, smiled even wider, and stopped drumming his fingers. "Even if you could do this, why would you?"

"It would be in return for leaving the TEC and abdicating any claim to its command."

The silence grew long. Klaus felt frozen in place. Eventually, Klaus asked, "What kind of deception is this?"

"We've been living a deception. I'm ending it. The TEC is crumbling, and I don't want anyone trying to resurrect it."

Klaus stopped smiling, leaned forward, and pulled the gamma laser out from under the desk. Jonah showed no surprise when Klaus pointed the laser at him. Murphy took an obvious step back from where Jonah sat.

"You will explain why you are here, Brother. Before I finish what you started fifteen years ago."

"Dimitri did it, Klaus." Jonah said calmly.

"Dimitri did *what?* *Sweat, you half-human monstrosity. Show some emotion. Don't you realize that I am finally going to kill you?*

Under the stare of Klaus' laser, Jonah told Klaus what Dimitri had done.

Klaus stood up, knocking his chair backward. "Why? Why would he have her—"

"He was our father, Klaus."

Murphy stared at both of them, eyes wide. Klaus felt his hand shaking, and he brought his other hand up to steady his gun arm. "You're lying," Klaus said.

"We're the result of Dimitri Olmanov's attempt to breed an heir. He had Helen Dacham killed, among other reasons, to foster a lethal rivalry between us. He didn't want two heirs."

"Sir," Murphy said.

Klaus swung the laser to bear on Murphy and said, "Shut up, he's lying."

"The irony," Jonah said, "is that Dimitri created us to avoid a succession battle. He was probably deluding himself. I was on Earth when he died, and for the moment I'm acting in his capacity. But from the tach-comms that preceded me here, I gather the TEC started eating itself alive the moment I left."

Murphy turned to look at Jonah.

"I don't believe you," Klaus said.

"My tenure couldn't last, even if the situation were stable," Jonah said. "It's only a matter of time before someone compares intelligence reports from Bakunin to those on Earth to trace my movements. Then I'll be challenged on who I really am." Jonah smiled. "In a way, you did kill me, Klaus."

"What are you talking about?" Klaus asked, looking away from Murphy.

"Sir, I think you—" Murphy began.

"You're not here to think!" Klaus yelled.

"Dimitri was careful to avoid tainting any potential heirs with heretical technologies. Claims of genetic engineering could poison any succession, especially a hereditary one. I have the office for the moment, but it will not take long for people lusting after power to realize—if they haven't already—that I am a ghost."

Ghost? It was a second before Klaus understood what Jonah meant. It meant that the Jonah sitting in front of him wasn't his brother. It meant he wasn't a part of this universe. The Jonah sitting in front of him was the result of someone traveling the wrong way through the old pre-Confederacy wormhole network. This Jonah was the result of his brother—or a version of his brother—trying to change his own past. It was literally impossible for this Jonah to be exactly the brother he knew. Legally, in fact, this Jonah didn't exist.

The realization was like a blow.

What that meant was that *his* Jonah Dacham, the Jonah who had killed Helen, the Jonah who had erased any ability to fix what his childhood had broken, *that* Jonah was beyond reach. That Jonah Dacham had traveled five, fifteen, or twenty years into a past that now had no causal connection to Klaus' present.

No, it couldn't end like that.

"You're lying," Klaus said. He turned the laser to face Jonah.

Jonah shook his head. "I don't want either of us to have a claim on the TEC. I want it to die, Klaus. Without Dimitri, or someone like him, it will die. We're not going to be Dimitris, Klaus. I can't redeem what we've done, but I can keep us from doing further harm."

Klaus closed his eyes. It was hard for him to think. There was too much to absorb. Jonah was lying. Jonah had to be lying.

"Sir, perhaps we should check—" Murphy never got to finish his statement.

"Shut up!" Klaus screamed, firing the laser. Even as he pulled the trigger, Klaus regretted what he had just done. By then, the act was long past retraction. The gamma laser's beam was only visible as a narrow heat shimmer in the air, marking the beam's passage long after the fact. Murphy was thrown against a wall of the office, not by

the beam, but by the explosion of boiling flesh erupting from his chest.

Murphy was a smoldering corpse before he slid to the ground, tracking blood across the holographic image of the Diderot Mountains. In response to his proximity, the office door to the roof opened, and Murphy's body draped itself across the threshold.

The door, damaged by the laser, tried to close. Blocked by Murphy's remains, it opened again, and closed, and opened . . .

"Murphy," Klaus whispered. He walked around the desk to where Murphy lay. Of all the marines, Murphy had been his only supporter throughout the whole operation. Murphy had rightly acknowledged his command. He would have followed Colonel Klaus Dacham to hell, because he was *Colonel* Klaus Dacham. Murphy hadn't abandoned him even when the other marines took the *Blood-Tide* by force.

Klaus leaned over Murphy's body. The door, opening, closing, back and forth, back and forth. The holo panel set in it was a surreal counterpoint to the mountains beyond. Reality, then holograph, reality, then holograph. In the holograph, the colors seemed more vivid.

"It's over," Klaus said. For the first time he really felt it was so.

"Yes, it is," Jonah said, behind him. Klaus turned to level the laser, halfheartedly, at his brother. Jonah was doing something to his right hand; it appeared he was prying up one of the chrome panels in his palm. With the cuffs restraining him, it looked like a clumsy maneuver. Klaus watched, but he didn't intervene. "I thought I'd try to give both of us a second chance." Jonah shook his head. "We've had too many already. We're both just too much of everything that's wrong with the Confederacy."

The panel came open with a pneumatic hiss, revealing a recessed hollow in Jonah's right hand. "Too much of our father in us," Jonah said, as he pressed a finger into the cavity in his hand.

"Good-bye," Jonah said as his right hand was enveloped in a halo of blue electricity. The holographic walls flickered, as Jonah's body jerked in a violent spasm.

Klaus dropped the laser because it had suddenly become hot enough to burn his hand. The laser sparked, flared, and melted into slag.

As the lights died, Jonah slid to the ground.

Klaus stood still. The office was completely dark, the walls blind and dead, the only light came from outside the now-frozen doorway draped with Murphy's corpse.

Klaus walked over to Jonah. Even in the dim light, Klaus knew he was looking at a corpse. Synthetic muscles had pulled into grotesque contortions under partially melted skin. Jonah's eyes were dark and clouded; the surface of one had cracked and charred slightly.

It was obvious what had happened. Jonah had an EMP device installed into his right arm. Klaus felt the chrome, and it was hot enough to burn. An EMP device was easy to disguise within otherwise innocuous electronics. Jonah had come here to smuggle it into Klaus' presence.

But why?

Klaus backed away from the body. Klaus, unlike Jonah, had no cybernetics in his body. He had no implanted machinery that an EMP could turn lethal. All Jonah had succeeded in doing was to engage in a painful variety of suicide.

Klaus looked around the office and wondered how widespread the damage was. He knew the specs of Jonah's old office, and the electronics were supposed to be hardened, but Jonah—even Jonah's "ghost"—knew more than enough to design a weapon to overcome them. Everything in the office—from the holo walls, to the communication, to the elevators—was dead.

Klaus slipped out the door, over Murphy's corpse, to get away from the smell of burning electronics.

The entire top floor of the residence complex was dead. His own personal aircar let out a pall of blue smoke when he slid open the canopy. Klaus shook his head and walked over to one of the emergency access doors. The door was fused shut. The door was locked magnetically, and the EMP had been powerful enough to weld shut the door.

That was when Klaus began to worry. Jonah had effectively trapped him here. He was out of communication with his people, the elevators were dead, and the only other exit was jammed.

Klaus backed away from the door.

Why would he do that? Kill himself to trap me here?

Klaus Dacham looked up to the darkening night sky in time to see a shadow glide silently across the face of Bakunin's largest moon. As his eyes continued to adjust to the dark, he watched the shadow slide toward him, black against a purple sky. As he watched, it grew, eating stars as it went.

Klaus knew what it was as soon as he saw it. He wasn't afraid. All the emotion had leached out of him. The one thought that crossed his mind was, *How appropriate.*

Klaus watched as five tons of polyceram monomolecular filament dropped from orbit. The central impact site of the circular net was a few meters north of the landing quad; otherwise it was perfectly centered on the GA&A complex.

Godwin Arms, and everything within a hundred meters of it—including Klaus, Jonah, and Murphy—was reduced to charred gravel the size of Klaus Dacham's little finger. The destruction ceased at a depth of thirty meters, a little deeper than the warehouse sublevels. The satellite photographs of the site would glow for a few days, and it would be a full Bakunin year before vegetation reclaimed the site, but other than that, the existence of Godwin Arms on the face of Bakunin was effectively erased.

FINAL EPILOGUE

Absentee Ballot

"They make a desert and call it peace."
—CORNELIUS TACITUS
(*ca.* 55–120)

CHAPTER FORTY-EIGHT

Peace Treaty

"All of war is unpleasant, including its end."
—*The Cynic's Book of Wisdom*

"What a beautiful fix we are in now; peace has been declared."

NAPOLEON BONAPARTE
(1769–1821)

Kari Tetsami walked out the northern perimeter of Proudhon, toward Mosasa Salvage. Her face was set in a grimace against the desert wind, her hand clutched the case at her side as if it were a life preserver keeping her from drowning in the reality surrounding her. She had been out of the hospital now for a month standard, just long enough for the skin over her wounds to assume a color resembling human flesh, though everything between her groin and breastbone was still hideously mottled.

But she was alive. More than she could say for Dom, or Ivor.

A month standard was long enough to learn to resent Bakunin even more than she had before she was shot. *Payday*, Jarvis had said. And damned if that word didn't sum up the whole fucking planet. Everyone out for theirs, and when the mercs of Proudhon didn't get theirs—

Tetsami never wanted to be that close to so many pissed-off mercenaries again.

In the month since she'd talked to Jarvis, Bakunin had managed to return itself to a chaotic normalcy. Tetsami had been through Jefferson City, and Godwin, and it was as if the invasion had never happened. Buildings had burned, wrecked vehicles were in the streets, certain corporations no longer existed, certain gangs controlled different territory . . .

But nothing had *changed*. A near-takeover of the planet hadn't changed a damn thing. It was the same people pulling the same shit with the same excuses.

Dom was dead, and it should count for something.

The salvage yard was the same as it had always been, ranks of dead spacecraft stretching out to the horizon. Now, however, every other wreck seemed to be some new military design. Tetsami passed dozens of contragravs with the turquoise and blue markings of Proudhon Spaceport Security.

That was the primary irony. This city had been the focus of the invasion, had controlled parts of it. Despite that, Proudhon had suffered the least change. The only sign of the conflict was the construction crews rebuilding part of the corporate headquarters of the Spaceport Development Corporation. The top floors of the central marble skyscraper had exploded sometime during the first stages of the invasion. Other than that, during the entire conflict, no one here had fired a shot in anger.

The only other change was the continued shortage of mercenaries in a city that was usually thick with them.

She walked the maze of wreckage, across black sand packed as hard as asphalt. Stagnant heat thickened the air, air so dry it sucked the sweat from her body. As she approached the central building, a glorified hangar, she felt the pulse in her neck, and her temple. Her mouth had gone dry long before she entered the salvage yard.

Do I have to go through with this?

Even as she had the thought, her decision was taken from her. The massive door to the hangar rolled upward, revealing the ebony, hairless form of Mosasa. Mosasa was accompanied by an equally bald, well-muscled white man whose black irises swallowed his pupils.

They're not men, Tetsami told herself. *They're machines, machines who have engineered the death of everything on this dirtball I care about.*

"We've been expecting you," Mosasa said.

I bet you have. Tetsami held her case in front of her like a shield while her other hand rummaged in her pocket. "You're all one AI, aren't you? You're all Random."

The pair glanced at each other in a gesture that prompted Tetsami to yell, "*Stop it!* Stop pretending to be human!"

"Tetsami," Mosasa began.

"I don't want to hear it!" Tetsami threw the case down between the three of them and pulled a control out of her pocket. "Either of you move, I press the button. Either of you lie, I press the fucking button."

The two constructs looked at her, not the case.

"I repeat, you are all Random Walk, right?"

Mosasa nodded, his earrings glinting in the midday sun. "Me, Ambrose, Kelly, Random Walk, are all—were all—a single gestalt AI."

Tetsami nodded. "That's what Zanzibar told me. There's a whole lot of shit you didn't volunteer until it was too late, wasn't there?"

"There were some things that we couldn't—"

Tetsami shook her head. "I don't want the justifications. Ivor is dead, Dom is dead, that's all I give a shit about."

"Yes," Mosasa said. "We were selective in what we revealed to people."

"Because that's how you manipulate events." Tetsami waited a moment before she yelled, "*Isn't it?*"

"Yes," both said simultaneously.

Tetsami nodded. "I've had a lot of time to think about this, I've talked to people, and I want to know exactly how much of this is your fault."

Mosasa took a step forward. "Tetsami—"

"*Don't you fucking move!* You haven't earned the right. You never told *me* you were an effing AI."

"You would have taken it badly."

She nodded. "I guess we're seeing that, aren't we? Now . . ." She turned to Mosasa's companion. "You're Ambrose, right?"

Ambrose nodded.

She turned back to Mosasa, even though she was effectively talking to the same person. "You had a mole in the

TEC chief executive's office—how much of all this was your fault?"

"That's hard to eval—"

"Were you behind the invasion?"

"That was inevitable. We could see it coming and we needed to—"

"Johann Levy was a turncoat. He recommended you."

Mosasa asked, "Is that a question?"

"You know what I'm asking." Tetsami's hand tightened on the control. "You've made so much out of predictive psychology—you know."

Mosasa nodded. "We used Levy. He was a portal for information."

Tetsami felt the anger burning through the wall of her abdomen, like the laser that had nearly killed her. "You've manipulated all of us, all along."

Mosasa didn't offer an argument.

"What about Dominic and Klaus? Did you set that up as well?"

"That was Dimitri's doing. They were his children."

Tetsami stared into the middle distance, thinking about the one real night she and Dominic had had together. She had never even gotten the chance to sort out how she'd really felt. By the time she'd learned of his return to Bakunin, GA&A was a smoking gravel pit.

Tetsami caressed the control with her thumb and said, "That doesn't answer my question. Klaus and Dominic? Your doing?"

"That began before we placed Ambrose. Dimitri Olmanov set most of those factors into motion."

"Dimitri's actions," Ambrose added, "rendered conclusion inevitable. We took it into account. We didn't engineer it."

"My father?" Tetsami asked.

"You must understand," Mosasa said, "we do not control people. We only anticipate their voluntary actions. Everyone chose his or her own path, Dominic and Ivor included."

"You set this Christ-blown bullshit up in the first place, you electronic hypocrite!"

"Much as anyone on this planet, we have been trying

to maintain Bakunin as a viable political entity. All that differs is our methods. If you must blame someone for these deaths, don't the two of them share some complicity?"

"Don't say that—" Tetsami started.

"Ivor volunteered for a suicide mission where not only he, but a fifth of myself was lost."

Tetsami refused to meet Mosasa's eyes, electronic or not.

"Dominic Magnus chose his own death twice."

"What?" Tetsami looked up.

"Dominic Magnus flew into the wrong end of a wormhole. It was the only way he saw that at least a version of himself could make it to the Terran Congress in time."

The surrounding desert sucked up sound, leaving Tetsami facing two sides of Random Walk in an empty silence. After a long time, she asked, "The Dominic who . . ."

"The Dominic who died at GA&A was a ghost. He wasn't the Dom you knew. That version of Dominic spent nine years in isolation, waiting for the Congress, and came from a universe different from ours in a few important respects."

"Different? How?"

"For one example, you died before this Jonah Dacham left Bakunin."

"But I—" Tetsami remembered her dreams of the Protean egg, of Eigne. Eigne had hinted at an endless series of universes, in many of which Tetsami didn't survive . . .

"The nature of ghosts," Mosasa continued. "Where their past overlaps the history they exist in, there cannot be a perfect match. Your Dominic didn't die at GA&A. He died when he crossed the event horizon of a wormhole in the 61 Cygni system."

Tetsami sighed. Maintaining the anger was fatiguing her. "I should set this off on general principles. Just for you playing God with all of us."

"Everyone tries to play God," Mosasa said. "It's just that some are better at it than others."

Tetsami smiled for the first time. "You arrogant SOB.

You know the *real* reason I ain't blowing us all into orbit?"

Mosasa shook his head.

"Come on, you and your predictive psychology should
be able to figure that one out."

Mosasa and Ambrose looked at each other in that irritating human gesture again, and finally Mosasa said,
"You've decided that it isn't worth it to take your own
life for the sake of revenge?"

Tetsami laughed, and was gratified to see an expression
of surprise on Mosasa—even if it was part of a program
to mimic human behavior. "Not even close."

Tetsami walked up and picked up her case. "The reason we're not a smoking crater is because this," she held
out her case, "happens to be my luggage, and this," she
held out the hand with the remote, "is my hotel key."

She turned away and began walking back to Proudhon.
As she did, she whispered, "Gotcha, bastards."

On her way back to her hotel, Tetsami stopped in a
little crater of a bar on one of the cul-de-sacs off of Arm-
strong Road. All the walking was making itself felt in her
gut, where the Jefferson doctors had rebuilt her abdominal wall and about a dozen meters of intestine.

It was still an alien sensation, even though she'd had
time to get used to the idea of her body rebelling. She had
spent most of her life in her head, her body was something she took for granted. But after her convalescence, it
wasn't just her wounds that gave her problems. She had
aches in muscles that weren't anywhere near the injury.
She tired easily. She felt as if, despite the doctors' efforts,
a good part of her life had leaked out on the roof of the
hospital. She felt old.

The bar where she stopped was typical, almost em-
blematic of the bars serving the spaceport crowd. Even
this early in the afternoon, the place was filled with
people—spaceship crew, mostly, whose biological clocks
weren't necessarily in sync with the planet's clocks.

Tetsami picked up a pitcher of local beer at the bar
even though she was supposed to stay away from alcohol.
The beer didn't count. Just one more little thing from the

war that everyone ignored, to Tetsami's annoyance. All the good breweries had been in the communes, and most communes were still smoking ruins. It would be years before that part of Bakunin rebuilt itself.

That's what the war did, Tetsami thought. *It nuked what was unique and admirable on this planet, leaving the common sleaze intact.* As she slid into a booth with her pitcher, she thought, *Maybe that's just what war happens to do.*

As soon as she got her shit together, she was going to take her leave of Bakunin. She'd been trying to do that since before she met Dominic Magnus, since before her life got so bent out of shape, since before the planet got so bent out of shape.

She still had no real idea of where she wanted to go.

It wasn't that her choices were limited. She'd made sure that her nineteen megs worth of assets were safely off-planet long before she'd been shot. Also, she had more on-planet assets than she knew what to do with. During her sidetrip to Godwin, Tetsami had stopped at the headquarters of the Bleek-Diderot Consortium. That was where she'd discovered the fate of everyone connected to the old Godwin Arms. The only people left there from the original group she and Dom had assembled were Zanzibar and Flower.

Zanzibar—after trying to recruit her back into Dominic's little enterprise—had provided her with another forty megs worth of currency, Ivor's share of Bleek-Diderot. It was a gesture that Tetsami had never expected, since there were no probate laws on Bakunin. She never asked about Dom's share, or why Ivor had ended up with a double share. She'd been too overwhelmed.

As she sat in the crowded, dark Proudhon bar, she still felt overwhelmed. She'd had a month to get used to missing both men, but the loss still hurt. The worst feeling of all was the idea that their absence finally freed her to leave the planet with a clear conscience— And that brought another wave of guilt.

Tetsami drained a glass of beer that tasted like dirty water.

"Tetsami! I thought I saw you come in here."

Tetsami looked up at a voice that sounded slightly familiar. She found herself looking at a redheaded woman as short as she was. The woman wore a leather jacket over a flight suit and it took Tetsami almost a full minute to recognize who she was looking at.

"Shane?" she asked hesitantly.

"Right the first try," Shane said, and slipped into the booth across from her.

"I didn't recognize you with hair," Tetsami said. Shane had allowed her hair to grow out. It was now curly, dark-red, and growing down to her shoulders.

Shane ran her fingers through it and said, "You're lucky you saw it. Once I get my ship, it'll either get cut or tied back severely. Serious nuisance in zero-g."

Tetsami stared at Shane and realized how little she really knew about this person. For all they had in common over the past half-year, they were practically strangers. "You disappeared," Tetsami said. "At least that's what Zanzibar said."

"I turned myself in," Shane said.

Tetsami set down her glass, "You what?"

"I handed myself over to the marines."

"Was that smart?"

"It was something I had to do. May I?" Shane reached for Tetsami's glass. Tetsami shrugged and handed it over. "I expected to be shot for a traitor." Shane topped off the glass from Tetsami's pitcher.

"Well, you weren't, were you?"

Shane shook her head and drained the glass in a fluid motion. Then she told her the horror story of the marines' assault on GA&A when the Confed support was withdrawn.

When she finished, Tetsami said, "They just let you go?"

Shane snorted. "A dishonorable discharge, permanent exile in lieu of imprisonment—not exactly 'letting me go.' "

"I'm sorry," Tetsami said, reaching back for her glass.

"Don't be. As Captain Fitzpatrick said, I seem to have a charmed life."

"So what are you doing here?" Tetsami asked.

"They dropped me off here when the *Blood-Tide* landed. I needed some reconstructive work. Been here ever since."

"I just got here myself."

"Going off-planet?"

Tetsami nodded, "Something I've been trying to do since before all this happened."

"Where to?"

"Anywhere, nowhere, somewhere else."

Shane cocked her head to the side and gave Tetsami a thoughtful look. "I've felt the same way about the Confederacy—or what's left of it."

Tetsami poured herself a beer and said, "Don't encourage me."

"I'm serious, I've spent over a month in this town trying to gather investors to purchase my ship."

"That's the second time you've mentioned *your* ship. What ship?"

"A colony ship. I'm going to rebuild one of the original ships that colonized Bakunin. They're still in orbit, and no one claims them or uses them."

Tetsami almost gagged on her beer. "Those things are over a hundred years old—"

"Cheaper than building a five-thousand-passenger ship from scratch."

Tetsami stared at Shane for a long time. "Five. *Thousand?*"

Shane shrugged. "Considering all the displaced communes on this planet, finding willing colonists isn't my problem. What I need is displaced capital, and that's somewhat more difficult."

"You're going to colonize a planet?"

Shane nodded. "I think this planet might have rubbed off on me. This will be the first privately funded colonization since the Confederacy was founded."

The audacity of what Shane was doing was stunning. It was probably a measure of the enormity of what Tetasmi had already gone through that she had no trouble taking Shane seriously. "Where is this ship going?"

"I have access to some information that's only shared between me, Random, and some Tau Ceti diplomats. I could broker the information to some arm of the Confederacy. Random insists I have an interest in the information, whatever that means. I long ago decided that I'm not turning it over ..."

"The artifact Zanzibar was talking about?"

Shane nodded. "From it I've targeted a cluster of five candidate systems, about fifty light-years beyond Helminth."

"Helminth? Fifty light-years? That's half again the diameter of the Confederacy ..."

"Of all the nearby choices I had, that is the direction in which the Confederacy is least likely to expand."

The two women sat there, looking at each other for a while before Tetsami said, "You know, I have about sixty megs that isn't doing anything. How're you fixed for crew?"

APPENDIX A

Alphabetical listing of sources

Note: Dates are Terrestrial standard. Where the year is debatable due to interstellar travel, the Earth equivalent is used with an asterisk. Incomplete or uncertain biographical information is indicated by a question mark.

Aristotle
    (384–322 B. C.), Greek philosopher.
Bakunin, Mikhail A.
    (1814–1876), Russian anarchist.
Bismarck, Prince Otto von
    (1815–1898), Prussian chancellor.
Bonaparte, Napoléon
    (1769–1821), French emperor.
Browne, Sir Thomas
    (1605–1682), English physician, writer.
Cheviot, Jean Honoré
    (2065–2128), United Nations secretary general.
Confucius
    (*ca.* 551–479 B. C.), Chinese philosopher.
Disraeli, Benjamin
    (1804–1881), English prime minister, writer.
Dryden, John
    (1631–1700), English poet, dramatist, critic.
Emerson, Ralph Waldo
    (1803–1882), American essayist, poet.
Engels, Friedrich
    (1820–1895), German socialist.

Euripides
>(484–406 B. C.), Greek dramatist.

Frederick the Great
>(1712–1786), King of Prussia.

Galiani, August Benito
>(2019–*2105), European spaceship commander.

Hannibal
>(247–183 B.C.), Carthaginian general.

Harper, Sylvia
>(2008–2081), American civil-rights activist, president.

Heine, Heinrich
>(1797–1856), German poet, critic.

Hobbes, Thomas
>(1588–1679), English philosopher.

Jefferson, Thomas
>(1743–1826), American statesman, president.

Johnson, Samuel
>(1709–1784), English lexicographer, essayist, poet.

Kalecsky, Boris
>(2103–2200), Terran Council president.

Lucretius
>(*ca.* 96–*ca.* 55 B.C.), Roman poet

Milton, John
>(1608–1674), English poet.

Nietzsche, Friedrich
>(1844–1900), German philosopher.

Paine, Thomas
>(1737–1809), American revolutionary, writer.

Pascal, Blaise
>(1623–1662), French geometrician, philosopher, writer.

Rabelais, François
>(*ca* 1483–1553), French satirist.

Rajasthan, Datia
>(?–2042), American civil-rights activist, political leader.

Reed, Thomas B.
>(1839–1902), American lawyer, politician.

Schopenhauer, Arthur
>(1788–1860), German philosopher.

Shakespeare, William
   (1564–1616), English dramatist.
Shane, Marbury
   (2044–*2074), Occisian colonist, soldier.
Shelley, Percy Bysshe
   (1792–1822), English poet.
Tacitus, Cornelius
   (*ca* 55–120), Roman historian.
Thoreau, Henry David
   (1817–1862), American libertarian, writer.
Tocqueville, Alexis de
   (1805–1859), French writer, statesman.
Voltaire
   (1694–1778), French writer.
Webster, Daniel
   (1782–1852), American statesman.
Wilde, Oscar
   (1854–1900), Irish writer.

APPENDIX B
Worlds of the
Confederacy

The Alpha Centauri Alliance

Number of member worlds: 14	Number voting: 13	Number prime: 10

Capital:

Occisis—Alpha Centauri	founded: 2074	a

Other important worlds:

Archeron—70 Ophiuchi	founded: 2173	c
Styx—Sigma Draconis	founded: 2175	b

The People's Protectorate of Epsilon Indi

Number of member worlds: 31	Number voting: 17	Number prime: 15

Capital:

Ch'uan—Epsilon Indi	founded: 2102	a

Other important worlds:

Kanaka—Zeta^1 Reticuli	founded: 2216	a
Shiva—Delta Pavonis	founded: 2177	a

The Seven Worlds

Number of member worlds: 7	Number voting: 7	Number prime: 5

Capital:

Haven—Tau Ceti	founded: 2073	a

Other important worlds:

Dakota—Tau Ceti	founded: 2073	a
Grimalkin—Fomalhaut	founded: 2165	x

The Sirius-Eridani Economic Community

Number of member worlds: 21	Number voting: 14	Number prime: 12

Capitals:

Cynos—Sirius	founded: 2085	x
Khamsin—Epsilon Eridani	founded: 2088	b

Other important worlds:

Banlieue—Xi Ursae Majoris	founded: 2146	c
Dolbri—C1	founded: 2238	d
Paschal—82 Eridani	founded: 2164	a
Thubohu—Pi³ Orion	founded: 2179	a
Waldgrave—Pollux	founded: 2242	d

The Union of Independent Worlds

Number of member worlds: 10	Number voting: 2	Number prime: 1

Capital:

Mazimba—Beta Trianguli Australis	founded: 2250	b

Non-Confederacy Worlds

Bakunin—BD+50°1725	founded: 2246	c
Helminth—Zosma	discovered: 2277	c
Paralia—Vega	discovered: 2230	d
Volera—Tau Puppis	discovered: 2288	e
Windsor—Altair	founded: 2146	x

Notes:
a = habitable earthlike planet
b = marginally habitable planet
c = possible site of Dolbrian terraforming
d = definite site of Dolbrian terraforming
e = site of Voleran terraforming
x = planet uninhabitable without technological support

S. Andrew Swann

HOSTILE TAKEOVER

☐ **PROFITEER**   UE2647—$4.99

With no anti-trust laws and no governing body, the planet Bakunin is the perfect home base for both corporations and criminals. But now the Confederacy wants a piece of the action—
and they're planning a hostile takeover!

☐ **PARTISAN**   UE2670—$4.99

Even as he sets the stage for a devastating covert operation,
Dominic Magnus and his allies discover that the Confederacy
has far bigger plans for Bakunin, and no compunctions about
destroying anyone who gets in the way.

☐ **REVOLUTIONARY**   UE2699—$5.50

Key factions of the Confederacy of Worlds have slated a takeover of the planet Bakunin . . . An easy target—except that its
natives don't understand the meaning of the word surrender!

OTHER NOVELS

☐ **FORESTS OF THE NIGHT**   UE2565—$3.99
☐ **EMPERORS OF THE TWILIGHT**   UE2589—$4.50
☐ **SPECTERS OF THE DAWN**   UE2613—$4.50